Renegade

Renegade

Cheyne Curry

P.D. Publishing, Inc.
Clayton, North Carolina

ISBN-13: 978-1-933720-47-0
ISBN-10: 1-933720-47-6

9 8 7 6 5 4 3 2 1

Cover design by Barb Coles
Edited by: Day Petersen / Verda Foster

Published by:

P.D. Publishing, Inc.
P.O. Box 70
Clayton, NC 27528

http://www.pdpublishing.com

Acknowledgements

I would like to thank Barb and Linda for helping me achieve my life-long dream. I would like to thank Day and Verda for their guidance through the editing process.

I would like to thank Mom.

Also, Dottie for her devotion and many years of encouragement to never give up on my writing.

Naomi, for her enlightenment.

Roselle, for her advice.

Renae, for her wisdom, support, and equanimity during my more stubborn phases.

Brenda, for her persistence, prudence, and unyielding love.

And The Raven, for starting it all.

For Paladin

"I want her dead!" Vincent DeSienna slammed the palms of both hands on his antique mahogany desk. The normally collected man's outburst startled the other man in the room.

Aldo Tartaglia, the family attorney, the consigliere to the DeSienna *brugad*, put his hand up. He made a motion that indicated they needed to keep their volume low. "When was the last time this office was...cleaned?" Tartaglia's bushy eyebrows arched to form an arrow toward his receding hairline.

"An hour ago. Don't treat me like an amateur, Aldo. Don't you think I'd check?"

"Under normal circumstances, absolutely. But these aren't normal circumstances." Tartaglia had walked into Vincent's office a moment earlier and sat down opposite his client. "What's going on, Vince?"

"Trace Sheridan. That's what's going on. I want that bitch in front of me. And then I'm going to kill her." His voice was cool, his demeanor shameless.

Aldo focused on Vincent DeSienna. Vincent was an impeccably dressed and charismatically handsome man. His Latin heritage was reflected in his olive skin, dark hair, and high-bridged Roman nose. If he had one outstanding feature, it was his cold, steel-gray eyes. When he pinned someone with those, that person knew he or she, most likely, would not get out of that room alive.

DeSienna stood and walked to the bar. He grabbed a decanter half-filled with bourbon and topped off a shot glass. A frustrated sigh escaped him and he held his glass toward his attorney. He nodded and downed the shot with a harsh growl.

Aldo joined him at the bar. "Still no luck finding her?" He took the decanter and poured Vince another shot.

"How can someone just disappear off the face of the earth like this? She hasn't shown up or called in to work, hasn't been near her apartment, no one has seen her or heard from her. None of my guys can find her. Everyone leaves a trail. She's just vanished."

"She pissed a lot of people off, Vince, maybe someone already capped her."

DeSienna swallowed the second shot and fastballed the glass into the wall across the room, where it shattered. "If that's true then I want whoever killed her found and brought to me."

"And then what? Kill that person for killing her?"

"Yes! Yes, because to be denied the pleasure of taking her out myself would be unacceptable. This is too personal. My father saved her from a street life of poverty. She was a fucking latchkey kid of a crack whore, for Christ's sake. My father took a chance on her; he welcomed her into our family with open arms. He was like the father she never had."

"Treated her like his own kid," Aldo said in agreement.

"Better," DeSienna said, bitterly. His resentment was ferocious. "He was so blinded by her, he never saw it coming."

"All due respect? Neither did you."

"And don't think I don't kick myself for it. I never liked her, Aldo, you know that, never trusted her, but my father kept telling me to get beyond it. He said I was jealous."

"I always thought it was because you wanted to get in her pants, and she wouldn't."

"No one with a real dick will ever get into those pants. Unless it's by force."

"Such a waste. It's a crime against nature a woman that gorgeous is a lesbian."

DeSienna glared at him. "Lesbian? She's a fucking dyke. She's got more balls than most of my men. My father is an old fool who was taken in by pretty eyes and a nice pair of tits. Ten years she worked for him. Ten years. Then, suddenly she breaks faith."

"She should have known that would be an automatic death sentence." Aldo rubbed his forehead.

DeSienna stopped short of laughing in his attorney's face. "Really? She should have known? Why? She set Nick up, got him busted, and then she entrapped Sal," DeSienna said, referring to his brother and his cousin, "and all my father said was: 'Maybe they needed a lesson.'" He walked back to his desk and sat on the corner. "Both times, it should have been me, too. The night she got Nick, I was supposed to be with him. Same thing with Sal. The night my father went to that warehouse, it was supposed to be me. I want to find her and end it before it is me."

Aldo had heard this same rant many times in the forty-eight hours since the *Capo di tutti capi*, Vittorio, had been arrested and held without bail. The fact that Trace Sheridan had orchestrated his arrest was a blow the old man wasn't easily recovering from. He had groomed the ambitious woman for greatness in his organization, had sent her to the police academy, pulled silent strings to get her assigned to Union City's finest, and used her to make evidence disappear in any case involving the DeSienna crime family. She was the perfect bad cop, until she turned.

"If someone hasn't already done it, she's a dead woman walking, Aldo."

"What I don't get is why? It doesn't make sense. She had it made with Vittorio, she was making money hand over fist. Up until a month ago, she was fiercely loyal to him and then, boom, she starts working for the commissioner. Do you think he got something on her and she worked out a deal?"

"He must have offered her more money," DeSienna said. His eyes moved to the left; Aldo recognized this as a sure sign he was lying.

"Vince, the commissioner could only wish he had more money to play with than your father. What aren't you telling me?" Aldo's tone was cautious but suspicious. DeSienna remained quiet. "Vince?"

"Maybe she suddenly got a conscience," he said, defensively.

"Only if it were surgically implanted. A conscience wouldn't have let her do what she did to Vittorio." Aldo studied his client. DeSienna's cold eyes reflected a hint of guilt. "Did you do something to start this pile of shit rolling downhill? Because that makes more sense to me."

"Are you accusing me of something, Aldo?" Vince gave the attorney his coldest glare, but Aldo was one of the few people it didn't work on.

"Vincent, I have known you since you were five and clinging to your father's pant leg. I know when you're hiding something. I'd rather you tell me now than later, before there's any more damage." Aldo's authoritarian inflection made DeSienna pause. "Maybe it's still salvageable."

DeSienna drew in a deep breath and let it out slowly. "It will only be salvageable when we stop her. And there's only one way to do that."

"What sent her on the warpath, Vince?" His question was met by dead silence. "Goddamn it all to hell, Vincent, tell me!"

"All right!" DeSienna yelled back. "I challenged her, okay?"

"Challenged? Or threatened?" Aldo asked, wisely.

"It may have come off sounding like a threat."

"May have. I see." Aldo nodded. "And just exactly what was this...challenge?"

DeSienna cleared his throat, his cockiness apparently in check. "The fucking bitch was always one-upping me with my father. I was so tired of hearing about Trace Sheridan this and Trace Sheridan that. He treated her like she walked on water. I'm his oldest son and he never gave me the recognition he gave her. She taunted me with that. So I told her to enjoy it while she could because I would make my father believe that she would turn on him and her pretty little ass would end up dead or in prison."

"You're not saying that actually scared her into beating you to it?"

"No. The bitch laughed at me. But ambushing her and nearly killing her and her detective partner must have."

Aldo put his hand over his eyes in disgust. "That was supposed to be gang-related. That was you? You and your ego. What were you thinking? That she would actually back off from you? She didn't get to be as ruthless as she is by being a stupid woman. Look what it's cost the family!"

"I know."

"You better find her."

"I know!" There was a tense silence between the men.

Aldo folded his arms. "Her mother's not hiding her?"

"Nope. We've been watching and listening."

"Friends? Lovers?"

"She doesn't have anyone permanent. Never has."

"Patrol partners?"

"Her latest one is in the hospital, recovering, and she hasn't been near him. Her only other partner got out of law enforcement after he got shot. He's like a scientist now or something. My sources tell me they don't communicate anymore."

"What if you don't find her?"

DeSienna looked at the family attorney, his confidence once again restored. "That's not an option. Trace Sheridan and I will see each other again. And I can't tell you how much I'll enjoy making that icy gaze turn to fear. That's what I want to remember the last time I look in that bitch's eyes."

Chapter One

Rachel Young blinked, at first thinking the sun was playing tricks on her, and then prayed the man lying face down on the ground in front of her was not dead. She approached the still form with caution and gently prodded him with the barrel of her gun. There was no movement. She looked for obvious wounds — such as bullet holes, slash marks, rope line around the neck — but saw no evidence of any attack, nor did she see any blood.

She took into consideration the recent sinister events in her life that prompted the concern this might be a ploy. If it wasn't, this man was hurt and she couldn't just leave him there to die, to suffer alone until wolves, buzzards, or God knew what else finished him off. Still guarded, she knelt down to study the situation more closely. Since Rachel saw nothing on the cowboy's back to indicate any injury there to be concerned about, she rolled him over with great effort to inspect his front.

She started at the man's boots, which didn't look like any cowboy footwear she was familiar with, then noticed that his denim trousers also seemed different...or maybe it was just the way they fit over the slender lower frame. As her eyes traversed up the inert body, her focus was suddenly drawn to his face. She had never seen him before and, having grown up in Sagebrush, she thought she knew everyone. The possible exception was the saddle bums who moved through town at any given time, picking up just enough work to earn them a sufficient amount of money to get them to the next town.

Her gaze centered on the drifter's striking face and her heart skipped a beat. The features were sculpted, with high cheekbones and a tan complexion that indicated possible Indian or Gypsy heritage. He had long dark eyelashes and shaggy, black hair cut in a style she'd never seen on any man in these parts. His nose was slender, almost feminine, but it seemed perfect on his face. His lips looked soft and they were slightly parted, which immediately made her heart pump faster. Emotion washed through her but it wasn't fear.

Her hand brushed down the cowboy's jawline. Rachel felt no stubble, no evidence of a beard, and she guessed, despite his long and well filled out form, that this man must be young or he did have some Indian blood. Transfixed, she had to mentally chastise herself to not spend so much time admiring his face and continue to search for injuries. Her free hand moved down to the stranger's denim shirt and felt for anything out of the ordinary. She wiggled a finger through a tear in the fabric and touched something odd. She unfastened the metal buttons and opened the garment to reveal an unusual looking wrap, a binding of some kind. She spotted a circle of blood approximately the size of her fist and figured she'd found the wound that had rendered the stranger unconscious.

Rachel brushed the odd stretchy material of the binding and put her fingers on the dark, moist area that appeared to seep blood. As she separated the layers of the wrap to see what type of wound she was dealing with, she reached skin and found a small jagged cut that did not look like a bullet hole or a knife slice. Her eyes grew wide when she noticed something else as well.

Cleavage.

Startled, she glanced back up at the fascinating face and found herself looking directly into intense, sky blue eyes. Before she could speak, a hand grabbed her wrist and held her in place securely, strength she was surprised to find in a woman.

"What are you doing?" the stranger asked tersely. Her voice was raspy and its register was a low alto, one that could be mistaken for a callow male.

Rachel was terrified and confused. "N-nothing...I...I was checking to see if y-you were hurt."

The dark haired woman must have realized how tightly she was holding Rachel's wrist, as she loosened her grip then let her go. Rachel lost her balance, fell back on her butt, and dropped her rifle. She scrambled backward, snatched up her gun, got to her feet, and fixed her weapon on the strange woman.

"Who are you? Why are you dressed like a man?" Rachel's voice was shaking but her aim was steady. *What in heaven's name have I stumbled onto?*

Trace Sheridan opened her mouth to answer, then stopped to push through the curtain that had dropped over her memory. What was she doing in the middle of a rural area she didn't recognize, outfitted like a man, held at antiquated gunpoint by a clearly scared, quaintly dressed woman? Obviously she had felt the need to don a disguise for some reason. She needed to stall until she could remember what the hell had happened to her. "How do you know I'm not a man?" she challenged.

"Well." The young woman hesitated. "You don't have any whiskers."

"All the men in my family have light beards." Trace scratched her chin for emphasis and moved to prop herself up on her elbows. She had to squint to protect her eyes from the sun, which was still high in the sky behind her inquisitor.

"And," the face reddened in embarrassment, "you have breasts."

Trace smiled at her. "How do you know that?"

"I was checking to see if you were hurt."

"Uh huh." Trace nodded, not taking her eyes off the woman with the gun.

"Are you in some kind of trouble?"

"Why would you ask me that?"

"Because you're pretending to be a man," her captor said.

"Shit." Trace speculated she was in disguise for some case she must be involved in, but what? "I guess I've already blown my cover." The observation was made to herself, but it was loud enough for the gunwoman to hear. She shook her head, disgusted with herself. Some cop. Not only was she caught, but sections of her memory seemed to have taken a leave of absence and prevented her from recalling the events that had resulted in her looking into the business end of a rifle.

"Answer my question." The young woman adjusted her hold on the shotgun and trained it on Trace as she slowly, stiffly shifted her position, still on her back and elbows.

Trace rubbed her eyes and then directed her attention to the woman who had her at gunpoint. The long, golden blonde hair, probably bleached lighter by the sun, was pulled back away from her face and shoulders by a ribbon. She had intelligent, penetrating, emerald green eyes and a lovely face. Her slender figure was covered from shoulder to toe by a dress that showed off her more than adequate bust line and trim waist, and then billowed out from there. When Trace's eyes moved back up the young woman's body and pinned her with a contrary glare, the jaw became set.

Trace put one hand up in surrender as she massaged the dull pain in her shoulder with the other. "Okay, okay, relax. You can put that thing down. I'm not going to hurt you or try anything. I promise." The rifle lowered but the woman remained vigilant. "Where am I?"

"Sagebrush."

Trace looked around and digested that information. *Sagebrush? Where the fuck is that?* She studied the gun-toting woman's attire and the relic she carried prompted a smirk. "What year is it supposed to be?"

"What?"

Trace moved her hand in a sweeping gesture and indicated the dress. She repeated, "Year...what year is it supposed to be?"

"It's supposed to be, and it is, 1879. Why don't you know that? Did you hit your head?"

"No, I'm serious."

The woman squinted at her and studied Trace as though she'd lost her mind. "So am I."

Her expression told Trace she wasn't joking. "*What!*" Trace's smirk disappeared and her stunned exclamation startled the woman, who once more leveled the weapon at her still mostly supine body. In response, Trace raised her hand again. *What the fuck is going on?*

How could I— Trace did her best to swallow her befuddlement and wondered how the hell she could explain her presence to a woman of, no doubt, parochial existence, when she had no idea herself how she'd come to be here. "No, it's — never mind. I'm just a little fuzzy from my...um...fall."

"You fell?"

She must have. She had a veiled recollection of plowing into the earth. She'd hit the ground with a bone-crushing thud, the force of which had evidently knocked her unconscious.

"Is that how you got cut?" There was a hint of concern in the voice.

"Cut?"

The tip of the shotgun indicated the bloodstain on her wrapped chest. "There."

Trace's hand instinctively went to her breast. "Well, shit." She reached inside the binding and felt around. "Yep. Damn it." As she scanned the immediate area, she spied a jagged rock she must have landed on. Thankfully, the wound wasn't bleeding profusely, nor was it any more painful than her entire body, which ached from the impact. She knew she'd have a bumper crop of bruises but was pretty sure nothing was wrenched, sprained, or broken.

"You curse a lot. And you still haven't answered my question."

Trace sighed. She knew she couldn't put the woman off any longer. "I'm not from around here, which I'm sure you already noticed."

"Where are you from?"

"Um..." Where was she from? *Think, Trace, think.* Then it came to her. Union City. However, if she said "Union City" and it was close by, no one there would know her and the woman with the gun on her would soon know she had lied. "Cottonwood?" *Yeah. That sounds like a plausible name.*

"I've never heard of it. Where is that?"

"Far from here?" Trace hoped it was.

"How'd you get here?"

"Uh...my horse threw me?" She looked up at the blonde and hoped she bought the explanation.

"Why do you say it like you're asking me? Did your horse throw you or not?"

"Yes. Yes. My horse threw me. You haven't seen him anywhere around, have you?"

Green eyes squinted, suspiciously. "What did he look like?"

Think fast, Trace. "He was a...pinto with a...um...brown mane and tail. Black saddle."

"Haven't seen anything like that around here. A painted pony, huh? You Indian?"

"Me? No." *Not that I know of,* Trace finished to herself. "Why? Do I look Indian?"

"Looks like you could have some Indian in you. Or Gypsy. So — are you running from somebody or not?"

What to do, what to do? Maybe this woman could help her until she figured things out. She certainly needed an ally. *Not only that.* Trace ran her tongue over her bottom lip and gave Rachel a more than appreciative once over. *Maybe I could introduce this little cutie to a bit of Sapphic pleasure once we get better acquainted.* Trace gave herself a mental slap. Those kinds of advances would probably get her hanged around here. *Son-of-a-bitch...finding companionship is going to be damned near impossible. What the hell am I doing here?* "Well...it's like this, I'll tell you if you put that gun down and we can get out of the sun."

The woman didn't budge. "You'll tell me now."

Trace knew she could be on her feet and disarm her inexperienced opponent in a heartbeat, but she also knew that would be a mistake. This woman wasn't a killer. She was afraid, Trace could sense it, could see it in her eyes, her posture. She certainly wouldn't make any points if she bullied her. Trace broke into her friendliest smile and shrugged in concession. "All right. May I ask your name?"

"Rachel Young."

"Rachel, I'm Trace Sheridan. And yes, Rachel, someone is after me." This was just a guess. She preferred to go with that explanation rather than tell Rachel the unbelievable truth as she knew it, and she had obviously been undercover for...something. *Why is my mind such a blur?*

"What did you do?"

"Actually? Nothing." Nothing that she could clearly remember. She was sure it had something to do with the vendetta the DeSienna crime family had against her, the dynamics of which she desperately wished she could recall. Just the nature of how she manipulated her profession caused someone to always be out to get even with her, but the DeSienna *brugad* had more reasons than anyone. Especially number one son, Vincent. She said the first thing that popped into her head. "I made someone very angry with me; I did everything I could to fix the situation, but nothing worked. So now he and his men are, well, gunning for me." That seemed to have a ring of authenticity to it. Maybe she had started to recover from whatever kind of amnesia she apparently suffered with.

Rachel's eyes widened in shock. "That would explain your disguise, but what could a woman possibly have done that was so bad it caused a posse to be looking for you?"

How do I explain this? "Because...well...where I come from, things are more, um, advanced. Women are allowed to be cops."

"What's a cop?"

"Police...uh...peace officers."

"Peace officers?"

The confusion on Rachel's face told Trace she didn't understand the term. "Marshals and sheriffs and deputies and jailers."

At first the younger woman nodded in comprehension but then raised an eyebrow in disbelief. She almost laughed. "You must think I'm a fool. Women can't be the Law. I've never heard of such a thing."

"It's true. I'm not lying to you. I was what is called a police detective in my town and—"

"Detective? Like Pinkerton?"

"No. Yes. Well, not exactly. It's sort of like that but I was more of a sheriff. I...uh...arrested some men who had friends and relatives that didn't like that very much and I think they want me dead." At Rachel's wide-eyed, alarmed expression, Trace added, "They are very bad men and they need to stay in jail. Their leader vowed to kill me and I knew he would, so...that's why I came here." Again, that sounded as though it could have been at least somewhat accurate. Vincent DeSienna wanted her dead long before she turned on his family. If that wasn't the reason, she knew she had always been a convincing liar.

"Will they come here looking for you?" Rachel's voice trembled with her sudden dread.

"I doubt it. At this point, they have no idea where to even start to look for me." *And, if this is real, they have no way to get here, either, I hope.*

"Then why must you keep dressing like a man?"

Good question. "Because...I can't guarantee he or his gang won't eventually ride through this area to search for me," Trace lied, her blue eyes almost pleading, which caused Rachel's cautious green ones to soften. "I know this is a lot to ask, because we don't know each other, but I need your help."

"What could I possibly do to help you?" Her voice was laced with skepticism. "I won't put my life in danger for someone I don't even know. Besides, I'm not sure you're telling me the truth."

"You're right. You don't know me and you don't know if I'm lying. I'm not asking you to hide me; I'm asking you to keep my cover."

"You said that before, something about your cover. I don't know what that means."

"My disguise. I need to stay here a while, a long while." At least until she could figure out what the hell was going on. "And I need to convince everyone that I'm a man."

"Why?"

Because I'm a woman who loves women, who behaves like a typical in-your-face, predatory male, and it will be safer for both of us. She gave Rachel a quick once over. Maybe. "Uh...hmmmm...well, first, as I said, if this man and his friends ride through town, they'll be looking for a woman, not a man. Second, as I also said, where I come from things are a lot more advanced. As an...uh...enforcer of the law, I am a lot more aggressive than any of your women and most of your men. Trust me, I need to live here as a man, otherwise men here will want to kill me, too." *Okay. That made sense.*

"I still don't understand."

"Well," Trace said, "I don't either, but trust me on this. You seem like a very kind woman, Rachel, and I'm pretty sure you wouldn't do anything to intentionally send me to my death."

"Of course not," Rachel said indignantly. "But I cannot have a man living in my home."

"Why? Is it your husband?"

"I'm not married."

"Really? A beautiful woman like you?" Trace's smile was engaging; the information delighted her. "Why not?"

Rachel cast her eyes downward. "I'm just not."

Trace noted that the redness in Rachel's cheeks appeared to be more of a burn than a blush. She knew there had to be a story behind Rachel's single status. Now was not the time to pursue it. "Like I said, I'm not asking you to hide me, just to keep my secret."

As if Rachel had not even heard her, she continued, her gaze still on the ground, "It's just not proper. And even though I know you're not really a man, the town wouldn't."

"It's okay; I understand."

Rachel finally relaxed her grip on the rifle. "Were you really a sheriff?" Her interest seemed genuine.

"Absolutely. If you have a Bible, I'll put my left hand on it and raise the right one to God."

That must have been the right thing to say. Rachel looked back over at Trace, her tone pensive. "I kind of wondered why you didn't seem to be afraid of staring down the barrel of my gun. Well...if anyone asks, I could say that I found you hurt and that I need to nurse you back to health."

"Yeah, that would work," Trace agreed hopefully. "Then the town could gradually get to know me."

"And I really could use some help with the land."

Trace cocked her head and shrugged. "You'd have to show me what you need done. I haven't ever worked land at all."

"You'd have to sleep in the barn."

"With what?" An unpleasant thought crossed her mind. The odor of pig, chicken, cow, and horse manure — or smelling like it — was something she didn't think she could get used to. "What else lives in the barn?"

Rachel appeared to be on the verge of laughing at the expression on Trace's face. "Nothing anymore. I had cows but they were all slaughtered," she said sadly. "Now it's where I keep equipment for the field. There's a small room in the back. You can stay there."

She took note of Rachel's demeanor when she mentioned the cows. Trace decided she would save that question for another time, too. "I really appreciate it, Rachel. Uh...would it be possible to get out of the sun now?"

Rachel seemed to think about it briefly before she lowered the rifle to her side and pointed it at the ground. "Okay. I should take a look at your cut, too. Looks like it needs tending to."

The thought of this adorable woman's hands on her made Trace eager to get to Rachel's house. *You can take the girl out of the sleaze, but you can't take the sleaze out of the girl.* Trace smirked.

As she stood, Trace unobtrusively studied Rachel. The blonde was at least seven inches shorter, had a nice body, judging by the limited amount the dress showed off, and was extremely pleasing to the eye.

If this wasn't some kind of weird dream, and if she was subtle, maybe she could make the most of landing a century back in time.

Inside the cabin, Trace appeared to be fascinated by everything she saw, though Rachel thought it was no better or worse than the homes with which the stranger must be acquainted. Rachel no longer noticed its somberness enhanced by the darkness of the log walls, the wood floor, and the small windows with the hand-made curtains closed over them. It was a neat and orderly provincial home, one that should have exuded warmth, but there was a hint of sorrow that pervaded the air. Rachel had become used to that, too.

"Sit over there and take your shirt off," Rachel instructed and pointed to a hard wooden chair pulled slightly away from the kitchen table. She only half paid attention to Trace, as she pumped water into a bowl.

Trace unbuttoned her shirt as she sat. "We hardly know each other." She laughed softly at her jest.

"Pardon?" Rachel's attention was focused on pulling a small glass jar down off a shelf in an anteroom, which included an iron claw foot bathtub.

"Nothing." Trace gingerly removed her denim top, feeling the strain of her jarred muscles and bones. She had started to show signs of bruising, which meant the pain would soon follow. She looked down at her wrap, saw the blood had absorbed into the material and spread over most of her chest. "Aw, Christ."

"I would appreciate it if, while you are in this house, you would not use the Lord's name..." Rachel stopped at the sight of Trace covered in only the bloody wrap from the waist up. It wasn't the condition of the wound that rendered her speechless; it was the condition of the bared body. "...in...vain."

"Sorry." Trace winced as she stretched out her arm and attempted to pull the kink out of the muscle in her shoulder.

Rachel had been a little shocked by Trace's height when she stood up to accompany her back to the cabin. That alone would make it a little easier to convince the town's people that she was a man, as Rachel had never before seen a woman that much taller than she was. She also noted the absolute confidence with which Trace carried herself, another trait she had only witnessed in men. A powerful aura surrounded this woman and it had Rachel a little flustered. Suddenly it didn't seem so far-fetched that the newcomer could have been someone with authority...like a sheriff.

Now, though, Rachel could see the actual physical strength in this strange woman, not just sense her power. She had muscles like a man, too...though not really. They were visibly defined as they moved under the woman's tanned skin, but they were not coarse or bulky. She also had strong shoulders, Rachel observed, before her eyes traveled down to the bare skin below the bloody wrap, to a torso, which was also sinewy without an inch of excess fat anywhere.

She forced her eyes back to the task of tending to the wound. Rachel was embarrassed and confused that she had openly gawked. At another woman. In a most unladylike way.

After she gathered gauze, a canning jar partially filled with a light liquid, a bowl of water, and a dry cloth, Rachel purposely avoided looking at her guest. Something about the woman made her insides shake. *What is it about this Trace Sheridan that's so unnerving?* She set her paraphernalia on the table and found her voice. "Um...we have to take that off."

Trace glanced down. "This?"

"Yes. I need to stop the bleeding and clean that wound. You don't want it to get infected."

Alert to Rachel's apparent unease, Trace said, "Listen, if you're uncomfortable with this, I can do it."

Suddenly indignant, Rachel shook her head. "No, I'll do it." She placed the cloth in water, unsealed the jar, and dropped the gauze in to absorb some of the liquid. "Doesn't that hurt?" she inquired, as Trace began to unwrap her binding.

"Right now, everything hurts." As Trace peeled off the last two layers of her wrap, Rachel quickly averted her eyes from the exposed breasts. This did not go unnoticed by Trace, who was charmed by Rachel's modesty. Her mouth curled into a slight smile, despite her escalating pain. She grabbed her shirt and slipped it on but left it unbuttoned. It covered her chest and the open garment allowed Rachel the freedom to work, undistracted.

"You didn't have to do that," Rachel said quietly, obviously grateful that she had.

"I know, but I feel better," Trace lied. "So...whatcha got there?"

Rachel plucked the gauze out of the jar and placed it directly on the oozing, jagged cut just to the side of Trace's right breast. Rachel was prepared for the quick flinch and sudden intake of breath from Trace as she put her free hand on Trace's shoulder for support. "It's nettle tea. It will stop the bleeding." She took Trace's hand and positioned it on the gauze. "Hold that there until I tell you to remove it."

"Tea will stop my bleeding?"

"Nettle tea will."

Rachel wrung out the wet cloth and began to clean the area around the wound. She stepped between Trace's legs for better access to the injury, a natural position under the circumstances and one in which Trace took restrained pleasure. Her face reflected her amusement as she watched Rachel studiously wash the blood from her chest and abdomen, gently but with enough pressure to get the job done. The proximity of their bodies was just too difficult to ignore. It was almost worth the pain she was in.

Rachel caught Trace's eyes on her as she leaned to wring out the cloth. "Why are you staring at me?" she asked quietly. She continued to rinse the cloth until the water ran light pink instead of deep red.

Why indeed. "Oh. I'm sorry. I didn't realize I was. You're just so efficient. Are you a nurse?"

"A nurse? No. I work here on the ranch. I grow vegetables and herbs and sell them to Luther Foster for his grocery store. Sometimes my neighbors come here for herbs and I sell them or I barter."

Engaging her in conversation appeared to make Rachel feel a little more secure, so Trace kept it going. "For what?"

"For necessities." Rachel submerged the bloody cloth again, wrung it out, and began one final cleansing of the area. "You can give that to me now," she said and took the gauze from Trace.

With her psyche still firmly planted in the twenty-first century, Trace almost asked Rachel how she dared to handle blood without gloves...and then she remembered — these were the days when bodily fluids weren't normally contaminated or potentially lethal.

Trace eyed Rachel as she knelt down to get a better look at the wound and inspected it thoroughly, oblivious to the position she was in. Trace was certainly conscious of it, though, and continued to subtly study Rachel as warm hands probed around the sore, open flesh. A lewd smile rose on Trace's face. *Heh, while you're down there...* But her fantasy was interrupted.

"Hmmm..."

"Hmmm? Hmmm what?" Trace looked down, surprised to see that the bleeding had stopped. "How'd you do that?"

"I didn't, the nettle tea did it. It has healing properties; it will make your blood clot. It was used a lot in the war."

"What war?" Two very wide green eyes stared at her in pure astonishment. *Uh oh.* Trace tried frantically to remember her American history. *Shit. The Civil War, you dolt.* "Oh, oh right, the war. War Between the States. Right."

Rachel shook her head and continued to inspect the cut. "Just how long have you been hiding out from these men, anyway?" she asked rhetorically, as a hint of sarcasm entered her tone. She stood up and placed the gauze into the bowl and set it aside.

Trace grinned as she watched Rachel return to the anteroom. This was really going to be interesting as she now realized another reason her presence in the past might not be such a good idea: she failed American history. Twice. "Can I button up now?"

"No. I want to put something on that." Rachel searched her shelves. "Ah. There you are." She reached up and plucked down another jar.

"What are you going to put on me this time? Coffee?" Trace teased.

"No. Honey."

Trace smirked and said, "Wow, we've known each other less than an hour and you're already calling me honey?" Rachel looked confused, then impatient and Trace was about to do some major back peddling when Rachel held up the jar in her hand.

"Honey. I'm going to put honey on you."

Shut up, Trace, just...shut...up. In another setting, a hundred years from now, you'd be in your glory. "And what will that do...other than get me sticky?"

"Don't you know anything?" Rachel smiled tolerantly. She removed the lid from the jar, dipped her fingers in, pulled out a glob, and paused before she applied it to Trace's wound. "Honey attracts water. Germs cannot live without water and they die. Which means no infection and quicker healing."

Impressed, Trace observed while Rachel scooped some honey off her fingers with her thumb and tenderly applied the gooey substance along the jagged cut. Finished, Rachel stepped back, then she stuck the fingers that never touched Trace's skin into her mouth and sucked the rest of the honey off them. Trace's jaw dropped and she crossed her legs tightly, not believing the rush that flooded her loins at Rachel's actions. She knew her new young friend had no clue as to how erotic that was.

"Let me get you something to keep that cov— What? Did that hurt? The honey shouldn't cause it to hurt more."

Trace realized that Rachel was not very worldly and must have mistaken her stricken look of lust for one of discomfort. She put a hand up to stop Rachel from getting as close as she had been before. "No," she rasped, "it's fine. Really. Thank you. Yes, something to cover it would be nice."

Rachel searched Trace's face with concern. "Oh. Okay." Hesitantly, she returned to the anteroom, found another patch of gauze and brought it back to her patient. "Would you like me to—"

"No," Trace answered so quickly it made Rachel jump. She held her hand out for the gauze. "I'll do it, thanks." She forced her voice to be calm. "You've been very kind, Rachel. Thank you." She placed the material over the honey and slowly stood up, beginning to feel like one big bruise. Trace reached over to the table and picked up her blood-soaked binding. "Where do I wash this? And, I suppose you wouldn't happen to have anything in your little bag of tricks to get the blood stain out of it?"

Rachel leaned against the table, head bowed. "You're making fun of me," she said softly.

Trace blinked and shook her head. "No, I'm not." She was surprised at how the thought of hurting this young woman's feelings affected her. Ordinarily, she would not have cared one way or the other, but for whatever reason, she felt almost protective of Rachel. *Where the hell did that come from?* She reached out and touched Rachel's shoulder, a gesture that made Rachel look up. "I'm not. I apologize if that's how it sounded," Trace said in a quiet voice. "I'm just a little...um...disturbed...about the events of today and the past few days...and my body aches, so please forgive me if I sound, uh, grumpy or...difficult. I don't mean to. Okay?"

Rachel nodded and, with what seemed like great effort, broke eye contact with Trace. "Okay." She tugged at the wrap in Trace's hand. "Let me do that for you. I'll wash it best I can. I don't think I'll be able to get all the blood out but...it'll be clean."

"Really, you don't have to—"

"No, I want to. You really should rest. You look mighty worn out. And you should give that cut a chance to start healing."

Trace couldn't argue with that; she felt tired and tendons and joints were starting to scream in protest at every movement. "If you're sure..."

"I am."

"Then I would really appreciate it if you would show me where I'll be sleeping, and I'll get out of your way."

"You're not in my way," Rachel said almost shyly. "But I'll show you to the barn."

It really wasn't a bad little room — other than being dim, dusty, and depressing. A cot-sized bed occupied one side, against a wall, and an old bureau stood against the opposite wall with a kerosene lantern that sat on top. It was a place to lay her head; she was thankful for that.

Rachel provided her with a linen sheet, a clean woven horse blanket, and a feather pillow, one of the two from her own bed. She also gave Trace an old nightshirt of her father's to wear so that she could wash and repair the hole in Trace's denim shirt. Trace's protests fell on deaf ears.

The long, white garment fit better than Trace thought it would, which made her wonder if Rachel had saved any of her father's other clothes that might be suitable for her to borrow.

Trace stretched out, her legs almost too long for the bed, and stared at the gloomy ceiling; her body actually starting to relax and settle to an acceptable throb. Her thoughts swirled at breakneck speed. It wasn't so much what she had gotten herself into, it was more how had she gotten herself into it. *Okay, despite not being able to remem-*

ber that part, like it or not, I'm here and alive...but can I stay that way? Her body hurt entirely too much and too realistically for this to be a dream, so somehow she had miraculously survived the deadly risk of time travel, an innovation she was pretty sure had not been invented, or if it had, no doubt was still in the stage of conception. Yet here she was. Her head was beginning to pound in response to her unanswered questions; more pain that she didn't need at the moment.

At first she thought she might have accidentally wandered onto a movie set and then, when she saw no evidence of production equipment or a film crew, she wondered if maybe she was the butt of a practical joke. Her colleagues were capable of it and pretty damned imaginative, but even as creative as they were and as merciless as they could be, they would not have let it go on this long. She had to acknowledge that she actually was in the late eighteen hundreds.

If she had to stay here, could she survive the meager, no frills existence she had been sentenced to?

She had forgotten that interior toilets were a luxury in this era and was not thrilled about having to utilize a stinky, spider-and-God-knew-what-else infested outhouse or find a tree marked "W". Laundry was done with a washboard, bar soap, and good old-fashioned elbow grease, and her baths would no doubt have to be taken in the nearby river. Until it got too cold and, hopefully by then, Rachel would feel comfortable with letting her use the indoor tub. If she was still here come winter.

She hoped she had just finished her period and wouldn't have to worry about that for a few weeks. *Shit.* She didn't look forward to dealing with that little fact of life, pretty sure tampons had not been invented yet, either, and almost afraid to ask her hostess what she did every month. Therein lay another problem. How could she cleverly find out what Rachel used to absorb the menstrual flow? If she came right out and asked her, how would she explain not knowing? And the cramps... *Damn it.* Some months those annoying, pulsating pains were so intense they could drop a moose. She wondered if Rachel had a natural remedy for that, too.

She certainly is handy. Trace couldn't help the indecent smile that crept onto her face. *Cute little thing, too. Not to mention a little bossy. Not that being bossy is necessarily bad; it means she has some spunk.* Shameless, a visual floated through Trace's mind that involved her, Rachel, and that feather bed in the room from which Rachel had retrieved her father's nightshirt. "Stop it, Trace," she chastised herself. "Keep your head out of your pants."

Trace knew reining in her hearty libido would be difficult, but anything else would be counterproductive to her survival. Rachel had opened her home to her, a stranger, an act of kindness for which Trace should be eternally grateful. To fuck that up in an attempt to indulge her carnal urges, which she was sure would backfire, would be idiocy. But that thing with the honey...Jesus, that was...unexpected, as was the physical reaction it evoked in her.

As attracted to Rachel as Trace was, she also needed to decipher that overwhelmingly alien feeling to protect Rachel. Where had that come from? Other than the desire to shelter her mother as much as possible, Trace had never once experienced that particular compulsion, except in the line of duty, but that was different; that was professional as opposed to personal. What was it about this...waif...that probed into a previously untapped side of Trace? That was something she would have to investigate further, as she was not sure she liked it. Feeling professionally responsible for someone else's safety was a lot different than feeling personally responsible. Trace was determined to be in total control of all her emotions and she resented this new one that had suddenly reared its unfamiliar head. Or did she? Maybe this was just one more thing she had to get used to if she could not find her way back to the twenty-first century. Maybe she needed to stop being so analytical and just let life happen.

Yeah, right. Trace sighed. *As if I ever let anything just happen.*

Another curiosity revolved around Rachel's father.

Obviously Rachel lived on this property alone and she used past tense when she spoke of him, so it wasn't hard to figure out her father was dead. But this darling, smart, skilled young woman, who possessed what looked to be a very nice body, was also not married. Dare she selfishly hope there was an alternative reason behind Rachel being unwed? Well, she could hope all she wanted, but chances were there was a perfectly good explanation for that.

And what had happened to the cows? There was anger in Rachel's voice when she said they had all been slaughtered, which indicated to Trace the cows had probably not been intentionally killed for meat. Something was going on here that gave Trace an uncomfortable feeling of foreboding. Her inquisitive nature would not permit her to let any of her questions lie idle for too long. Later, when she knew Rachel a little better, she would ask.

There was a soft knock on the door. "Come in," Trace called, and tried to sit up. The pain that wracked her body advised her that staying supine would be a much better idea.

Rachel entered almost timidly, carrying a tray that held a bowl of something, a thick slice of what Trace guessed to be homemade bread, and a steaming cup of some mildly aromatic liquid. "Hi," she said quietly. "I thought you might be hungry, so..." She shrugged, knowing the proffered tray spoke for itself.

As Rachel neared the bed, Trace pushed herself up slightly until her back rested against the wall. She couldn't repress the sharp intake of breath when she moved.

"That's what I thought, so I made you something to help with that." She set the tray down on Trace's thighs.

"Soup and tea?"

"And charoset bread to dip in the soup," Rachel added. She pointed to the cup. "That's peppermint tea with rue and wood betony. It'll help with the pain."

"And the soup?"

Rachel smiled. "That'll help with the hunger."

Trace had to smile at that obvious conclusion. She picked up her spoon and sampled the chowder-like substance. Her face lit up. "Mmm. Potato soup." Her absolute favorite soup in the whole world. How odd this would be the first meal this insightful young woman would bring her. She took another spoonful, then a bite of the deliciously sweet bread. "This is really very good." She glanced up at her beaming hostess. "Thank you."

"You're welcome. How are your injuries?"

"Let's just say they're there and leave it at that. I've had bruises before. They'll go away."

"Should I take a look at your cut?"

Trace stopped mid-taste. The thought of Rachel that close to her again, those nimble fingers on her skin, was too much. "No...um...I'm pretty sure that's fine also. But I appreciate the offer." She resumed inhaling the contents of her bowl and her bread. She had not realized how hungry she was.

Rachel smiled and stood silently for a few minutes, encouraged by Trace's enthusiasm for the small supper she had prepared. "Your binding and shirt are washed and hanging on the line right now. They should be dry before nightfall. I also fixed the tear in your shirt."

"Thank you again. You're very kind," Trace said with sincerity.

Rachel bowed her head and stepped back. She shrugged slightly. "It's nothing really. I enjoy it...helping people."

Trace studied her, finding her shyness irresistibly endearing. "Well, you're obviously good at it."

Rachel nodded her thanks and indicated the tray. "I'll be back for that later. Drink your tea. It'll help you sleep."

Trace shook her head and watched Rachel leave. She knew there had to be a good reason why no man had snatched up this exceptional woman and made her his wife.

Rachel returned a little over two hours later with Trace's clothes. She was pleased to see her new friend sound asleep, a soft snore emanating from the sprawled form. She had not told Trace that charoset was made from apples, walnuts, cinnamon, honey, and a few other ingredients, and that together, though mainly the walnuts, the combination amounted to an effective sedative. She wisely assumed that, had she known, Trace would have refused the calmant, not wanting to crack the tough façade she maintained, another more male than female characteristic that puzzled Rachel.

She picked up the tray from the floor and set it on the bureau. Stepping back over to the bed, she looked down at this strong — however vulnerable at this point — individual and folded her arms. What was her story? What had really brought this very handsome woman, pretending to be a man, to the edge of Sagebrush and into Rachel's life? *Whatever the reason, it will reveal itself soon enough.*

As she watched her unusual guest sleep, an unexpected warmth enveloped Rachel in an oddly satisfying way. When she awoke that morning, she certainly could not have predicted that she would have someone to take care of by the time she went to bed, someone to cater to regardless of Trace's protestations that she didn't want Rachel to go out of her way. Trace had no way of knowing that her hostess was grateful to have someone to fuss over again. Until today, even she had not realized how very much she missed that.

Rachel felt a coolness in the air and knew the mid-April night would get chillier. She pulled the blanket over Trace's long body, retrieved the tray, and left the room.

Chapter Three

A hideous noise infiltrated Trace's sporadic sleep and jolted her into sudden consciousness. The sound assaulted her ears again and she flew out of bed, regretting it the minute her feet hit the floor, having forgotten about the large contusion that was now her body. The piercing, shrill racket echoed again and, in her fuzzyheaded state, prompted her to immediately think someone was being murdered. Or worse. She forgot where she was and she danced around the room in search of her Glock 22, confused at not being able to find it. Realization hit her and the memory of the day before whipped into her mind. She quickly recovered and her first thought was of Rachel, that she needed help.

She raced out of the barn, toward the house, and nearly slammed into the object of her concern, having to grab her before she knocked her to the ground.

An amused expression crossed Rachel's face as she was held up and steadied by a wild-eyed Amazon. "Morning," she said calmly.

Trace held Rachel at arm's length for inspection and frantically asked, "Are you all right?"

"I'm fine." She scrutinized Trace. "Are you all right?"

Trace ran a hand through her unruly hair and wondered if she looked as demented as she suddenly felt, with her unlikely armor of a gooey, disheveled nightshirt and cowboy boots. She dropped her arms to her side and looked around, bewildered. "I'm...fine. What the hell was that noise?"

Rachel stepped back cautiously and continued to observe the addled woman. "What noise?"

As if on cue, the horrendous sound cut through the air again and penetrated Trace's eardrums, setting her teeth on edge, making her cringe. "That noise. What the hell is that?"

Rachel tried very hard to stifle a laugh. She cleared her throat, she said, "That is a rooster."

"What the hell is wrong with it?" Trace asked, her breathing slowing.

"Nothing. Roosters always crow at first light."

"Why?"

Rachel cocked her head at Trace in disbelief and said, "For coming from a town that's supposed to be ahead of the times, you sure are reactionary." Immediately responding to the irritated look on Trace's face, Rachel hastily added, "But maybe you don't have roosters there."

Trace folded her arms. "Is it going to do that every morning?"

"Of course, silly. That's what roosters do."

Her expression didn't change. "Why?"

Rachel nervously fiddled with the fresh eggs in her basket and then focused on checking each shell for cracks. "Well...the Bible says the rooster crowing at dawn is a symbol of the daily victory of light over darkness, good over evil." She looked up at Trace and caught her rolling her eyes. "Why did you do that?"

"The Bible. Uh huh." She squeezed her eyes shut tightly as the rooster crowed one last time. "How would you feel about chicken for dinner?"

Okay, so she shouldn't have made the remark about killing the rooster, not that she would have actually murdered the bird given the opportunity. But rising every morning before the sun was even up was going to be hell, her body clock being regulated to a swing shift schedule.

And what a temper little Miss Rachel has, Trace thought, as she put on her freshly laundered denim shirt and buttoned up. It was just a question. She was used to working in the dark; why couldn't she start her "chores" in the afternoon and work late into the evening?

Damn, that wrap really hurt. She stretched her sore muscles as much as she could, pretty sure that the pain was from the injuries her body sustained from that fall to the ground and not the binding itself. God, she hoped not, knowing she would have to live with being wrapped every day regardless. She also needed a full bath. Rachel had left a cloth and bowl of water in her room sometime before she awoke and Trace cleaned up the honey that had smeared all over her chest during a night of obvious restless movement. But she still felt sticky. And just plain icky, in general.

And now she felt obligated to have breakfast — a meal she hated and usually skipped altogether in favor of sleeping a little longer — with her madder-than-a-wet-hen hostess.

Trace sighed heavily and walked to the cabin with a slight apprehension that suddenly made her smirk. She had gone up against some of the most sordidly vicious criminals the streets had to offer, and now she was nervous about facing an itty bitty ranch girl? *Well,* Trace pondered, *Rachel was quite irate when she stormed into the house after the dinner suggestion and the sleeping late question. And then I guess I poured gasoline onto the fire after she quoted the Bible again, something about laziness and I, being the up-at-the-crack-of-noon person I am, told her what she could do with the "Good Book".*

Trace leaned against the thick frame and watched Rachel putter determinedly around the stove, evidently still angry. Why the hell she wanted to feed Trace after she obviously made light of her faith as evidenced by spouting Bible verses was beyond her. Trace hated to apologize as it implied making mistakes, and mistakes showed weakness. This would be the second time in less than twenty-four hours that she had sincerely apologized to Rachel. It was rare when Trace openly admitted error twice in a year. Twice in one day was unheard of. But she needed this young woman's help and couldn't get that by pissing her off. And, for reasons beyond her understanding, she really didn't want Rachel upset with her. At least, not this early in their budding alliance.

Trace cleared her throat and knocked on the door as she stepped inside the cabin. "Uh, Rachel? I, uh, I apologize for my words earlier." Her voice was low and modulated. She wanted to indicate that she was, indeed, sorry for being thoughtless and offensive, but not for having what would be, around here, an unpopular opinion regarding the Bible. That was something Rachel would have to live with if she wanted Trace to continue to keep her company and help out around the place. "I was just a little unnerved by that bird and I was tired and I still hurt and—"

"And crabby. Don't forget that one," Rachel snapped. She was still facing the stove, her hands on her hips.

"Okay. Crabby. Yes, I was certainly that," Trace said, thinking she would have to make a conscious effort to be more congenial in the mornings, especially since there wasn't going to be a way to get out of waking with that damn rooster.

"And surly."

Rachel's tone had not lightened any as she slid the contents of the skillet onto a plate with bread on it. There was also what looked like a cup of coffee next to the plate, which made Trace's eyes light up. She took a small step toward the table as Rachel placed the pan back onto the stove.

"Surly, right. I thought we established that." She so wanted to grab for that cup but was pretty sure Rachel wasn't done verbally pouting. Maybe if she reached for it very slowly...

"And blasphemous!" Rachel whirled to face her, prompting Trace to pull her hand back so fast, she struck herself on the shoulder. Rachel pointed a finger at Trace, threatening impalement. "If you live here, you will have respect for the Lord's Word and the book that it's written in."

Trace hadn't realized it while it was happening, but the little spitfire had just backed her up against a wall. She wondered if it was safe to even eat the eggs Rachel scrambled for her. "Okay, okay..." Hands in front of her, she gestured her surrender. Rachel's eyes flashed indignantly, as if daring her to dispute her behavior. "Okay. I'm sorry," Trace reiterated softly.

Rachel started to turn back toward the table when she heard Trace draw in a breath. Obviously thinking Trace was going to protest or argue, Rachel spun back and held up her index finger again in warning.

"Okay, all right, I've got it: no bashing the Bible."

"And no taking the Lord's name in vain."

That was going to be a tough one, but Trace wasn't going to admit it at that particular moment. "Got it." She stayed put while Rachel walked back to the table and sat.

Rachel looked over at her. "Well, are you going to come eat or not?"

Trace prudently kept her mouth shut as she walked to the table and joined her fiery little hostess. She picked up her coffee cup and had it halfway to her lips when she noticed two very annoyed green eyes looking at her. Wisely, she silently set the mug down and allowed Rachel to take her hand.

Rachel bowed her head and closed her eyes. "Lord, we humbly thank You for Your offering of this food. Amen." She let go of Trace's hand and began to eat.

Trace studied Rachel for signs of anything else that might come between her and her caffeine. When Rachel said nothing and continued to eat, Trace finally got her first swallow of coffee. It was horrible. It was bitter and grainy and, well, thick. But when her mercurial breakfast companion looked to her for approval, Trace smiled convincingly. "It's wonderful. Thank you, Rachel."

Oh, boy.

One of the good things about Rachel, Trace quickly discovered, was that she only simmered briefly before she boiled over, and then it was done. She said her piece about Trace's attitude and before breakfast was finished, she was fine. The breakfast — with the exception of that sludge she called coffee — was quite tasty. Once she felt safe to finally dig in and eat it.

She was going to ask Rachel about washing up when Rachel told her the first thing she would like her to do. A bath seemed futile if she was going to spend the morning on a sweaty horse, checking the perimeter fence for holes or breaks. Other than that, it sounded simple enough.

Until she walked into the stable and realized she would have to saddle up a woolly mammoth and actually sit on top of him, guiding him to where ever she needed to go. Trace knew she would not be able to manipulate this male animal as easily as she could male humans. Her arms fell to her sides in defeat. The closest she had ever been to a horse was the carousel in the amusement park outside of town. And she couldn't exactly ask Rachel, being as she was supposed to have been thrown from a horse.

Suck it up, Trace, she thought. *How hard can it be?*

An hour later, if she could have picked up the damned horse and thrown him, she would have. She was positive the beast was laughing at her, not that she blamed him. She was grateful Rachel had occupied herself with housework and cleaning the chicken coop and had not come to check on her.

In the previous sixty minutes, she had attempted to saddle the horse. She had studied the leather seat intently, as if it was going to speak to her and give her explicit instructions. When it didn't, she glanced at the horse, who just as suspiciously eyeballed her in return. Then she grabbed the saddle by the horn and the cantle and pulled it off the post where it rested, expecting to hoist it onto the horse's back just like John Wayne did in the movies. It never occurred to her that the damned thing would weigh almost thirty-five pounds.

She tugged it backward and freed it of its support. Momentum caused her to lose her balance and unintentionally thump down on her behind, where she found the saddle unexpectedly on her lap. "Shit!" As if her body needed any more bruises. Her sudden action provoked the horse to prance to the side a little and snort at her. "Shaaaadduuuup," she told him, as she snickered at herself.

Trace stood up and brushed the straw off her jeans, then bent down and picked up the saddle. She held it, getting used to its weight. When she felt confident, she slowly closed in on the horse, a beautiful — and large — Palomino, and stood next to the animal's left side. At least she remembered that mounting a horse was always done on the left, so it was natural to assume, any other kind of approach should probably be done on the left, also. She took a deep breath, lifted the saddle with concentrated strength and threw it up toward the horse's back, only to have it smack the animal on his left flank as it sailed over him and onto the floor on the other side. Which caused the horse to protest indignantly and dance, quite spiritedly, around her a few times, stopping directly in front of the door to his stall, trapping her inside. She was positive she saw a "fuck you" look in the animal's big brown eyes. She and the horse repeated this strange ritual from several angles.

She stood there making faces in contemplation and rested her hands on her hips, frustrated. "Look, buddy, work with me here, okay?" she addressed the horse, who always seemed to return to his position between her and the doorway. "All I want to do is take you out for a nice ride...with me on your back. If I knew how to ride bareback, I would. But I don't, so it'll be a lot easier if you just give me a break, okay?" She picked up the saddle once again. As fit as she was, her biceps twanged from the continuous lifting of the awkwardly balanced item. "I don't see why we can't be friends."

Her impatiently fake smile was rewarded by another snort, and the clever animal quickly sidled over to her and pinned her up against the stall wall with his right flank. It happened so fast, Trace had no time to react, other than dropping the saddle, but suddenly there she was, unable to move with the side of the steed's belly tight to her. "God, this is worse than a Laurel and Hardy movie," she said, and started laughing. Pushing the animal only resulted in his moving closer, if that was possible.

"Very funny, very cute. Okay, you've shown me who's boss. You can move now." He didn't budge, other than to bob his head up and down several times. "Don't piss me off. A glue factory isn't entirely out of the question for you, you know." Trace started to get angry when shoving and raising her voice obviously didn't impress him. "Listen, Mr. Ed, I'm not fucking around here! Move!" Which he did. Closer to her, which really restricted her mobility. Maybe she shouldn't be pissing him off.

"Move, you big bag of bones! I'm not kidding here!" Trace grunted and groaned, as great effort was put into getting the obstinate animal to move. "You big jackass, you're not supposed to be this stubborn. Move, you son-of-a-bitch!" Trace pushed her body against the horse with all her might, the Palomino oblivious to the bothersome creature in his space. "Augh! God da—"

Rachel cleared her throat audibly, loud enough to interrupt the ranting woman and get her attention. There was an abrupt silence.

"Gosh darn it," Trace said, as she banged her head against the horse's side. How was she ever going to explain her way out of this?

Trace figured Rachel must have been en route to the house from the chicken coop when she heard the angry voice filtering out from the stable. Rachel probably wondered why she hadn't gone out and checked the fences yet. She had quickly learned that Rachel was an inquisitive woman so, of course, she had to come to check out the odd circumstances. She could only imagine how it looked as the horse had Trace ensnared at an angle, the top of her head and her long legs next to the horse's hindquarters, the only visible part of her.

"Um...what are you doing?"

The earnest question came from the disembodied voice of a sweet, innocent woman who, Trace knew, was about to make a fool of her. Or, more accurately, highlight the fact that Trace was doing an excellent job of making a fool of herself. *First the rooster, now the horse. Maybe working with animals is not going to be my forte.*

There was no way out of it. Humility raged through her normally cavalier persona and Trace started with a little chuckle. "Heh. Well, uh, it's like this...I tried to saddle him and he wouldn't cooperate."

Rachel stepped forward and easily coaxed the horse away from a brooding, embarrassed Trace. "First," Rachel began, showing signs of smugness, "you have to be smarter than the horse." She scratched the big steed under his chin, then leaned in and kissed him on the bridge of his nose. She turned to Trace. "Were you actually trying to put a saddle on him without a blanket first? No wonder he rebelled."

"Well...um...we do things differently where I'm from," she said, wondering how long she would be able to use that as an excuse.

Rachel raised an eyebrow. "Your horses must not last too long." She lovingly ran her hand along the side of the horse's head. "Did you even try to groom him first?"

"Uh..."

Rachel shook her head and picked up the brush. "You act like you've never saddled a horse before. You sheriffs have someone do that for you?"

Trace knew an escape route when she saw one. "Yes, that's it — we have a saddle person who does all that for us." She studied Rachel intently as Rachel removed dirt from the horse's throatlatch and neck, and then moved to his girth with a hard-bristled brush.

"Pick up that soft-bristled brush there and just do everything I do," Rachel instructed.

Trace picked up the brush and mimicked everything Rachel did. "Now...we're doing this because..."

It took a minute for Rachel to realize she was supposed to finish the sentence. "If he's not groomed first, he could get sores in his weight-bearing area. This keeps his skin in good condition, brings the oil up, keeps his coat healthy. Always start on his left side, always make sure he sees and hears you, and always talk to him soft-like when you're doing this." Rachel waited and when she heard no noise coming from her taller companion, she straightened up and looked at Trace, waiting. "Well?"

"Well what?"

"Talk to him."

Trace scrunched up her face. *Is she kidding? I can barely hold a decent conversation with people.* She was grateful none of her co-workers were there to see her. She looked at Rachel, then at the horse and then back to Rachel like a deer caught in headlights. She opened her mouth to protest but nothing came out, so she snapped it shut. Trace glanced at the Palomino and cleared her throat. "Uh...heh...hi there, horsey...nice horsey," she started, strained. She put her hand up to pet the animal but he pulled his head back abruptly and snorted again. Trace stepped back. "See? He just doesn't like me."

"Don't much blame him. He knows you don't like him."

"Wh—? No, I like him. I do." *I just don't have any experience around the damned things*, she wanted to say, *and the damned horse is taking advantage of it.*

"His name is Chief," Rachel said. "And we'll work on your charm later," she added dryly.

While both women continued to groom the cantankerous animal, Rachel advised Trace on the etiquette of horse care: what specific equipment was for, safety tips to avoid getting kicked, how to clean the hooves and comb the mane and tail.

Rachel then instructed Trace on how to properly saddle Chief, how to fasten the cinches, how to adjust the stirrups, and how to stay on the horse's "good side" as she was doing this. While Trace concentrated on that task, Rachel fit Chief with his bit, bridle, and reins. When it was time to ride out to the property line, Trace mounted Chief and did her best cowboy imitation and made a clicking noise with her mouth and kicked her heels into his haunches. The horse did not budge. Undaunted, she tried again, knowing Rachel was watching. Chief stubbornly remained in place.

Rachel rolled her eyes, stepped up to Chief and slapped him hard on his hindquarters. The animal responded immediately and lurched into a gallop out of the stable, nearly sending Trace backward onto the stall floor. But she hung on. And did something she had never done before: she prayed.

By sheer luck, Trace did not fall or get thrown from the horse's back, though it certainly wasn't from Chief's lack of trying. She swore the animal waited until she eased up on her death grip around his neck and chose that particular time to jump over something, anything, the last object being a small shrub he could have just as easily moved around or galloped over. When he landed, she thwacked down on the saddle so hard, her jaw slammed shut and rattled every tooth in her mouth.

When Chief abruptly halted, it was less than a foot away from the rail fence and it was only flat out leg strength that kept her from sailing over the horse's head into the wooden barrier. Infuriated, Trace fluidly slid off the saddle and marched up to the front of the animal, staring him in the eyes.

"What the fuck is wrong with you!" Her fists rested on her hips. She stared the horse down, the rage and terror so visibly on the surface that she was actually vibrating. "Are you trying to kill me?"

Chief snorted, then bent down and began munching on the high grass beneath him. Trace sputtered at the animal's utter disregard for her safety and obvious lack of response to intimidation. She was so furious, she couldn't get any words out. Trace paced and screamed and continued to wear a path beside Chief until she calmed down. She took a deep breath and stopped in front of the horse again.

"Okay, look, you've had your fun. You've made your point, but we're not getting anywhere. I'm trying to help out your owner, here." She paused as Chief looked up at her accusingly. Trace glanced skyward in exasperation, then back at the Palomino. "Okay. So she's helping me out. Christ, what are you, a psychic?" She stared at Chief then looked heavenward. "I don't believe this...I'm trying to reason with a fucking horse." Trace slowly reached over to touch him, to hopefully signal a truce or make a connection.

Nodding his head up and down wildly as if to avoid her hand, Chief backed away, turned around, and trotted back toward the house, leaving Trace frustrated and alone in the huge field.

"Son-of-a-bitch!" Trace yelled. She stomped her foot, balled her fists up by her sides and watched helplessly as Chief disappeared from view. *Great. Now I'm stuck here, wherever "here" is.* She knew she was still on Rachel's land and maybe if she'd been paying more attention to where she was going or where she'd come from instead of concentrating on hanging on for dear life, she might have been able to find her way back. But it wasn't as if the damned horse had taken a straight line. He had carried her on a high speed tour of woods, through a shallow part of the river, and across what seemed like miles of flat, grassy land. Hopefully, if she wasn't back by dark, Rachel would come looking for her. On a different horse.

That merry ride had done nothing to help the soreness and the aching her body was now barely tolerating. Concerned that the bouncing around may have re-opened her wound, she slipped her hand between the buttons of her shirt, feeling a minor seepage. "Damn it." She swore softly, then broke into a smile at the memory of Rachel sucking the excess honey off her fingers. She wasn't too sure she could see that again and actually stay in her seat.

Trace looked around at the fertile landscape that surrounded her — the range of grass, trees, a river, and skies a deeper blue than she'd ever seen. She took a deep breath and realized she had been inhaling fresh air for probably the first time in her life. She savored the moment, sighed, and then began to walk along the rail fence in the direction from which she had come. Common sense told her that at some point it had to bring her back to the house and its owner.

In the two hours she walked along the fence, she found a few minor breaks in the railings, none of which appeared to be anything more than rot or normal wear and tear. However, just before the river, she stopped and closely inspected a large fifty-foot gap that most certainly looked as though it had been purposely created, almost as if the fence had been mowed down. Rails and splintered wood were strewn about as though a herd of buffalo had trampled through. For the first time, that phrase finally made sense to her. The damage did not appear to be accidental; it looked malicious.

She stood there and scratched her head, wondering how that might have occurred when she heard the pounding of approaching horse hooves. She turned toward the sound and was relieved to see Rachel cantering up to her on Chief.

Rachel pulled up on the reins and slowed the horse to a stop. "You know," Rachel said, mildly amused, as she rested her arms across the saddle horn, "one of the main reasons I need you here is so that I can get work done at the house while you do the field work. It isn't of much help to me if I have to come out here and do your work, too."

"Don't you have any other horses?" Trace asked, glaring at Chief.

"Sure do. I have four others. Chief is the best, though."

"That's not particularly reassuring," Trace said, looking down, showing tiny signs of chagrin.

"And he was already saddled. So...what happened?"

"I have no idea. I got off him and he took off."

"I meant the fence," Rachel said.

Trace looked up at her while Rachel surveyed the destruction. "Oh. I don't know. I was just thinking about that. Stampede, maybe? Do you have those around here?"

"Where there are cattle, there are stampedes."

"Think that's what happened, then?"

"More than likely," she responded, her tone disgusted. "But I don't think it was an accident."

"Why?" Trace's curiosity was genuine.

"I just don't, that's all."

It was Rachel's expression that made Trace hesitate. Her face was a palette of emotions: anger, apprehension, and something that definitely did not belong — shame.

What the hell is going on here?

There was a reason this young woman lived on this big stretch of land by herself...no parents, no husband, slaughtered cows, destroyed property. Something didn't add up and it was obvious Rachel was not going to be forthcoming with the details. At least not yet.

"Come on, let's go back, have some dinner and then you can come back out here and start fixing this break."

Oh, goody. Manual labor. Hopefully she could muddle through mending a fence better than she could saddle and ride a horse. Speaking of which... "Do I have to ride Chief?"

"Better get used to him. He's the fastest and the strongest." Rachel held out her hand. "Haul up here."

Trace looked at Rachel's extended arm as though it were an electric eel, and blanched. "You mean ride? Together?"

"Well, yes. You do want something in your belly before you start working, don't you?"

Trace was hungry and Rachel was a good cook. Hopefully, she hadn't made any coffee. She looked up at Rachel. Hmmm...why was she balking? Considering how close their bodies would be... *Trace, you are such a hound,* she admonished herself. She stuck her foot in the stirrup, grabbed the offered hand and swung her tall, solid body snugly behind Rachel's.

"Hold on," Rachel commanded.

Before Trace had time to react, Rachel kicked Chief into gear. She had no choice but to hold tight to Rachel's waist. If she hadn't been so terrified, she would have enjoyed the proximity much more.

Chapter Four

Dinner consisted of homemade bread and a hearty stew, thick with meat and sliced vegetables. Trace was surprised to find the stew also loaded with fresh basil and garlic. She loved how those two herbs flavored just about anything to her liking.

Rachel was a chatty little thing, Trace discovered as she devoured her meal. Surprised at her own ravenous appetite, she just listened and ate while Rachel rambled on about seasonal flowers coming up in her garden. She then moved on to the novel she was reading, *Wuthering Heights,* and debated with the air the virtues of Emily Brontë's writing.

After two hefty helpings, Trace desperately needed something with which to cleanse her mouth. Swishing fresh apple cider around just wasn't doing it. She waited for Rachel to take a breath in her solo conversation and finally jumped in when Rachel took a sip of her beverage.

"You wouldn't happen to have an extra toothbrush lying around anywhere, would you?"

Rachel set her cup back on the table and squinted into the vivid blue eyes. "Toothbrush? One of those things with a bone handle and boar's hair bristles?"

Well, that certainly didn't sound like something Trace wanted to stick in her mouth. "Is that all you have?"

Rachel stood and picked up their bowls and carried them to the bucket to be washed. "I don't have one of those. They cost a lot of money."

"What do you use to clean your teeth?" She almost dreaded the answer but knew, whatever it was, she would have to abide by it because her teeth were feeling pretty fuzzy and her mouth tasted like what one might remove from Chief's stall with a pitchfork.

"Depends on what I have available...baking soda or chalk."

"Chalk?" The thought of chalking her teeth was not an appealing one, but neither was never brushing her teeth again. "Well, then, which do you have that I could clean my teeth with right now?" Rachel's expression made Trace realize that brushing twice a day was not going to be feasible. Nor were regular hot showers or daily "constitutionals" in the comfort of one's own indoor bathroom, timely shaving, douching, or reaching into her refrigerator after a shift to crack open a cold beer or two.

Oh, the challenges...

Trace placed clean gauze over her oozing wound, then reluctantly left the house to utilize the "facilities" again. She was grateful that an old Farmer's Almanac with a hole punched in the corner was hung on a nail in the outhouse for the sole purpose of wiping one's self. It sure as hell beat drip dry and she didn't even want to think about how long she'd have to sit there or what she might have to use for anything more complicated than emptying her bladder. Old jokes about corn cobs suddenly sprang to mind and she shuddered at the thought.

Trace used the outdoor pump to rinse off her hands and headed into the barn where, together, without much conversation, she and Rachel lifted rails, posts, and stakes onto the light, uncovered wagon. They then loaded it with an axe, shovel, nails, string, and a mallet. Rachel hitched Chief up and sent Trace on her way.

Twelve half-round pine rails, eight feet long, hung over the end edge of the five foot flat bed wagon. Placed on top of them were six posts that extended only a foot longer than the rails. Trace let the horse lead her back to the area by the river where the fence line had been destroyed. Maybe if she didn't try to be in charge, she and Chief might be able to suspend their hostilities. That would be nice, since the horse was getting on her last nerve.

Rachel told her these were the only prepared rails and posts she had; any other mending would have to be done with freshly split wood. *Which means I'm probably going to have to find a Home Depot.* She laughed ruefully. *Or at least a logging place that will sell me pre-cut fencing.* She giggled. *Or chop the damn things myself.* That stopped any frivolous musing altogether. Oh, well...if she hadn't been in shape before she got here, she had no doubt that would change. Soon.

Rachel had been somewhat vague and non-committal regarding the possible reason for the damaged barrier. *What was it she said?* Trace climbed down from her perch and walked back to the portion of strong standing fence to inspect it. *It was probably the neighbors not being very neighborly.* That was an understatement, she was sure, kind of like Trace saying her hundred and some-odd year jump back in time was just a little glitch in the space/time continuum.

Never having built or repaired a fence, Trace studied the simple structure so that she would have an idea as to how to begin. It looked easy enough, she deduced: the rails inserted into holes in the posts that seemed to be held in place by their own weight. She walked the fence line — or where it should have been — and was relieved to see that only two posts had been splintered beyond repair; the rest were still intact. The ground holes that held the posts were still there, and all it would take is a little more dirt to support the standing post.

Five hours later, as the sun set, Trace was finished and pretty darned proud of herself, not to mention pretty darned sore and exhausted. Riding a horse had used muscles she hadn't even known existed, and combined with the lifting, hauling, dragging and balancing of the posts and rails, the day's activity had taken its toll. She looked around one last time at her handiwork and nodded. *Not bad for a novice.* With the splintered wood cleaned up and loaded back on the wagon, she climbed into the driver's seat and yanked the reins to the right. Chief snorted and sauntered back toward the main house. *Huh. I fixed the fence without incident and the horse hasn't given me a hard time. Things are looking up.*

She wondered what Rachel might have prepared for supper. She didn't care, as long as it was edible and plentiful. She felt so hungry she could have chewed on the reins all the way back and convinced herself it was jerky.

Thirty minutes later it was pitch black and she was back at the barn, barely able to move off the wagon. Her muscles had tightened up to the point where they felt locked in place. Not one to complain or show pain, Trace inhaled sharply as she landed on her feet, concerned her back was going to give out before she could unhitch Chief and get him back to his stall.

She had just hung up his tack when she heard, "I kind of expected you back before sunset. I was getting a little worried. Everything okay?"

Rachel's voice was soft, concerned. Despite her discomfort and her body's demand for rest, Trace found herself grinning. She took in air — breathing from her diaphragm, hoping not to show how miserable she really felt — and turned around. She plastered a smile on her face. "Everything's great," she fibbed, and hoped she had not missed dinner.

"How much did you get done?"

"All of it," Trace said indignantly. *Does she think I'm incapable?*

"All of it? Oh my Lord, no wonder you're moving like you're wading in a lake of molasses." Rachel was astounded. "I never expected you to do it all, Trace, just to start it, maybe get two or three done."

"What?" Trace said weakly. "I just thought..." She leaned back against the wall and exhaled in frustration, deflating. "Augh."

Rachel placed a hand on her arm. "Next time, I'll be more clear." She tugged lightly on Trace's shirt. "Come on, wash up and let's get something in your belly, and then let's see if I can get you to feel better."

For the first time, Trace was glad that wouldn't have the double meaning she would typically have hoped for. She was just too damned tired.

Trace sat at the table, barely able to hold her head up as Rachel set another big bowl of leftover stew before her. The heavenly heat rose and caressed her olfactory sense. Her first bite provoked an almost sensuous moan at the tasty array of vegetables, meat, and gravy-thick liquid. After a famished Trace had eaten most of the contents of the bowl, she finally spoke. "Rachel, this is wonderful, thank you."

"You're welcome." Rachel beamed. "One of my specialties is rabbit stew."

Trace stopped mid-spoonful and looked up at her. "Rabbit? That's the meat in here?"

Rachel was puzzled by the expression on Trace's face. "Yes."

"This wouldn't be one of those cute little bunnies around the side of Chief's stall, would it?"

"Yes. That's what they're bred for. Food."

Trace put the spoon down and wiped her mouth with her hand. "Thanks. Think I'm done."

"But you didn't finish..."

"It's... I'm fine... I'm...too tired to eat any more."

"Didn't you like it?"

"It was delicious, Rachel, really." Except that during her fiasco with that stubborn horse earlier in the day, she had made friends with the six rabbits in that cage and even named them: Peter, Flopsy, Mopsy, Cottontail, Bugs, and Thumper. She couldn't bear to think which one she might have just eaten.

Rachel cleared the dinnerware from in front of Trace, who put her head down and rested it on her folded arms on the table. Moments later she felt a hand on her shoulder. "I know what will make you feel better."

"A sledgehammer to the forehead?" Trace muttered.

"Heavens, no."

Rachel looked horrified, not realizing Trace was joking. The twenty-first century sense of humor did not make the nineteenth century woman laugh. Yet.

"I have a jar of peppermint oil that I want you to take to your room and rub on the areas that ache. You'll feel better by morning." At Trace's skeptical look, she added, "The menthol from the peppermint leaves soothes irritation and ache."

Trace sat up and cocked her head. "How do you know all this stuff?"

Rachel smiled warmly. "The Bible."

"You learned all of this healing and nutritional stuff from reading the Bible?" Trace's tone was one of doubt.

"Absolutely. The use of peppermint can be traced back to Moses and the burning bush—"

Trace put her hand up and said, "All right, I believe you." She slowly, agonizingly stood up and turned toward Rachel. "What I really need is a full body massage." She said it as a thought out loud, never expecting a response.

"I agree, but my supply of olive oil is low. Otherwise, I'd give you one," Rachel said.

Trace nearly lost all semblance of decorum and restraint. She had to bite her lip, close her eyes and shake the X-rated thought out of her R-rated brain. "You have olive oil?"

"Yes. It's precious and I'm very lucky that I can even get it. Elizabeth Reddick, my neighbor, has three mature olive trees. Her grandfather planted them when he was a young man. Elizabeth's husband made her a kind of press and that gives us both our supply for a while."

Rachel's explanation of how she could possibly afford olive oil being of such meager means meant nothing to the twenty-first century woman who could walk into any store and pluck it off the shelf. Trace was still focused on the thought of Rachel's skilled fingers sliding all over her body. She looked Rachel directly in the eyes. "You were going to massage me with olive oil?"

"Yes."

"All over?"

"Yes."

Her expression was so innocent. Trace blinked back her lascivious thoughts from becoming spoken words. "That's in the Bible?"

"Yes. Olive oil massaged into the skin has wonderful healing powers, more long-term than peppermint."

Once again, the image of Rachel's hands rubbing oil deeply into Trace's skin made her shiver. A hint of a smile graced her face as she passed Rachel and rested a hand on the shorter woman's shoulder. "I think we're luckier you just had this." She accepted the small jar from a perplexed Rachel, thanked her, and retreated to the barn.

Rachel checked on Trace before she turned in for the night and, quietly watched her industrious guest sleep. She could smell peppermint in the air, and was glad that Trace had taken her advice and applied the healing oil to the areas of her body that hurt the most. Trace's exhaustion was obviously overwhelming and she slept hard, never even waking when the rooster crowed at the break of dawn.

Because of all the work Trace had done the day before, and assuming how much discomfort she must now be in, Rachel decided not to disturb her. She'd checked on her at least three times since gathering eggs at sunrise and Trace had not shifted from the position she had fallen asleep in the night before.

Rachel prepared breakfast, and was about to go rouse Trace to feed her before the day wasted away, when sudden nausea took hold of her and she barely made it outside. The smell of eggs cooking had never bothered her before but they were sure making her sick now. She didn't actually heave anything but it rose to her throat threateningly.

Halfway to the stove, the queasiness returned and Rachel raced back to the front porch, not able to keep the contents of her stomach from spewing forward. She missed a sore and sleepy Trace by mere inches.

"Yeow!" Trace jumped aside. "Whatever you had for breakfast, don't make me any," she joked, then wished she hadn't. She watched helplessly as Rachel held her belly and lurched and trembled until finally the sensation subsided. By that time Trace was on the porch, holding blonde hair away from a pale face with one hand, her other hand on Rachel's back. "You okay?"

Rachel nodded and straightened up, her eyes tearing uncontrollably. "I don't know what's wrong. I must be coming down with something."

"Stomach flu?" Trace asked.

Rachel looked at her in alarm. "Influenza? I hope not."

Trace kept a hand on her back and slowly ushered Rachel into the house and to a chair. "You look pretty peaked. Can I get you anything?"

Before Rachel could respond, bile rose in her throat again and she clamped her hand over her mouth. Trace reached a long arm over to the bucket, grabbed a clean bowl, and got it to Rachel just in time but not before she got splashed by vomit.

"Not exactly the bodily fluid exchange bonding moment I had hoped for," Trace mumbled, almost inaudibly.

When Rachel's stomach finally appeared to be more stable, Trace left the bowl in Rachel's lap and brought over a rag she had dampened under the indoor pump. Trace gently wiped Rachel's face and then rested the cloth against the sweaty forehead.

"What can I get you to help with that upset tummy there?" Trace asked, still squatting by Rachel's chair.

"Ginger powder. I have some in a jar over there." A shaky finger pointed toward the anteroom. "There should be hot water in the tea kettle. If you would be kind enough to get me a cup, I'll mix it together and it should help."

Trace placed Rachel's hand on the rag and guided it back up to her forehead. She fetched everything Rachel asked for and placed it on the table in front of her. Rachel was still weak and looked a little green around the gills as Trace knelt before her again and felt for a fever.

"You're clammy," Trace announced. "Could have been something you ate."

"I haven't eaten anything yet," Rachel stated, taking in big gulps of air. She poured some powder from the jar into the steaming cup of hot water, stirred it with a spoon, and left it there as another wave of nausea washed through her.

Wracked with dry heaves, she bent over at the waist and rested her head on her lap. Trace gently placed her hand on Rachel's back and stroked up and down her spine. "It's okay. You're okay," Trace comforted in a soothing voice. "Do you need to go lay down, Rachel?"

"No," came the muffled response, "I'll be okay in a moment... soon as I get some ginger in me..."

When Rachel made no attempt to raise her head, Trace took the cup off the table and stirred the contents, blowing on it to cool it enough for Rachel to sip. When it looked like it was drinkable, she smoothed Rachel's hair. "Come on, try some of this... You need to get something in you to make you feel better."

Rachel managed to lift her head slightly, just enough for Trace to slide the cup in. Trace held it to Rachel's lips, patiently waiting until Rachel took a drink, then another, then took the cup in her own hands, sitting up slowly. A few more sips and Rachel closed her eyes. "Thank you, Trace."

"Sure. You okay?"

"I think I will be," Rachel said weakly.

"Good. Listen...I, um, need to bathe. Do you have anything I could use for soap? And my clothes smell of sweat. I hate to ask this but I have nothing else to wear... Do you think I might be able to borrow something of your father's until I can wash my stuff?"

Rachel nodded. "You know where his clothes are. You're welcome to wear anything that fits."

"Thank you." She placed her hand over Rachel's and stood. "Anything I can do for you?"

"No...I'm...I'll be fine. The ginger is helping." Her voice was still weak, but stronger than before. As much as she appreciated Trace's ministrations, she was grateful when she was alone again to dissolve into her shame.

As she entered the bedroom to search for clothes, Trace looked back at Rachel and studied her intently. Rachel stared blankly toward the anteroom and clutched her cup with both hands, as tears streamed down her face. The look of despair on the young woman's face was heartbreaking and Trace felt compassionate and powerless at the same time. Something bad had drawn a blanket of desolation over this house and this lovely young woman. Trace could feel it, taste it, and putting her own personal mystery aside, she was going to find out what it was. A good bath would help her think.

The area of the river where Trace chose to strip and bathe, then wash her clothes, appeared secluded enough. This was going to be a new experience, public exhibitionism, and although most likely her only audience would be some wildlife and vegetation, she still felt exposed and vulnerable. She remembered reading stories or seeing movies regarding the Old West that had mischievous packs of boys who would spy on individuals washing themselves in rivers and the like, and steal their clothes. Should that happen, it would mean Trace would have to move on, a thought that instantly made her sad. This situation she had fallen into with Rachel was as close to perfect as she would probably get until she figured out what was going on. She needed Rachel and, although she didn't yet know why, Rachel needed her.

The water was cold at first, but refreshing, and Trace let her skin adjust to the temperature before she moved about underwater. The motion drained the stress from her body. Although it felt heavenly, she decided not to stray too far from her clothes, just in case.

She was thankful it was a nice warm day as she scrubbed herself with lye soap — not quite the "Ocean Breeze" scent she was used to, but since she'd smelled like something akin to a rancid wart hog, before she entered the water, she could deal with the thick but cleaner aroma of a smoking coal stove.

She was not used to washing her hair with soap. It was bad enough it wasn't shampoo, but with no conditioner to tame her normally unruly mop, she could only imagine the results. Thankfully, she sheared off her very long locks to give her a more masculine appearance for the undercover assignment she must have been working on, so she had less hair to deal with. And it wasn't like she felt she had to look particularly attractive for anyone...except maybe Rachel, which was probably a wasted effort.

Once Trace had finished rinsing the minute amount of lather out of her hair, she waded back toward the rocks where her belongings were piled. She began to scour the shirt, jeans, socks, wrap, and boy briefs she was so fond of. Satisfied that they were as clean as she could get them, she cautiously emerged naked from the water, toweled off with a large linen cloth Rachel had provided, and quickly dressed in a bulky flannel shirt — much too warm for the mild, early Spring weather — and a pair of worn blue denim pants that were at least one size too big. She chose those specific items in case she happened to run into anyone between the river and the house, so that her ample chest, without its binding, wouldn't be so noticeable.

As Trace walked barefoot back to toward the barn to hang her clothes to dry, she marveled once more at the crisp, unpolluted air and the untainted setting that surrounded her. *If only the world didn't have to change in a way where it ravaged Mother Nature.*

As she rounded a corner, the cabin came into view and she observed Rachel on the porch shaking out a small, woven rug and then going back inside. Rachel's expression was still troubled. Whatever was going on there, Trace was determined to find out and fix it.

She shook her head in disbelief. Had she only been here a little over a day? It felt like so much longer. The enigma of how she got here had begun to plague her. How could she be in the twenty-first century one day and in the nineteenth century the next? Had she encountered some sort of time warp? Were there really such things? The theory of a time warp was as plausible as thinking the time travel was the result of a time machine. Was it her choice to leave behind what she recalled to be a troubled existence? Were there actually ways to do that? And no matter how she had gotten here, Fate had landed her smack dab in the middle of Rachel Young's distraught life. Except she didn't believe in Fate.

Maybe she needed to start.

Rachel placed the throw rug on the floor by the indoor pump and wondered when Trace would be returning; it was time to go into Sagebrush to get some supplies. The thought of going to town did not inspire a good feeling in her. It would be the first time she would be in town since before the...incident. Well, at least the Cranes had left for Dodge City on their lengthy drive to take their cattle to auction and she didn't have to worry about running into any of them for a while. Especially Ben. Panic seized her at the thought of him, and the horrible memory of what he'd done to her nearly caused her to faint. She held on to the back of a kitchen chair for support and waited for the crippling sensation to pass.

Trace would be with her; that gave her some consolation. And then she wondered why. She felt safe in the presence of the chivalrous woman she hoped everyone would believe was a man. She admitted she liked having Trace around, even if she did have some decidedly strange habits, and was a little...spoiled. As for Sagebrush and this outsider, there would be questions...and speculation...and definitely talk. Oh, yes, the town was good at that. She knew there would be gossip soon enough anyway; a little more at this point wouldn't matter.

A slight taste of ginger bubbled up into Rachel's throat and she swallowed it back, reliving the morning's queasiness. Just that reminder, and what it meant, caused tears of guilt to sting her eyes. She couldn't be carrying Ben Crane's baby, couldn't be! Yet just as sure as she knew the day was long, she knew she was with child. Her monthly curse should have come and gone eleven days before and she was never late. And now she was sick in the morning, like her cousin Charlotte, eight months before she bore twin girls, and her best friend and neighbor, Elizabeth, before she twice miscarried.

Rachel wiped her eyes with her apron, took a deep breath and looked skyward. *Why did this have to happen?* She always considered herself a devout Christian, never did anything that would embarrass the church, the congregation, or disgrace her family, never betrayed the teachings of the Bible, never turned her back on God. Why did she feel as though the Lord had turned His back on her? First her father suffered so horribly before he died, then her mother was taken from her, then her fiancé was accidentally killed, and then...that night. It seemed like the devil himself was after her.

And who really was this Trace Sheridan and why did she feel so secure with a total stranger, a woman, of all things? Rachel heard footsteps on the porch and turned to see Trace enter the cabin.

"Well, I feel better, cleaner," Trace said.

"Good." Rachel smiled absently.

"How about you? Feeling better?" Trace's concern was genuine.

"Oh, yes," Rachel lied. "Much."

Chapter Five

The decision to go into town was not an easy one. Rachel had no doubt that Ben Crane had made good on his promise to announce to all of Sagebrush that he'd, to put it bluntly, engaged in intimate relations with her. A week ago, Elizabeth had come to return a pie tin and would not look Rachel in the eye. Her husband Matthew demanded she hand the plate to Rachel and leave immediately. The expression on Matthew's face was one of disdain and disgust, Elizabeth's, one of question and confusion. Cousin Charlotte, her only living relative, had moved away from town two weeks ago with her husband and babies, and never even bothered to come say goodbye. And when Isaac Tipping brought the last order out from his father's store, even though he was young, he looked at her differently, too, probably shocked by the not-so-nice things that were being said about her in the stockroom. They should all know better, but obviously they didn't. Or didn't dare not to believe Ben Crane's claims.

Rachel couldn't understand how anyone could actually believe she would willingly submit to Ben Crane, especially as their families had been at odds for years and she had adamantly and publicly turned down his marriage proposals. Crane's flagrant womanizing was no secret and neither was Rachel's engagement to the dashing, and much more upstanding, Thomas Baines. Why anyone would think she would allow the town pig into her bed, when she had denied that privilege to her own fiancé, was beyond all reasonable thought.

But then, what had really happened defied all reasonable thought. She had not invited Crane anywhere near her private chambers or her body, and he had taken what he wanted without her permission or her consent. And now she was disgraced. She had heard stories about that sort of thing happening to other women and always thought they must have done something to encourage such behavior. Because she wasn't that kind of girl, she never thought something like that could happen to her.

And Ben was a Crane. Nobody went against the Cranes — not the sheriff, the circuit judge, or even Reverend Edwards. Bad things happened when a Crane did not get what he wanted; she was living proof.

If she could stay on the ranch the rest of her life without ever going into town again, she would. If only that was a viable solution. It was not, and she steeled herself to face the stares, the whispers, the treatment, and everything that went with her sullied reputation. And now she was going to show up in town with a total stranger sitting by her side.

She sighed. If that weren't enough, it was complicated by the fact that the man everyone would see was really a woman, pretending to be a man and they both hoped no one would catch on. Trace, as a woman, could have been easily explained away as a distant relative come to visit, but Trace as a man would create a little more stir...as if she needed anything more added to the pot. Rachel wished they didn't need to maintain the masquerade, as her life would be so much easier if her companion would drop the façade. Still, she had given Trace her word that she would keep her secret.

A month earlier, it would not have caused as much talk. Cowboys frequently passed through town looking for work, and there was no question that Rachel needed the help. Her father had hired saddle stiffs all the time, especially during harvest, to work the land with him, repair things that needed fixing, help transport the modest herd of cattle to auction; in short, to do whatever needed to be done that required an extra pair of hands. But with the systematic elimination of the ranch's resources and Rachel's livelihood, and the boasting of Ben Crane, the townspeople would surmise that there would be only one thing she could be using as currency to pay the stranger...herself.

It was humiliating that she would now be thought of like that, devastated that a place that her ancestors had helped settle — where she was born, raised, schooled and almost married — could turn on her so suddenly. The best she could do would be to face down her detractors as best she could, deny everything and hope the knowledge that it was a blowhard Crane running her name into the ground would make a glimmer of difference in what people believed deep down inside.

Regardless of the consequences, Rachel and Trace were on their way, the wagon pulled at a leisurely pace by Moses, an old workhorse Rachel normally only used to go to town and back. At his advanced age he wasn't good for much else, but she didn't have the heart to sell him and she couldn't shoot him.

As they ambled along, Rachel stole a glance at Trace and felt a puzzling but welcome sense of calm. Trace looked very convincing in the pin-striped cotton, collarless work shirt and blue denim trousers she'd gleaned from Rachel's father, though the jeans needed to be held up by suspenders. Trace's binding had dried quickly in the sun so she was wearing it underneath the shirt, and Rachel had fixed her up with a neckerchief to help disguise her lack of Adam's apple. A black straw cowboy hat with a three and a half inch shapeable brim was pulled low on Trace's forehead in a persuasively menacing dip. It was a little big for her but she wore it well and it added to the illusion of her being male. Strangely, once they had started out, Rachel felt more comfortable with the concept of the town thinking there was a man living on her property, despite the perception of impropriety. Hopefully it would make her seem not quite as powerless as she had been on her own.

Trace felt like they were Charles and Caroline Ingalls from *Little House On The Prairie* heading into Walnut Grove.

Rachel had properly covered her head with a pale green bonnet that tied under her chin. It closely matched her green and white gingham "going to town" dress that Trace thought looked absolutely adorable on her. Anyone riding upon them would assume they were the perfect couple, and suddenly, unexpectedly, Trace wished they were. That revelation struck her like ice water in the face and she quickly looked around her, then skyward. *Where the hell are all these outlandish notions coming from? First protective, then nurturing, and now commitment?* She shook her head as if that would clear away the recent epiphanies.

"What's wrong?" Rachel asked.

"What?"

"What's wrong? You look...I don't know...startled."

"No, I'm fine. So, what are we going to get in town?"

"I need flour, bacon, rice, coffee, tea, sugar, dried beans, dried fruit, hardtack—"

"Hardtack? What's that?"

"It's pilot bread...um...like a cracker... You've never had hardtack?"

"If I had, would I ask you what it is?"

Rachel's eyes narrowed. "Sometimes your tone leaves a lot to be desired."

Trace was about to argue that point when she realized her companion was right. She smiled and said, "I'll try to be more aware of that."

"Try hard," Rachel said before continuing the list. "Salt, corn meal, corn — parched and ground, saleratus—"

"Saleratus?"

"Baking soda," Rachel amended, "and one small keg of vinegar."

"A keg?"

"I use it for a lot of things; it doesn't last long."

"I think of keg, I think of beer," Trace said and wished she had one at that moment. "The town got a saloon?"

"Yes, Wilbur's, but you don't want to go there."

"Why wouldn't I?"

"Because that's where the men go—" She looked at the man-disguised woman seated next to her. "Maybe you going into Wilbur's wouldn't be a bad idea."

Yeah...a damned bar. Woo hoo! Now we're talking. And if they have a pool table... Have pool tables been invented yet? Trace was pretty sure they had. All she needed to do was play a game or two of eight ball and that alone would be convincing enough. They never would believe a woman could play pool like she could. Maybe she could even hustle some money.

As if Rachel read her mind, she piped up, "Or maybe it's not such a good idea..."

Trace noticed that the closer they got to the outskirts of town, the more restless Rachel got. "You okay?"

Rachel nodded apprehensively and said, "People are going to talk; just don't pay them any mind."

"You mean about me?"

"Well...yes. They might say other things, too. I live alone and people like to gossip."

"Would it be easier for you if I just stayed back on the ranch?" Trace asked, trying to read the meaning behind Rachel's words.

"Easier? Yes. But then if anyone rode by or came out and saw you, it would seem as if I was ashamed of something and trying to hide you, or hide what you appear to be, a man, and that would only make things worse."

They rode a few more minutes in awkward silence until Trace decided that she needed to know. "Rachel, why are you alone on that big place? I gather your parents are gone, but since I've been here, I've gotten the feeling something's going on. Mind telling me what it is?"

Rachel looked away and inhaled deeply. She held her breath in for a long moment before expelling it cautiously. "I just had a run of bad luck the past year, that's all. It's still hard to talk about it. All I'm trying to say is people are guessing about a lot of things and don't know, so just bear that in mind when you hear gossip."

Not the answer she wanted but it would have to do. For the time being. "Okay. Is there a pawn shop in town?"

"Yes. Right next to the bank. Joseph Turner owns it. Why do you need to go there?"

"Because I don't have any money, but I have a few items of jewelry I'd like to pawn."

"Trace...um...I don't have much, but if you stay on and help me with the ranch, what I have I'll gladly share."

Trace smiled at the generous offer. "I appreciate that, Rachel, but I think it wise that I have my own money." *Who knows when I'll need to suddenly pick up and move on?* Her heart sank at the thought of leaving. Trace saw an expression of concern on Rachel's face. "What?"

"It's just that Joseph Turner is a very nosy man; thinks he knows everything and wants to know everything that he doesn't already think he knows."

"So what you're saying is: don't tell him anything and don't listen to anything he tells me."

"Yes. Please."

"Want to give me a hint as to what I might hear?"

"How would I know that?" Rachel snapped defensively.

"I just thought you might have an idea, that's all." Trace's response was more composed than it normally would have been if someone jumped down her throat like that for no apparent reason.

After another several seconds of silence, Trace felt Rachel's hand on her arm. "I apologize, Trace. I haven't been in town for a while and I know there will be questions about you..."

Trace could not ignore her body's reaction to the light touch of Rachel's fingers on her bicep, even though it was through fabric. Goosebumps rose everywhere and she was grateful for the binding that covered her traitorous, telltale nipples. She briefly covered the smaller hand with her own. "Don't worry about it, okay? I'll handle anyone who decides to be...disrespectful."

The look on Trace's face left no doubt that she meant it.

As Moses lumbered his way around the corner onto Main Street, Trace stared, rapt, at the boardwalk that connected the general store, mercantile, saloon, blacksmith shop, and livery stable with the butcher shop. She turned her gaze in the opposite direction and, across the street, she surveyed the three story hotel, the shorter bank edifice, a pawn shop, the barred windows of the sheriff's office and jail, and several other merchant shops, with a small chapel separated from the rest of the buildings by a good two blocks.

The blatant gawking by the townsfolk began as soon as the wagon passed the first couple. Rachel nodded politely but received no such courtesy in return.

Trace turned to Rachel. "They seemed kind of hostile, not to mention rude to you. What's their problem? Is it me? Is that what you tried to warn me about?" Clearly simmering on Rachel's behalf, she went on. "I know I've only been here two and a half days, but you've shown me nothing but unconditional kindness, minus a few ecclesiastical conditions," she added, smirking. "I don't know what these folks are thinking, but I'd like to smack some sense into them."

"Pay it no mind, Trace. Just ignore them; I do."

Stopped in front of Foster's Grocery, Trace stepped down and, in a very gentlemanly manner, assisted Rachel from the wagon. Rachel thanked her demurely and handed her the reins. She then walked to the back of the wagon and assessed the goods she had brought to sell or barter as Trace tied the reins to the hitching post.

Luther Foster, the grocer, stepped out onto the wooden sidewalk in front of his store and wiped his hands on his apron. He glanced briefly at Rachel then eyed Trace with suspicion.

"Afternoon, Mr. Foster. I brought you your usual order." Rachel indicated the baskets of spring vegetables; asparagus, fennel, fiddle-heads, mustard greens, watercress, radishes, and sweet onions. Her tone was pleasant. Maybe if she pretended everything was fine, it would be.

"Rachel." He acknowledged her with an absent nod as he inspected Trace, who glared back at him. "Mrs. Reddick dropped by a jar of olive oil for you to pick up when you came by." He then cleared his throat. "I'm not sure I'm gonna be able to take your vegetables any-more."

"Why not?" Trace's voice was calm but strong.

"Who's this?"

"This is Trace Sheridan, Mr. Foster. He's helping me out on the ranch for a bit." She had to consciously remind herself to refer to Trace as "he".

Foster frowned and returned his attention to Rachel, ignoring Trace's outstretched hand. "He staying out at the spread with you?" His disapproval was obvious.

"Yes, but he's—"

"Sleeping in the barn," Trace supplied, interrupting Rachel. She stepped forward. "And I'm right here, Mr. Foster. You can speak to me directly."

The grocer was angered by Trace's insolence but retreated a pace when she stepped up onto the boardwalk in front of him, as she tow-ered over him by several inches. "O...Okay..." He avoided looking her directly in the eye. "How is she paying you?"

"Paying me? She feeds me and gives me a place to lay my head, that's how she's paying me. I'm sure you don't have a problem with that." The fierce blue eyes bore a hole through him.

Rachel was taken aback by how Trace could go from accommodat-ing to intimidating in no time at all, and she was temporarily speech-less at how easily this woman stood up to a man. She began to understand why Trace thought the men in Sagebrush would want to kill her. Maybe their reaction wouldn't be quite that dramatic, but no woman ever stood up to a man like that, or challenged one like that. Rachel knew if Luther Foster had any idea Trace was female, he never would have backed down, especially since he had a tendency to be a bit of a browbeater, specifically toward women.

Despite that, Rachel liked Foster, was grateful that he continued to purchase her crops after everything that had happened on the ranch. She knew the Cranes had threatened him and he ran the risk of having his home and business burned if he didn't comply. But Foster had been her father's best friend, and if Rachel didn't provide him with produce, he'd have to get his vegetables from a grower in Jefferson City, twenty miles north of Sagebrush. Also, if he lost his store, everyone in Sagebrush, including the Cranes, would be affected, so she was pretty sure that the threat against him was an empty one. She wasn't quite so optimistic about the future of her own commerce.

Foster cleared his throat as he addressed Trace. "No. No problem with that." He began to regain his composure as a small crowd of his neighbors gathered to watch the exchange. He was a man who liked being the center of attention when he was on the up side of the situation, but never when he appeared to be a fool.

"Now, why don't we try this again?" Trace stuck out her hand.

Foster looked at it, then back up into the unyielding expression on the flawless face. The question clearly not a request, Foster accepted the handshake. Trace's grip was firm.

"Trace Sheridan."

"Luther Foster." He was a rotund man, prone to sweating with no apparent provocation. Now he was perspiring profusely. Wisely, he allowed Trace to drop the handshake first. "Where you from, Mr. Sheridan?"

"Cottonwood."

"Never heard of it. Where is that?"

"Far from here," Trace and Rachel chorused. Trace looked surprised as Rachel joined her on the boardwalk.

Rachel smiled to herself at the look of relief on the grocer's face. "Trace, why don't you go tend to your errands and Mr. Foster and I will work out the problem, hmmm?" She laid a gentle hand on Trace's forearm.

Trace nodded, not taking her eyes off Foster. "Only if you're sure..."

"These people are my friends, Trace," Rachel assured her, hoping to make a point not so much to Trace but to Foster and the others who had stopped to watch. "I'm sure."

Trace searched Rachel's face for any hint that she should stay. Finding none, she patted Rachel's hand, nodded to Foster, left the boardwalk and headed toward the pawn shop.

"What's going on, Rachel?" Foster asked, after the wagon had been emptied and they were in the privacy of the grocer's small office. He sat down, opened his cash box, and counted out the few coins he owed her after he deducted the cost of the goods she purchased.

"What do you mean, Mr. Foster?"

The grocer shook his head grimly and said, "First, Ben Crane comes into town just before the drive to Dodge City and tells anyone who will listen at Wilbur's that you and he...well," he lowered his eyes, "you know." Flushed, he handed her the payment for the produce, "And then you bring a total stranger to town with you, surly as a grizzly, looks to be at least half Injun. People are talking, Rachel, and now they'll talk more." Foster marked the exchange in his account book then stood as Rachel put the money in her purse.

"It isn't true...what Ben Crane said, Mr. Foster. You know why he said those things."

"Even if it ain't true, Rachel, he's a Crane and no one's gonna call him a liar."

"Not to his face, anyway," Rachel finished for him.

"Precisely. But he's got the town talking. And now this? What would your daddy say if he knew you had what looks to be a half-breed living out at your place? Don't matter where he claims to be sleeping, it don't look right, a man out at your place..."

"I need the help, Mr. Foster. I can't do it by myself anymore. Daddy used to hire drifters to help out certain times of the year, you know that. If he couldn't do it alone, no one should expect me to!" Her voice rose with each word.

"I know, Rachel, but it just ain't proper." He wiped sweat off his brow with the back of his hand. "If you'd just sell that place to the Cranes, you wouldn't have to worry—"

"Mr. Foster, I should slap your face for suggesting such a thing," Rachel said boldly. "If my daddy heard you say that..."

Foster put up his hand. "I know. I know what your daddy went through to keep that spread out of their hands. But it's time to be reasonable, Rachel. They're going after you a little bit at a time. You can't win. It would be different if you had any hope at all, but you don't."

"We'll see about that, Mr. Foster." Her bitterness was clear.

He watched her leave and sighed in despair. "Rachel, I swear you've inherited your daddy's pigheaded ways and his knack for trouble."

Trace recognized the three gilt balls that glittered above the doorway to the pawn shop. The customary symbol hadn't changed over the centuries. She entered through the open doorway and was hit with a thick, musty odor that nearly made her sneeze. Trace blinked a few times, rubbing her nose as she took in her surroundings. This wasn't like any of the places she'd seen in her lifetime. This shop actually had some semblance of order, decency, and credibility. She browsed through the items that had been placed on deposit in exchange for cash: various styles and sizes of shawls, bonnets, undergarments, dresses, suits, and shoes. There was also bedding, musical instruments, clocks, tools, guns — which she would look at later if she had the time — and furniture. The jewelry was in a display case in front of the proprietor. A tall, skinny, jowled man with thin hair, he looked like he was straight out of a Washington Irving novel. Trace deduced that he was the Joseph Turner Rachel had talked about. He stood when she approached the counter. He still had a pen in his hand, and on his modest desk there was an open book that appeared to be his ledger.

"Afternoon," the man said, in a twangy voice that was immediately grating. "What can I do for you..."

They stood there and assessed each other. For a brief second, Trace was worried he might not buy into her act.

"...Son?"

Trace took a breath and artfully lowered the pitch of her voice. She didn't want it to sound fake, but she sure as hell didn't want to sound feminine, either. It was different with the grocer. He had pissed her off and her voice always dropped an octave or two when she was angry. She reached into her breast pocket and took out two wedding bands she'd found in her jeans. They'd been wrapped in a tissue, along with other unfamiliar articles of jewelry. The fact that she didn't recognize them as anything she'd ever owned, and they looked like they might be authentic to the eighteen hundreds, indicated to her that her time journey must have been preplanned. *Another little piece of the puzzle that is now my life.* She placed the 18-karat gold bands on the counter. "I'd like to pawn these."

Turner looked the items over, then picked them up and felt the weight, the substance. "Might be able to do somethin' for you. Where'd you get them?"

"They were my...mother's. She's gone now and I need the money." Trace felt an unexpected pang of guilt. Her mother wasn't deceased but it might not be long before she was, with Trace not there to keep her from indulging her crack addiction.

Joseph Turner performed a cursory authenticity examination of the rings, including biting down on the bands. "Don't think I've seen you around here before."

"You haven't. I'm from Cottonwood."

"Cottonwood? That's a full month's ride from here, isn't it?"

The question stopped Trace for a minute. Had this man really heard of a Cottonwood, or was he already living up to Rachel's description of a know-it-all? "About that, yeah."

"What're you doin' in this neck of the woods? Just passin' through?"

He'll find out sooner or later, might as well be now. "I'm staying out at the Young place, helping out on the land for a while," she said.

Turner responded with a raised eyebrow. "Is that so? Out there with Miss Rachel? Just the two of you?"

"For the time being. I got hurt and lost my horse. Miss Rachel found me and kindly fixed me up. I need a place to stay for a while and she needs some work done. It's the least I can do." Trace made sure her intention was clear. She pinned Joseph Turner with eyes like blue steel and said, "And that's all. You understand?"

He shrugged and never attempted to hide his lascivious grin. "Whatever you say."

Trace seethed quietly but held her temper. "How much can you give me for the rings?"

"You need a loan for these or do you want to get paid outright? I mean these would be excellent collateral for—"

"No. Thank you. Just the money." Trace was sure his interest rates were quite high, even in this time period. He wouldn't make any profit otherwise. As she was sure the pieces held no sentimental value for her, there was no need for her to buy them back.

"I think I can give you, hmmm, fifty dollars each."

"What! Just fifty dollars?" The look in the man's eyes at the outburst told her that it had been an honest offer. She remembered where she was and quickly capitulated. "I'm sorry. My mother said they were worth more. Fifty dollars apiece is fine."

Turner nodded, looking slightly ruffled by Trace's flare-up. He took a step backward toward his small, open safe and set the rings on his desk. He sized up the young man in his shop and said, "Got some redskin in you, son?" He bent over and pulled a cash drawer from the knee-high iron vault.

"Not that I know of," Trace answered wearily. "No Gypsy, either. Maybe a little Greek."

"Oh, Greek, yeah. I would've guessed that eventually." Turner removed the correct amount in bills from the drawer and stepped back up to the display case and held them out to Trace.

The money looked very different from what she was used to. "Could you count it out for me, please?" She paid close attention as he did to ensure he gave her every cent she was entitled to.

The pawn shop proprietor grinned. "Ah, can't add, huh? No problem."

"No." Trace tried to keep her annoyance in check, but her tone was not without an edge. "I can add just fine. I can count and spell and read, too. It's just...we're strangers and I'm protecting my interests."

Turner was impressed by the admission. "Not everyone would have the guts to say that and 'spect me to keep goin' with the trade. It's as good as callin' me a cheat." The skeletally thin man proceeded to count out the balance of the money and handed it to Trace. "There you go. All there."

"Thank you." Trace looked at the pawnbroker and hesitated. After her attitude regarding her scholastic abilities, she didn't want to appear to be stupid. "I'd like to have a beer at the saloon; could you give me one of these in smaller change?"

"Yep. That I can do." Turner exchanged one of the bills for coins.

"How much you get charged for a beer in this town?"

"Five cents for a cream ale. How much do they charge in Cotton-wood?"

Trace shrugged nonchalantly. "The same. I was just making sure." She folded the paper money in half and shoved it, and the coins, into her shirt pocket. "Well, thank you. It's been nice doing business with you."

"So...how long you think you'll be stayin'...out at the Young place?"

She immediately saw the question for what it was — the pawnbroker being a busybody. "Don't know. When I got thrown from my horse, I got me a puncture wound." Trace indicated the area on her chest. "Have to make sure that's all healed up before I...move on. Plus, Ra...Miss Rachel needs a hand out there. Since she helped me, it's only fitting that I help her."

"So you expect to be movin' on? Not goin' back to Cottonwood?"

"No. No need to go back there. My family is gone now." She smiled at him. "Who knows? Maybe I'll take up residence here in Sagebrush."

Turner grinned back. "What's your name, son?"

"Trace. Trace Sheridan."

"Joseph Turner. Nice doin' business with you, Trace Sheridan." The pawnbroker extended a long, bony hand, which Trace briefly accepted. "Always good to welcome a hard workin' cowboy to town."

"Thanks." He seemed sincere but Trace didn't trust him completely. There was something about him she didn't like, though she couldn't put her finger on it. She nodded in polite departure and left.

Chapter Six

Rachel decided to run some other errands while Foster prepared her order, and then she needed to find Trace to help her load it onto the wagon. She needed to walk off some anger, and bypassed the butcher shop, where she would purchase some bacon later. She ended her walk at Molly Ledbetter's dress shop. Molly was a gray-haired grandmotherly-type who had been very close to Rachel's mother. Rachel knew, regardless of the rumors and gossip, Molly would welcome her, offer her a cup of tea, and probably give her some excess material she always just happened to have lying around so that Rachel could make herself something pretty.

When Rachel entered, the bell on the door clanged. Molly Ledbetter looked up from hanging a woven waist jacket on a rack. Her eyes twinkled as she smiled warmly at the daughter of her dearly missed friend. The reaction of the two shop patrons wasn't as congenial.

Rosalie Beauregard glared at Rachel in condemnation then turned to her daughter, Suzanne. "We might have to leave."

Rachel knew the mousy, brown haired, Suzanne well. They'd grown up singing in the church choir together. Rachel had always thought they were close until, because of pressure from her gold digging mother, Suzanne became engaged to Seth Carver, Ben Crane's cousin. That made it extremely difficult for Rachel to maintain a civil relationship with Suzanne or anyone in her family.

Suzanne caught Rachel in town one day, about a week before Ben Crane's fateful visit to the ranch and confided through tears that her marriage was not her idea. She begged Rachel not to hate her. Rachel knew how domineering Rosalie was, and how Suzanne's father would kowtow to his wife, not to mention how the family would benefit by being associated with the Cranes. Suzanne didn't stand a chance.

"Good afternoon, Suzanne," Rachel said, knowing the young woman probably would not dare to respond. "Mrs. Beauregard."

Rosalie stuck her nose in the air with an emphatic "Harumph!" and wrenched Suzanne's arm backward, pulling her toward the door. Her skittish daughter blinked apologetically at Rachel but stayed silent. "Molly? Are you going to allow this kind of person in your store?"

Molly Ledbetter gave Rachel a patient look and then turned to Mrs. Beauregard. "What kind of person is that, Rosalie? Certainly you wouldn't be referring to the daughter of my very best, dear departed friend?"

"Well, honestly, Molly, she's out there on that ranch, all alone, entertaining men...sullying her family's good name. It's disgusting."

"Unlike your daughter, who's being whored out to Seth Carver so you can get your talons into the Crane fortune?"

The look of shock on Rosalie's face and the look of near amusement on Suzanne's were priceless. "Well! I never!"

Molly looked pointedly at Suzanne and responded, "Well, you did, at least once."

"Molly Ledbetter! See if I ever shop here again!" Rosalie spat vehemently.

"Suit yourself, Rosalie. If you're going to be more judgmental than the Lord concerning my other customers and people dear to me, then I would prefer that you go to Jefferson City for your dresses from now on."

"You'll regret this," Rosalie said as she pulled Suzanne to the entrance. The younger woman mouthed the words, "Bye, Rachel," before being yanked out the door by her mother.

Rachel looked ruefully at Molly and said, "I'm sorry, Miz Ledbetter, I didn't mean to cause trouble."

"Oh, honey, you didn't cause that." Molly waved her hand at the vacant space left by Rosalie and Suzanne. "I've never had much use for John or Rosalie Beauregard. Both of them always thought they were more high and mighty than anyone else in this town, even before they got involved with the Cranes."

"Yes. Poor Suzanne. She's the one coming out on the short end of all this."

"Girl needs to get a backbone. Needs some of that Young stock in her." Molly smiled, winking at Rachel. "Now, come have some tea with me and tell me what you've been up to, because I surely don't believe what I've been hearing."

Walking into Wilbur's Saloon was a surreal experience. Trace pushed through the hinged, swinging doors like cowboys did in so many of the western movies she had watched as a kid. She took in her surroundings: the dirty wooden floor; the four large round tables, obviously used for card playing; several smaller tables just for sitting and drinking; a long, well-stocked bar up against the wall; a piano against a staircase that led up to what Trace assumed were rooms occupied by a prostitute or two. But sadly, no pool table. Trace strolled purposefully up to the bar, aware that she was collecting a few stares along the way. *So what else is new?*

The barkeep, a bear of a man probably Trace's age with, stringy dark hair and a thick brush of a mustache, smiled at her. He wiped off the space in front of her with a damp rag.

"Howdy," he said in a voice that belied his build. It was adolescent, like a teenage boy still going through puberty. She couldn't help but smirk. Not because of his unusual tone or because if he sounded like that, she could relax and not worry about her own timbre, but because he actually said "howdy".

"Hi," Trace responded.

"What can I get ya?"

Trace shrugged then remembered what the pawnbroker called it... "A cream ale would be good."

"What kind?"

That stumped her. She didn't think she would actually have options. Any experienced beer drinker would know his ale, so she said, "First time here, give me your most popular."

"That would be Handel's. Good choice. Coming right up." The big man pulled out a mug and poured a pint of foam.

Trace wanted to tell him to tip the glass and aim the stream against the opposite side, but she felt that might be overstepping her boundaries. Incredibly, when it was set in front of her, the head was barely a quarter of an inch. "Thanks. How much?"

"Five cents."

Trace laughed. *A nickel for a pint of beer. Maybe this isn't a dream at all; maybe I've died and gone to heaven...well, except for the no indoor plumbing thing.* She removed a handful of coins from her breast pocket and set down a silver dollar. "Keep the brew flowing, my friend, and what I don't drink you can have for a tip."

The barkeep's face lit up and he let out a gruff laugh. "Stranger, you're welcome in this saloon any time. I'm always grateful for a new customer, especially if he turns into a regular and a good tipper to boot." He extended his big, beefy hand. "Silas Boone."

Trace accepted his hand in her own firm grip, sizing up this big ape of a man, she immediately thought, *What's your mama's name? Bab?* She wanted to ask him if he was any relation to Daniel Boone, but as she couldn't remember if that character really existed or was just folklore and, if he was an actual person, had he been born yet. *I should have paid more attention in history class.* She wisely decided to keep the conversation short and to the point. "Trace Sheridan."

"Where you from, Trace Sheridan?"

"Cottonwood." And then, before he could ask, she added, "It's far from here." She released his hand and took a sip of her beer. It wasn't bad, but it was different. A little thicker than she was used to, no doubt from less filtering and dilution than in modern times. It could have been colder but she wasn't complaining. It was beer.

"How 'bout a shot of bug juice to go with that ale?"

Bug juice? Trace could only imagine what kind of bug. "Uh, no thanks. I think I'll pass."

"What brings you to this neck of the woods, Trace?"

"I was just passing through but my horse threw me and took off and I got hurt, so I'm staying out at the Young ranch, recovering and working off my debt to Ra— Miss Rachel for fixing me up. Plus, I need to earn enough money to get another horse so I can move on." *Perish the thought*, her brain piped up suddenly.

A strange look clouded Silas' face. "You out there at Frank Young's place? Alone?"

This was getting tedious. Trace looked the bartender square in the eye. "Yes. I am. Look, Silas, I intend to be around for a while and I'm just staying at the Young place, sleeping in the barn — alone. There's nothing going on between Miss Rachel and me. But if there's something I should know about, I'd like to hear it."

"No, no..." The big man shrugged and looked down. "I just heard she's had some trouble out there, that's all."

"What kind of trouble?"

The bartender glanced back up at her and shrugged again. "If she didn't tell you then I suppose it ain't my place to."

Trace studied him. She knew Silas wanted to say something to her about it, but then she stiffened as she felt somebody sidle up next to her. She never took her eyes off the barkeep and observed with more than mild interest that Silas slowly backed away.

"That's right, Silas, you don't want to be tellin' tales out of school."

Aware that she was being scrutinized by the man standing to her left, Trace relaxed her body and psychologically prepared herself for a fight. The vibe she got from the man was extremely confrontational. *Go ahead, fuckwad*, she thought. *Start something I can finish.* She stared straight ahead and took a long drink of beer. Never physically acknowledging the man, Trace said, "Something I can do for you?"

"Yeah, you can tell me what you're doing out at Frank Young's place."

Trace did not move a muscle and took another sip of beer. She kept her voice steady and even. "First, Frank Young is dead, so I believe that would make it Rachel Young's place now, and second, what business is it of yours?" It was then she turned toward the man and regarded him with a defiant, cold blue glare. Her eyes fell on the star stuck to the man's rawhide vest. Unimpressed, she looked up at his craggy face.

Even though he stayed put, Trace saw in his eyes that she'd made him take a mental step backward. He suddenly seemed intimidated. She guessed that he had expected her to feel more threatened than she was when facing The Law. The man squinted at her. "My business is ol' Frank was a good friend of mine and he wouldn't like no Gypsy man living out there with his daughter."

"Well, Sheriff, I'm not a Gypsy and before you ask or assume, I have no Indian blood in me, either. What my heritage is doesn't concern you." Trace noticed the dead silence that engulfed the saloon where only seconds before there had been the sounds of conversation, glasses clinking, laughter, and poker chips flying across tables. "What should concern you — especially since *ol' Frank* was such a good friend of yours — is the condition that property is in and that poor girl has nobody out there to help her. When was the last time you or anyone else checked on *ol' Frank's* daughter?" She knew she was being sardonic but she couldn't help herself.

The sheriff at least had the decency to look slightly embarrassed. "It's...uh...been a while. But Isaac Tipping delivers feed out there once a week and he would have told someone if she needed help," he countered defensively. "It would be in your best interests, son, to move on. Quickly."

Trace didn't like him. She'd dealt with many snakes in her time and this man had reptile written all over him. "Is that advice, Sheriff, or a threat?"

"Right now, it's advice. Don't let it become a threat."

Now that she had pegged the cretin for what he was, she smirked and calmly took another swallow of beer. "I don't take kindly to threats, Sheriff." *Where is this dialogue coming from? I never talk like that — "take kindly"? What's next? Am I going to not "cotton" to things?* She had to consciously stop herself from laughing. "I'll move on when I'm damned well ready, and not before." She neither raised her voice nor changed her expression. She certainly didn't want to end up behind bars her first visit to town, but she also needed to establish some rules of her own — and being threatened and bullied just wasn't going to fly.

The sheriff looked flustered and Trace guessed he wasn't used to people not cowering in his presence. Not only didn't she flinch, she didn't even break a sweat. It wasn't difficult to see that the sheriff was perturbed.

"Suit yourself." The sheriff turned to the bar. "Silas, gimme a shot of bourbon."

She watched with interest as the bartender frowned, grabbed a bottle with a pale brown liquid and poured it into a small glass. He placed it in front of the lawman, who tossed it back with practiced ease.

The sheriff pushed the glass forward and cleared the liquor residue out of his throat. "Well...better get back to it," he announced to no one.

"Drinking on the job?" Trace commented in amused observance and knew she was close to stepping over a line. If nothing else, she liked life on the edge. It kept her juices flowing.

"You're a brazen fella, ain't ya?" the sheriff asked.

"I've been known to be," Trace answered pleasantly. She turned to lean against the bar and studied the faces of the customers in the saloon.

The sheriff shook his head and smiled. "Just keep buildin' that big ol' chip on your shoulder, boy. It's gonna give me great pleasure to knock it off."

"It's going to give me greater pleasure to see you try," Trace countered congenially. She and the sheriff locked stares. He didn't look at all happy with her, but she made sure her expression told him she was not backing down.

He stood rigid and scanned the interior of Wilbur's, his expression daring anyone to look back at him. No one did. Then he panned back to Trace's icy blue eyes. "You watch your step, son. Ain't smart what you're doin'. I have no doubt I'll see you in my jail before you leave Sagebrush. That's if you leave Sagebrush." And with that, he pushed out through the doors.

All eyes followed the sheriff until he was gone and then focused back on Trace. Oblivious, her concentration still on the door, she said, "He's kind of an asshole, isn't he?"

The stillness nearly swallowed her up. When she finally looked around the room, she saw that everyone had been struck mute by her statement and they all stared at her, dumbfounded. "What?" she asked, bewildered. Surely they'd all noticed that the sheriff was an asshole.

"You got some sand, boy," Silas said, breaking the silence as Trace turned back to face him. "Nobody talks to Ed like that. 'Specially not nobody who don't even wear a six gun on his hip."

She shrugged and took another few swallows of her beer. *Who would have thought I'd need to be armed just to come to town to get groceries?* She guessed she needed to go back to the pawn shop at some point and buy a gun. Unless Rachel had one back at her place. "He doesn't scare me. He's a bully with a badge."

"Which is the worst kind. He's got the law to back him up."

"Only if he makes up the laws as he sees fit," Trace commented. Slowly the din of the saloon began to rise again as the patrons went back to what they'd been doing before the exchange between Trace and the sheriff. Trace drank down the rest of the pint and signaled Silas for a refill, which he readily provided.

She had not realized until that point how hazy with cigarette, cigar, and pipe smoke the interior of the bar was. It burned her throat and she remembered that these were the days when no one knew how hazardous tobacco was to one's health, and if she couldn't explain that to them, there was no way she was going to convince them that breathing secondhand smoke was just as bad. Smoking was a nasty habit she was glad she'd never picked up. She had tried it a few times and each attempt made her a little more nauseated than the last. After one final lightheaded, overly queasy moment, she decided cigarettes were not for her and she never touched them again.

She suddenly wondered what was happening in the twenty-first century, knowing life was obviously going on without her. She wondered how her absence had been explained. She wondered if there was a way for her to return and if there was, would she? Something had made her decide to run, to miraculously leap through time. But what? She hated not knowing.

Feeling melancholy, she thanked Silas for the refill and drained half the glass in two swallows. She fleetingly wondered if she'd ever have an ice-cold beer or a hot shower again.

Chapter Seven

Rachel and Molly sat opposite each other in the small back room of the dress shop. They drank hot tea and shared a corn meal muffin.

"Now, Rachel, I've known you since you were in pinafores and pigtails and you've never lied to me. Least not that I know of. Don't think you're going to start now. What's all this I've heard about you and that turd with lips, Ben Crane?"

Rachel couldn't help snickering. Molly was nothing if not colorful. "What has that serpent been saying?" She tried to sound aloof but she knew the moment she heard the words, they would hurt deep in her bones.

"He's saying that he showed you the pain and glory of consummation, and that you warmed that bed like a fire on a cold night." When Rachel bit her lip and bowed her head, the older woman erupted. "Oh, Rachel Frances Young, you did not give yourself to that touch hole!"

Rachel shook her head and the tears flowed without warning. "No, Miz Ledbetter, I certainly did not," she choked out.

"Then why in heaven's name are you crying as if you did?" When Rachel couldn't answer her, Molly reached over and gently lifted Rachel's chin and waited until the emerald green eyes met her weary hazel ones. The look of shame Rachel wore was not guilt but mortification. The anguish in her eyes caused Molly's breath to catch and when she spoke, there was a lump in her throat. "Oh, my Lord, child, what did he do?"

Staccato words struggled out between gasps and sobs. "He hurt me real bad, Miz Ledbetter."

The dressmaker enfolded Rachel in her arms and began to rock her comfortingly. "Why that no good son of a snake! What happened?" Molly's voice was tightly controlled as she tried to hold back her fury. She didn't want Rachel to think she was judging her. "If I had Ben Crane in front of me right now, I'd kill him with my bare hands. Isaac Tipping told everybody that you looked terrible bruised when he delivered to your place last month, said you told him you fell off that new mustang of yours. Was it really Crane what did that to you?"

"Yes, ma'am. He...he...well, Rosie had just foaled and I was on my way back to the house from the stable and he came up behind me and...he grabbed me...and dragged me back inside the barn and took me like a wild animal..." She was hysterical, first at the recollection and second at the relief of finally being able to tell someone the truth.

Molly's arms stiffened. "Are you telling me that Ben Crane knocked you about and had his way with you?"

Rachel nodded her head against the older woman's shoulder. Her mind replayed that night in vivid detail and she wondered if the memory of it would ever go away. She had to talk about it.

"It was a little over a month ago. He tried several times to call on me that day but I wanted none of him. The more stubborn he was, the more determined I was. He called me a pigheaded woman, told me he was getting to be the town joke and was being humiliated by some of the more brazen comments aimed at his masculinity. I told him it didn't have to be that way if he'd just learn to take no for an answer and forget about me. Later that night, after he'd been drinking at Wilbur's, he showed up after dusk, and that's when he caught me leaving the stable.

"I fought him as hard as I could. I screamed and struggled and begged, but he wouldn't pay me no mind. Clearly I was no match for his strength and nothing I said could stop his drunken attack." She stopped as sobs shook her. She recovered a bit of her composure and continued. "By the time he finished, I hurt so bad, I nearly passed out from the pain."

She had been weak and terrified, in shock, ashamed and didn't know what to do about it. Crane, reeking of stale whiskey and bitter tobacco, rolled off her, his smug arrogance clearly lacking any remorse. He staggered to his feet, pulled his trousers up, then sank back to his knees and drew back his arm. She cowered and wanted to cover her face but she was unable to get her limbs to respond. She waited to feel the blow of his fist again but something stopped him.

"'Now look at ya,' he'd said. 'Ain't too good for me now, are ya? You're a nice piece of tail, Rachel, and I'll make sure the whole town knows it, too. I'll make sure if you don't marry me, then no man will want ya.' And, with that, he'd left the stall, mounted his horse, and ridden away.

"I laid there for several minutes after he was gone, frozen. My mind left me and I felt crippled. I couldn't believe what had just happened. I...I still can't. I couldn't stop crying." She determinedly brushed flowing tears from her cheeks. "My dress was in tatters. As I tried to sit up, every movement was torture, every inch of me was in agony." She winced as she recalled brushing straw and hay out of her hair and how her hands wouldn't stop shaking as she gingerly touched the cuts on her cheek and lips. And then there had been the blood on her dress. There had been so much blood.

"I was a virgin, Miz Ledbetter," Rachel sobbed as the older woman held her. "My mama brought me up respectable."

"I know, dear. You were saving yourself for your wedding night with Tommy. If he hadn't died, you two would have been hitched long ago and this never would have happened." She hugged Rachel more tightly and said, "Lord, help me, those damned Cranes. They're never going to stop. And that damned Ed Jackson, he'll never do one thing to any of them. My word, child, if I'd had any idea, I'd have been out there to see you."

"Mr. Ledbetter needs you here," Rachel managed to get out, knowing it was true. The dress shop was connected to the Ledbetter residence, which made it easy for Molly to frequently check on her husband, who was confined to their bed or a chair by the bed.

Three years earlier, a strapping Harvey Ledbetter had been shot while he assisted Rachel's father in a territorial dispute with the Cranes. The bullet hit his spinal cord, paralyzing him from the waist down. Since no one could prove who fired the shot, Sheriff Jackson said he couldn't arrest anyone, and since it was a property issue, he really should keep his nose out of it. Since then, with Harvey nearly as helpless as a baby, Molly Ledbetter didn't stray too far from her home.

"Please don't tell anyone, Miz Ledbetter, please!" Rachel pleaded. "No one will believe me and I'll be disgraced."

"Shhh, shhh, Rachel. Everybody will believe you. They all know what those Cranes are capable of; the problem is that no one will speak out against them. But now that Ben has spread his damned lies about you—"

"But those I can deny. I did not give myself to him in that manner and because everyone knows Ben's reputation, there's a chance they might think it's just him boasting. If it gets around that he truly did... have me...it won't matter how it happened and you know that. People will feel sorry for me but it won't stop them from gossiping. And I'll be thought of just like one of those pleasure girls at the sporting house over Wilbur's. Just like Mrs. Beauregard said."

Molly shook her head in frustration. "It isn't right, you having to live out there all alone, having to deal with all this hell on earth. Why'd the Lord see fit to take Tommy from you? They wouldn't be doing this if Tommy had made it back and married you."

The presence of Thomas Baines, Esquire, would have put a damper on the Cranes' brutish behavior, no doubt about that, Rachel thought. But it obviously wasn't meant to be. If a marshal's stray bullet during a train robbery hadn't killed him, there was a better than even chance he would have met his Maker at the hands of one of the Cranes. Rachel leaned away from Molly and wiped her tears away with a delicate handkerchief. She took a deep breath. "I'm not alone anymore. At least not presently."

Molly was surprised. "You take on a hand?"

"Yes. Well, kind of." She again consciously reminded herself to refer to Trace as male. "Rosie and her baby got out a couple of days ago. I went looking for them and came on this drifter got thrown from his horse. He was hurt so I brought him back to the house and fixed him up, and he's going to stay and help me out with the land."

"What do you know about this stranger?" Molly asked cautiously.

"Only that he's not from these parts and that he's willing to stay around, hole up in the barn, and help me out for a while."

"How you gonna pay him?" Rachel's pursed lips caused her to say, "I know, you're not like that, child, but everyone else will wonder, 'specially after Ben running off at the mouth."

"Just feed him and give him a place to lay his head. That's all he wants. Lost his horse and wasn't wearing any guns when I found him lying there, hurt."

"Sure he's telling you the truth?"

"He's been here almost three days and he hasn't tried anything yet. He's already fixed the break in the south fence. I really don't think he has any dishonorable intentions." *If she only knew...*

"Well, hopefully, he'll still be around when the Cranes come back from their drive. A man out at your place won't exactly be popular with them, 'specially not Ben, but it might make them think twice before they try anything again. Young buck, is he?"

Rachel shrugged, then nodded. "Young enough."

"Young enough for you?" There was a hint of a twinkle in Molly's eye.

"Molly Ledbetter! That's the last thing that'll happen between me and this man!"

Trace knew she should get back to the wagon to help Rachel load up, but the beer had started to taste very good and despite the setting, she was starting to feel like herself again.

After his apparent initial shock at seeing Trace standing up to the sheriff wore off, Silas returned to his talkative self and before long she had the lowdown on just about everyone in town. Curiously, though, any subject that bordered on the Young family and their land was deftly avoided.

She just finished her last swallow of beer when the sound of running footsteps above them drew everyone's attention to the staircase. A half-clad, voluptuous redhead appeared and shouted frantically, "Someone come quick! It's Jed, I think he's chokin' to death!"

Several people ran for the stairs but Trace beat them all as her training and instinct kicked in without a second thought. She followed the redhead to a room at the end of the hall. Trace flew through the open doorway and nearly skidded on the slick wooden floor. She found a distinguished looking older man sitting on a rumpled bed, silver serving tray in front of him that held a platter showing evidence of a partially eaten meal. His face was beet red, his eyes were popping, and his mouth was open but not a sound came out. *Yep*, Trace thought, *he's definitely choking*. The redhead began to smack him roughly on the back.

"No!" Trace yelled. "You'll just lodge it deeper!" Trace rushed over to the silver-haired man, and pulled him to his feet. She moved behind him, put her arms around him, found the right spot and performed the Heimlich maneuver.

As the onlookers watched in horror and fascination, a piece of steak flew from his mouth. Weak and gasping for breath, the half-naked man began to cough. Trace removed her arms but kept one hand on his back, in case he needed continued support.

"What the hell you doin', son?" a voice bellowed from the doorway. Another white-haired man shouldered through the crowd and into the room. "What were you trying to do, break the mayor's ribs?"

Trace looked at the man she'd just saved and then at the prostitute, she shook her head. *The mayor. It figures.* "No, I was saving his life," Trace stated calmly to the man who resembled pictures she had seen of Mark Twain.

"Squeezin' him like a bear's savin' his life?" the man continued, outraged.

"Shut up, Amos, you jackass!" the mayor sputtered. "Jesus H. Kee-ryst, whatever this young man did was the only thing got that darned piece of meat out of my gullet." He nodded at the redhead. "Cassandra pounding on my back like that only made it worse."

Trace glanced at Cassandra, who shrank back against the wall. "Hey, she tried," Trace offered. That elicited a smile from Cassandra, who held her short silky robe closed in the front.

Silas stepped into the room, hands raised in the air. "Okay, show's over; let the mayor have his privacy." Despite the grumbling that followed the bartender's command, the room cleared out and Silas closed the door behind him. That left Trace, the redhead, the mayor, and the other older man in the room.

"What's your name, son?" the mayor asked, now breathing normally.

"Trace Sheridan."

The mayor extended his hand and said, "Jedediah Turner."

"Turner?" Trace accepted the limp handshake. "Any relation to the pawnbroker?"

"Ah, you've met my baby brother, Joseph." The mayor ran his hand through an unruly shock of white hair. "I know what you're thinking, everybody does — we couldn't look any more different if we were strangers."

It was the truth, Trace thought. Other than a slight resemblance around the eyes, they didn't look related in the least.

"Him and me had different mamas." He looked back in the general direction of the prostitute. "Cassandra, bring me that bottle."

The redhead obeyed and handed him the unmarked bottle.

"Now, Jed, take it easy on that stuff..." the other man began, only to be immediately cut off by Jed Turner.

"Amos, will you shut the hell up! Your mouth flaps more than a duck's ass." The mayor looked at Trace for the first time. "Why, you're a handsome feller, ain't ya? Bet you got the ladies swarmin' 'round you like bees to honey."

You have no idea, Trace thought.

"Unlike me, who has to get me arms that are willin' only if they're bought." He stated it matter-of-fact, no shame in his voice. "Have a shot of this bug juice with me."

What's with the freaking bug juice, Trace thought. "No, thanks, I'll pass."

"Suit yourself." He took a hearty swallow from the bottle and made a long, satisfied rasping noise as the liquid burned its way down his throat. "Trace, you met Doc Smith yet?"

Trace shook her head. "Not officially, no." She extended her hand but the doctor brushed by her and sat on the bed next to the mayor.

"Jed, let me check you out now—"

The ornery mayor slapped his hand away and took another swig from the bottle. "Damn it, Amos, get away from me before I bean you with this bottle! Now shake this boy's hand before I tell your wife you were in here playin' poker."

The doctor's face took on an even more sour expression. "Don't need to make his acquaintance. He won't be stayin' around long enough for any of us to get to know."

The mayor looked up at Trace then over at Amos Smith. "Why is that?"

"Yeah." Trace folded her arms and also looked at the doctor. "Why is that?"

"You were given some good advice by the sheriff," Smith said. "I suggest you take it."

Jed Turner briefly studied both Trace and Smith, then focused on Trace. "What's goin' on?"

Trace squinted at the doctor with unmistakable suspicion and directed her conversation toward the mayor before actually looking his way. "Your sheriff has suggested I move on, out of town."

"Really? Huh. Do you want to move on, son?" The mayor sounded sincere.

"Sagebrush is starting to grow on me. If I move on, I'd like to do it when I choose and not because someone suggests it."

"Then I think you should stay," the mayor declared.

"But, Jed, he's livin' out at—"

"I don't give a good goddamn where he's livin'. If he wants to stay then he should stay. This is still my town, ain't it?"

"Well...yes, but Ed—"

"But, nothin'! Ed Jackson's as much of a horse's ass as you are." Turner looked up at Trace. "You wanted by the law, son?"

"No, sir."

The mayor looked back at the doctor. "Then you tell Sheriff Jackson he can go plumb to hell. He won't be runnin' anyone out of my town, and surely not anyone who just saved my life." With that, the mayor stood up and reached for his pants. "Guess I won't be finishin' my dinner. Kinda lost my appetite." Turner stepped into his trousers. "Goddamned Ed Jackson. Nothin' but a big bag of wind. If those Cranes weren't behind him, he'd be runnin' out of town the other way with a stripe down his backside."

Trace ignored the mayor and the unfriendly doctor who tried to fuss over him. She looked over at Cassandra and nodded. "You okay?"

Startled by a question being directed at her, Cassandra lifted her wide green eyes to engage Trace.

Before she could answer, the mayor piped up, "Of course, she's fine. Why wouldn't she be? I'm the one who damn near choked to death." He snapped his fingers toward his shirt and the redhead picked it up without hesitation and helped him put it on.

Trace tried not to look disgusted at this blatant display of false gender superiority. She chewed the inside of her cheek to stay quiet. After all, the mayor was on her side...but just exactly what that meant remained to be seen.

"How's it you came to learn that little bear hug trick, anyway?" The doctor spoke to her in a tone that was a little more friendly than before, but not much. "You got some doctor trainin'?"

"Um...no, nothing like that. Just some little thing I picked up in my travels."

"How's it work?"

"Well...here." Trace positioned her arms around the doctor and he flailed and pushed her away.

"I don't want you bear huggin' me! Show me on Cassandra."

An eyebrow shot up as Trace assessed the redhead with the hourglass figure. And the way Cassandra ogled her in return, it was obvious the prostitute was more than agreeable to the request. She practically leapt toward Trace with an obliging grin on her face.

Trace stopped her at arm's length and turned the redhead around, instructing as she slowly demonstrated. "First you wrap your arms around the victim's waist." She made a fist and placed the thumb side of her fist against the redhead's upper abdomen, below her ribcage and above her navel and tried not to think about the heavy breasts that touched her forearms. Trace focused on her task and grasped her right fist with her left hand and pressed into Cassandra's upper abdomen with a quick upward thrust, which made the prostitute gasp with surprise. Trace minimized the pressure, so as not to do any harm. "You don't actually squeeze the ribcage," Trace explained. "You confine the force of the thrust to your hands and then you repeat until the object is expelled."

Cassandra tried to lean her body back against Trace, who was able to get her lesson across without molesting the nearly nude prostitute, although embracing the woman, regardless of the circumstances, did make Trace's mouth water. She snapped out of it and gently let go of Cassandra, smiled politely, and stepped back. "Understand?" she asked the doctor.

"Makes no sense to me," Smith spat back.

"Don't have to make no sense if it works," the mayor observed and put on his suit jacket. He walked up to Trace and clapped her on the shoulder. "Thank you, son, for helpin' me live to see another day."

"You're welcome, Mr. Mayor."

"Mr. Mayor," Jed Turner repeated, cackling. "Polite feller, too."

"He wasn't so polite to Ed," Doc Smith muttered and followed the mayor out the door.

"Nobody should be polite to Ed, he don't deserve it, the damned fool." Jed Turner yammered out into the hallway.

Suddenly Trace and Cassandra were alone in the room. Trace was about to ask a few questions about the mayor and the doctor when the prostitute let the robe slide off her body and posed seductively. Trace couldn't help but stare at the natural — she noticed — redhead while her brain adjusted to the situation. Cassandra was not an unattractive woman by any means, and although she was more plump than Trace was usually drawn to, her body wasn't unpleasant. Her first attempt to speak produced no words, so she cleared her throat to try again.

Cassandra purred, "How 'bout one on the house? Seein' as you just saved my best customer and all."

Trace took one last look at breasts that begged to be fondled and lips that looked like they could suck the nose cone off a 747 and reluctantly nodded her head toward the doorway. "I'm...uh...really flattered, Cassandra, and maybe some other time, but right now, I should get back to the store." But her feet seemed glued to that spot on the floor.

Cassandra appeared surprised that anyone would turn down a free roll in the hay. "A young, healthy man like you doesn't want," she looked down at her naked body, then back up at Trace, "this?" She smiled suggestively. "I've never had anyone turn me down before, not for free, and definitely not anyone as good lookin' as you. Why, you're so handsome, you're almost pretty. I'm gonna make a pledge to you, Trace Sheridan. If I don't get you in my bed right now, I'll get you in my bed before you're run out of town."

It was only when Cassandra took a step forward and reached out to cup a piece of anatomy Trace didn't have that she shook herself out of her mini-fantasy and ducked out the door. "Thanks anyway," Trace tossed back over her shoulder. She removed her hat and wiped her brow. It was a close call and one that she put in her mental archives to avoid in the future.

Back downstairs, she took time to accept a quick round of "goodbyes" and "good jobs" before exiting the saloon. Yes. She would definitely have to purchase a gun. If for nothing else, to use the bullets to bite on in situations like this. In addition to all the other adjustments, she wondered if she'd ever have sex again as long as she lived.

Trace found Rachel waiting impatiently in front of Foster's Grocery. She suppressed a smile. It amazed her how they'd already fallen into a rhythm with one another. She felt a sense of relief at seeing Rachel and when Rachel finally saw her, the same look of relief crossed her face. That mollifying sensation stopped abruptly when Trace got close enough to see that Rachel had been crying.

Her protective nature provoked her temper to flare immediately and she reached out and touched Rachel's arm. "What's wrong? Did that grocer make you cry?"

Before Trace went off half-cocked to give Luther Foster a piece of her mind, or worse, Rachel grasped Trace's arm and urged her back around to face her. "No, Mr. Foster did not make me cry. I visited with a dear friend of my mama's and it was just...sad...that's all." She watched Trace's eyes soften.

"Oh. Okay. I just thought...he was such a jerk to you and all..." She wanted to pull Rachel into her arms and comfort her but common sense stopped her. First, they were in public view of the whole town, and second, Rachel probably wouldn't appreciate it. Unfortunately. Despite the offer she had just turned down at Wilbur's, she would have welcomed this particular woman into her arms.

Trace couldn't help the bawdy grin that found its way to her face when she placed the jar of olive oil onto the wagon. As she drove back toward the ranch, she visualized Rachel massaging her. Her thoughts were interrupted by the sound of Rachel's voice.

"Trace?"

"Yeah?"

"You want to pay attention to guiding Moses? Otherwise we're going to end up down by the river. I swear that horse would live there if I ever set him loose."

"Oh...sure." She forced herself to pay attention and noticed that they were about twenty feet off the dirt road, heading to the left. She pulled the reins slightly to the right and the horse obediently wandered back to the path.

"What were you thinking about?"

"Nothing...just, um, daydreams."

"Daydreams?"

Change the subject, Trace, the sooner the better. "Rachel, do you own any guns?"

"My father left me with two Colt Peacemakers, a Sharps, a Winchester, and a carbine. Why?"

"Until I buy my own, can I use one of those?"

Rachel cautiously gave the requested permission. "Of course, but why? Did something happen in town?"

"No, no." *Oh hell, with that grapevine, she'll find out soon enough.* "Well, sort of."

"Sort of?" She stared at Trace in alarm.

Trace looked for a way to minimize the event when she did a double take at Rachel's expression. "No, Rachel, everything's fine, really. I just kind of had a run in with the sheriff..."

"Oh, no." Rachel closed her eyes. "Not Sheriff Jackson." She shook her head and let her chin drop. "I leave you on your own for a few hours, and you aggravate the one person I'd have preferred you not run into, that revolting excuse for a man—"

"Aha! So you know he's an asshole," Trace said triumphantly. Rachel reacted to the vulgarity by glaring at Trace, an action that Trace ignored. "He threatened me, told me to move on if I knew what was good for me. Can you believe that?"

"Because he found out you were staying with me?"

"Yes." She searched Rachel's face for a clue. "Why is that?"

"I told you how people would react—"

"No, it was more than that. Because when I saved the mayor's life, the doctor—"

"Wait, what?" She grabbed Trace's arm. "You saved Jed Turner's life? What in heaven's name went on over at the saloon?" Rachel listened, absorbed, to Trace's adventures at Wilbur's.

"So, how is it that no one is surprised that your mayor is choking on his lunch upstairs in a prostitute's room?" Trace asked pointedly.

"Oh, Jed eats his lunch up in Cassandra's room most every day; everybody knows it. He's a crusty old bird, a widower who never remarried. Not that any of the widow women in this county would ever hitch up with him. Everybody just looks the other way, but he wouldn't care if they didn't."

"How did somebody like that get to be mayor?"

"He inherited the job from his daddy. Got elected after he'd already had it for a month because no one else wanted it."

"And who are the Cranes?" Trace did not expect the intake of breath and the deathly quiet that came from the woman beside her. Trace looked at her companion and found her pale and staring straight ahead. "Rachel...who are the Cranes?"

"I really would rather not speak of them."

"Just saying their name seemed to strike terror in the heart of everyone I met, and since the sheriff mentioned them in his warning to me, I'd kind of like to know." Rachel's expression told Trace that the name struck terror in her heart, too. Softly, she said, "I would really appreciate knowing what I might face with these Cranes."

"They...they're not nice people."

"I gathered that. Are they responsible for the destruction of the fence I fixed yesterday?"

"I believe so, yes."

"Why?" Even though Trace tried to be gentle with her questions, her adrenaline was pumping pure fury through her veins. "I was just threatened. Don't you think I have a right to know?"

Rachel sighed. "Jacob Crane is a cattle baron. He owns most all the land east of Sagebrush. Everyone this side of town has sold their land to him. Except me."

"And the reason you haven't sold?"

Rachel's eyes flashed in indignant anger before she spoke, the words coming out in stiff bites. "My great-grandfather settled this land when the first frontiersmen came here. Everything I have today was built on the sweat of my ancestors. Jacob Crane moved his family and his cattle business here just a little over a decade ago. They've been forcing everyone off their lands ever since."

The tone of Rachel's voice and the expression on her face told Trace that this was delicate territory, so she tried to tread lightly. "Forcing, or buying people out?"

"Oh, they're offering money, but if you say no, things happen."

"What kind of things?" Even as the words left her mouth, she knew. The empty barn, the vandalized property...the death of her parents, perhaps? *Great. I left one turf war that besieged my job on a daily basis only to step into another one that might cost me my life. Different stakes, same principle.*

"Some things I can't blame on anyone, not even the Cranes. My husband-to-be was shot by accident during a robbery on a train. Just a few months later, mama and papa got sick and the doc couldn't save them. None of that was the Cranes' doin'." She glanced at Trace, who listened raptly. "Before papa died, though, the Cranes were after him to sell them the land, and there were a number of incidents like the broken fence line."

The more Rachel related, the more Trace's heart ached for her. *This poor woman has been through enough.* "And they have been after you ever since you inherited?" As Moses clopped through the entrance of the Triple Y ranch, Trace looked around at the deceptively serene setting.

"Yes," Rachel responded with a rebellious lilt.

"What did they offer you?"

"Their most recent is fifty thousand dollars for just the land, plus an extra thirty-five hundred for the house and improvements."

Trace thought back to the era they were in and that Rachel might be able to start a very comfortable life on that amount. "That's a nice little chunk of change, you—"

"I will not sell to them!" Rachel's bellow overrode anything Trace might have said. She folded her arms stubbornly across her chest and they endured the next few minutes in awkward silence.

"Why is it so important for them to have your land?"

"Because it runs smack dab in the middle of the path of their cattle drive."

"Can't they go around your property?"

"Sure. But every extra mile runs that much more meat off the steers."

The injustice of Rachel's situation ignited the fire in Trace's belly. It had been a long time since she'd stood up for the underdog, and she loved a good fight. These Crane people were probably not going to stop until Rachel gave in, or ended up dead. Trace looked over at the fierce set of Rachel's jaw and knew she now had another reason, other than personal obstinacy, to stay put. "When are these Cranes due back?"

"Shouldn't be for another four or five months, more or less. It normally takes three, but I heard they were going to take some time to buy some stock that might be good for racing as well as for working their range."

As the wagon stopped in front of the house, Trace smiled confidently at Rachel. "Then it looks like we have our work cut out for us."

Chapter Eight

While Rachel busied herself making dinner, she put Trace to work arranging the items that were brought back from town and depositing them in their proper places. Finding out where everything went formed the substance of the conversation between the two women and when Trace was done, she went to the barn to remove her wrap. Left alone in the kitchen, Rachel made biscuits and popped them into the oven while she contemplated the events of the day.

She was not surprised that her fears had been realized; Ben Crane had made good on his promise to taint her reputation. However, being right about it didn't make it hurt any less that people actually believed it. Maybe if she continued to deny it, the gossip would go away. *Sure, and maybe babies really do come from cabbage patches.*

She felt both drained and relieved at having spilled her soul to Molly, but she had left out one very important detail. She unrealistically hoped she was mistaken about being with child and until she was positive, no one needed to be the wiser. What she was going to do after that was too much to think about just yet. At least to think about out loud.

Luther Foster's words stabbed at her, though, telling her she should give in to the Cranes. He knew what her family had been through to keep Jacob's hands off the Triple Y. Any rational person would have just taken the money they offered and let them have the ranch. But her resolve went way beyond what anyone else considered rational. Small as it was in comparison to other spreads in the area, the Triple Y meant too much to her to just give it up. Her grandfather, her father, and she herself had been born in that house and it was all she had left of her family. It was her home and she stubbornly did not care what the Cranes wanted. She had paid dearly for her defiance — slaughtered cattle, burned crops, hamstrung horses, and the most devastating blow of all, rape. She was done paying.

Which brought her to consider the strange and strong woman who now lived on the ranch. Just the knowledge of the existence of another person on the property — especially one believed to be a man — would stir up a hornets' nest. Trace had made a conspicuous entrance into the Sagebrush community by saving Jed Turner's life, an act that would be hailed by some and cursed by others. And, by ruffling the feathers of the sheriff, she was positive Trace had unintentionally poked at that hornets' nest with a very stout stick. She didn't know why...but despite the gravity of the situation, something about that made her chuckle.

Trace's unsolicited protectiveness of her in town also evoked a fond smile, and thinking of it, and of Trace, she felt a warmth surge through her that should not have stirred her blood the way it did. She was confused by the alien emotion and disturbed because this was not the first time she had experienced it. Rachel reasoned that it was more than likely because she had to think of Trace as a man. Still, it didn't make it any less troubling that she wished Trace would take her in her arms and make all the troubles go away.

Trace was not used to being bound down for so many hours and her injuries, though healing well, were nonetheless still healing, and parts of her skin cinched into the binding remained tender. She was fairly certain there would be no visitors to the ranch so she was unconcerned about going braless. If someone did show up, she would deal with it, but right now...it would be pure bliss to free her poor corralled breasts.

She reflected on the tenor of the town as she had experienced it. It was a lot tamer than what she was used to, but still unsettling. The bartender liked her, as did the pawnbroker and, of course, his half-brother, the mayor. The woman named Cassandra really liked her, but the doctor and the sheriff did not. On the other hand, neither His Honor nor Rachel had anything good to say about the overbearing man who wore the badge. And everyone in the saloon had seemed afraid of him.

Ed Jackson was a bad cop. If anyone could readily recognize one, it was Trace, having spent a good portion of her law enforcement career playing both ends against the middle, selling her services to the highest bidder. Her lip curled into a predatory smile. She had been a better bad cop. Jackson was obviously in the back pocket of the Cranes. She knew what that was like and no matter how ruthless these Cranes were, they couldn't be as abominable as the DeSiennas or the other modern day criminals she had to deal with on a daily basis. If she was going to stay in Sagebrush, she wasn't going to allow herself to be restricted by anyone or anything. She glanced toward the house and sighed. Oh, yes...she definitely wanted to stay here.

She suddenly realized she had a chance to redeem herself. Right now. Even though she wasn't in her own time where the people she had hurt could benefit from her change of heart, she had an opportunity to make up for past sins. If Sagebrush's above-the-law family wanted to hold the county hostage, she could deal with that. She was used to it. Except this time she would be on the side of the angels.

As she walked back to the house, she vowed to herself that Rachel would never again have to worry about the Cranes. Talk was cheap, so she would have to prove she was as good as her word, as she was quite sure the nineteenth century Rachel would never believe a female would be able to hold such a powerful clan at bay. But to be successful, Trace would have to get herself back in shape while learning a whole new way of life. She took a deep, cleansing breath. *God, I love a challenge.*

The supper conversation was strained but not in a way that represented anger or awkwardness. Each woman was lost in her own individual thoughts and neither really seemed to notice the other one was not talking much. After the delicious dinner of hearty, thick corn chowder with bacon and biscuits, Rachel did the dishes while Trace went to the stable to make sure the horses had food and water.

When Trace had finished filling up the trough, she strolled outside the stable and stretched the lameness out of her bones. Movement caught her eye and she saw Rachel disappear behind the west corner of the house. Curiosity got the better of her and Trace followed her up to a knoll. Joining Rachel on the other side of the slanted hill, Trace saw several small tombstones. Roughly etched on three of the stones were the names of Rachel's mother and father and Thomas Baines. Rachel kneeled down and silently cleared away grass that had grown wildly around the base of the granite markers.

"Your fiancé is buried here, too?"

"He had no family left but mine. Not that we were any relation, of course. He was sixteen when his folks were killed coming back here on the stage. They'd been in Kansas, at a service for Tommy's grandmother."

"How were they killed?" Trace bent down and helped brush dirt off the stones.

"Word got back to town that they were ambushed by Indians, but I don't believe it. The Pawnee settlement just outside town has never caused any trouble and there hasn't been an Indian uprising since the Plains nations got together at Little Big Horn. Least not around these parts." She looked over at Trace. "That's why people aren't trying to run you out of town 'cause you look like you could have some Indian in you. Any tribes left around here are all friendly."

"So why would someone lie about how those folks died?"

"Because everything was slaughtered, including the horses. Even if it was a renegade bunch, Indians wouldn't have done that; they would have taken the horses with them."

"Where are his parents buried?"

"They aren't. Stagecoach was set on fire; wasn't enough of them left to bury. What made everybody suspicious was it was Seth Carver came to town with the news."

Trace straightened and rubbed the side of her neck. "Who is Seth Carver?"

"He's Jacob Crane's nephew." Rachel went back to pulling weeds. "Mr. and Mrs. Baines were also holding on to their land and didn't want to give it up. After they died, Tommy couldn't keep up with running the ranch by himself, and was forced to sell. He used the money to go to law school. He was on his way back here to marry me and hang out his shingle when he was killed. He was going to fight the Cranes legally, try to stop them."

"And how would he have been able to do that with a crooked sheriff so obviously supporting the Cranes?"

Rachel looked up at Trace. "He would have found a way; he had to do what was right. Even though no one else had the gumption."

Tears glistened in Rachel's eyes and Trace could not decide if it was due to her grief over the loss of her fiancé or her determination to not become another casualty of the murderous Cranes. This hardened Trace's resolved to take them down.

One at a time, if she had to.

The next morning showed Rachel an entirely different Trace. She was up with the rooster, dressed and grooming the horses before Rachel had to resort to guilting her out of bed with numerous wake-up visits, each one guaranteed to be a little less friendly than the previous. In fact, Rachel was so surprised at this unexpected behavior that when she passed the stable and heard whistling, she nearly dropped the eggs she had gathered. Not quite sure what she would find, she cautiously stepped inside and observed Trace brushing Chief with an enthusiasm that she hadn't previously seen her display. The way the horse glanced over at his owner, he looked a tad nonplussed, too.

"Uh...morning...?" Rachel squinted to make sure her eyes weren't playing tricks on her.

"Good morning," Trace responded brightly.

Nope. Not an apparition. "Um...you all right?"

Trace smiled at the hesitancy in Rachel's tone. "Couldn't be better. Thought I'd get Chief ready and then after breakfast, I'll ride him around the perimeter and see what else needs fixing."

"You *want* to ride Chief?"

"Didn't you say he was the fastest and the strongest?"

"Yes, but—"

"Then he and I need to get used to each other because we're going to be spending a lot of time together." She lightly slapped Chief's muscular flank. "Aren't we, you handsome creature?"

Rachel shook her head in speechless confusion. She could have sworn the look in Chief's eyes said, "Help me."

"I didn't go into the other section where your mustang is. He seemed pretty restless but I've already brushed Moses and I was going to groom Rosie but she's pretty protective of that precious little baby she's got in there. Have you named her yet?"

"No, I was waiting to see..." *...if I needed to sell her to keep the place going*, she finished to herself.

"How about Zelda?"

"Zelda... I've never heard that name before."

"It's my mother's name."

"You want to name a horse after your mother?"

"Sure, why not?"

Rachel couldn't think of a reason, so she shrugged. "Um...okay, we'll call her Zelda."

"Really?"

"Really."

"Cool. Thanks." Trace continued to vigorously run the bristles over Chief.

"Cool?" Rachel repeated and cocked her head. "It's hotter than a whipped boy's behind this morning."

"No — cool...it means, uh...it's an expression of approval where I come from. When something is cool, it means it's—" she nodded her head for emphasis, "okay."

"Then why don't you just say it's okay? You talk strange sometimes, Trace Sheridan." Smiling, she turned around and headed back toward the entrance. "Don't saddle him up before breakfast," she called back.

"Okay."

Rachel stopped and looked back at Trace, flustered. "You mean, cool?"

"No, I mean okay, I won't saddle him up until after breakfast." Now it was Trace's turn to smile as Rachel shook her head, perplexed.

After Trace had washed up at the outdoor pump, she walked into the house to find a very pale Rachel at the stove, holding her stomach.

"Still feeling a bit ill, huh?" Trace asked as she approached the table, which held only one plate of bacon, eggs, and pancakes dripping with butter and honey. There was also a cup of what Trace was sure was criminally horrible coffee. Maybe she could use some of that honey to make a difference in the taste, although she doubted it. She returned her attention to the plate of greasy food that smelled unbelievably delicious and, despite the amount of bad cholesterol she knew she would ingest, she couldn't wait to start shoveling it in. "I can feel my arteries harden as we speak," she mumbled as she pulled out the chair. "You're not going to eat?" Trace asked, acknowledging the absence of a second plate on the table.

"I'm not hungry," Rachel said weakly, and ran for the door.

Trace looked down at her breakfast and with Rachel's regurgitating sound effects out on the porch, she muttered, "Neither am I, anymore."

She checked in the pantry, located the container of powdered ginger and brought it back out to the table. She set the kettle on the stove to get the water heated, then went out to the porch. Rachel was bent over at the waist with her hands resting on her knees.

"I'm okay, Trace," Rachel said hoarsely, not looking at her. "Go back inside and eat."

Trace placed a hand on Rachel's back and pulled the long blonde hair away from Rachel's face. "I've got the ginger out and the water boiling for you."

Rachel wiped her eyes with her apron then ran it over her mouth. "Thank you. But I'm not so sure I can go back in there right away. The smell is making my belly roil."

Trace helped her straighten up and led her over to a wooden porch chair. "No worries. I'll bring the drink out to you."

"You don't have to do that." The gratitude in her voice belied her demurral.

Trace smiled at her and said, "I don't have to do anything except eat, shit, pay taxes, and die."

"Lord, Trace, your language..." Rachel sighed. "I can't remember the last time anyone was this kind to me," she admitted weakly.

Trace prepared the soothing solution the way she had seen Rachel do it the day before. She brought a steaming cup back out to the porch and handed it to Rachel, who was still looking quite peaked. "I can't remember if I've ever met anyone I've wanted to be this kind to before."

"Please go back inside and eat," Rachel said. "It's not as tasty when it's cold."

Now that there were no vomiting sounds, Trace found she was hungry again. "If you're sure you are going to be all right..."

"I'll be fine in a bit...soon as I get this down."

"If you keep feeling like this, maybe you should go to the doctor."

"No," Rachel answered quickly. "I'm sure I'm fine."

Breakfast, despite having cooled, was still palatable, and Trace ate every bite, knowing she would need the energy. While Rachel, feeling better, cleaned up the kitchen, Trace looked through the chest where Rachel kept her father's clothes for something less encumbering to wear than her denim shirt. It was going to be a muggy day, and Frank Young most likely had something appropriate to wear in such weather.

She found some dirt-stained, worn cotton shirts that she pulled out and draped over her arm. If Rachel was agreeable, she would cut the sleeves off and use them to work in. She also looked over Frank's pants. She was probably going to have to sacrifice comfort for decorum, as she was pretty certain men didn't alter blue jeans to wear as shorts in the eighteen hundreds. Not that she had to worry about her legs giving her away. If she didn't see a razor soon, they'd be hairy enough to pass for a man's. The jeans were at least one size too big for her and she didn't think she would get any points for being trendy by holding up cut-offs with suspenders. Their next visit to town, she would have to buy some clothes that fit.

As if Rachel had read her mind, she addressed Trace from the doorway. "Those dungarees might be more suitable if I took them in a bit."

Trace saw that Rachel had a little more color in her face and that she was holding a rifle, the barrel pointed at the floor. Rachel gingerly ran her thumb over the Sharps' hand oiled forestock.

"You might want to take this with you. Needs to be cleaned but it was the last one I used and that was only a week ago, so it still shoots good." Rachel jerked back the brass slide-hammer to be sure Trace would have bullets at her disposal. She fingered the metal button embedded near the handle before turning it over to Trace.

"Am I going to need this?"

Rachel shrugged. "You never know. Irritating Ed Jackson probably wasn't the wisest idea. Can't have you riding into a mess of hot lead."

"No, we can't have that," Trace agreed wryly. She examined the eight-pound weapon. The .54 caliber cartridge rifle had a thirty-inch round blued barrel attached to a one-piece walnut-finished stock with three metal bands. She noticed it had fixed front and adjustable rear sights. The overall length was about three and a half feet. *Interesting little trinket. Do I dare admit I have no idea how to shoot it? Still, it can't be that difficult if a little slip of a ranch girl can do it. I'll take it with me and practice.* "What about handguns?"

"What?"

"You know...um...a revolver, a, uh, a six-shooter..."

"Oh, the Colts. Sure, but I thought you might want something that could reach past six-gun range."

"Good idea...but I am more used to using a handgun, a six-gun, than I am a rifle." She drew a deep breath. "Actually, I'm a little rusty at both. I've been traveling a while and could use some practice."

"Oh. I don't have a lot of extra bullets, but you're welcome to what I have."

Setting the Sharps across the bed, Trace thanked Rachel with a nod. "You said I could help myself to anything of your father's that fit. I found these shirts and—"

"Oh, I meant to take them out of there, cut 'em up and use them for rags."

"Can I have them?" At Rachel's hesitant expression, Trace explained her plans for the shirts. With Rachel's blessing, and her shears, a half-hour later Trace had some sleeveless garments to work in.

Out of the corner of her eye, Trace could see that Rachel was watching intently as she saddled up Chief with very few mistakes. Trace was sure that Rachel would also be surprised when she heeled the horse into a canter as though she'd been doing it all her life. She was a quick study and normally only had to have things demonstrated once and she could pick it up from there. It was important to Trace to impress Rachel and as she trotted away on Chief, she hoped she was.

Fixated on the two forms as they galloped away from her, Rachel was dazzled for a lot of reasons, one of which was not being able to deny that Trace was a breathtaking specimen of womanhood and someone that she should not feel so infatuated with. She automatically blamed these disquieting feelings on misplaced effects from her pregnancy. It certainly couldn't be anything else.

When Trace and Chief were out of sight, she went back inside the house to start her chores. Wondering if Trace liked plums, Rachel thought that she might bake a damson pie.

Despite the trouble she had growing inside her, she suddenly felt like she had a life again.

Trace was pleased at Chief's cooperation. Maybe just like any other male she had dealt with in her life, she had to show him who was in charge by letting him think he was the boss. Trace chuckled at that and headed back to the house for repair materials. She'd discovered three minor wear and tear breaks in need of immediate fixing.

Fortunately, she had not needed to use the rifle, but because of Rachel's warning, practicing until she became proficient with the Sharps and the other firearms was no longer optional. However, she held off on target practice because she didn't want to waste ammunition, which she might actually need to defend herself. She would take a trip into town and use some of the money she got from the rings to buy bullets or the materials she needed to mold and load her own. In the meantime, this afternoon, she would learn the joys of splitting rails.

Under Rachel's direction, Trace found the tools she needed in the barn — an axe, an eight-pound sledgehammer, and three four-pound wedges. Carrying the implements to the logs gathered behind the house, near the wooded area close to the river, Trace figured out she needed fourteen rails to fit into holes in the still standing posts. She used Moses to help her move the logs from the pile onto the ground where she could work on them.

After Moses had pulled four logs free of the stack, Rachel took him back to the stable while Trace assessed the amount of work ahead of her. She needed to split the wood into four sections as even as she could get them. Rachel returned to observe and stood back, crossing her arms. Though she didn't come right out and say it, Trace figured she anticipated the worst. Her first advice was, "Finish up with the same number of fingers and toes you started with." Rachel told her that hitting a knot tended to split the wood crooked, so Trace looked over the unsplit timber for knots, so as not to drive her wedge through one. She placed the wedge vertically in the exact center of the butt end of the log and tapped it in with the maul until it stuck. She lifted the sledgehammer over her head, and brought it down in a straight, square blow that jolted her from her toes to her teeth. Recovering from the aftershock, Trace saw where the log had cracked a good two feet from the end.

"Hey, look at that. Not bad, huh?"

Rachel couldn't help but smile at Trace's undisguised thrill at what she had done. When Trace leaned down, reaching for the wedge, Rachel said, "Use another one. That one's stuck."

"Stuck? Did I hit it too hard?"

"No," Rachel said and laughed. "You did just fine. Put a second one there." She pointed to the end of the crack. "Hit it again like you did the first one and you should open that original split another two or three feet. That should free that wedge there," she pointed to the first one, "so that you can jump it to keep splitting it until the trunk breaks into two halves. Then you just split the halves."

Trace did as she was told and split the trunk into four nearly equal rails. Two hours later, panting like a workhorse, she had cut sixteen rails, had blisters that stung like they were on fire and an upper body ache that rivaled the one she'd had her first week at the police academy.

She wiped her brow with the back of her arm, set the maul down, and admired her work. Her arms and her back were killing her, but looking at what she had accomplished made her quite proud of herself.

An ice cold beer would have tasted great.

As Rachel placed her pie on the porch to cool, she thought it might be a good idea to check on Trace, to see how she was doing. Again, she was a bit startled at the fact that Trace was on her last rail and she admonished herself because it should not have surprised her. Trace had already proven she was as robust as any man, and had muscles as taut as her rotund grandmother's corset laces. Watching the firm, nicely defined muscles shift beneath Trace's skin as she wielded the sledgehammer provoked a sudden acceleration of her heart rate.

Rachel approached Trace and held out the cup of water she had brought for her. Nodding her thanks, Trace took the small tin container and tried not to gulp the cool liquid. As Rachel took a step closer, Trace smiled. "I wouldn't get too close if I were you...or at least stay upwind of me."

"Nothing wrong with good, hard-earned sweat," Rachel commented as she inspected the rails. "I do think you may have a calling for this kind of work."

"Thank you...but," Trace said, studying her blistered and bleeding hands, "I don't think I want to do this too often. Haven't you ever heard of plywood?"

"Of course, I have. Plywood's been around since the days of the Pharaohs. But why pay money for what we already have?" She gestured to a forest full of trees behind her. "You should notch those rails a little so the fence will fit tight."

"I think I'll wait until tomorrow; my hands are a little raw now."

Rachel took Trace's hands in her own and examined them carefully. "I thought you were wearing those gloves of my father's."

"I was but they were too big and kept slipping. That's what started the blisters in the first place."

Rachel shook her head. "You're awfully tender-fleshed." She looked up at the raised eyebrow of her taller companion, and added, "for someone who's supposed to fight outlaws."

"Yeah? Well, give me a couple weeks and I'll amaze you with these hands," Trace commented innocently, then froze, closing her eyes as though she had said something wrong.

"I'm sure you will," Rachel answered in a voice that came out much huskier than she had intended. She absently ran her thumbs lightly over Trace's fingers. Locking gazes with Trace, Rachel swallowed hard and abruptly dropped the sore hands. Slowly pulling her eyes away from the much too engaging blue ones, Rachel bowed her head and stared at the ground. "It'd be better to notch 'em now. Tomorrow your hands will hurt too bad." As she walked away, she called over her shoulder, "When you're finished, come on to the house. I'll fix you up."

She watched until Rachel had gone inside. *Well that was interesting. What the hell was that about?* She didn't think Rachel was flirting, at least not consciously. But the moment Rachel had become aware of the connection between them, what was it she had seen in Rachel's eyes? Definitely not disgust. It could have been fear. It was indeed shock, but...at what? She read the uncertainty in Rachel's expression. Yet it was difficult for Trace to decide if Rachel was offended or bewildered by her own behavior, or, dare she hope, curious.

She would have to monitor her interaction with Rachel carefully. She in no way wanted to overstep any boundaries and she breathed a sigh of relief that she had not resorted to being her often obnoxious and flirtatiously bold self. That worked fine for her in her own time, but it would not be received well here.

Trace shook it off. Of course Rachel wasn't interested; it was dehydration mixed with wishful thinking. The poor woman had been through so much and Trace's sudden appearance in her life and the unusual circumstances under which they were sharing space had to be confusing, at the very least. *You need to keep your damned libido on a short leash, Trace.* Her sudden surge of frustration motivated her through scoring both ends of each rail until fourteen out of the sixteen were done.

Rachel could not get inside the house fast enough. When she knew she was completely out of Trace's sight, she braced herself and held on to the back of a chair. She let out the breath she'd been holding since she dropped Trace's hands. *What in Heaven's name just happened out there?* Had she just made a subtle overture toward Trace? No. No, she couldn't have; she wasn't like that. She didn't think about women like that. She had heard about women like that and no, she definitely was not one of them. She couldn't be. She had been engaged to be married; she had been in love with her fiancé. She liked kissing him, being in his arms, and had dreamed of...other things...they might do together. No, it was settled. She was not that kind of woman. It must be her innards being all messed up that made her feel all crazy inside.

Yes, that must be it...that must be what made her belly flutter and heart clench whenever Trace was around. It must be knowing deep inside that Trace was a protector that made her feel so safe in her presence. Had to be that baby growing inside her that discombobulated everything in her body and head, making her feel a kind of kinship, like she had known this woman her entire life. That, and her desperate loneliness. Trace had filled a gap in her life Rachel hadn't even acknowledged was there until she realized that if Trace moved on, everything would seem twice as empty as it had before. How odd, when she had only met this woman days ago.

Embarrassment burned in Rachel's cheeks. *Good Lord, what must Trace have thought?* Well, obviously Trace wouldn't think anything peculiar about her, she reasoned. After all, Trace knew she had been engaged. She comforted herself with that information and smiled. She moved to the stove and put the water on to boil before gathering what she would need to dress Trace's blisters.

When Trace entered the house, she smelled two distinct aromas other than herself. One was the freshly baked sweetness of a fruit pie with brown sugar, and the other was the rather overpowering scent of garlic.

Rachel was busy at the table using a granite mortar and pestle to crush fresh cloves of garlic and was heating olive oil in a small iron pan.

"Let me guess...pasta Italiano for supper and apple pie for dessert," Trace cracked. In response she received a blank stare from Rachel.

"I didn't think you'd want supper after the late dinner just a couple of hours ago."

Although it was true that Rachel had prepared them a very filling meal just before Trace split the rails, she had worked up an appetite and was a little disappointed, especially with the smell of garlic in the air. She suddenly longed for a huge dish of shrimp fettucini alfredo.

"Would you do me a favor and take the kettle off the stove? I thought we might have some tea with our pie...and it's not apples, it's damson plums."

Trace did as Rachel asked. "I've never had a plum pie before but it smells delicious." She was secretly grateful that what had happened in the yard was obviously not going to be mentioned. "And the garlic?"

"...is for your blisters."

"For my—" She stopped herself. In the short time she had been there, she had learned to not question Rachel's methods of healing.

"I'm going to make an oil to rub onto the blisters and I have a comfrey salve to put on the open sores. If you don't rub it all off before or during sleep, your hands should feel better by morning. We'll see how they look tomorrow."

Trace poured the water and steeped two cups of tea while Rachel cooked the garlic and olive oil concoction for five minutes, let it cool, and then strained it into a small jar, letting it sit before cutting a slice of pie for each of them.

"Mmm, Rachel, this is wonderful," Trace complimented, a mouthful of pie still not swallowed. "You really are an excellent cook. And baker."

"Thank you." Rachel blushed. "I thought you'd like it."

Nodding, Trace took another bite and was glad they were having tea instead of coffee. Sooner than later, she needed to ask Rachel to please allow her to make the coffee. So far, it was the only thing Rachel didn't do well.

Chapter Nine

Rachel told Trace how to treat her blisters instead of doing it for her. Since Rachel was usually physically demonstrative toward her, Trace figured it was because of the interchange between them that afternoon. And as Rachel seemed compelled to touch her whenever they interacted, Trace snickered to herself that Rachel almost had to sit on her hands while directing the salve application.

It was dusk before the solution had seeped in and started to dry. As the sun set, Rachel lit candles in every window, then lit the parlor lamp and took up her sewing. When she began to mend one of her dresses, Trace picked up a deck of cards and started to play solitaire at the table.

"How do your hands feel?"

"They burn a little but," Trace smiled, turning a card over, "I'll live." She looked up. "Tell me about Sheriff Jackson."

"Ed? Other than him being an insufferable know-it-all, more crooked than the letter Z, pretty adept at manure-spreadin' and having an abundantly abysmal personality, what would you like to know about him?"

Chuckling, Trace turned over another card. She didn't know why she bothered to play solitaire, she never won. "What's he like when he's backed into a corner?"

"That doesn't happen very often. Only strangers who don't know him think they can do that and they don't stay in town too long. There was this one time, though. Billy the Kid rode through. Went to Wilbur's for a couple of shots of whiskey before moving on. Seems Ed didn't know who he was and, thinking he can bully anybody he wants because he works for the Cranes, he made the mistake of shaking his finger in the Kid's face."

Billy the Kid. Wow. Thought he was just a folk legend. "What happened?"

Obviously tickled by the story, Rachel giggled. "Billy grabbed his finger and, um, shall I say 'escorted' him out to his horse, shoved the barrel of his six-gun practically in Ed's big mouth and demanded he mount up. Some of the boys the Kid rode with accompanied Ed out of town and acted like they were going to kill him. Obviously they didn't, but I don't think Ed's saddle dried out for a month." Rachel tied off her thread. "Ed doesn't know what to do when he runs up against men who aren't scared of the Cranes. And nobody — especially not the Cranes — is going to go up against Billy the Kid, so Ed was on his own." Rachel glanced over and saw Trace move a card to be able to lay another one on top of it. "Trace Sheridan! Did I just see you cheat?"

Trace looked up into surprised green eyes and smiled. "Why, yes, I believe you did."

"Doesn't that make you feel guilty?"

Trace mulled it over for a half second and shrugged. "Nope." Of all the things she'd done that should have made her feel guilty, cheating at any card game was not even in the top one hundred.

Although Rachel seemed perfectly fine at breakfast, Trace had awakened in the middle of the night to the sounds of intense heaving. Sitting opposite her at the breakfast table, Trace observed that other than Rachel being a little pale, her stomach seemed settled. *Whatever Rachel has, it's a strange kind of bug.*

Trace's blisters had drained and dried and her cuts were closing up. Her hands were sore, but not like they would have been without Rachel's natural remedies. Rachel's advice to notch those rails yesterday was wise. She wasn't too sure she would even be able to hold a hammer today, much less swing one. Which meant she wouldn't be able to grip a gun, so target practice was also out. But she still might be able to check out the weapons and clean them.

Trace laid the two Colts, the Winchester, and the carbine on an old tattered cloth on the table and studied them. Rachel brought her the cleaning equipment and then went to tend to the household chores. Used to more advanced paraphernalia, Trace noted that even as archaic as the materials were, they were sufficient to get the job done. Plus, dismantling and cleaning each weapon as best she could would help her to get to know these guns before she actually had to use them.

She didn't normally shoot a revolver, but had been required to familiarize herself with them at the academy and, along with her automatic service weapon, she had been timed in taking them apart and putting them back together in firing condition.

Trace found the guns were essentially in working order and with the exception of the Sharps, they were all quite dirty.

She picked up a long brush that resembled a pipe cleaner with a thyroid condition and affixed a tiny, well-oiled patch of cloth to the end. She ran the rod through the individual chambers of the cylinder of one of the Peacemakers.

It feels almost blissfully domestic, she thought. She did all the "butch" things while Rachel prepared the meals, washed dishes, pots and pans, mended, darned, swept, dusted, made the bed, washed and ironed the clothes, refilled the lamps, and built fires in the evening. She smiled at the thought of Rachel being her "wife", then immediately choked on a swallow of hot tea that went down the wrong pipe.

"Are you okay?" Rachel quickly dropped her dust rag and grabbed a cup to fill with water at the pump.

Trace waggled a hand to indicate she was all right. "I'm fine... really..." She accepted the water and took a few sips. *Where the fuck are these ruminations coming from? Wife?* Just the word made her choke again, prompting Rachel to pound her on the back. Trace's eyes widened with surprise that such small hands could pack such a vigorous wallop.

Moments later, when it was clear she was going to live, Rachel returned to dusting and Trace went back to her weapon cleaning, and revisited the thoughts that had caused such a reaction in her. *What's going on? I've never entertained any desire to settle down with anyone. Ever. It just isn't in my make up.* Sneaking a glance at Rachel, two words crept into her head: *until now.* She needed some air.

Rachel looked over at Trace in concern when Trace stood. "Are you sure you're okay?"

"Uh...yeah. I think the bore oil fumes are getting to me." Trace pointed toward the door. "I'm just going to step outside for a little while."

"Is that a good idea? You're awfully pale."

"Maybe what you have is contagious," Trace said.

Rachel snorted softly and went back to dusting.

Outside, Trace took several gulps of air. She hadn't even known Rachel a week; she could not have possibly developed feelings this deep for her. And yet...the thought of Rachel not being there evoked an emptiness inside her that was beyond explanation. *No, no, no! This isn't happening; I am not falling in love, I am not falling in love...* Yet when she closed her eyes, she saw Rachel and the different things she did, her different expressions. A fond smile appeared on Trace's face, a warmth surging through her she had never felt before. *Fuck me to tears*, Trace thought, sighing helplessly, *I'm falling in love.*

Great. Now what? Talk about closeted.

She was living in an era when she was pretty sure there had to be jail sentences for homosexuality, and if there wasn't, whatever punishment the town took upon itself to administer would undoubtedly be severe, if not deadly. Fortunately, no one had a clue that she was a female, so that particular issue was not a problem. No one knew but Rachel. The only one who really mattered.

She began to pace. *What am I going to do?* It was different when it was just lust. That was old hat to her, it was emotionless...but love? She'd never been in love before, but she somehow knew that there was a point of no return in that phase which was why she always fought against it. She couldn't be in love with this woman. Rachel was straight and naïve and sweet and good, not at all the type of woman Trace normally hooked up with, and the very idea of her having these kinds of feelings for Rachel would no doubt horrify and terrify the poor girl. In reality, it terrified Trace. She thought she had gotten past having "things" for heterosexual women years ago...although she never had much of a problem with curious straight women. But Rachel was different, regardless of what had happened the day before.

Trace knew she had a powerful presence, that she could be intimidating and she could pour on the charm without half trying. She had always been a very successful flirt, especially when it came to attractive women. It was second nature to her. But she was always in control. Always. Where Rachel was concerned, she felt anything but in control. That had never happened before. Which brought up another reason for her panic.

"This was such a mistake," she whispered, frustrated. "Why am I here? Why can't I remember anything?" The only thought that came through with any clarity was that if she hadn't come to this time, she would probably be dead. *But what does that mean?* She wondered if she would ever get her memory back.

Maybe I should just leave. I have enough money to buy a gun and a horse; hell, I could even steal one or two of Rachel's guns and one of the horses. She leaned against a post, crossed her arms over her chest, and looked down at the weathered wood of the porch floor. She couldn't do anything to bring this wonderfully kind woman any added pain and strife.

And what would be the consequences of her moving on? The benefit was that somewhere she might be able to find a place to settle down where her sexual proclivities would be welcomed by a woman or two. The problem, however, was that whoever it was, she wouldn't be Rachel.

The disadvantages heavily outweighed that measly personal advantage. Rachel would be alone again, and defenseless. What was left of her livestock and crops would likely be destroyed and she would be forced to give up her home. And Trace's departure would look as though she had knuckled under to the sheriff's "request", falling in line behind the rest of Sagebrush in allowing the Cranes to run her life. She inhaled deeply. If she had not permitted that with much more powerful twenty-first century criminals, she would be damned if she would allow it with a group of nineteenth century rubes.

"Trace?"

The voice interrupted her train of thought and she looked up to meet inquisitive green eyes. She wondered how long Rachel had been there, watching her.

"Are you all right?"

Christ, she's beautiful. She committed Rachel's face to memory. Trace grinned. "Yeah. I'm fine. Thanks. I was just coming in." And when Rachel returned a relieved smile, Trace knew right then and there she would never voluntarily leave this woman.

When the small arsenal of four weapons were cleaned and reassembled, Trace picked up one of the revolvers. Hand guns with cylinders fascinated her. She had always wondered why people chose to use them when, in her opinion, automatics were so much quicker, more accurate, and, with the higher caliber, packed much more firepower. Or maybe she convinced herself of that because she had been lazy. By being able to slap in a clip, she could pop off more rounds faster and not have to worry about counting to six and stopping to use a speed loader. Now that she was in a situation where she had no choice but to use this magnificently authentic Colt Peacemaker in her hand, she knew she needed to get comfortable with it and become more than competent at firing it.

Trace decided that tomorrow, if the cuts on her hands were better, she would take the new rails out and repair the fence and then, if she was up to it — and definitely after a bath — ride into town and buy ammunition and a gun belt, and look over whatever else might come in handy. She glanced over at Rachel, who had dozed off in her chair. Poor kid was obviously exhausted. *No wonder, what with trying to keep this place up and running all by herself. She must have literally made herself sick and tired.*

Trace's expression softened as she studied Rachel. She appeared so unguarded, so unblighted, so powerless...yet she had endured, so far, against the brutal and obviously merciless Cranes. But it had clearly taken its toll. She sighed and shook her head. *Well, no more, if I have anything to do with it. I will move a mountain, one shovel at a time if necessary, if it means peace for Rachel.* As Trace passed the chair, she reached down and pulled the knitted shawl up around the younger woman's shoulders and then stepped out onto the porch, sitting down on one of the well worn, solid wooden chairs.

Trace propped her feet up on the railing and inspected the clean Colt Cavalry single action .45 Peacemaker. She felt the weight. Even with bullets the revolver wasn't exactly heavy but it was sturdy, something she attributed to the nickel plating and the walnut grips, which had seen better days but were certainly not in need of replacing. The barrel, cylinder, and frame were very strong and when she put it back together, she'd noticed that the mechanics seemed as close to perfect as she would probably ever see in a gun like this: cocking, indexing, firing...all were very smooth. She pointed the Colt at a slender tree opposite her in the distance, looked down the six-inch barrel and lined up the sights. She might just get used to this, as soon as it stopped hurting to close her fingers around the grip.

Rachel was busy preparing a chicken pot pie for supper and Trace was bored with just hanging around, waiting for her injuries to heal. She used what was left of the garlic concoction from the day before and rubbed the oil into her skin. She then wrapped her hands with cloth and pulled on the suede work gloves she hadn't used the day before. She donned heavily stained overshoes several sizes too big and went to muck out the stable.

All the horses, except the mustang, were out in the pasture, so Trace did not have to be concerned about being trapped again, like that first day with Chief. By the time she reached the final stall, the one occupied by the feisty Spanish horse, her pitchfork had poked quite a few eye-watering, nose hair burning pockets of fecal ammonia, making her flinch every time she came across one of the fresh, steaming piles or the moldy, rotting matted clumps.

Trace entered the stall of the horse that had tentatively been named Rio because he had been found by the river. The two stubborn mammals stared each other down. "Don't even think of starting with me," Trace said in a husky alto. "I like being in here even less than you do."

It must have been her unyielding attitude that made Rio ignore her and go back to chewing on hay. He was even cooperative when she needed to get around him. When she was finished, she pushed the wheelbarrow to just outside the stable entrance and went back into the stall to replenish Rio's food staples before going out to round up the other horses and get them back inside for the night.

Rio was a beautiful animal. Standing at slightly above-average height, he was a smoothly muscled, hearty, chestnut-colored horse. Trace smiled at him, respecting his space, identifying with the mustang's reputation for tenacity, endurance, and adaptability. She decided she wanted Rio to be her horse. Maybe she could eventually talk Rachel into that little notion. She suddenly sensed another presence and Trace spun around to see her favorite little blonde standing at the entrance, hands on her hips, surveying the stall.

"Gosh, Trace, this looks nice and tidy. You did a fine job," Rachel said. "Makes me wonder if you were telling the truth about never having done any of these kinds of chores before. You always do such a good job."

"Thank you." Trace grinned. She was amazed at how even a little praise from Rachel could make her heart swell. Rio barely acknowledged his owner and went back to eating.

"How are your blisters?"

"A little sore but not bad."

"You probably should have given them a little more time to heal."

"Yep, probably. But I couldn't just hang around doing nothing. Idle hands and all that."

Rachel folded her arms and nodded her head toward Rio. "Looks like he doesn't mind you."

"Yeah...speaking of that—" At the sound of an explosive, rolling flatulence, Trace looked up to see Rachel staring at her with eyes as big as pie tins. Defensively, she said, "It was the horse!"

The odor that accompanied the sound encircled them both and they made a mad dash for untainted oxygen. Outside the stable, Trace took a deep breath of fresh air.

"Okay, that was just wrong," she said, wiping the sting away from her eyes.

"I think he's still getting used to the oats," Rachel said.

So am I, Trace thought, *but I don't smell like that.* At least she hoped she didn't. "I think I'd best wait a bit before I bring the other horses back to their stalls."

"Well, I came to tell you supper's ready. But since I've seen pall-bearers look happier than you do right now, it won't hurt it to cool a bit until you get your appetite back."

"No, no. You worked too hard to let it sit and get cold. Just let me get these clothes off and get washed up, and I'll be right in." Trace patted Rachel's arm reassuringly, then headed in the direction of the barn.

Rachel watched Trace's retreating form and ran her fingers lightly over the skin that Trace had touched, feeling goosebumps. She smiled. She'd never experienced anything like this before. Not able to explain her reaction, Rachel thought it best not to try. She went back to the house to set the table, an unexpected spring in her step.

After dinner, Trace offered to do the dishes but Rachel wouldn't hear of it. "Why don't you just go on out to the corralled pasture and bring the horses in?"

Sure, Trace thought, *so they can mess up those nice clean stalls.*

Trace led a lazily trudging Moses into the stable, followed by Rosie and her shy baby, who seemed determined to play peekaboo with Trace from behind her mama. A surprisingly cooperative Chief brought up the rear. She secured them all into their stalls and stopped long enough to talk softly to Zelda, who still hid behind Rosie but seemed as fascinated with Trace as Trace was with the filly.

Finished, Trace knew she could not go to bed smelling the way she did. She didn't know how Rachel managed to sit opposite her all through the meal without throwing up again. The thought had no sooner crossed her mind than she heard the sounds of vomiting. Trace picked up her pace and rounded the corner to find Rachel bent over at the waist, depositing her supper in the bushes by the outhouse. By the time Trace reached her, Rachel was finishing up with a few dry heaves.

"Rachel, I don't like this..." Trace said as the pale, drawn face focused on her.

"I'm all right."

"No, you're not. You're obviously very stressed."

Rachel cocked her head. "Stressed?"

"Yeah...um...out of sorts, upset, agitated."

Rachel nodded. "Well, that is the truth." She was silent for a minute and then, for no apparent reason, she started to cry.

"What's wrong?" Trace asked, alarmed.

"I'm afraid you're going to leave."

Trace pulled Rachel into her arms and held her securely. She smoothed her hair as Rachel wept silently against her shoulder. "Shhhh, shhhh, it's okay," Trace soothed. "I'm not going anywhere. I'm going to help you fight these Cranes, help you keep your land."

Again Trace was experiencing a new aspect of herself. She had never been an outwardly affectionate person, yet she didn't hesitate for a second to give Rachel physical comfort. Normally, she considered herself to have all the gentility of a NASCAR wreck. Rachel was drawing out a side of her she never knew she had.

There also was no hesitation in Rachel's acceptance of this reassurance from her. Rachel settled into her embrace without reservation, Trace noticed, as if touching in this manner was an everyday occurrence. She might have pondered the significance of that further but Rachel was hit by another wave of nausea and she pushed herself away from Trace rather than risk spraying her. Trace was surprised there was anything left to spew.

Later that evening, after Trace had taken a discreet, naked plunge in the creek, preferring the strong smell of lye soap over the more pungent odor of manure, she sat on the porch with Rachel, listening to the crickets and the frogs, and the occasional howl of an animal or two. By the light of the full moon, they discussed Trace's plans for the next day. Under different circumstances, it could have been very romantic, which is exactly what Ed Jackson must have thought when he rode up to the house.

Both women stood at the sound of slow hoofbeats approaching, Trace immediately alert to Rachel's stiffening posture. When the glint of the sheriff's badge became distinct, Rachel became visibly disturbed.

"What could he want?" she said in a voice just loud enough for Trace to hear.

When Jackson got close enough that his features could be recognized, he spoke, his tone arrogant and condescending. "Rachel." He nodded to her. "Mr. Sheridan." He regarded Trace with a sneer. When neither woman acknowledged him with a word or a gesture, he said, "Am I interruptin' somethin'?"

It was the disrespectfully blatant leering at Rachel that caused Trace's fingers to curl into a fist. Rachel must have sensed her barely contained wrath and stepped forward. "Nothing but an evening's discussion about tomorrow's chores."

Jackson did not hide his disbelief. "Right," he said with a smirk.

"What is it we can do for you, Sheriff?" Trace's voice was even less friendly than the lawman's.

"I just thought, as a courtesy, I'd tell Miss Rachel, here, that her fence is busted over by the south end of her property."

"Yes, I know that," Rachel spoke up. "That's old news, Sheriff. If that's all you came for—"

"Now there ain't no need to be inhospitable," Jackson said. "With all the mysterious things happenin' out here, I would think you'd want to be just a little more sociable to—"

"Mysterious? There's nothing mysterious about anything that's happened here, Sheriff," Rachel spat, unable to hold on to her forced composure. "You know very well who's responsible for slaughtering my herd and crippling my horses, for burning most of my crops, for..." She stopped abruptly as if rethinking what she wanted to say to him. "And you know, despite how sociable I became to you, you wouldn't lift a finger to stop them. You disgrace that badge!" She shook with anger, but a gentle hand at the back of her elbow allowed her to recover some semblance of calm.

Jackson didn't seem fazed in the least by her outburst. "Why, Rachel, your respect for the law is right heartwarmin'."

"She has respect for the law, Sheriff. That doesn't mean she has to respect the man badly representing it. That respect is not automatic, it has to be earned. And it sure looks to me like you're a long way from doing that."

Trace's words got Jackson's attention and he narrowed his eyes. "You know, Sheridan," he began, "I don't like you. Didn't like you from the moment I laid eyes on ya."

Imitating Ed's drawl, Trace almost smiled. "Well, Ed, that just plumb hurts my feelin's." Rachel turned her head away, presumably to keep from laughing, and Trace swallowed her own smile.

"Why, Sheriff," Rachel said, "you look madder than a centipede with bunions. You probably haven't been defied by anyone since that incident with Billy the Kid." Trace was sure that if steam could come out of Jackson's ears, plumes would be sending smoke signals.

He managed to rein in his temper. "Ain't no way some half-breed, Gypsy-lookin' drifter's gonna get my back up." He took a few deep breaths and then said, "Say, Rachel, I just come from a nice dinner of roast cur at the Beauregards' and I'm a mite thirsty. Why don't you favor ol' Ed with a nice big shot of bug juice and I'll be on my way."

Rachel sighed and turned to go inside when Trace's arm blocked her way. In a voice loud enough for Jackson to hear, Trace asked, "Do you want to wait on him? Because he can be on his way without the bug juice."

They both heard the squeak of leather as the sheriff shifted in his saddle. In a tone barely above a whisper, Rachel said, "I just want him out of here with no trouble. I know this will do it." She gently pushed Trace's arm down and entered the house.

"Now, you listen to me, boy," Jackson started, once Rachel was out of sight. "Let me tell you somethin'. If Rachel wasn't here, I'd cut you down where you stand. I still could. No one would call me on it, except Rachel, and no one would believe her. Well, they might, but it wouldn't matter. I'm just wonderin' how big a talker you're gonna be up against the Cranes...'specially Ben. He's got a temper, 'specially when it comes to that pretty little blonde in there. It'll be fun watchin' that boy teach you some manners." He looked at Trace, expecting more of a reaction than a bland, bored stare. "That sweet, young thing may be warmin' your bed for now, and you might be feelin' like a stud 'cause of it. Hell, I would be—"

Furious at the implication, words became strangled in Trace's throat. It was okay if she had designs on Rachel, but for some scrote like this crooked lawman to assume they were sleeping together turned her damned near homicidal. It took a great deal of self-control not to pick up her chair and slam Jackson upside the head with it.

"...but if I was you? Enjoy it while you can because when those boys get back from Dodge and find you here, I guaran-damn-tee you'll be like a field mouse with a cat at his tail. And...well, let's just say you keep shootin' off your mouth like that to those boys, and you might wind up on the end of a rope over a cottonwood branch. Now, ain't that just befittin', seein' as how that's where you say you're from," he continued, oblivious to Trace's rage.

Trace was about to rebuke him with a tirade that would make his head spin when Rachel stepped back out onto the porch and over to the first step, and handed a glass to the sheriff. Jackson swallowed the double shot in one huge gulp, belched loudly and tossed the glass unexpectedly to Trace, who caught it effortlessly. Her smooth reflexes drew a raised eyebrow from the sheriff and that was all.

He touched his index finger to the brim of his hat, smiled and nodded at Rachel. "You have a good night. And don't forget about your south fence, there." He guided his horse away from the house and trotted into the shadows of the trees in the distance.

Both women watched him go. Rachel broke the silence. "Man's got a grin like a rabid dog."

Through clenched teeth, Trace said, "I don't like that man. I don't like the way he talks to you, I don't like the way he looks at you, and I don't like the way he threatens you."

Rachel seemed a little taken aback by Trace's furious, almost possessive tone. She returned her attention to the dark woods. "They say when a snake rattles its tail, you ought to kill it. Unfortunately, if you cut the head off that particular snake, several more would grow back. I'd shoot him for trespassing but that would only get me a cross planted above my brow." She sighed and swatted away a black fly, which, with its many relatives, had begun to annoy them both. When Trace also attempted to bat several away, Rachel said, "Blessed things are as big as buzzards. Let's go inside. I'll make some more tea."

"Rachel, what the fu— heck is bug juice?"

"Whiskey."

"Whiskey?" She followed Rachel inside, closing the door behind her. "Why don't they just call it whiskey?"

Rachel shrugged. "Why don't you just say 'okay' instead of 'cool'?"

Good question. Rachel's simplistic approach to things was always enlightening, and she had a feeling that seeing life through Rachel's eyes would force her to re-evaluate her own way of thinking in the days to come.

Chapter Ten

Trace spent forty-five minutes having a cup of tea with Rachel and then headed for her room in the barn. She was tired and should have been sleepy, but unnerved by the sheriff's unexpected visit, she was only just starting to calm down. She lay awake, staring at the ceiling for several hours until the normal night sounds faded into the recesses of her subconscious; something didn't feel right.

A little after midnight, one noise stood out from the rest and the detective in Trace immediately reacted to it. Like a phantom, she silently slid out of bed, donned her clothes and boots, and crept out to the barn door that she'd left ajar. Every nerve in her body was totally aware and ready for anything. She automatically monitored her breathing and went on peripheral alert, scanning the limited area she could see for the source of the noise. It was then she saw two shadows in close proximity to where she stood.

"Ed said just to scare 'em. Maybe drag the Gypsy out of bed and whale the bejesus out of him in front of her."

"What about Miss Rachel?" the second male inquired. He sounded young and a little unsure.

With a lascivious snicker, the first voice said, "As much as I'd like to have a little piece of that myself, Ed said to leave her alone. But if she gets too rambunctious, she might have to be taught a lesson."

That was all Trace needed to hear. She stepped forward on her left leg, shifted her weight and let loose with a front jump kick, snapping her right leg up at the knee and striking the door with the ball of her foot with such force, the door lurched outward. It stopped with a resounding crack when it slammed against two bodies, knocking them to the ground. She quickly moved outside and faced the dazed men, who both wore black hoods with eye holes.

"Come on, boys," Trace said, beckoning them. "I'm ready for my lesson now."

Both men staggered to their feet. "He was supposed to be in the house," the shorter one whined.

"Never assume," Trace advised, in an almost playful tone of voice.

The taller, obviously older of the two men barreled toward her, fist cocked. Trace stepped aside and let him pass. Under his own momentum, he tripped and fell face first into the grass.

"Too bad that cowardly mask doesn't have a hole cut out where your mouth should be. You deserve a dirt sandwich right now," Trace said. He jumped back on his feet pretty quickly, angry and embarrassed.

"What the hell's the matter with you, boy?" he addressed his companion who just stood there, unmoving. "Get him!"

Trace glanced at the smaller of the two and decided he wouldn't be a problem. Almost timidly, the shorter man advanced at her from one side as the other man charged at her from the other. A deceptively fast roundhouse kick caught the older man on his right cheek and sent him flying backward, stunning him as he once again hit the ground. While he shook that off, the younger one drew back and propelled his fist forward with the intention of punching Trace.

She caught his fist mid-thrust and twisted it in a direction nature never designed it to move. As she brought him to his knees, he yelled for mercy. With little effort, she could have broken his arm.

While Trace was occupied, the taller attacker mistakenly believed he could gain control of the situation. When he was about two feet away from Trace, she back kicked him away from her and he once again found himself on his ass in the dirt. He pounded the ground in frustration, stood up, and drew his gun.

Trace heard the click of the hammer being cocked, and spun her prisoner around so that he was in front of her, wrenching his badly sprained arm into a choke hold against him. She found herself looking into the muzzle of a well-worn pistol. Regardless of its appearance, she was sure a bullet fired from it at such close range would be deadly.

"If you shoot me, he dies."

"And the second shot will be you joining him."

Surprised at the sound of a new voice, all three looked around to see Rachel, her nightshirt covered by an unbelted cotton robe, on the porch with the carbine trained on the taller man. Her voice was steady, angry; there was no doubt she meant what she said.

Trace couldn't help smiling. She had no qualms that she could have handled the situation just fine on her own, but Rachel coming to her "rescue" made her nearly burst with pride. The man holding the pistol lowered it to his side.

"Good boy," Trace said. "Now lay it down and kick it toward Rachel." When he hesitated, Trace tightened her hold on his partner, who howled in pain. "Do it."

He reluctantly obeyed and Trace was about to pull off the hood of the man in her grasp when they heard a rustling from the woods and the sheriff appeared, atop his weary horse. Jackson's expression couldn't settle on fascination or disappointment. One hand was on the reins and the other rested on his gun belt near the holster. "Put the gun down, Rachel." He looked directly at Trace. "There'll be no killin' here tonight."

Not releasing her prisoner, Trace's eyes became slits as she said in a deadly tone of voice, "You son-of-a-bitch. You sent them here."

"Why, I don't know what you're talkin' about, son." His expression betrayed him.

She tightened her hold on the younger intruder and he cried out again. "Really? I heard these two say that this was what you wanted. But if they're lying, just what are you doing out here in the middle of the night?"

Jackson shrugged. "Been reports of wolves around, attackin' the hen houses after dark. I heard the commotion. Noise travels a fair distance this time of night."

"How convenient," Trace said. "I think these men were here to do your dirty work. If you've got a problem with me, Sheriff, then get down off that horse and take it up with me." Then she added, "Man to man," nearly gagging on the words.

"I don't mind sayin', you got some imagination there, Sheridan."

"I don't mind saying you're a consummate liar there, Jackson," Trace countered, not flinching.

The naked insult made him stiffen and his hand moved to the handle of his Colt, still holstered but the threat was there, nonetheless. He looked up at Rachel. "Thought I told you to put that gun down."

"You're on my property without an invitation," Rachel told him firmly. "I'll lower my rifle when you leave."

In a flash, Jackson's revolver was out and aimed at Rachel. He glanced quickly at Trace and said, "One move from you and I'll shoot her."

It surprised Trace that the sheriff had taken such a chance, and then she remembered the chauvinistic time she was in, a realization that was punctuated by Jackson's next words.

"Don't ever threaten me, missy. When I tell you to do somethin', you do it. Now put the gun down."

"Don't do it, Rachel," Trace said.

"Don't listen to him. He ain't on the business end of my Colt. I ain't gonna tell you again, Rachel."

"He won't shoot you, Rachel," Trace said.

"You sure about that, son?" Jackson asked. "She's got that carbine lookin' right at me. I need to defend myself. Especially when all I'm doin' here is tryin' to protect her fowl from gettin' ate up."

"You are so full of shit, Sheriff, I'm surprised your eyes aren't brown."

Jackson smiled, "Gotta tell ya, Sheridan. You got some sand. I don't like ya, not one iota, but you don't scare easy. I 'spect that'll change in a few months, but for now, I'm damned impressed." He turned back to the woman standing on the porch. "Rachel?"

To Trace's dismay, Rachel slowly lowered the gun. Trace let her head drop.

"Sheridan, let him go." He cocked the pistol, extending his arm in Rachel's direction. "Now."

"Stop aiming that at her and I will."

"You ain't in no position to be givin' the orders here."

When Trace didn't move, a shot rang out and the bullet seared into the porch at Rachel's feet, just missing her. She jumped back with a frightened yelp, immediately covering her mouth to stifle a scream. "Rachel!" Trace pushed her prisoner to the ground and started toward the porch. Jackson then turned his revolver on her, which stopped her in her tracks.

"I didn't touch her. She won't be so lucky next time if she don't do as she's told." He smirked at Trace. "And neither will you." Jackson turned his attention to the two hooded men. "You fellas get movin'. Don't be caught out here again. You may not be so lucky, either." The sheriff's tone was patently insincere. "Git! Go on, now!"

As both men ran until they were out of sight, Trace turned back to Jackson. "They attacked me on private property; they had malevolent intent. Why didn't you arrest them?"

"Malevolent intent? Looked to me like you was gettin' the best of 'em."

Trace looked over at Rachel, whose hand still covered her mouth, tears brimming at her eyes. At that moment Trace could have killed Ed Jackson without a second thought. "I want to press charges against them. I want you to arrest them."

"And just who am I supposed to arrest? They were masked, they can't be identified."

Seething, Trace pinned him with a murderous glare intended to make his back hairs rise. "You fucking bastard," Trace said through clenched teeth.

"Nice talk in front of a lady," Jackson said, tickled that he was able to rile Trace to such a state and not run the risk of getting hurt.

"I'll apologize to Rachel later," Trace said and fixed him with a threatening gaze. "If I ever catch you on this land again without permission, I'll fucking kill you."

No one had ever looked at him like that, not even any of the Cranes in their most hostile moments. He couldn't hide the bit of tremor in his voice when he said, "That a threat?"

"No. That's a promise."

He aimed his gun at Trace. "Maybe I ought to kill you right now, save the Cranes the trouble."

"You do and Rachel will shoot you right off that flea-bitten thing you call a horse. Is killing me worth losing your life?"

Jackson shot a dubious glance at Rachel, then focused steadily on Trace. "She'd go to jail."

"And you'd still be dead."

Jackson holstered the sidearm and jerked the reins, causing his horse to start walking at a slow pace. As he passed Trace, he said, "Let this be a warnin' not to cross me, son. Things can get out of hand right quick. As I said...you got lucky tonight. You both did. I think you need to reconsider movin' on."

"And I told you I'll move on when I'm ready, and not before."

"We'll see about that." He heeled his horse to a trot and rode off in the direction the two men had taken.

Trace scrambled onto the porch and enveloped Rachel in a tight embrace. "Are you all right?"

She felt Rachel nod against her. "I'm sorry," she said tearfully into Trace's chest. "So very sorry."

Trace leaned back to look into those expressive jade eyes that said everything, but Rachel wouldn't look at her. "Sorry for what?"

"For getting you into this."

"You didn't get me into anything; I chose to stay here. I chose to do this, to fight this battle with you. How you've been doing this all by yourself amazes me. At first I thought you were just being stubborn. Now I see that you're very brave and very strong."

"You really think so?" Green eyes finally blinked up at her.

"Absolutely...but I have to ask you — why did you put your gun down?"

"It wasn't loaded. I woke up because of the ruckus out here, looked out the window and saw what was going on, and grabbed the first rifle I could get my hands on. I remembered it wasn't loaded after I was already pointing it at that man. I was hoping just the sight of it would settle things down."

Trace pulled Rachel into another hug and closed her eyes, grateful that Rachel hadn't been hurt. Releasing her, Trace bent to pick up the carbine. "We'll make sure everything's loaded from now on. I don't think we can take the chance this won't happen again." She looked back at Rachel. "Did you recognize anything about either of those men?"

"No. But I'm positive they're from Crane's spread. About a dozen cowboys stay behind during the drive to tend to the ranch and make sure nobody does any harm to the property or the Crane women." She crossed her arms and studied her companion briefly. "Trace?"

"Yeah?"

"Where'd you learn to fight like that? I've never seen a woman whup the tarnation out of any man before, much less two men at the same time."

Trace shrugged. "Some of it's instinct, some of it's training. I needed to learn to defend myself for my job." She rested a hand on Rachel's shoulder. "Are you sure you're okay?"

"Yes. I'm..." she almost smiled, glancing shyly up at Trace through light eyelashes, "...cool."

Trace ruffled Rachel's hair affectionately. "Yes, you are. You're very cool, indeed." She held out the carbine and Rachel took it.

"Trace?"

"Yes?"

"Thank you."

"You're welcome." Their eyes locked; Rachel was the first to look away.

"Trace?"

"Yeah?"

"Would you, um, stay in the house the rest of the night? In case they come back?"

Trace brushed her dark hair out of her eyes with a lazy stroke of her hand and thought about what that would have indicated to her just a week ago and how she would have taken advantage of the circumstances. Now? Hell, yeah, she was still desperately attracted to Rachel but she was, at that particular moment, more concerned for Rachel's welfare and safety. "Sure. I'll bunk down on the sofa."

"There's a bed in the loft."

"I know. But if they come back, I want to meet them head on."

"Oh. Okay. Thank you. Again."

Trace nodded and closed the door behind her. *You can thank me when they're no longer bothering you.* She smiled reassuringly at Rachel and went to retrieve all four guns so she could load them.

Trace woke to the smell of something burning on the stove. Flying up off the couch, knocking the carbine, which had been resting upon her chest, to the floor, she grabbed a linen napkin, folded it over several times and removed all three pans from the heat. She waved the smoke away and looked around for Rachel.

"Rachel?" There was no answer. "Rachel?"

"Out here," came a weak response.

Trace found her seated out on the porch, in one of the chairs, bent forward at the waist with her head on her lap. Her pasty, clammy exterior revealed the details of her nauseated, unpredictable interior. "Glad I like my breakfast well done," Trace said.

Rachel raised her head high enough to rest it on her hand. "Sorry. I was going to surprise you with corn meal, fried potatoes, and fried apples, but the smell just soured my belly."

Trace knelt by Rachel's chair. "Are you sure you don't want to see a doctor?"

"No." She looked at Trace while she silently debated with herself about something, something she might want to say. Then she returned her focus to her lap as though she had changed her mind.

"Can I do anything for you?"

"Ginger tea would be nice."

Trace smiled kindly. "Coming right up."

After Rachel's nausea subsided, she helped Trace hitch Moses to the wagon. With the assured guess that the invertebrate sheriff and his band of not-so-merry chickens would not return to do their bullying in the light of day, and that Rachel would be fine with a loaded shotgun and pistol within reach at any given time — and the promise that she would use them — Trace headed for town.

On her ride into Sagebrush, she pondered Rachel's nausea. It wasn't constant but it was daily. Odors seem to trigger it but she also got sick at night, apparently waking from a sound sleep when there were no smells to provoke the vomiting. Although Rachel was clearly a hard worker, she seemed exhausted during the day, abnormally so for someone in such apparently good physical shape. And she made frequent trips to the outhouse. She balked at seeing a doctor, which meant she was either afraid, or knew what was wrong. Since Rachel didn't seem to be fearful of much other than the Cranes, Trace figured it was the latter.

Rachel was reluctant to talk about her chronic stomach distress and Trace had not pushed. The idea of Rachel being chronically ill was not something Trace wanted to think about, as she was already too attached to the young woman. Then another thought flitted into Trace's mind.

Could Rachel be pregnant? No. She shook her head in dismissal of the speculation. There was no man in the picture. Her fiancé had been gone too long, and Rachel didn't seem like the type of woman to have indiscriminately slept with anyone who was not a constant in her life. No, it had to be something else. *When she's ready to talk about it, she'll let me know what's wrong.*

As Moses sauntered along, Trace checked the position of the Colt and the Sharps, ready for anything. Fortunately, she made it to town without incident, not sure what might happen once she got there.

Her first visit was to a shop next to the livery called Nathan's Saddlery, where, after trying several on, she purchased a black cowhide prairie cartridge belt, which had twenty-four loops to hold extra .45 Colt ammunition. With it, she bought a floral carved skirted holster with a retaining strap, and a matching hand-stitched Bowie sheath with simple tooling that was fitted onto the rig. From the moment she buckled the gunbelt on, it felt natural, as though it had always belonged there. She recalled her first week as a cop on patrol, how the other rookies complained about the awkwardness and getting used to the weight of wearing a rig and she had felt as though that gun on her hip, and the Sam Brown utility belt, had grown there.

After the saddlery, she hit the gunsmith shop where she bought several boxes of .45 caliber rounds for the revolver and cartridges for the Sharps and then bronze shell casings, fine black powder, primer, propellant, and wads so she could load her own bullets.

Trace then went to Joseph Turner's pawn shop, where she bought an eight-inch Bowie knife, the blade three fingers wide, a couple pairs of well-worn, softened suede work gloves, a few assorted items that caught her fancy, and a guitar. She didn't know why she felt compelled to get it because she hadn't played one in years, but once she had the hand-crafted rosewood instrument in her possession, it was clear to her that the reason didn't matter.

Her next stop was to Tipping's Feed and Grain to pick up Rachel's standing order. She introduced herself to Caleb, the proprietor, who seemed friendly and accommodating.

"Mr. Tipping, I'm much obliged that you've been helping out Miss Rachel, but from now on, I'll be picking up the feed, so deliveries no longer need to be made out to the ranch."

Caleb nodded. He looked around and spotted his son. "Isaac, come help this fella fit Miss Rachel's order into the wagon."

With downcast eyes, Isaac sidled toward the door. "Can't. I got some other things I need to do right now, pa," he said, making a hasty exit.

Embarrassed, the older Tipping apologized for his son's uncharacteristic rudeness. "Don't know what gets into youngsters these days. Always runnin' off somewhere. I can give you a hand, if you like."

"Thanks, but I can handle it myself." Trace paid for the feed and led Moses around to the back of the store. She parked the wagon alongside others outside the stockroom and began lifting the sixty pound sacks.

Halfway through the loading, Isaac Tipping stepped out into the supply area, oblivious to Trace's presence among the other customers loading supplies. Trace took a break and observed the teenager with more than a casual interest. He had the same voice, was of similar height, had the approximate build of one of the hooded trespassers, and, most telling of all, his right arm was in a sling.

"How'd you hurt your arm?"

The voice startled the boy but when he saw who it was, he was terrified. He looked like he wanted to run, to get as far away from this person as he could, but he stayed where he was. Head bowed, eyes scanning the floor, Isaac said, "Got thrown from a horse yesterday."

Trace was sure he probably felt as though he'd been dragged behind a fast stallion. The young man's timbre was identical to that of the intruder she'd had in a choke hold.

Yep, she confirmed to herself. *That's one of the sheriff's henchmen from last night.* "Did you now?" Trace made sure she sounded as though she didn't believe him. "If I go back in there and ask your father, is that what he's going to tell me?"

Isaac didn't respond. It was obvious to Trace that he knew that she knew what caused his injury. The teenager could still not look her in the eyes.

"Was your father the man with you?" Trace knew he wasn't, as the physical and vocal characteristics didn't match, but she was pretty sure the boy would react to that. If the kid had a conscience, he would protest his father's innocence, inadvertently admitting his own guilt at the same time.

"No!" the teenager said defensively, and then looked skyward, realizing his mistake.

"You feel good about what you did last night?" Trace inquired with more calm than she felt.

"No, sir," Isaac answered. "I like Miss Rachel. Please don't tell her it was me."

"Then why?"

He lowered his head again. "Cranes are trying to get a cut of my pa's store. Sheriff Jackson said if I did this, he'd hold 'em off."

Trace unconsciously grit her teeth, both angry and sympathetic. She sighed and returned to loading the rest of the order onto the wagon. "Are you telling me the truth?"

"Yes, sir," Isaac said emphatically.

"Who was the man with you?"

"John Carver." Responding to Trace's blank stare, he offered, "Mrs. Crane's brother."

Trace nodded, absorbing the information. "If the sheriff ever asks you to do anything like that again, I want you to come tell me. Okay?"

"Yes, sir. But what good's that going to do?"

"You let me worry about that." Trace lifted the last burlap bag and looked over at the chagrined teenager. "And Isaac?"

"Yes, sir?"

"Don't worry about your father's store." At the boy's questioning stare, she wanted to say, "There's a new sheriff in town," but instead she actually found a smile for him. "Just...don't worry."

Isaac acknowledged Trace's words without expression. He was obviously still embarrassed by the whole incident. Instinctively, though, Trace knew she had an ally if she needed one. *One down, the rest of the town to go.*

Errands accomplished, Trace stopped by Wilbur's to have a drink. It was a calculated visit — not only to have a beer before she returned to the Triple Y, but to take in the atmosphere of the town again, to get the latest gossip from Silas and anyone else who might have loose lips while they imbibed.

Because of the huge tip Trace had left on her last visit to the saloon, Silas gave her a shot of whiskey on the house. Not one to be ungrateful, Trace accepted it graciously and slammed the small glass of liquor back, swallowing the nasty substance that felt like it seared a path all the way down her throat. She could not keep her eyes from watering as she set the empty glass back down on the bar.

Silas laughed. "Blaze a trail clear to your gullet, did it?"

"So that's what you call bug juice, huh?"

"No, the bug juice is over there with the red-eye. What you just had was what we like to call rotgut."

"I can see why," Trace rasped, chasing the burn with a few gulps of ale.

"It'll put hair on your chest."

"Yeah. Just what I need." Trace drained her mug, tossed the affable saloon keeper twenty-five cents and pushed out the swinging doors. On her way out, she passed the sheriff on his way in. She saw that Jackson immediately took in the fact that she was now armed. Trace imagined Jackson probably hoped she didn't handle a gun as well as she wielded her fists and feet. She looked forward to the chance to show him.

Trace and Jackson glared at each other but neither spoke. However, Trace did notice that the jovial mood in the bar immediately became somber at Jackson's dour presence. It didn't take a rocket scientist to see that the sheriff was not a popular man. She would use that to her advantage.

Trace checked to make sure everything was secure, then climbed into the driver's seat and directed Moses back to her new home.

Chapter Eleven

Trace decided not to tell Rachel about Isaac Tipping's involvement in the event of the night before. Not just because the boy asked her not to, or because she felt it would accomplish nothing other than to cause hard feelings, but because she understood the position Isaac had been put in. She had been in similar situations when she was a teenager. If someone had given her a chance to change back then, she might have grown up with a different set of values. No, Trace would keep Isaac's secret for now.

She needed to figure out a plan, think of something to turn the sheriff's game against him and, ultimately, against the Cranes. She needed to find a way for Rachel to keep what was rightfully hers with no more problems, and to help the people of Sagebrush get their town back.

Once again, she was bewildered at her abrupt personality change. Before she arrived in the eighteen hundreds, she was on the side of whoever had the money to pay her, and thought nothing about the consequences of her unscrupulous behavior or her corrupt actions. She'd felt little concern about how her decisions might trickle down and affect the helpless people...like Rachel. When Detective Trace Sheridan embarked on her life of crime, she did so with Robin Hood-like noble intentions. Greed and power kept her there. And now, suddenly, a twelve year career of shame burned white hot within her, causing her to almost choke with rage at her own arrogance, ignorance, and rapaciousness.

Continuing to beat herself up for things she couldn't change was futile, and a total waste of her time and energy. Acknowledging the error of her ways and moving on with a determination to improve was the only way to regain her self-respect and to, hopefully, help save this town. She needed to use the knowledge and experience she had gained from surviving on the wrong side of the law, and put it to use on the righteous side. Trace realized this might mean she might still have to fracture an ordinance or two in order to make things right, but if it all resulted in change for the greater good, and she could redeem her prior bad acts, it would be worth it.

After she unloaded the purchases she had made in town, Trace piled the rails she had split onto the back of the wagon and headed out to repair the south fence.

Two hours later, she was back in the barn, unhitching Moses and leading him to the stable. Before she returned to the house, she ensured all the horses were in their stalls and had enough food and water, and checked the tack to see what was in need of conditioning and what needed to be cleaned.

Trace made a mental note that some of the equipment looked a little worn and, worse yet, dry. She reminded herself to ask Rachel where she kept the saddle soap and make it a point to work on that within the next day or two. Though she was new at being around horses and their equipment, she was not a novice at caring for leather; her gunbelts, holsters, sheaths, and boots needed attention from time to time, depending on how often they were used.

After dinner, Trace and Rachel sat out on the porch. Rachel ripped the seams out of her father's pants to take them in so that they would fit Trace better while Trace tuned her guitar.

"Do you hunt, Trace?" Rachel asked, breaking the cozy silence between them.

"Hunt what?"

"Game. You know...food."

"No. Do you?"

"I've had my share of dinners on the hoof." She glanced over at Trace who was picking the scale on her new toy. "I don't like to, but sometimes I've had to. Do you fish?"

"Nope."

"Do you want to learn?"

"Nope." Trace looked back at Rachel, met her eyes and smiled. "But something tells me I'm going to whether I want to or not."

Rachel returned Trace's grin. "There are a couple of willow poles in the barn. Tomorrow we'll go fishing."

"Do I have a choice?"

"Not if you want to continue to eat here." Rachel was still smiling as she returned to her sewing.

Trace chuckled. *This feels so...comfortable.* She finally had the guitar tuned and strummed a G chord. "Mamas, don't let your babies grow up to be cowboys," she sang, her voice clear and strong. Warbling a few more verses, she stopped to retun an E string. She looked over at Rachel, who appeared a little stunned. "What?"

"You have a very nice voice."

"Why, thank you, ma'am."

"I've never heard that song before."

That's because it hasn't been written yet. "It's a standard where I come from."

"What's a 'trucks'?"

"What?"

"A 'trucks'. In your song. There was something about drivin' ol' trucks. What does that mean?"

"Oh. Truck. It's like a strong wagon that moves with the power of a couple of plow horses."

Rachel tried to picture it and shook her head. "Don't think I've ever seen one of them."

"No, I would guess you haven't. They're very rare right now." *In fact, downright non-existent.*

Rachel nodded and said, "Well, it's nice to hear music around here again. My mama used to play piano in church and sing."

"Do you sing?"

"Only on Sundays, in front of Pastor Edwards." She set her sewing aside. "Would you like a cup of tea?"

"That would be very nice, thank you." She watched as Rachel went into the house. Rachel had asked Trace to spend the night on the sofa again, saying it made her feel very protected the night before. Trace agreed without hesitation. She was pretty sure there wasn't much Rachel could request of her that she would refuse. She sighed. It was all so very...domestic. Once again, she shook her head in bewilderment and went back to plucking out notes on her guitar.

Inside, the water was almost to a boil as Rachel filled the metal tea ball. Swamped by strong cramps and a wave of nausea, she held her belly tightly until the feelings passed. Rachel listened to Trace singing right outside the window, and argued with herself about whether or not to tell Trace about the baby. She had talked herself out of it that morning, and now she talked herself out of it again. She didn't want to even think about the possibility of Trace getting disgusted with her and leaving. She couldn't bear that. Rachel placed the steeping teacups on a tray and returned to the porch as Trace finished up a song about a stairway to heaven.

"That was a beautiful song, Trace. I've never heard that one, either."

"Another classic where I come from."

"Sounds like you have a lot of fond memories of where you come from."

"Some."

"If you felt like it wasn't dangerous to go back there, would you?"

Would I? Good question. Would I return to the twenty-first century if I had the option? She took a deep breath, inhaling clean, fresh air, and looked out at an unspoiled sunset. Then she looked over to her right, into the emerald gaze of someone she would never want to expose to the modern world. She stared into the trusting eyes of the woman she suddenly felt she wanted to spend the rest of her life with. Right there. Forever.

"No," Trace answered softly. "I like it right where I am."

"Good." Rachel smiled shyly. "I like you right where you are, too."

"Really?" Trace tried to gauge the intent behind the words. She knew what she wanted them to mean, but she was sure it was just that Rachel was grateful for her presence, thankful to have someone, anyone, finally on her side, who felt no misgivings about getting involved in this mess. Trace knew she made Rachel feel safe. If Rachel felt any more than that, chances were she hadn't realized the full implications of it.

"You're good company, and you work hard. And you're not afraid of anything. I'm very appreciative of the first two," she shook her head, "but I don't know how foolish that last one may be."

Chuckling softly, Trace sipped her peppermint tea and went back to playing her guitar. Without warning, a current of sexual need galvanized her center and then radiated outward through every nerve in her body. She impatiently waited for the sensation to pass. It didn't. She broke out into an unexpected sweat and knew she needed to excuse herself to take care of this urge, privately and quickly. Putting the instrument aside, she took another sip of tea and stood up. "I...uh...need to use the outhouse and, uh, then I'm going to get washed up at the river and be back in for the night." She began to edge away.

"Right now?"

"Uh...yeah..." She stretched and faked a yawn. "It just hit me how tired I am."

As Trace descended the steps, she knew Rachel didn't exactly believe her but she was positive she didn't have a clue as to the real reason for her hasty departure. She skipped the trip to the outhouse and headed for her room in the barn.

Trace leaned against the closed door — in case Rachel had chosen to follow her, it would ensure she wouldn't get walked in on — she unbuttoned her jeans and slipped her hand inside her underwear. She closed her eyes and envisioned the beguiling little blonde. It took her no time at all to relieve the pleasurable, almost painful pressure. Measurably less tense, she waited for her breathing to moderate, then grabbed her night clothes and headed to the river to bathe.

The next morning, Rachel awoke to find Trace up and about and the coffee already made. Tired, she dressed sluggishly and cooked some oatmeal, carefully suppressing any signs of the nausea that threatened. Later, she watched through the kitchen window as Trace set up practice targets. At different intervals on tree stumps and other fixed objects, Trace placed blocks of firewood, rusted tin cans of various sizes, old pieces of furniture which had been broken or had fallen apart, and chipped dinnerware. The targets were arranged so that she would shoot away from the house, barn, stable, and pasture. Rachel smiled at that. If Trace missed, the only thing in danger of getting shot would be assorted vegetation.

She went out to the porch to get a better view. Mesmerized by how confident and methodical Trace was, she also couldn't keep her eyes off the nicely defined bulging arm muscles every time she lifted anything off the ground that required a little effort. She blushed furiously when she realized she was darned near ogling Trace, and returned to her chores inside, only to find herself drawn back to the window.

Oblivious to her confused admirer, Trace set up and readjusted marks before and after shooting at them. It seemed to take her no time at all to get used to the weapons.

After two hours of listening to gunfire, Rachel returned to the porch to call Trace in for lunch, but stood watching with interest as Trace gripped the Colt in a manner she'd never seen before. Trace had the revolver in front of her at arm's length, holding the .45 with her right hand, her left arm bent and clasping her right wrist. Rachel knew that a shooter took careful aim when using a rifle, but she'd only seen pistol shooting either from the hip or with an extended arm, the gun positioned somewhere between the waist and shoulders. Trace's form and style, which Rachel could only assume was to result in a more smooth and precise shot, obviously worked because her accuracy was flawless.

Trace fired off all six bullets in rapid succession and debris from the targets splintered outward when the slugs hit their mark dead in the center. An appreciative grin split Rachel's face. *Is there anything this woman can't do?*

That afternoon, while Rachel cleaned out the chicken coop, Trace busied herself with rigging up a boxing bag in the barn. She took two empty burlap feed sacks, threaded them together with leather thongs, stuffed in a layer of hay for padding around the exterior edge and filled the middles with dirt for weight. She tested the weight by adding or removing contents until she was satisfied with the heaviness and resistance. She secured the opening of the bag by tying a thick hemp rope tightly around it; she tossed the end of the rope up over a solid beam and pulled the rope toward her, hoisting the bag until the bottom was about eighteen inches off the ground. That gave her about six feet of content to work with. She looped the rope over a hook in the wall and then assessed her makeshift innovation. It wasn't great, but it would have to do.

Trace ripped pieces from an old discarded linen sheet and wrapped her hands, then fitted Frank Young's oversized suede gloves over them for protection. She began to work out and unmercifully abused the hanging sack in place of a sparring opponent. Trace felt good to be moving, throwing punches, snapping kicks, practicing what she felt she had been born to do — fight. Ironically, Trace never felt more at peace than she did when she was fighting.

Sharing tea every night on the porch at sunset was a welcomed ritual, Trace thought as she plucked out a few tunes on the guitar. She knew Rachel had never heard most of the songs before, and the meaning of quite a number of the lyrics were no doubt alien to her as well. Eventually, Rachel got to the point where she stopped asking questions regarding what Trace sang about and just seemed to enjoy the private concert.

What also became routine was Trace sleeping in the house. Within a week, she progressed from the barn to the couch to the loft. She was never without one revolver or one rifle within reach and made sure that Rachel was equally prepared. Just in case.

She had yet to start bathing in the house and would continue to use the river until Rachel invited her to use the clawfoot tub in the anteroom.

Trace got up every morning when the rooster crowed and ran on a path she had created with the help of Moses and a rake. It took her approximately one-half mile around the house, the barn, the stable, and the perimeter of one of the corralled pastures. Rain or shine, she jogged on that path and circled it at least ten times. She knew she needed to be in her best shape if there was to be a confrontation — and she had no doubt there would be one, if not many. She also worked out with her punching bag before she began her chores.

Every third day, she reluctantly but faithfully mucked out the stalls, checked the tack and equipment for needed upkeep, became friendlier with all the horses, continued to gain Rio's trust, and encouraged Zelda to become less shy around her. Every day, she saddled Chief and rode around the boundaries of the property and checked all the fence lines. Every five days, she took target practice, getting better and better with the Colts and rifles, until it was unusual for her to miss anything she aimed at. Every sixth day, she hitched Moses to the wagon and directed him into town. She dropped off vegetable and herb orders to Luther Foster, picked up whatever supplies, groceries, and necessities were required for the next week, then finished up with a beer or two at Wilbur's. She mainly went every week for the trip to the saloon. Silas kept her up on all the gossip and goings-on. She slowly became more sociable with the townspeople, deliberately integrating herself into the quirky, rural, Sagebrush groove, deftly avoiding the sheriff. Or maybe it was the other way around.

Avoiding Jackson didn't mean she stayed ignorant of his whereabouts or activities. There was always someone willing to volunteer what the lazy, no-good sheriff was up to.

As the days and weeks passed, Trace and Rachel became much more comfortable with one another, as though they had always lived together and shared space. Their interaction was always respectful, mutually gracious, and even though it bordered on flirtatious, it never crossed that line into anything more. Trace was sure Rachel meant nothing by it and was afraid that expressing her own feelings would be too overpowering for the already overwhelmed young woman. For the first time in her life, Trace Sheridan thought about the impact of her actions on someone other than herself.

Every day Rachel suffered from some form of nausea and then went on about her day as though nothing was wrong. Every day, Trace became more certain of the reason behind Rachel's sickness. Somehow, the virtuous Rachel Young was pregnant.

Chapter Twelve

Trace returned from her rounds of the property and entered the house with the intention of advising Rachel about the break in the north fence. She was sure it was nothing but wind damage, but it needed to be fixed, just the same. She was about to call out Rachel's name when she heard the sound of a soft snore coming from near the hearth. Trace quietly stepped closer and observed Rachel asleep in her mother's rocking chair. A small flame flickered in the fireplace and Trace's breath caught at the vision of Rachel's natural beauty and innocence enhanced by the glimmering light. She wanted to reach down and take this woman into her arms. *Oh, if only we were in another time.*

Trace knelt by the chair and placed her hand over the one resting in Rachel's lap. Squeezing it gently, so as not to startle her, Trace said, "Hey...Rach?"

Her voice stirred the slumbering woman. Slowly shifting her in chair, the green eyes fluttered open, pure and unguarded, lazily focusing on Trace, capturing her with a warmth that rivaled that of the heat from the late afternoon fire Rachel had started to take the chill out of the room. With a voice hoarse from her most recent dry heave session, she said, "I fell asleep."

"I see," Trace said softly. "You've been doing that a lot lately. You okay?"

Rachel's free arm unconsciously settled across her belly. "I'm... I'm fine. Why?"

The movement did not go unnoticed. Trace's voice was tender, compassionate. "Rachel, are you...preg...with child?"

It was the kindness and lack of judgment in Trace's expression that brought tears to Rachel's eyes. She bowed her head, humiliation flowing through every fiber of her being. "How...how did you know?"

Trace pulled up a foot stool and sat down, then took Rachel's hand firmly in her own. Rachel didn't pull away. "Well," Trace's voice was soothing, "you're tired a lot, you have morning sickness, backaches, frequent trips to the outhouse. I recognize the symptoms." Trace brushed a few tears from the delicate cheek, then cupped her jaw. "You don't have a husband, you don't have a boyfriend...a beau...no man in your life that I've seen any evidence of...yet you're going to have a baby. How does that happen?"

Rachel turned away from Trace's touch and cried even harder. "I can't talk about it. I'm so ashamed."

"Ashamed? Why? What do you have to be ashamed of?" Trace pressed gently. "What did you do?"

"I don't know," hysteria was rising in her voice, "but I must have done something because he came here and took me and—"

"What? Wait — who 'took' you? When? What happened?" It was not what Trace expected to hear and the thought of it brought pain to her heart and an angry knot to her chest that held her lungs hostage.

"I can't talk about it, Trace; I can't."

"Yes, you can. You can talk to me."

Rachel shook her head, unable to speak.

Trace's eyes flashed, dark and stormy. "You were raped, weren't you? You didn't willingly have relations with the father of your child, did you?" Rachel's only response was a soft whimper. Furious, but not at Rachel, Trace tried to swallow her wrath. She laid her head on Rachel's hand, counted to ten, and then looked up at her distraught friend.

"Rachel, you have no reason to feel ashamed, do you understand? You didn't do anything wrong. You were raped. You're not pregnant by choice. It's not your fault; you didn't do anything to deserve it."

"How can you know that? You weren't there."

"If you can't tell me, let me guess what happened. You were somewhere, probably here, minding your own business, going about your day, when this man came out of nowhere and forced himself on you. You did not invite it, you did not ask for it, you did not want it...but it didn't matter. He took what he wanted. You fought him, you screamed 'no' and 'stop' and he ignored you. And he hurt you. He violated you against your will."

Rachel stared at her, wide-eyed, her voice barely audible as she stuttered, "How...how did you know that?"

"Because I used to arrest guys like the one who did that to you. It's always the same story. I know all about how they work."

"No one's ever going to believe me."

Trace took both of Rachel's hands and held them to her chest. "I believe you. I know what happened."

Silence enveloped them; the only noise in the room was the crackling of the fading fire. They looked at each other for a long time, eyes locked, an uncharacteristic boldness simmering in Rachel's. Trace's stomach fluttered and her heart flipped, which went along with the pleasurable sensations that were gathering in her groin. She wondered if Rachel felt the same. The electricity in the air was a good indication that she did. Rachel was the first to look away. Trace was sure Rachel was blushing, but in the dim glow of that wavering light, it was difficult to tell. Then Rachel spoke in such a hushed tone, Trace almost didn't hear her.

"You're so wonderful to me...why can't you really be a man?"

"Why? What good would that do?"

Suddenly shy, Rachel turned away, gripping Trace's hand tightly. "I would marry you."

Trace swallowed hard, stunned. She was nearly strangled by her overwhelming want for this woman, and suddenly she was possibly within reach. "You...you would?"

Rachel nodded but couldn't look at Trace. "Does that shock you? It does me."

Trace cleared her throat. In a voice thick with desire, she answered, "Um...no, it doesn't shock me." Trace knelt by Rachel's feet, placing her forearms across Rachel's lap and interlacing their fingers. Rachel's breath caught but she didn't pull away. "Rachel, where I come from, it doesn't matter if a couple is a man and a woman, a man and a man, or a woman and a woman. All that matters is who your heart falls in love with."

Rachel was not able to tear her eyes away from the magnetic pull of Trace's gaze. "I'm not sure I understand..."

The connection between them was undeniable. "I think you do." There was an indecipherable silence, so Trace gently pressed her case. "Just don't limit yourself, that's all I'm saying. Just like you can't make yourself love someone if the feeling isn't there, you can't always control who you fall in love with. The people in my town understand that."

"Where you come from, two women or two men can get married?"

How to explain the civil union as opposed to marriage in terms a nineteenth century woman would understand? Frankly, though she herself was more than a hundred years progressed beyond Rachel's awareness, it still confused the hell out of her as to why there had to be a difference, so she simply said, "Yes."

"Two women or two men are allowed to publicly love each other as man and wife do?"

"Yes." It was a lie, and it wasn't. Again, much too complicated a subject to get into. Besides she was masquerading as a male, so it seemed somewhat incidental.

"Are...are you one of those women?"

"I've never been married to a woman but, yes, I have had love affairs with women."

Rachel suddenly looked like she wanted to bolt from the room. Trace felt a slight tug, as though Rachel might yank her hands away, but then another expression took over — curiosity.

"Rachel, please understand. I would never hurt you. I'd never do anything to make you uncomfortable, never do anything to make you ask me to leave."

Rachel relaxed and pressed her hands more securely into Trace's. "I know that. I know you would never hurt me." Rachel took a deep breath and asked, "Do, um, you think about me like that?"

Trace rested her forehead on their joined hands, then looked up. "Would it frighten you if I said yes?"

Rachel flushed, cleared her throat awkwardly. "No," she whispered.

Trace squeezed Rachel's hands. "Good. So...what are we going to do?"

"Do?" Rachel's voice squeaked. "Um...about what?"

"Your delicate condition. You're not going to be able to hide it much longer."

Rachel hung her head. "I don't know. I don't want this baby. It's a part of someone horrible. But the good Lord gave me this child to carry, so I'll do what I have to do."

"You know what?" Trace began gently. "I was born from a similar situation. My mother was a prostitute, a whore, just like the women on the second floor at Wilbur's. She never knew who my father was. Where I come from there are legal ways to...uh...get rid of the baby before it's born, but she chose to keep me. And...here I am." Trace's smile was sincere. The unexpected confession registered silently, and Trace suspected Rachel was unsure of how to respond to it.

"It will be hard to raise a child alone here. It'll just bear out everybody's presumption that I'm wayward," Rachel said, finally.

Trace lightly massaged Rachel's fingers with her thumb. "You don't have to raise this child alone." At Rachel's questioning stare, Trace said, "Let me make a suggestion, and hear me out before you say no."

"Okay."

"Everybody in town thinks I'm a man. Thank God they do. And they already suspect we've more than likely been intimate. Let me marry you and give you and the baby a name and respectability."

"Me marry you? How could that be respectable? You're a woman."

"Yes, but only you and I know that. We'll get married, and when you do meet a man you'd like to spend your life with — if you do — I'll leave," Trace promised, knowing that would be the most difficult thing she would ever have to do. The stillness suddenly seemed deafening and she reluctantly slid her hand from Rachel's. "Well, you think about it." Trace stood up and stretched. "Would you like some coffee?"

"It's okay, I can make it."

"No," Trace responded, a little too quickly. "No, I'll do it. You sit still."

"There's nothing wrong with my coffee," Rachel said playfully.

Trace made a hideous face. "No, not if it's your last request before the hanging," she said. "Your coffee would kill you first."

"Fine, then you make it," Rachel said, trying to sound indignant. It didn't work. With Trace staring at her, eyebrow raised, Rachel broke into a grin.

"By the way, there's a small break in the north fence. I don't think it was anything other than wind. I put a temporary barrier there, but I'll have to go back and repair it tomorrow."

Rachel nodded. "Thank you."

"Sure." As Rachel stood, Trace gently grasped her elbow. "Are you going to tell me who did this to you?"

"No." Rachel crossed her arms and went on through to the kitchen to get the coffeepot for Trace.

That's okay; I'll find out myself. And I'll start with everyone associated with the Cranes.

Did I really suggest Rachel marry me? The weight of her proposal hit her like an anvil dropped from the top of a ten story building. *Marriage?* Despite a few disastrous attempts at a relationship, Trace's longevity, and faithfulness, barely lasted much beyond foreplay. And now she wanted to actually marry someone? Well...as a matter of fact, yes, she did. And not just "someone"; she wanted to marry Rachel Young. The more she contemplated it, the more elated she became.

Trace had never before felt like her heart was trying to burst through her chest and every nerve ending was standing at attention. When she looked at Rachel, she had no control over her body's reactions.

It was the most wonderful feeling Trace had ever experienced, and she'd experienced a lot. She smiled and blushed deeply, thinking that no one who knew her in her own time would believe she was capable of such emotion. Seeing Trace smile was not unusual; seeing Trace turn red was.

"What are you thinking about?" Rachel asked, then, as she considered what Trace might have been daydreaming about, she became a telling shade of crimson herself.

Not missing Rachel's reaction, Trace shrugged, her face showing the remnants of a smirk. "Just thinking about how delicious supper was and what a good cook you are."

That threw her off. Stammering, Rachel was able to get out a shy, "Thank you." Nibbling on her bottom lip, she avoided Trace's gaze and went to make their nightly tea.

There had been a significant change in their relationship in less than an hour. Trace's willingness to marry her had displayed a selflessness neither of them expected. Rachel had presumed that when Trace discovered she was a mother-to-be, it would not matter how the baby was conceived. She would pack up and move on, appalled. She never even considered Trace would stand by her without reservation, and so she had once more been surprised by Trace's compassion.

And then there was the other revelation.

Her entire body flushed as she thought about the other momentous development between the two of them. This extremely handsome and capable woman was in love with her. Trace didn't have to say it for Rachel to be able to feel it. And the main reason Rachel felt it was that she was in love with Trace. In love. On the one hand, it scared her witless. What if anyone ever found out Trace was not a man? Two women loving each other the way a husband and wife did just wasn't right; it wasn't natural. Yet it felt like the most natural thing in the world. And it thoroughly excited her, almost unbearably. Not even Tommy had aroused the feelings within her that Trace did, now that she acknowledged them for what they were.

The emotions swamping her made Rachel's knees weak and she reached out to hold on to the table for balance. Sneaking a look at Trace, Rachel was relieved she had not noticed. She was not yet ready to openly confront her feelings for Trace.

A deep roll of thunder growled over the house and Rachel was glad for a commonplace topic. "Storm's getting close. Are all of the horses in?" Her voice was shaky but she hoped Trace would think it was nervousness due to the worsening weather.

"In and fed, tucked in for the night and read a bedtime story. Zelda kept wanting a drink of water, but I knew it was only because she didn't want to stay in bed. But Rio seemed quite snug."

Rachel favored Trace with a feigned glare of reprimand and then she chuckled. "Well, don't be so sure. That mustang is not fond of the wind when it howls like that; I'm sure the added noise just makes him more restless."

"Will he get destructive? Should I go out there and stay with him until the storm calms down?"

"If I thought it would do any good, yes, but this might go on all night. We can't baby him or we'll be out there all the time."

"I like that horse, Rachel. I'd like to make him my horse...if that's cool...okay...with you."

Rachel crossed her arms and studied Trace. "He's cantankerous. He's not really wild but he's not tame, either. If you can break him, he's yours." She sighed. "I'm certainly in no position to break him myself." She looked toward the window as a bolt of lightning lit up the sky.

About four seconds later, more thunder cracked and rumbled and the rain drummed heavily on the roof. Trace placed three more logs over the two already aflame, stoking the embers so that the dry wood easily caught fire. It almost immediately took the dampness out of the air.

"Tomorrow, I thought we could have rabbit stew again. Or maybe we could spit-cook it."

Trace's expression revealed that the idea was not agreeable to her. "Do we have to? I mean, it was tasty, Rachel, it's not that but...they're just so damned...I mean, darned cute."

This made Rachel smile. "Why, Trace Sheridan, you big baby," she teased. "You can beat up men without a second thought, probably kill them if you had to, but you can't stand the thought of hurting a little bitty bunny?" Rachel knew that Trace didn't like to be challenged, and hated being teased, but the truth of the irony in her words forced a frustrated smile from Trace.

"We never did go fishing like I wanted. We need something other than vegetables to eat, Trace. You don't hunt, but even if you were able to kill some game, something tells me you've never cut out a steer for slaughter. I need the chickens for the eggs. We can't afford to keep buying our meat, and soon, without supplement, the canned goods in the pantry won't last as long as they should."

"I have money," Trace said.

"For how long? You don't make any money helping me out here, and once what you have is gone, it's gone."

"Rachel, what happened to your cattle?"

She sighed. It was time for Trace to know. "We had five cows, two calves, and one steer. They were grazing in the south pasture. I went out to herd them in and they were all gone. Not rustled, slaughtered. It was awful." She shuddered at the memory. "That night I got a visit from Gideon Crane and two of his ranch hands. Told me if I'd sold my land to his daddy that never would have happened. I reported it to Ed Jackson and he told me I couldn't prove who did it, that even with Gideon saying what he did, he didn't admit to anything."

Trace nodded. "And your crops?"

"Everything in the north sweep, which was most of the vegetables plus a field of corn, was burned to the ground. Now I tend to what I can keep an eye on from the house, which doesn't leave me much to sell to Mr. Foster. And before you ask, I had four other horses, but they were spitefully crippled and had to be destroyed."

"All because the Cranes want your land and you wouldn't sell?"

"Yes."

"It stops here and now, Rachel. I promise you. It's done."

The conviction in Trace's oath was unshakable, and it sent a shiver down Rachel's spine — both for the sincerity of the pledge and the passion with which it was made. She could only shake her head. Trace couldn't possibly have any idea what she was up against. Tonight before bed, she would pray for Trace.

Chapter Thirteen

The subject of marriage didn't come up again the following week, nor did either talk about her discovery of being in love with the other. The conversation the night of the terrible storm had been soul baring, but because it was also new and uncharted territory for both Trace and Rachel, for entirely different reasons, the topic was deftly avoided as each woman was not exactly sure how to broach it again for fear of making the other one uncomfortable.

Both desperately wanted to openly analyze their feelings, but neither dared to bring it up, just in case the exchange had been born of sympathy or misplaced chivalry.

Rachel believed that Trace's feelings were genuine and she wondered whether the depth of them was at all as frightening to Trace as it was to her. She was still trying to come to terms with the fact that she was actually in love with a woman. She started out every morning arguing with herself about the moral implications of her feelings, and how they just had to be something else. Every night, after spending concentrated time with Trace during the day, she would go to bed believing her feelings could not be anything but love, regardless of Trace's gender.

Their interactions were friendly while remaining infuriatingly neutral. Any potentially volatile subject was cautiously danced around, but that didn't stop their thoughts — about love, or about Rachel's pregnancy. Still, other issues needed to be attended to that occasionally diverted them.

The most immediate dilemma for Trace was that she got her period. It was utterly unwelcome, not just a figurative pain but a literal one, as well. She'd always had a rough time with first day cramping, as though the contractions were trying to eject one or both ovaries. Rachel, true to form, had a remedy: peppermint herb boiled in milk and drunk hot. It worked...until it wore off. Rachel made sure this concoction was in abundant supply, as Trace's menstrual distress appeared to debilitate her and make her very grumpy, indeed.

As for what was used to deal with the blood, that was something Trace was definitely going to have to improve on. The menstrual belt and cup Rachel had, were fine and dandy, if one wore a dress. However, with Trace wearing trousers, the rig just would not work. Instead, Trace made the best of rags she wrapped around small beds of cotton, washing the materials out nightly and discarding the batting that could not be cleaned and re-used. She constructed ten of these little pads so she would always have one to change into, fastening them in place with safety pins.

It was spartan but it absorbed the flow and, for the most part, kept the blood from leaking through to her jeans. Accustomed to wearing tampons, the pads made her feel like she had a king-sized pillow between her legs. It took some adjusting but, putting it in perspective, it was a minor cog in this new wheel of life Trace was incorporating herself into.

As the days passed, Trace was very industrious, making the most of her time. She efficiently completed her daily chores, each one getting easier with practice, not to mention patience. Every morning, after grooming the horses, Trace saddled up Chief and checked the perimeter fence, dutifully noting and fixing any weakness or damage in the property line. Returning, she mucked out the stables when they needed it, cleaned the rabbit cages, noting that Mopsy and Cottontail seemed to be getting a little heavier every day, and ensured that the horses had enough to eat and drink. Then she would assist Rachel with anything she needed to have done around the house or grounds.

Every afternoon, in accordance with Rachel's instructions, she worked with Rio to gain his trust. She had plenty of carrots and apples to offer him, treats he began to look forward to whenever Trace was near him. Conditioned by living in the wild since birth, the mustang had learned to listen for predators and his ears would go up as soon as anything approached him. He quickly attuned to Trace's scent and the sound of her gait, and reacted accordingly whenever she appeared.

Trace sensed that he was beginning to feel confident with her, especially when he allowed her to gently run her hands all around his head and neck, but only after he got his treats. She knew he associated the tasty delicacies and relaxing massage with her, showing him he had no reason to fear her. This became a ritual with Trace speaking to him soothingly and lovingly, to the point where if she wasn't with him by a certain time every afternoon, he would poke his head over the stall door and look for her. Trace began to look forward to the time she spent with the mustang; she seemed to find a spiritual buoyancy in her connection with him.

Every other day, in the late afternoon, Trace would work in an hour of target practice with all four weapons. She was altogether proud of how efficient she was with guns that were so different from what she was used to. She checked her ammunition and made a mental note that she was going to have to start loading her own bullets and be a little more frugal with her supply.

Trace spent whatever free time was left busily perfecting a coarse prototype shower out of a wooden beer keg with holes in it, suspended by a hemp cord over the limb of an oak tree. Connected to the barrel was a crude version of an elevated sluice, where water from an offshoot of the river about twenty yards from the house could be pumped through and then held by a valve to stop or regulate its flow. When the small floodgate was lifted by yanking on a string accessible to the person standing underneath the cask, a stream of pent up water would rush into the keg and drain out through the tiny openings Trace had created with a large nail. For privacy, she built a wooden stall that would enclose the showering individual, covering them modestly from shins to shoulders.

Her reward for the innovative contraption was Rachel's reaction when it was done and Trace demonstrated how it worked. Rachel clasped her hands together and squealed in delight.

Every evening, after supper, Trace and Rachel would sit on the porch and drink tea while Trace serenaded Rachel. Sometimes Rachel would request a repeat of something she found catchy and worth listening to again, but most of the time she just let Trace play and enjoyed the music. Trace had a voice unlike any Rachel had ever heard, so clear and deeply soulful, impressively always on key, with a range of several octaves.

Rachel's suggestion that maybe Trace should sing in the church choir brought a raised eyebrow and a look that needed no commentary.

Over the next couple of days, Trace continued to work with Rio. Never known for her patience, even she was surprised at her equanimity with this animal. She certainly did not have it with Chief, nor did he exhibit it with her. They had reached a state of mutual tolerance and that's how it stayed. There was no doubt he was Rachel's horse and very loyal to her. As for Trace and Rio, both human and horse were finding great solace in each other's company.

With the exception of being attached to a neighbor's dog when she was a child, Trace had never bonded with any animal and could only now understand how rewarding it could be. The repugnant thought of anyone doing harm to the mustang — or Rosie, Moses, Chief, and the precious little Zelda — horrified and infuriated her. Recalling that Rachel's other horses had to be destroyed because of intentional maiming by the Crane clan made her even more determined to get even with the bastards.

When it was time to go into town again, Trace had a list of personal errands she needed to attend to, in addition to the usual business that took her to Sagebrush. First, she intended to see Joseph Turner at the pawn shop. Depending on what transpired there, she would open an account at the bank, talk with a few businessmen in town, and then get what she needed for the ranch, buying a few extras — like a soft, French-milled soap that was lightly perfumed with lavender as a gift for Rachel. The look she anticipated on Rachel's face would be worth the small extravagance. She wondered how long it had been since Rachel had received or bought herself something nice.

Trace tended to the last of her list and was loading the feed and mercantile supplies on the wagon. Isaac Tipping was nowhere in sight, which Trace found a bit unusual. She finished the chore and looked over at the saloon. She was hot and tired, and a beer would taste very good. Rachel was not going to start supper until dusk, so one mug shouldn't do any harm. She secured her load, patted Moses' neck affectionately, and strolled across the street to Wilbur's.

It was still hard to believe that she actually lived in the Old West. Staying on the ranch was definitely a reminder, but coming into town was the clincher. She stepped up to the bar and Silas grinned at her and poured her an ale.

Her masculine façade was working, no doubt about that. She was being taken for a tall, graceful young man and, no matter how much she protested, one of possible Native American descent or of Gypsy heritage. Not that it mattered to her. She certainly would not have been ashamed of being either. It was the deprecating prejudice with which it was always stated that bothered her. Besides, for all she knew, she could be part anything, as her father's bloodline was a mystery. She knew her mother was of Greek descent and that's what she attributed her darker features and complexion to, but the piercing azure eyes must have been a paternal trait as her mother's lifeless orbs were chocolate brown with gold flecks.

Whatever they thought her origins were, she knew her appearance was deceiving, and anyone who confused her lithe, angular — for a man, anyway — frame for inexperience and weakness would be making a deadly mistake. Hopefully, the scumbag who had raped Rachel would make the mistake of thinking that her youth and lighter weight would make her an easy target. She had already proven to two men and the sheriff that they didn't.

Just the thought of that ugly incident, how horribly violated and destroyed Rachel must have felt, set Trace's teeth on edge and made her quake with rage. She nearly choked on her first swallow of beer.

"Why, hell, Trace, you look as ornery as an undertaker in a ghost town. What's that expression for?" Silas cracked, pouring a shot of whiskey for himself. He held the bottle up to her.

Trace shook her head at his offer, remembering her last encounter with that nasty stuff. "Nothing that this can't cure." She smiled, slightly raising her glass.

"Or that." Silas nodded toward the staircase.

Trace followed his gaze and saw Cassandra bounding down the stairs, making a beeline for her. She couldn't help but smile at the red-head's blatant attraction to her and unbridled enthusiasm every time she saw her. Cassandra was not a bad looking woman — light-skinned and green-eyed, with full rosy lips and a generous mouth that Trace could only imagine what it could accomplish. It would be nice to take some comfort and ease some of the sexual tension that had built up to nearly volcanic proportions, but there were two problems with that: the first being, if Trace allowed Cassandra to service her, her secret wouldn't be a secret for very long; and second, Cassandra wasn't Rachel.

Cassandra stopped her gallop and sashayed the last five or six feet to Trace's side, making an obvious show of her arrival. Leaning an elbow on the bar, the prostitute pursed her lips at Trace. "Buy a lady a drink?"

Trace bowed her head, smiling in mild disbelief. She looked back up into clearly interested eyes, that today were taking on the color of her dark green dress. "I guess if I see a lady anywhere around, I'll be sure to do that."

The five male saloon patrons and Silas laughed uproariously and Cassandra pretended to sulk until Trace reached over and gave her upper arm a brief squeeze. "You know I'm just kidding, right? What'll you have?"

"You." Her expression was sultry and practiced.

Cassandra stepped so close to Trace, she could feel the prostitute's breath against her neck. Trace took a subtle step away. "You can't drink me."

"Wanna bet?"

That drew a round of "Ooooohs" from the boys in the bar but Trace didn't blink. She gave the redhead an appreciative once over and smiled again. "Cassandra, I'm sure you could make my toes curl if I gave you a chance."

"Well?"

"Sorry. Although I'm sure your charms exceed most men's wildest dreams, I'm not going to give you that chance."

"Why? Don't you like me?"

"It ain't that, Cass." Joseph Turner, standing by the staircase, jumped in. "Trace, here, is getting his toes curled by Rachel Young."

Trace pinned him with a glare, the force of which should have knocked him clear across the room. In a voice even and definite, she said, "Mind your manners, Joseph. Miss Rachel is a lady. I won't have anyone talking about her like that."

"Come on, you're telling us you're living out there on that big spread, just the two of you, and you and her have never—"

"Never what, Joseph?" Trace interrupted, not believing the idiot didn't get the hint to shut up.

"You know." Grinning lewdly, he gestured obscenely with his hands.

"I told you no, Joseph. Miss Rachel is a lady. She's nursed me back to health and given me a place to stay and that's all."

"Well, you're probably better off." Cassandra shrugged. "Word has it she's no virgin."

"Word has it?" Trace snapped. "Whose word?" Trace's captivating eyes turned ice blue and she was no longer playful.

"Well," Joseph said, "Ben Crane, for one. He said he's had her and she's real...uh...spirited in the bedroom."

"Who the fuck is Ben Crane and why would he say something like that?"

The sheriff had mentioned Ben specifically. Trace wanted to know more about him. She scanned the room, letting each and every one of them know that a line had been crossed.

Cassandra mistakenly thought she could soothe the savage beast in Trace. She reached out for her and said, "You don't want to mess with Ben Crane, Trace."

Trace swatted the prostitute's hand away, a motion that startled everyone, most of all Cassandra. Trace glared at Joseph. "I said, who the fuck is Ben Crane?"

They all exchanged glances. Silas cleared his throat. "Uh...the Cranes are cattle barons, Trace. They run this town. When they're here."

"That much I know," Trace said, still not impressed. "And the Cranes, including Ben, are away, heading up their cattle drive to Kansas, right?"

"Right," Joseph said. "They get fifty dollars a head delivering them to Dodge City. They round 'em up and drive 'em once a year and this is that time. They own most of the property that surrounds the town. All except for the Young spread."

"And that spread — which Rachel won't sell — is right in the middle of their drive route, which adds an extra half day to their trip east," Silas added, reiterating information Trace was already aware of, and then he said something she didn't know. "Ben asked Rachel for her hand a few times, hoping it would take care of the problem of Rachel not selling, but she turned him down every time. Guess he finally gave up."

Gave up, my ass, Trace thought. An idea started forming in her mind, putting together some missing pieces of the jigsaw puzzle that was Rachel's life before she'd entered it. "So why would this Crane dickhead say what he's saying?"

It was obvious the normally amiable Trace was not at all rational about this particular subject and the atmosphere in the room changed. The tension in the air was thick and suddenly everyone in the saloon looked like they wished they had somewhere else to be. Including Cassandra, who still acted a little stung by Trace's rejection.

"Look, Trace, Crane told us he's had Rachel...that's all I'm telling you," Joseph said with finality.

"And you believe him?"

"Why would he lie?"

"You tell me." Trace glanced from face to face, her eyes challenging every one of them. No one said a word. "Okay...just for shits and giggles, let's say he had her. What's the problem?"

They all exchanged looks with one another, then back at Trace, each one looking embarrassed. It was Silas who finally spoke. "Well...come on, Trace...you wouldn't want a woman who's already been—"

"Don't even think about finishing that sentence, Silas," Trace warned. "First, that's an insult to Cassandra, and second, if what this Crane asshole said is true, why does that make her undesirable and not him?"

Even the three men playing poker at the table against the stairs looked up at that one, but no one responded to her question.

Laughing caustically, Trace said, "Let me get this straight, he beds her and he's a big stud and she's a whore? How come he's not considered a whore?"

"You're kidding, right, Trace?" Silas asked, a nervous little laugh getting caught in his throat.

"No, I'm not," she said, agitated. "Women are sexual beings. They have wants, needs, desires, just like men. But, no, we can't allow women to express that, to behave just like us because then we lose control over them." Out of the corner of her eye, Trace noticed Cassandra smirk and look down at the floor. "Men come in here and pay for the pleasure of Cassandra's services and that's okay. We all just look the other way because that's what men do. But women...the minute they show any sign of enjoying the sex act like a man does, deriving any pleasure from it at all, she's a whore, a hussy. She has to be a virgin on her wedding night but we don't. Ain't right, guys," Trace told them.

Joseph, Silas, and the other men all snickered. "Damn, Trace. How you talk sometimes." Silas shook his head.

"Yeah, yeah, but let's just look at this for a second. Say this prick Crane is telling the truth and he and Rachel got romantic and frisky one night and they had...relations. Who are you going to respect more? Rachel, who most of you have known since she was born? She's a good, kind, law-abiding woman who's had some pretty horrible things happen in the past year, who may have made a mistake with Crane. Or him, who slept with her and bragged about it to everyone, knowing it would ruin her good name? I don't see where there's even a choice here, boys."

Amazingly, her words apparently sunk in and they all seemed to consider what she'd said.

"But," Trace added, employing what her last patrol partner used to tell her was one of her most annoying traits — rubbing salt into an open wound, "I still think either he's lying or he took her against her will."

Matthew Reddick, one of the younger men playing poker, put his cards down. "Uh...Trace...are you accusing Ben Crane of rape? Because that could be real dangerous around here."

Knowing she'd hit a nerve, Trace almost smiled. "I'm just throwing out the possibilities. You draw the conclusion yourself. Somehow, just hearing how you talk about this Crane pig tells me that Rachel wouldn't willingly give him the time of day, much less give him anything else — if you understand me. And," she said, her voice steady, "make no mistake: the threat of a Crane being pissed off at me doesn't scare me. Bullies never scare me."

Cassandra shook her head. "If the Cranes don't scare you, then you're a fool."

"Yeah...maybe, but I don't want to hear any more of that talk about Rachel Young. She's a good, decent woman and she's been a saint to me. And regardless of what this fucker, Ben Crane, says, I can guarantee she had nothing to do with him and it's just sour grapes on his part."

Silas smiled. "Kind of sweet on her, ain't ya, Trace?"

Knowing she was blushing, Trace broke into a smile. "Well...yeah...I mean, shouldn't I be? Look at her. She's beautiful."

Matthew Reddick folded to a bobtailed flush, cleared his three dollars in winnings off the table and stood up, putting the money in his pocket. He passed Trace with a smile. "Ya know, Trace? She deserves to finally have something good in her life again. Rachel's a good woman." He clapped Trace on the shoulder and left the saloon.

Chapter Fourteen

One beer turned into four and it was just past dusk when Trace steered Moses to the hitching post outside the front door. She could smell supper as she hopped down off the wagon and decided to unload the supplies afterward. She unhooked the old horse and led him to the barn and strolled back to the main house.

"Hey," she greeted Rachel as she walked in.

Rachel smiled brightly at her as she finished setting the table. "Hi. Go get washed up. I thought you were going to be late."

"Yeah, me too, for a minute." Trace moved to the pump and basin. "Kind of lost track of time at Wilbur's."

Barely concealing a wider, rib-busting proud grin, Rachel said, "Yes, I heard you defended my honor there today."

Stunned, Trace looked over at her. "How did you find out?"

"Elizabeth Reddick came over to visit. Brought us an apple pie. Matthew hasn't allowed Elizabeth to come over here in almost a month. She said Matthew got home from playing cards and told her that Joseph Turner was saying some things about me that weren't very nice and you almost hit him."

"I didn't almost hit him. I felt like it...but I restrained myself. Good Lord, people have big mouths around here."

"So...did you defend my honor?"

Trace looked over at the radiantly beaming young woman. It was contagious. "And if I did?" She was about to wipe her hands on the towel when Rachel's smile turned to a stern smirk. "What?"

"Wash your hands again, Trace Sheridan, and this time use soap." She pointed at the basin. "Those hands are not clean."

Trace held them up, displaying both palms and then knuckles. "They may not be clean, but they match," she said in a playfully defensive tone. Shrugging in defeat, she returned to the pump. "You didn't answer my question," she continued, scrubbing her hands in an exaggerated manner with a gritty borax powder. She was looking forward to Rachel's reaction when she gave her the perfumed soap.

"If you did, I just wanted to say thank you," she said almost timidly as she placed a bowl of steaming potatoes on the table.

Trace studied the beautiful woman. "You're welcome," she replied, her tone loving. "Rachel, was it Ben Crane that raped you?"

It came out of nowhere, like a hard slap. Rachel stopped in her tracks. "Leave it alone, Trace," she said, her eyes pleading and fixed on Trace. "Ben Crane is a dangerous man."

"Ben Crane doesn't scare me, Rachel. I've dealt with hundreds of Ben Cranes. He's an overgrown bully, and bullies never scare me."

Rachel was panicked. "You have no idea what he's capable of. He's a very powerful man, him and his father and brothers. You don't want to make a Crane angry. They run this town; they keep money flowing into this town as well as take it away. No one in Sagebrush, no matter how much they hate the Cranes, will back you up if you cross a Crane—"

"Hey, hey..." Trace's voice was loud enough to be heard over Rachel's rising hysteria, but soothing enough to let her know she wasn't arguing with her. "The town is afraid of them, I get it. They're not nice people, I get that, too. And they own Sagebrush so, in a way, they are holding the town hostage, I understand. But that doesn't give them the right to antagonize, intimidate, or rape anyone."

Rachel took her by the shoulders. She was crying. "Please, Trace, I'm begging you, don't go up against the Cranes. They'll kill you." She was sobbing, and her voice broke into a desperate whisper. "I can't lose you."

The impact of that hushed confession stunned Trace into momentary silence. She pulled a desolate Rachel into her comforting arms, rubbing her back with one hand while tightly holding Rachel against her with the other. The response from the frightened woman simultaneously surprised and excited her —Rachel held her back, almost intimately, like a lover, burrowing into her uninhibitedly as though releasing her would cause her to vanish into thin air. "Shhh, shhh, it's okay...I'm not going anywhere... I promise." Trace consoled her, absently pressing her lips several times to the top of Rachel's head, an action that came naturally.

Rachel's body stiffened and Trace closed her eyes, mentally cursing herself for stepping over that line. She knew that whatever Rachel may have been feeling, it was new and bewildering and complicated, and she was trying not to force her rapidly growing love and libidinous feelings on her. As strong as Rachel was, she was still very fragile. Holding her breath, Trace waited for Rachel to make the next move.

No immediate reaction or response was forthcoming, but neither did Rachel move out of Trace's embrace. Allowing the moment to play itself out, she waited in silence until Rachel finally cleared her throat nervously.

"Trace?"

A thousand thoughts swirled in her mind, but one seemed stronger than all the rest: Rachel would ask her to leave, regardless of not wanting to lose her. Trace was disgusted with herself for not having more self-control. In modern times, her gesture would have meant nothing; right here, right now, it said much more than she felt Rachel was ready to handle. Her voice leaden, she said, "Yeah?"

"Did you mean what you mentioned last week?" Rachel's voice was muffled but her question came out clearly.

"I said a lot last week...what specifically?"

"About...getting married."

It was Trace's turn to freeze, mostly from confusion. Never in a million years would she have ever expected this from the traditional, moral young woman. She stepped back, putting herself at arm's length from Rachel. Trace gently placed a finger under Rachel's chin and lifted, forcing their eyes to meet. "What about it?"

"I want to get married...if you still want to." She drew a deep breath. "I'm glad it's out. I've been thinking about your offer since you brought it up that night of the storm. It's been difficult to think about anything else." She tried to look away from Trace but she couldn't. The expression on Trace's face was priceless.

"If I— Of course, I still want to. Why do you want to?"

"I've been thinking about what you said and...I know you would be good to me, protect me, take care of me. I know I won't find a husband, especially not being...with child. And nobody has to know the truth except you and me." Trace's hand was caressing her face and Rachel closed her eyes and leaned into the touch.

"I'll never hurt you, Rachel. And I'll make sure no one else ever hurts you again." She stepped closer and lightly massaged Rachel's belly. "I'll raise this child as my own."

Rachel fell into Trace's arms again and hugged her fiercely. "I feel so safe with you. I don't care if you're a woman."

Trace looked skyward and mouthed the words, "Thank you." The two women's eyes captured each other's again and Trace said, "I know you mean it."

"I do mean it. I don't care. I just never want you to leave me."

"Sweetheart, I'll be here as long as you want me here, need me here." Trace didn't know when things had changed, but she wasn't about to question or try to analyze it.

"I think I'll always need you," Rachel said, looking down, "...always want you."

A surge of pure rapture washed through Trace, coursing through her veins like water through a fire hose, jolting her between the legs like nothing before. Heat radiated outward, igniting every nerve. She couldn't tear her eyes away from the flawlessly beautiful face.

"Would...you..." Rachel's voice was shaking, "...kiss me? Like a man kisses a woman?"

"You mean, like, romantically? Like lovers?" Trace's voice was hoarse, desire for Rachel overwhelming her.

Blushing, Rachel smiled. "Yes...like that."

"Then let me kiss you like a woman kisses a woman. Romantically. Like lovers."

Receiving willing permission from Rachel's eyes, Trace leaned in and met Rachel's lips tentatively, tenderly. She let Rachel get used to the sensation, get comfortable with the idea before she attempted to deepen the kiss. Her lips were soft, wanting. When Rachel's arms snaked around Trace's neck, pulling their bodies even closer, Trace took that as a cue to move forward with the kiss.

Swept up in Trace's passion, Rachel returned the kiss as though it were normal for her to be standing in her kitchen wrapped in the arms of a woman, as if she'd been kissing women her entire life.

Trace opened her mouth, licking gently over Rachel's bottom lip. Startled, Rachel stilled for no more than a second, and then mimicked Trace's action. Not being able to contain a smile, Trace moaned into Rachel's mouth and fervently pursued the inexperienced woman's tongue, her own dancing with it. Rachel must have liked that, too, because she began to match Trace move for move with as much, if not more, enthusiasm.

It took every ounce of self-control Trace possessed not to let her hands roam over every inch of Rachel's body, not to act even remotely aggressively with her, as she would have with her modern conquests. That would, no doubt, frighten Rachel, something she knew she would die before doing, die before allowing Rachel to equate the act of love-making with violence, which was the only experience Rachel had ever had. As Rachel's body melted into hers, Trace continued to explore every fraction of Rachel's mouth, stopping occasionally to lightly suck on her tongue — which made Rachel's knees grow weak. Rachel pushed back from Trace, separating their lips as she grabbed on to Trace's denim shirt for support and nearness. They touched foreheads, panting, almost gasping for air.

"Oh my Lord," Rachel breathed.

"Are you okay?" Trace exhaled, sure she should be asking herself the same question, wondering if Rachel would understand the signals her loins must be sending her body.

"I...I've never been kissed like that before. It was as wonderful as I thought it would be." She smiled and flushed. "Oh, my, I'm not sure I can describe what you just stirred up inside me."

Trace blinked back her astonishment. "You've thought about kissing me?"

Turning a deeper crimson, Rachel nodded shyly. "Yes. Often."

Trace took Rachel's hand and pressed it to her hammering heart. "Feel that? That's what your kiss just did to me. Thinking about kissing you has been almost as bad. Why didn't you say anything before now?"

"I didn't know what to say, how to bring it up. I was embarrassed. I mean...I knew women like you existed, but I've never personally met...one...before. But when you told me about you, it made me think...and...I think, um, I think I might be like you."

Trace led Rachel to the table where supper was growing cold, she gestured for Rachel to sit. Trace squatted by her side. "You're telling me you think — romantically — you like women better than men?"

"I don't have much to compare it to, some courting, some kissing and, well, except for—" she bowed her head regretfully, "you know... but nothing has ever made me feel the way your one kiss just did."

Trace reached up and cupped her chin, provoking another shiver in Rachel as their eyes met. Bringing the younger woman's fingers to her lips, Trace kissed every one. "Rachel Young, will you marry me?"

Rachel tumbled into Trace's arms, knocking them both back onto the wood floor, Trace cushioning the fall with her own body. Both women were laughing, Rachel practically fusing herself to her new fiancée.

"I take it that's a yes?" Trace asked, knowing if her smile was any wider, her face would split.

"Yes! Yes, I will marry you, Trace Sheridan!" Rachel spread butterfly kisses all over Trace's face before their lips met, reigniting their desire.

Trace knew she had to stop them now or she wouldn't be able to stop. She sat up, carefully bringing Rachel with her so that Rachel was sitting on her lap. "So," she inhaled then exhaled to regain her equilibrium, "when do you want to get married? And how do we do that here?"

"We need to talk to Pastor Edwards. There shouldn't be a problem."

"That easy, huh?"

"Well, yes. And we have to see the circuit clerk and recorder at the mayor's office. Did you think getting married would be difficult?"

"Believe me when I tell you that me marrying anyone was the last thing on my mind."

"You never wanted to get married?"

The look of amazement on Rachel's face was precious. "Not until now." Trace smiled at her, giving her a playful squeeze. "How soon can we do this?"

"Someone's eager," Rachel teased demurely, running a hand through Trace's thick, dark mane.

Caught off guard, Trace laughed. "Well, yeah...for a lot of reasons." She pinned Rachel with an undeniably lusty gaze. Without realizing it, Rachel crossed her legs, as though damming up the pool Trace was sure was gathering there. Rachel looked almost puzzled, as if she was not quite understanding her body's reaction. Trace's mouth went dry as all the moisture in her body headed south. She gingerly lifted Rachel off her, stood up, and assisted her fiancée to her feet. "You're going to start showing soon," Trace laid her hand across Rachel's abdomen, "and I'd like everyone to think this is my baby."

"I'd like everyone to think that, too." She stood on her tip toes and kissed Trace on the cheek. "I'll make you believe this is your child. I love you so much, Trace Sheridan, I think I'm going to burst. You've made me the happiest woman alive!"

Maybe the second happiest, Trace thought, as she lovingly embraced Rachel's warmth.

Neither ended up doing much damage to the very nice supper Rachel had prepared, because they were both too excited. It was difficult to keep their eyes off each other, to refrain from holding hands so that they could consume their food, to hold back from clearing the table by crawling over it to kiss each other. Again. Sexual impulses were new to Rachel and not acting on them was new to Trace.

Rachel couldn't stop thinking about Trace's lips touching hers...or what would happen next, even though she knew Trace would not rush her into anything.

This was an epiphany. She had never felt like this, not even with Tommy. His kisses had been pleasant, if a little anxious and sloppy. Even in his eagerness, as charming as he was, his overtures were comparatively boring with what Trace had just showed her. And she couldn't think of the brutal, violent way Ben Crane had kissed her. She shuddered and bile rose in her throat at just the thought of being touched by him. Shaking that nightmare from her consciousness as much as possible, Rachel focused on the woman sitting across from her.

She realized she didn't have the sexual sophistication Trace most likely had, but as she sat opposite the dark beauty, Rachel knew that was to her advantage. The very idea of Trace teaching her, well, *everything* brought a deep, anticipatory blush to her cheeks and an urgent heat to the lower half of her body. Enlightenment, indeed.

Trace had not experienced such spontaneous euphoria since her senior year in high school when she had boldly kissed her androgynously cute P.E. teacher — a woman she had a wicked crush on — right in the middle of being reprimanded by her for hogging the basketball during practice. She never thought about that unexpected moment without getting butterflies in her stomach and a foolish, shit-eating grin on her face...kind of like the one she was sporting right now.

Helping Rachel clear the table, Trace affectionately kissed the top of her head and squeezed her shoulders before she went outside to unload the wagon.

Now that she had proposed — something she never believed she was capable of either offering or accepting — she was thrilled about getting married. Her, the woman who had always said that marriage was another word for "ownership". The thought gave her pause. Was that what this was about? Did she want to possess Rachel, claim her as her private property by right of conquest? No, she detested that kind of behavior. And yet, she knew as sure as she was standing there that she didn't want anyone else to have Rachel; just the thought of it caused pain to claw at her heart. *This may all be new to Rachel, but it's all pretty foreign to me, too.*

Before Rachel Young entered her life, the idea of spending twenty-four hours a day, seven days a week with anyone was ludicrous, unacceptable. Now, the thought of spending one minute away from her seemed unbearable. Shaking her head at how one person could change her so completely, and in such a short period of time, Trace finished stocking the pantry shelves with her trademark raised eyebrow smirk.

When she finished, she stepped back out into the kitchen with her hands behind her back, approaching Rachel who was putting the dishes away. With uncharacteristic reserve, Trace cleared her throat to get Rachel's attention. Rachel turned around and tilted her head in question.

"I brought something back for you from town," Trace said. The anticipated expression of wonder appeared on Rachel's face.

"You... Did you buy me a present?"

"Mmm hmm." Trace inched closer.

"What is it? Let me see." Rachel attempted to dance around Trace's back but the taller woman simply moved with her. "No fair, Trace. It isn't nice to tease me."

Amused at Rachel's eagerness, Trace said, "I'll give it to you for a kiss."

Rachel stood stock still, goosebumps rising. She crossed her arms over her chest to cover hardening nipples. "How about you give it to me and if I like it, then I'll give you a kiss."

"Oh? You feel you're in a position to barter?"

"I do. Because I know you want to kiss me just as much as I want to be kissed."

Shrugging, Trace nodded. Either way, she was going to get her wish. "Close your eyes and put your hands out," she said.

Rachel did as she was told and Trace brought her hand around and placed the tissue wrapped gift in Rachel's palms.

Rachel's eyes widened in surprise and gratitude as she recognized the wrapping. "Oh...Trace," she said, holding the soap up to her nose and inhaling its fragrance. Her eyes blinked back up at the incredible blue ones that looked into her soul. "You're so sweet, I could eat you with a spoon."

She has got to stop saying stuff like that, Trace thought, knowing Rachel had no idea of the double meanings to things she so innocently said. "Now, where's my kiss?"

Eyes brimming with tears at Trace's thoughtful gesture, Rachel almost jumped into her arms. "Thank you," she whispered, lifting her face.

Trace's lips brushed Rachel's lightly, tauntingly, then claimed them for a slow, sweet, lusciously deep kiss that had Rachel quivering and eager for more. The response from Rachel left Trace breathless and almost too light-headed to stand. When Trace pulled back, she saw Rachel's eyes were sparkling.

"My body hungers for you, Trace," Rachel confessed in a hushed tone, as though she were embarrassed by her desires. "You've stirred something way down inside me. I've never known a need so blind and demanding."

As the words came from someone quite inexperienced with being in touch with her own sexual feelings, Trace found Rachel's declaration enticingly erotic. She was about to suggest the possibility of taking things to the next level when Rachel said, "But I want to wait until we can be together in our, um, marriage bed."

Trying not to let her disappointment show, Trace put the brakes on her carnal urges. Knowing that the request was important to Rachel, she exhaled and nodded. She caressed Rachel's face and kissed her forehead. "Can we get married tonight?"

Rachel hugged her fiercely. "Don't think it's not killing me, too, 'cause it is."

Smiling indulgently, Trace knew it was going to be an impossibly long night.

Trace awoke to the sounds of her bride-to-be retching downstairs. She quickly slipped into some clothes and climbed down from the loft. Rachel was outside on the porch, bent over at the waist, dry heaving into the bushes.

The sun had at least one more hour before debuting another day and the morning was dawning clear and crisp, a fact that was contradicted by Rachel's profuse sweating. Trace could tell Rachel sensed her before she actually saw her or felt Trace's hands on her back. She gently pulled Rachel's hair away from her face and held it while Rachel experienced another round of convulsive nausea. When she was finished, she turned slightly and sat on a porch chair, holding her belly and looking up at Trace pathetically.

Trace's expression was helpless, sympathetic. "Oh, sweetheart, I wish there was something I could do to make you feel better."

"Just your being here makes me feel better."

"Why don't you sit here and take in the fresh air. I'll go heat up some water and get the ginger." Trace received a weak nod in response and disappeared into the house. She returned a few moments later and sat in the chair opposite Rachel. "So, Rachel, what else is going on with you? What else are you feeling?" Trace reached over and gently massaged Rachel's shoulder. "Craving anything special or different to eat?"

Startled, Rachel looked up into caring blue eyes. "Yes. Something, anything soaked in salted vinegar. How could you know that?"

Trace smiled patiently. "It's a well known symptom of pregnancy. Just like you starting to take more and more trips to the outhouse, you being tired all the time, soon your back will start to ache." Rachel's expression confirmed the presence of Trace's list of subtle physical changes. "What about headaches?"

"Yes."

"Are your breasts tender and swollen?"

"A little. I...I get cramping, too, and I don't know if that's normal. I don't want there to be anything wrong with the baby."

"Are you constipated?" Laced with concern and compassion, Trace's voice was not intrusive.

"Yes," Rachel admitted shyly. "I'm not used to talking about my body's inner workings with anyone except Doc Smith and my mother."

"It's okay, sweetheart. All of that sounds very typical. Your cramping is most likely due to your being constipated, and that, along with you having to pee more frequently means the baby is beginning to press against your bowel and your bladder. Unfortunately, it's only going to get worse. I'm sure the baby is fine, but it's growing, Rachel, and we need to get married before that baby begins to show."

She flattened her nightshirt across her tummy and displayed what she thought was a slight bump. "I'm already starting."

Focusing on Rachel's lower abdomen, Trace couldn't really see any obvious bulge, but Rachel must know her own body. Even if it was just bloating, Trace could not help an excited grin. Moving off the chair, she knelt alongside of Rachel and looked up into glistening green eyes. "May I?" Her hand hovered a few inches above Rachel's belly.

"Yes, of course," Rachel answered, breathless at Trace's request.

Trace laid her palm across the material covering Rachel's stomach. Knowing the baby was probably only slightly larger than a walnut at this stage, Trace didn't expect to feel any movement but it didn't matter. It almost felt like her son or daughter was growing inside this beautiful woman with whom she was desperately in love. Trace leaned in and lovingly planted a kiss on Rachel's tummy before looking up into the eyes of her bride-to-be. "I love you," she said simply.

"I love you, too," Rachel answered in a fierce whisper. "What ever did I do to deserve you, Trace Sheridan?"

"Oh, no." Trace shook her head, smiling as she stood up. "I'm sure it's much more what did I do to deserve you." She leaned down and tenderly kissed Rachel, who did not resist.

"How could you want to do that after what I was just doing?" Rachel wondered out loud.

"For better or for worse," Trace responded, caressing Rachel's face. Trace went back inside the house to take the boiling water off the stove. When she walked back out onto the porch, Rachel was standing. She handed Rachel the steaming cup and stood behind her, wrapping her arms around the still slender waist. Rachel leaned back into the strong, comforting body. Together, an intimate silence surrounding them, they watched the sun rise.

Chapter Fifteen

Trace and Rachel were on their way to town. Rachel needed to stop in at Molly Ledbetter's dress shop and ask her about possible alterations on the wedding gown she was bringing to her. But first they would go by the church; Rachel didn't want to put off talking to Pastor Edwards about performing the marriage ceremony. Trace was not nearly as enthusiastic about going to meet the preacher. She was sure that getting the cleric's blessing would involve a promise to join his congregation. Trace couldn't keep a frown on her face. She looked over at her bride-to-be, who was seated quietly next to her, obviously lost in thoughts of her own. If it paved a smoother path to the altar, she would go to church on Sundays — whatever it took to make Rachel happy.

The past couple of days had been extremely productive. Though she was still riding Chief, the breaking of the mustang was coming along just fine, and her afternoon workout with the punching bag was not only getting her back in physical fighting shape, but helping to discipline her psychologically, as well. It was also perfect for working off some of the sexual frustration and energy that built up, now knowing that she could and would have Rachel in her bed very soon.

During Trace's last visit to Sagebrush, she'd pawned two more of the jewelry items that had traveled with her through time. She still had plenty of cash left over from her first visit to Joseph Turner's shop, but her plans for the Triple Y would require quite a bit of spending. If she was going to become the man of the house, so to speak, security for the property was going to be done her way.

After speaking to Pastor Edwards, with Rachel most likely spending a good portion of the afternoon being fitted for her wedding dress, Trace would check to see if her order had come in to the mercantile. It only had to be brought in from Jefferson City, which was a five hour wagon ride away, and her order had gone out by horseback the day after she'd placed it. After that it would be off to Wilbur's to throw back a few ales, maybe play a hand or two of poker and check on the progress of her under-the-table deal with Silas. She had not yet said anything about her plans to her future wife, knowing Rachel would fret unnecessarily at the tauntingly insolent challenge it would present to the Cranes.

With the exception of kissing, which they did a lot, the physical boundaries of the engagement had been set. Trace frequently shoved her hands deep into her pockets to keep from touching her betrothed inappropriately. They discussed plans for their wedding in practical terms. She would absolutely defer to Rachel concerning any aspect of the ceremony because Trace had no idea how any of it should go. Even in her own century, Trace had never been a part of a wedding, other than as a guest, so she would have to follow Rachel's lead.

Trace wanted to get Rachel an engagement ring, but Rachel told her that the money could be better spent in more necessary areas...like food and supplies. It was Rachel's desire to wear her grandmother's wedding band, which had been passed down to her mother and now sat in a small, red velvet-lined jewelry box in Rachel's bedroom. Fortunately, she and her mother were the identical ring size and the thin, rose gold band fit nicely on her delicate hand.

Frank Young's wedding band did not fit Trace, however. The thick, plain gold band was at least two sizes larger than Trace's ring finger. As it was Rachel's wish that Trace wear her father's band, it would have to be resized. She hoped the goldsmith in town would be able to refit it for her with little difficulty.

Also in the wagon, folded neatly between two shawls, was Rachel's mother's wedding dress. She was taking it to Molly Ledbetter's to be altered so she could wear it. Fortunately, Minnie Young had been a smidgen taller and a little thicker around the waist than Rachel, so when she'd tried it on two days earlier, the saffron taffeta oval-printed gown fit almost perfectly, well enough so that she didn't want it taken in anywhere. Rachel was lucky to have a figure that didn't have to be cinched into a corset, although a bone bodice underneath would certainly make the dress look nicer. However, with a baby now growing inside her, she would sacrifice style for comfort. What she hoped Molly would be able to do was provide crinoline petticoats and turn the high collared gown into one with a moderate sweetheart neckline. If she couldn't, that was okay, too, just the satin, lacy underskirt would be fine.

Nearing the outer edge of Sagebrush, Rachel boldly reached over and slipped her hand in Trace's, interlacing their fingers and squeezing. Trace brought Rachel's fingers to her lips and kissed every one, only letting go of Rachel's hand when she absolutely had to.

Trace glanced around at the familiar scenery as she guided Moses down Main Street. Passing the barbershop, she observed the same four older gentlemen she always saw, sitting outside gossiping. If she didn't know such things had not been invented yet, she would have believed they were human-looking animatronics. The old boys sat in the same order, in the same relaxed, lazy positions, always seeming to stop speaking when she passed and all simultaneously nodding their heads, the only part of their body which seemed to move at all. It happened precisely in the same sequence every time she came to town.

Noticing what Trace was looking at, Rachel smirked, reaching up and ruffling the shaggy locks that hung below Trace's cowboy hat.

"Obviously, your hair has not seen a barber's shears in a while. You may need to stop in there before the wedding."

"Spare me. You can trim up my hair."

"Well...I used to cut my father's; I suppose I could cut yours."

"No supposing about it, I'm not setting one foot in there."

Moses plodded past the bustling entrance to the hotel where at least three people were having their luggage loaded onto the stagecoach. Trace shook her head. *A real, live stagecoach with gilt lettering on the side... Unbelievable.* She observed a few cowboys standing around talking, rolling cigarettes or spitting out disgustingly long streams of tobacco juice into the street in front of Wilbur's. Above them, leaning over the second floor railing and shouting down at the virile young men were at least three pleasure women from the bordello over the saloon. Cassandra wasn't among them, Trace noted, guessing that the voluptuous redhead must be entertaining the mayor since it was approximately dinner time.

The old horse moseyed past the deserted telegraph office and headed straight toward the small wood-constructed, whitewashed church. Trace looked over at Rachel, who was quietly studying her, and she had the sudden urge to lean over and kiss the blonde beside her, her heart rate picking up at the mere thought of it. But taking such public liberties, especially before they were married, would only lend credence to the popular rumor that she and Rachel had probably shared a bed already. Suddenly, without warning, a blush crawled up Rachel's face and she looked away, smiling.

Chuckling softly at Rachel's naughty grin, Trace adjusted her collar, wanting to undo the top button. She felt like she was being strangled. There had been a mild argument before they left the house when Rachel insisted Trace trade her sleeveless cotton workshirt and dungarees for go-to-meeting clothes. Trace was stubborn but finally compromised by donning one of Frank Young's not-so-freshly boiled, button-down white shirts and a clean pair of denim trousers that Rachel had taken in so that Trace no longer needed suspenders. Before they left home, sighing wistfully in obvious appreciation of Trace from head to toe, Rachel told Trace that she looked mighty handsome. And somewhat jittery. As they approached the church, she still felt uneasy.

Rachel watched Trace remove her hat and mop some sweat off her brow with a faded red bandana that had also been her father's. "Why, Trace, you're sweating like a whore going to election. There's no need to be nervous. Pastor Edwards is a very nice man."

"I am not nervous," Trace said nervously, as Moses slowed in front of the church.

Trace stepped into the seemingly unoccupied house of worship behind Rachel and looked around at the antiquated setting. It had an unexpected charm and character, and a warmth she was very surprised to be able to actually feel. She hoped the atmosphere reflected the attitude of the minister in charge of this multi-denominational church.

"Pastor Edwards?" Rachel called out, her voice reverberating around the empty chapel. "Trace, remove your hat," Rachel prompted in a low voice.

Trace took the hat off and twirled it in her hands. Rachel reached out, snatched the hat and held on to it, glancing up impatiently at Trace, who grinned sheepishly.

Rachel took another couple of steps forward into the main aisle that divided the ten rows of pews. "Hello? Pastor Edwards? It's Rachel Young."

There was still no answer as Trace moved up behind Rachel, suddenly getting the urge to whistle. So she did. Until she looked down into the exasperated green eyes of her fiancée. "What?"

"Good Lord, Trace, you act like you've never been in a church before!" Rachel scolded.

She was about to say she was surprised the sky hadn't fallen the instant she'd stepped over the threshold, when a middle-aged man appeared in a doorway off to the right. "Got *his* attention, didn't it?" Trace countered, her voice hushed.

"Hello?" He squinted, then, recognizing Rachel, he smiled affectionately. "Rachel! I'm so happy to see you. It's been a while." Meeting her halfway down the aisle, he took Rachel's hands, in a gentle, fatherly manner.

"Yes, sir, I know. I really have no excuse, other than it's been a bad couple of months at the ranch."

"I know. I've heard. The Lord forgives you, Rachel."

Peter Edwards' tone was appeasing, which irritated Trace, who was caught rolling her eyes by her annoyed bride-to-be.

Trace shrugged defensively and began focusing on other objects in the church — like the pulpit, the crucifix on the wall behind it, and the one small stained glass window above the cross...and, *Wow, nice use of exposed beams in the ceiling.* Which was obviously more necessity than fashion statement. A sudden poke in the ribs drew her attention back to a pair of curious and, as much as she hated to admit it, wise brown eyes.

"Pastor Edwards, I would like you to meet Trace Sheridan...the man I am going to marry."

A hand had begun to extend toward Trace and now was quickly withdrawn. "Marry?" Edwards tried his best not to glare at Trace before fastening his gaze at Rachel. "This is...abrupt. Why, I didn't even know anyone was courting you since Thomas passed on."

Rachel nodded. "Yes, I am sure it does seem quite sudden, but Trace has been courting me for a month now and, well, I don't want to wait. We're in love and we would like to be joined in holy matrimony as soon as you can arrange to do it."

Again, Edwards gave Trace a once over, then looked back at Rachel who had a determined set to her chin. "But, Rachel, I have never seen this man before. We don't know him. Does he understand...do you understand that marrying you might get him an audience with the Lord?"

It annoyed Trace enormously when people talked around her as if she was not even in the same room with them. "Uh, hello...I'm right here."

Linking her arm with Trace's, Rachel said, "I know him, Pastor Edwards. And I do not think that I could find anyone better suited to me." She winked reassuringly at Trace, who instantly calmed.

"I don't know, Rachel..." He suspiciously studied Trace. "How long have you been in Sagebrush, Mr. Sheridan?"

She suddenly felt like a specimen in a biology class. "About six weeks or so," she grudgingly answered,

"You got here a little over a month ago and you've been courting her for a month? You don't waste any time, do you? Where are you from?"

"Cottonwood."

"Never heard of it. Must be far from here."

"It is."

"Is Trace your full Christian name?"

"Trace is my name, yes." She knew how ministers liked to use the complete name of the individual they were addressing or speaking about, and she would be damned if anyone other than her mother would ever call her Tracey. Her middle name, Lee, was both masculine and feminine, so that wouldn't have been a problem, but she wasn't going to volunteer that, either. Someone calling her Tracey Lee would take her back to being seven years old, when she'd flushed her mother's cigarettes down the toilet and Zelda repeated the name over and over as her little behind got whaled on. Whenever she heard "Tracey Lee!" she knew she was in trouble. She did not need that reminder here.

"Where is your family?"

"All I had was my mother and she's gone now." A tiny stab of pain seared through her heart at realizing that might very well be the truth. "I left there because I had no more reason to stay and I ended up here."

"What is it that you do?"

"Currently, or as a trade?"

"Both."

"I am a ranch hand, as of the last month, but before that I was a...well...kind of like a deputy sheriff."

Edwards eyes widened. "A sheriff?" He was clearly shocked. "A sheriff..." He said it again, as though trying to digest the idea. "Like Ed Jackson?"

"I was nothing like Ed Jackson," Trace responded evenly. But that was a lie. She had been exactly like Sheriff Jackson...only more corrupt and better at it.

A broad smile bloomed on the preacher's face and he let loose a boisterous guffaw that startled both Rachel and Trace. "Rachel, you have made my day! You're going to marry someone who used to be a lawman! That will certainly ruffle a few Crane feathers. I cannot wait to see the look on Benjamin's face when he returns from Dodge City and you are no longer available to him."

"I was never available to him, sir," Rachel replied, respectful but indignant.

"I know that, Rachel," Edwards said kindly. "Diabolic intent runs through the blood of those Cranes, especially Benjamin. Don't think for one second I ever believed any of those sinful stories Benjamin was spreading about you. But he is going to be madder than a flea without a dog when he gets back here and finds you married." His tone of voice was quite tickled as he looked at Trace. "And to someone he cannot immediately get a rise out of, I would suspect."

"No, sir, I am not easily intimidated."

"That's good, son. You're going to need a backbone to face down this man — and I use that word loosely. You're also going to need eyes in the back of your head, because these Cranes are sneaky and not honorable. You sure you're up to that?"

"Yes, sir. I want to marry Rachel and I will be privileged to take on all the responsibility that goes with it," Trace told him with sincerity.

The reverend smiled at Trace, eyes twinkling mischievously and clamped a big hand on Trace's shoulder. "And all the glory, too, I suspect," he chuckled, winking at Rachel.

"Pastor Edwards!" Rachel's cheeks burned with embarrassment.

Joining the minister in laughter, Trace decided she liked this man. His slightly off-color insinuation was not accompanied by any kind of leer or vulgar innuendo. It was more like he was just stating an obvious fact. Even as aghast as Rachel was at the pastor's implication, she could not stop herself from smiling through her moral indignation, even if she still exhibited a mortified blush. "It's a guy thing," Trace appeased, hoping she'd never have to say that again.

"Well, come on back to the parsonage and let's talk about getting you two hitched. Mrs. Edwards was just baking some raisin bread when I left. We can enjoy that and some tea while we go over the details. I'll let Henry over at the mayor's office know that you two will be stopping by later."

"Who's Henry?"

"He's the county circuit clerk," Rachel said, as they followed Edwards out of the church.

"And the town crier," Edwards added.

Rachel nodded. "Worse than Joseph Turner."

"Oh, my yes," Edwards agreed. "I don't know who you have or haven't told, but once Henry knows, everybody will know." Nodding in amusement, the minister turned to Trace. "If you know what you're up against and still want to marry this woman, you've got a spine, boy. My hat is off to you. Maybe there's hope for this town yet."

During a nice visit with Pastor and Mrs. Edwards, Trace had to literally choke down every bite of the dry-as-a-bone raisin bread with several gulps, requiring several refills, of tea. She could not wait to get to Wilbur's Saloon for a mug of ale.

They agreed on a small wedding to be performed on the upcoming Wednesday evening, which was only two days away. In private, Trace had to convince the amiable reverend that she had not yet had relations with Rachel, and therefore had not caused Rachel to be in a family way, and that the reason for the hasty ceremony was that Rachel wanted to be married and settled before the Cranes returned from their drive, and Trace wanted to get married quickly because, well, you know, wink, wink, nudge, nudge. Edwards bought it.

Trace had not lied and hopefully this baby would not be born early, because it was going to be suspicious enough when Rachel delivered well before nine months from Wednesday night. She knew people always counted. They would attempt to persuade everyone that the full-term, full-size infant was really premature.

Trace walked Rachel to Ledbetter's dress shop. She wanted desperately to lean over and kiss her senseless, and from Rachel's expression the feeling was mutual. They stood on the boardwalk letting life pass them by unnoticed, until a customer emerged from the store and snapped them out of their connected daydream. Sighing, Rachel stepped back, turned, and disappeared inside the shop.

Trace moved on to the goldsmith's, where he measured her finger. When Trace told him to keep the gold extracted from the band and paid him a twenty-five cent piece as a good faith tip besides, he promised to have the ring ready in about two hours.

She strolled to the mercantile where she found that only half of her order had come in and if she wanted the rest, she would have to go to Jefferson City to get it herself. The man who usually drove the wagon with supplies once a week had two lame mules. Trace knew it was useless to get angry; a man certainly couldn't do much about lame mules, other than let them heal. She considered how soon she would need the other half of her order and debated whether it could wait. She decided she would rather have it all before she began the project she had in mind. It looked like she would be taking a trip to Jefferson City.

The idea of Rachel being alone at the ranch all night long did not sit well with Trace, especially with the shitstorm their marriage was going to create. The newlyweds-to-be were upping the stakes and would have to be extra vigilant. She wondered if Rachel would like to go with her, spend the night, and then come back.

Looking up, she met the curious eyes of Isaac Tipping.

"What can I do for you, Isaac?" Trace asked, more politely than she felt.

"Need some help loading that?"

Trace stopped and studied him. He appeared straightforward. "Sure. But don't get cut. Those edges there will draw blood if you're not careful."

Isaac nodded and cautiously picked up a coil and placed it onto the back of the wagon. "What is this stuff?"

"Barbed wire."

"What do you do with it?"

Again, Trace scrutinized the young man. Was he asking out of curiosity or was he scouting again, doing dirty work for the Cranes? His arm had obviously mended, as he had no problem lifting and moving. Had she really changed his mind about a life of crime or did he just agree with her to pacify her? She might as well tell him; it would probably be all over town by the time they got back to the Triple Y anyway. "It's a fence."

"A fence?" He stopped loading and looked intently at the mass of spiky wire curled in circles and tied with strings of hemp. "Miss Rachel already has a fence on the property."

"Yes, she does...a fence that doesn't seem to mean diddly to a certain family."

Isaac cracked a smile. "Diddly?" He shook his head. "I've never heard that word before. I like it." He continued loading. "So, you gonna put this up to stop them?"

"Well...it sure as hell will surprise them. At the very least, slow them down."

"Uh...Mr. Sheridan?"

"Yes?"

"I was inside when Mr. Taylor told you that only half your fence was here. I have to go into Jefferson City on Thursday to pick up some staples and supplies for my father. If you'd like, I could pick up the rest of your fence and bring it back for you. I could even bring it out to the ranch, if you want."

"Why would you want to do that?"

He hung his head. "I did a bad thing, and I sure would like to make up for it. Now maybe I ain't right in the head, but I think I would rather be on your side than do anything again for them awful Cranes." He looked back up at Trace. "If you'll let me, I want to help you fight them."

Even though he seemed sincere, Trace hesitated. "That will be dangerous, Isaac. I don't think your father would approve."

"I'm all growed up and haired over, Mr. Sheridan, I been a man for almost a year now, even had myself a painted lady on my last birthday," he said indignantly. "Did her up right nice, too."

"That's just a little too much information, Isaac."

"I don't need my father's permission to do anything. I'm trying to save my father and my mama and the store. You're the only one willing to help me do that. So, you tell me what needs doin' and I'll do it."

Trace looked him over again. He was shorter than she was, hadn't really filled out yet but...she could work with him, get him in shape. An army gets built one person at a time. "Okay, Isaac. Tell you what...I'd appreciate it very much if you picked up my order in Jefferson City. When you get back, we'll talk about how we're going to fight these Cranes, okay?"

"Really?" His voice cracked, causing him to curse under his breath but he recovered quickly.

"Really. Wouldn't say it if I didn't mean it."

"Thank you, Mr. Sheridan."

Isaac thrust his hand forward and Trace shook it, almost laughing at his enthusiasm. He returned to loading the barbed wire with a fervent energy he hadn't displayed before.

"Call me Trace, okay? If we're going to work together, you can't be calling me Mr. Sheridan all the time."

He nodded. "All right, Trace."

"And Isaac?"

"Yes, Trace?"

"Have you ever been a best man before?"

"Married!" Molly Ledbetter bellowed. "Who are you marrying? That drifter ranch hand? You said that was the last thing that would happen between the two of you."

Rachel beamed. "That would be the one."

Molly held Rachel out at arm's length and looked her over from head to heels. "Rachel Frances Young...you are radiant. I do believe you have fallen in love."

"Yes, ma'am, I do believe I have. I've never felt like this before, not even with Tommy, and I cannot wait to marry Trace," Rachel said dreamily.

"When's the wedding?"

"Wednesday evening. Pastor Edwards will be presiding."

Molly dropped her hands to her sides. She looked skeptical, almost disappointed. "That's right quick, Rachel...any reason for that?"

"I know what you're asking, Miz Ledbetter, and I have not had Trace Sheridan in my bed. He has been nothing but a gentleman. We're waiting for the wedding night."

Molly sighed with relief. "I believe you, girl, I just had to ask. Why so soon then?"

"Just want to be all settled in as a wife before the Cranes get back."

"You know Ben's heart will be black with jealousy."

"Then that's just something Ben's going to have to find peace with."

"You'll be more likely to see angels fly out of his behind," Molly commented dryly. "That young man you're marrying, does he have a notion as to what he's getting himself into?"

"Yes, ma'am, he's aware and he'll be ready for it all."

"Think about it. You already lost one man to an untimely bullet, you don't need to be a widow on top of it."

Rachel followed Molly to her counter, knowing she was fretting about her like her mama would have. "I deserve to be happy, Miz Ledbetter. I deserve more choices than Ben Crane or spinsterhood. Trace Sheridan is the only one to come along who isn't afraid of the Cranes."

"He crazy?"

"No. He's just sure of himself."

Molly laughed ruefully. "Being too sure of yourself can be deadly in Crane territory. Let's hope he won't be joining the other ones, who were too sure of themselves, in the Almighty's Kingdom." She turned around to see Rachel pouting. "Now, Rachel, I'm not trying to be downhearted; I just don't want to see you go through this again."

"I don't want it to happen, either, surely I do not, and with Trace, I don't think it will. No disrespect, Miz Ledbetter, but I would like you to help fit me into something I can get married in, so could we not talk about me choosing a mourning dress before you alter my wedding dress?"

Molly pulled her into a warm hug. "You're right. I am sorry. Here you come to me with this wonderful news and all I can do is be discouraging. I do apologize, Rachel. You are all I have left of your mama and I just want what's best for you." Taking Rachel's hand, she tugged her toward a fitting room. "Now, let's see what we can do for you."

Chapter Sixteen

Trace was finally able to get to Wilbur's. She was beginning to really like the place, the atmosphere being a combination of folly and unpretentious raunch. She was happy that she had been accepted into the fold, for the most part, held in rather high, if silent, esteem for standing up to Sheriff Jackson, and becoming known for her generosity with gratuities for the bartender.

There was a reason for her tipping. Bartenders always had their fingers on the pulse of life that circulated through their realm. Trace learned quickly that Silas was the go-to guy in town for information and deals. The more benevolent she was with the affable barkeep, the more she could count on him feeling obligated to help her out. And she knew he genuinely liked her, so that helped. She also knew that he had to trust her implicitly to assist her in doing anything that would defy the Crane empire. She smiled to herself. *Yep. An army, one person at a time.*

Trace stepped confidently through the hinged half-doors. There was an animal strength about her, an almost feline grace in the way she moved that was hard to ignore. She scanned the saloon for familiar faces, friendly and hostile alike, and unfamiliar individuals who might be up to no good. As she did not know who was owned by the Cranes and who wasn't, she had to depend on Silas and her own sixth sense to tell her when someone might have a desire to cause her problems. Trace expected trouble and did not want to be blindsided.

Trace moved to the bar where a grinning Silas Boone already had a full mug of ale waiting for her. She noticed a table of Native Americans in the corner by the staircase. She wasn't sure whether or not that was unusual, but no one in the bar seemed to pay any extra attention to the four men dressed in pullover shirts that looked to be made of deerskin, leggings bordered with what she hoped was horsehair, and knee-high rawhide-soled moccasins. Three of the Indians wore their long, jet-black hair tied back away from their faces, and one, who appeared to be considerably younger than the others, let his silken dark mane flow freely. They were all watching Trace with more interest than menace and that intrigued her. Did they also think she shared a partial heritage with them?

Trace slapped a couple of dollars on the bar. "Silas, a drink for everyone on me. I'm getting married." A sudden stillness enveloped the saloon. She wondered if that had more to do with her impending nuptials or free booze.

"Married? You and Rachel?" The silence seemed to be balancing on Trace's response.

"Yes, sir, and I consider myself a lucky man." Trace turned around to face the other patrons. "Anybody have a problem with that?" Her tone wasn't so much defiant as it was clarification of who was okay with the news and who wasn't. Trace wanted to know just what she was up against and wanted to memorize the faces of the men who didn't seem agreeable to her union.

"Trace," Matthew Reddick spoke up, shattering the breathless quiet, "as long as you keep the bug juice flowing, you can marry Silas if you want."

Laughter filled the room, but not from Silas, who wasn't sure whether he should laugh or not.

"Trust me when I say this, Matthew: Silas just isn't my type." That was followed by another round of snickers, this time with Silas joining in. As Trace studied every man carefully, she saw no one who appeared to object, even by expression. Nodding triumphantly, she turned to face Silas. In a hushed voice, she asked, "Whatcha got for me?"

Leaning in, the bartender inclined his head toward the table of four who had caught Trace's attention when she walked in. "I don't know how you feel about dealing with Injuns..."

"I have no problem dealing with anyone as long as they don't cheat me."

"These boys won't do that. I've dealt with them before. Injuns are notional. They act on the moment if they think somethin' works in their favor. And these boys don't want no trouble with the white man if they can help it. Treat them fairly and they'll respect you. Do them dirty and they'll get revenge one way or another. They may be peaceful now but I don't think it would take but the weight of a pup's turd to turn them back into savages."

"No one likes to be taken advantage of, Silas. I'm sure they've had their fill of it. If they did get savage, I'm sure they'd have every right to do so."

Silas shook his head. "They're gonna like doing business with you."

"I hope so." She took a sip of her beer. "What do they think of the Cranes?"

"They think the whole bunch is lower than a snake's belly."

Trace's grin was sly. "Oh, really?" She raised an eyebrow in amusement. "Very good to know."

After the quartet finished their second shot of whiskey, compliments of Trace, they rose from the table and left the saloon, nodding to Silas on their way out.

"Where are they going?" Trace asked, a little surprised that they had not even acknowledged her.

"Simmer down there, cowboy. They just wanted to get a good look at you. Buying them whiskey was a good idea, too. It'll make them much more willing to barter with you." Looking into questioning blue eyes, he said, "Don't worry. Your deal is as good as set. They'll find you."

Rachel pushed back the curtain of the dressing room and stepped out into the store to the anticipatory gaze of Molly Ledbetter. The admiring look on the older woman's face told Rachel the dress was perfect. In fact, she was sure she saw a tear on Molly's cheek. She cocked her head inquisitively. "What?"

"Oh, Rachel," Molly said, folding her hands together, "you will be the most exquisite bride. If only your mama and daddy could be here to see you."

"Does it really look good?" Rachel slowly spun around.

Molly had pinned a lacy, satin ecru petticoat beneath the dress and strips of pale beige velvet that she would sew into the cuffs and collar. She had tried to talk Rachel into wearing a fitted bone bodice but Rachel declined. She persuaded Rachel not to go with the sweetheart neckline, and opted to remove just the high collar so as to leave it respectable. After all, people would be talking enough about the abrupt ceremony, Molly told Rachel, she would not need to give them anything more to go speculating about.

"Just a full crinoline underskirt and it should be all you need to make it befitting the beautiful woman you have become." She smiled warmly at Rachel. "But, Rachel, I declare you could wear a sackcloth and make it look pretty. Now you go take that off before your intended bursts through that door and sees you. That's bad luck, you know."

"Yes, ma'am, I know." Rachel looked at herself in the full-length mirror before stepping back into the dressing room to change. She was glowing and happy and in love. Just the way a bride and expectant mother should be.

"I hope this young man is worthy of you, child," Molly said, as Rachel gingerly removed the garment.

Rachel did not want to dislodge the pinning or get poked by one of the sharp little varmints, either. "The way this town talks, and you haven't heard anything about Trace?"

"Oh, I've heard things...I just wasn't sure whether or not I should listen to them."

Rachel's curiosity got the better of her. "Like what?"

"That he is a restless soul with a gambler's appetite for trouble. It scares me a little, Rachel, because you really don't know anything about him."

"I know he would hammer down the gates of Hell for me. I know he will love me and protect me and do his best to keep the Cranes away from my...our land."

"That's another thing. He marries you and he takes over your entire spread. You sure that's not all he's after?"

"I couldn't be more positive." Rachel emerged from the dressing room and handed the garment to Molly. "Are you sure it's not expecting too much to have that done by Wednesday?"

"Child, I will make the time to finish this. You're like my own flesh and blood getting married. I am invited to the wedding, aren't I?"

Shyly, Rachel clasped her hands in front of her and swung slightly back and forth. "I need a witness, Miz Ledbetter. Would you be my matron of honor?"

Molly stopped dead in her tracks. "You don't want an old thing like me to stand up for you, girl. I'm sure Elizabeth Reddick would be pleased to do it."

"But I don't want Elizabeth, I want you."

Tears stung Molly's eyes for the second time that afternoon. She reached out, taking Rachel's hands in her own. "I would be honored."

By the time Trace went to pick up Rachel, she had won four dollars at stud poker, arranged a bachelor party Tuesday night at Wilbur's, bought a couple more rounds of drinks, picked up the wedding band at the goldsmith's, and met with the Indians in the alley next to the livery.

Through them, she could purchase a herd of cattle. They were the only available resource that wasn't controlled by the Cranes. She could get fifteen prime cows and steers for fifty dollars a head. Although she could afford the full seven hundred and fifty dollars, that would deplete her resources, so instead she gave them one hundred ninety dollars in cash, the rest to be handed over when the cattle arrived, and bartered the use of the ranch land for planting and hunting for the balance of the cost.

The land the tribe inhabited was mostly dirt and rock and not good for growing much of anything. The Indians would be allowed to hunt on the Young property and have access to wood from the dense forest. Trace also promised them a quarter of the yield from the corn field she intended to plant the next week. The solemn foursome considered it a good deal. They shook hands on it and Trace walked away hoping if she ever needed them as warriors and allies, they would be there for her. If they despised the Cranes as much as most of the town did, their skills would come in very handy indeed if the rebellion she could see slowly growing became a reality.

Trace walked into Molly's to collect her fiancée and was not surprised to find Rachel and the kindly proprietor having tea. Trace's heart swelled at the absolutely adoring expression on Rachel's face when she spotted her. Rachel jumped up and flew into her arms, hugged her fiercely, then led her back to the small table where she had been seated.

"Molly, I'd like you to meet the man I'm going to marry, Trace Sheridan. Trace, Molly Ledbetter, my mama's best friend in the whole wide world."

If Molly had any questions about whether or not these two young people loved each other, they were answered. The betrothed couple could have heated the store with their obvious affection.

"My goodness, you are a handsome devil, aren't you?" Molly remarked, scrutinizing every inch of Trace's face. She stood up, her full height coming to Trace's shoulder. "Just promise me one thing."

"What's that?"

"That little gal you're holding is very special to me. She's had a lot of awful things happen to her the past year or so. Don't you become one of them."

"No, ma'am, I do not intend to." Trace's gaze was steady. "I promise you right here, right now that I'll die before I let anything bad happen to her. And I don't have plans to die any time soon." She gave Rachel's shoulder an extra squeeze.

"Amen," Rachel responded.

Molly's eyes softened. "You have my blessing. Not that you asked for it, or need it, but I approve. And, Rachel, I think your mama and daddy would have, too. Looks like you got yourself one hell of a stallion here."

As images of just exactly what that meant filtered into her brain, Rachel blushed and smiled coyly. "Me, too." She looked up into Trace's eyes. "Guess I'll be finding out soon enough."

Now it was Trace's turn to be embarrassed. She had no doubt she could live up to the label, but it was a tad uncomfortable mulling it over in the presence of a woman old enough to be her mother. Clearing her throat, Trace said, "We need to get going before — what's his name, Henry? — before he goes home for the day."

"Oh, that's right, you have to register with Henry," Molly shook her head. "Hope you weren't expecting to keep this quiet. That weaselly garter-sleeved puke just has to put his eagle-beaked nose into everybody's business. He's just damned unpleasant. Why, he is so ugly, it'll hurt your feelings just to look at him."

"Miz Ledbetter, that's not very nice," Rachel said, then lightly slapped Trace in the arm for laughing. "Henry can't help his looks; he has to make do with what the good Lord gave him."

"Well, the good Lord must've had it out for that boy because his personality matches his face and there just ain't no quit in ugly." Molly picked up the cups from the table and put them on the counter. "You two get going, get your registering done. Don't hold that hedgehog up or you'll never hear the end of it."

Rachel left Trace's side long enough to embrace Molly. "Thank you, Miz Ledbetter. I'll be back Tuesday night for the dress."

"Now don't you worry, girl, that dress will be perfect. Just like you."

"How much do I owe you for the alterations, so I'll know what to bring with me?"

"The only thing I want from you, Rachel, is to give me some babies to spoil."

Trace and Rachel exchanged a knowing glance. "We'll start working on that Wednesday night," Trace said, winking at her bride-to-be.

It was an almost perfect day. Almost. As Trace settled Rachel on the wagon seat, she was approached by Sheriff Ed Jackson and Mayor Jed Turner. Jackson looked smug; His Honor looked uneasy. They stopped a few feet away from Trace.

"Well, well, well, I hear congratulations are in order." Jackson's tone conveyed that the last thing he felt was benevolence.

"If you are referring to my upcoming marriage, then yes," Trace said, not friendly at all. After the trouble Jackson had already caused, she didn't feel the inclination to be "right neighborly" toward him. She nodded to Turner. "Afternoon, Mayor."

"Trace," Jed said, looking as though he wished he were anywhere but there.

"Actually, I was referrin' to knowin' that you'll be in my jail before you have a chance to walk down that aisle."

Trace handed the reins to Rachel, then turned and nonchalantly leaned against the wagon, studying the sheriff. "And why would that be?"

"Trace," Mayor Turner spoke up, clearing his throat uncomfortably, "Ed here got a telegram from Cottonwood. Said there's a five thousand dollar price on your head."

"What!" Rachel was stunned.

Trace shook her head at Rachel, putting her hand up to stem any further frantic reaction. "He's lying."

Jackson sneered. "Is that so?"

"Yeah, that's so," Trace shot back, trying to keep her cool. She wanted to tell this bastard that if there even was a Cottonwood, she wasn't from there, had never been there, so there was no way there could be a bounty on her. "I'd like to see this telegram."

"You don't need to see it. Who do you think you are, challenging me? I'm the law around here, son, and if I say it's so then it's so, and you just need to take my word for it!" Jackson yelled, obviously thinking the elevation in his voice would emphasize his authority.

Trace burst out laughing, riling the sheriff to the point of veins bulging in his neck. "You can't be serious. Take your word for it? Does anyone actually fall for that?"

"Damn you, Sheridan, I'm the sheriff and if I say it's so, then it's so!"

"Mayor? Have you seen this alleged telegram?" Trace focused on Jed.

"Well, no. Ed just came and got me and told me about it and said we needed to arrest you before you left town."

Trace beckoned the mayor over to the side, out of hearing range of Jackson, who appeared to be close to hyperventilating, and addressed Turner in a hushed voice. "Mayor, you know the sheriff has it out for me. You know the sheriff is stuck up the Cranes' asses and is pissing his pants to think that Ben is going to come back to town and find Rachel married and he couldn't do anything to stop it. There is no telegram, there is no price on my head, and I give you my word that I will not leave town. When that moron produces a legitimate telegram from..." She had to think up a name quickly. Looking up she saw the silver gilted spheres of the pawn shop. "...a telegram from Marshal Silvers saying that there is, then and only then will I surrender to that piece of shit wearing a badge."

Nodding, Jed turned to Jackson. "Ed?"

"Yeah?"

"Who sent you that telegram from Cottonwood?"

"What?" This question clearly surprised him, if the tone of his voice was any indication.

"You hard of hearin'? I said, who sent you that telegram? What's the damned sheriff's name?"

Too much hesitancy confirmed the mayor's suspicion, cleared Trace, and infuriated the devious sheriff, who was caught in his lie. "Uh..." Jackson had obviously not expected to be questioned.

"Thank you." Trace smiled triumphantly, hauling herself up to the seat beside Rachel. "You boys have a nice day." With that, she snapped the reins and Moses started clomping forward. Rachel proudly linked her arm with her fiancée's and smiled sweetly at both men.

They weren't even a wagon's length away when they heard the mayor turn on the sheriff. "You horse's ass! What the hell ails you? Maybe you want to make a blasted idjit out of yerself in front of that Sheridan feller, but I sure as hell do not!"

"B-but Jed...you know what will happen when Jacob and his boys come back and Rachel is married. I'm trying to do that boy a favor."

"You're trying to save your own crooked hide, you imbecile. Next time, don't bother me, 'less you got proof. I'm fed up to here with your horseshit."

"Trace? I know you knew that Ed was lying because you would obviously know if there was or wasn't a bounty out for you, but how did you know how to trap Ed like that?" They were well beyond the outskirts of the main street.

"Because he thinks he's smarter than everyone else, and those he isn't smarter than are intimidated by his connection to the Cranes."

"You do know that he'll probably show up at the wedding and object."

"On what grounds?"

"He won't need any. He's Ed Jackson."

"Oh? Well, we'll just see about that."

Rachel decided not to question whatever Trace had up her sleeve. Trace had not steered her wrong yet and Rachel fully believed that Trace would not let anything disrupt their special day. Leaning her head against Trace's shoulder, Rachel closed her eyes, dreaming about Wednesday night.

"Rach?"

"Uh huh?"

"I asked Isaac Tipping to be my best man."

Opening her eyes, Rachel looked up at Trace. "Really?"

"Well...I don't really know anyone that well and Isaac seems to be a good kid. Plus, he wants to help around the ranch a little bit."

"Doing what?"

Trace chewed on her lip, her tone cautious. "Helping me fix up the fence."

"I thought the fence was all fixed."

"It is. We're going to reinforce it." At Rachel's confused expression, Trace explained, "I bought barbed wire."

"Barbed wire? Wh—"

"Some of the order is in the back," Rachel turned around to look, "and Isaac is going to pick up the rest on Thursday, then help me put it up."

Rachel's expression was inquisitive rather than suspicious. "When did you decide this?"

"A little over two weeks ago. Rachel, the land needs protection and we can't be everywhere at once. With barbed wire wrapped around the fence, no one will be able to just crash through, not without causing damage to their herd or their horses. And if they want to deliberately knock it down then that will make them extra work and a project they will not be able to complete without me noticing."

"You've thought a lot about this." Again, it was an acknowledgment rather than a question.

"Yes. If we're going to take a stand, we need to start now, before the Cranes get back. I want everyone to know we mean business. And Rachel...I think I can turn people in this town around, I really do."

"What do you mean?"

"I mean...it sounds like everybody is damned tired of being run by the Cranes. I think all they need is a little incentive to make it stop."

"And you think you can be that incentive?"

She looked at Rachel and smiled reassuringly at her. "I know I can."

Rachel wanted to believe that was true, but since Trace had never dealt with the Cranes, Rachel felt she had a reason to be skeptical, and very afraid. Time would definitely tell.

Chapter Seventeen

The next day, Tuesday, both women had a full day ahead of them. The morning began with a kiss, an affectionate embrace, and a big breakfast. Trace observed with loving amusement that Rachel could not contain her building excitement at their approaching wedding. So much to be done, so little time in which to do it.

The first order of business, in which Trace impatiently indulged Rachel, was to fit into Frank Young's wedding trousers with the satin pinstripe running the length of the outer seams at the waist and an inch at each inseam. While Rachel pinned the black cotton slacks, Trace stood fidgeting. Once the fitting was done and she stepped out of the pants, she pulled on work clothes and went out to get on with her daily chores and then start on the fence repair.

Trace came bouncing back into the house, around noon, with an announcement. She found Rachel in her bedroom, hanging up the wedding trousers. Practically gushing, she said, "Guess what? We're the proud grandparents of five baby bunnies. They're so cute." She grabbed Rachel's hand and led her out to the stable, where they stopped at the cages containing the adult rabbits and the furry, squirming newborns.

Rachel could not help smiling. "Yes, they are adorable. And so are you, you big, tough softie," she teased. "Just don't get too fond of them. Soon enough those tiny critters will have grown and will be on your dinner plate."

Sighing, shoulders slumping, Trace said, "I was hoping if you came out here and actually looked at how precious they are, you might reconsider that option."

"I've seen baby bunnies before, Trace." She rubbed Trace's back in empathy. "I do agree that they're precious, but they aren't pets. They're food."

The very idea of it horrified her. "I don't see how you can look at something that cute and still butcher it."

Curling her fingers around Trace's, Rachel slowly pulled her back toward the house. "I just don't think about it," she said quietly. "Come on, you have some clothes to try on."

Trace followed Rachel into the downstairs bedroom where she tried on the pants. They weren't perfect but fit well enough to complement Trace's tall stature. Thanking Rachel with a kiss that neither woman wanted to end, Trace reluctantly went outside and hitched Moses to the wagon, loaded tools into the back, and drove out to the property line that had been the hardest hit by the Crane's outbound cattle drive.

She carefully affixed the barbed wire to the wooden posts; the resulting barrier looking ominous. Trace had completed about fifty feet of fence when she heard the unmistakable sound of hoofbeats drawing nearer. She smiled when she recognized Isaac Tipping on a gorgeous, well-muscled, Arabian.

"Hey, Trace," Isaac greeted.

"Hey, yourself, Isaac."

Openly admiring Trace's handiwork, the teenager grinned. "So this is how you do it, huh?"

"Yep." Trace sighed, glad to be able to take a break. "When you bring me the rest, I'll put you to work. But you'll need some good strong gloves and tools like these." She indicated the implements at her feet.

"I can get them from the store. Trace?"

"Yes?"

"I'm invited to your gatherin' tonight at Wilbur's, ain't I? I mean, bein' your best man and all."

"You allowed to be in Wilbur's?"

"Hell, yeah," he said indignantly.

"Then I would be proud to have you there, best man." Needing to return to the house and take a shower before going into town for her bachelor party, she loaded everything back onto the wagon. "Isaac, I have a favor to ask of you."

"Anythin', Trace, you just name it."

"Don't be so quick to agree. It will involve you not coming to my party."

Isaac's shoulder's sagged. "What is it?"

"Matthew is going to bring Mrs. Reddick by here this evening to keep Rachel company while we're in town. Now you know the sheriff doesn't like me and I don't trust him and, since he is not invited to the celebration tonight, I want to make sure he doesn't come poking around here, bothering the ladies. When I go to town, I'll have a five gallon can of eggnog spiked with two quarts of whiskey. If you meet me by the gate, I'll make sure you have some of that if you'll find a place to keep yourself hidden and keep an eye on the women. It's a big responsibility and there aren't too many I can trust to do it."

"What would you want me to do, just watch the house?"

"Yes. And if Ed Jackson, or anyone you recognize to be associated with the Crane clan comes anywhere near the house, I want you to ride into town as fast as you can and get me. Think you could do that for me?"

He shrugged, weighing his options out loud. "Hell, eggnog and whiskey? That'll sure beat the flat ale Silas would serve me. Although I won't get to see Cassandra do her harlot dance for you..."

Harlot dance? Trace hadn't thought of that. "I'm sure you'll have plenty more opportunities for that," Trace assured him. What she was asking of him was a very grown-up responsibility and she hoped he would feel honored and proud that she'd trust him to do this. It would give him the chance to start proving himself to her.

As though he was thinking the exact same thing, Isaac's chest suddenly puffed out. "Yup. I could do that for ya."

"Great, thanks, I appreciate it."

They agreed on a time to meet and shook on it, and Trace climbed on the wagon and turned it toward home.

Before Trace took her shower, Rachel insisted on trimming her hair. Trace was initially apprehensive about it, but realized Rachel couldn't do a worse job than she assumed she'd done on herself, whenever that had been. She couldn't even remember chopping off the hair that had hung down to the middle of her back. She immediately forgot about the haircut when Rachel stood in front of her, concentrating on the top of her head, standing between Trace's open legs to be able to reach.

The part of Trace's hound-dog nature that controlled her libido in the past, reared its head as her face was eye level with Rachel's breasts. Thankfully, Rachel could not see the lustful grin Trace displayed as she gazed longingly, just imagining their look, their feel. *Just one more day, Trace*, she told herself. *Just one more day...*

Taking a cold shower, something she was getting used to, Trace considered that her next invention would be to figure out how to heat the water. She dried off and dressed in brown linen trousers and a beige button-down shirt with dark brown stripes. Due to Isaac's unintentional warning about Cassandra possibly getting closer to her than she would really like, she rolled up a pair of socks and stuck it in her underpants. It looked and felt ridiculous, but after some adjusting, Trace was sure it would serve its purpose should she accidentally, or intentionally, get cupped by the prostitute. Reflexes would be able to get Cassandra's experienced hands away before she had a chance to explore.

Brushing her hair, she decided she liked the trim Rachel had given her, still longish and full but not unkempt. She had gotten used to the shorter hair, just like she had started to get used to her body hair growing wild. After all, she was pretending to be a man and men didn't shave legs and underarms. She had to admit it was a little awkward at first, especially wearing sleeveless shirts, but it certainly helped with the illusion. Tomorrow, though, she would be clean-shaven, smooth for her bride, for her wedding night. Just thinking about that prompted Trace to give herself another splash of cold water.

While Trace was showering and dressing, Rachel prepared the eggnog and whiskey concoction, which would be Trace's contribution to the gathering at Wilbur's. Since Silas couldn't close the saloon and Trace didn't want to be paying for drinks for cowboys who weren't a part of the celebration, they agreed on the spiked beverage as a compromise. If the small group of men wanted anything else, they could buy it themselves. It was the best they could do with an event planned on such short notice.

Descending from the loft, Trace approached her bride-to-be, whose eyes roved over her with hungry appreciation. "My...don't you look...just good enough to eat."

Trace chuckled. "You've got to stop saying stuff like that." She stepped closer to Rachel and took her in her arms.

"Why? You want me to admire you, don't you?"

"Oh, absolutely. It's just...you don't realize the meaning of your words sometimes."

Rachel cocked her head. "My meaning, or how you interpret my words?"

Good point, Trace thought. She knew Rachel would not comprehend the vulgarity of her interpretation and she was not about to introduce her to that aspect of her personality...at least not yet. She preferred Rachel in her pristine state of mind. The idea of Rachel knowing as much as she did about the vile side of human nature was distressing. For Rachel to maintain her inviolate oulook after everything that had happened to her showed Trace just what kind of woman she was dealing with; she didn't want her to change. She enveloped Rachel tightly in her arms and kissed her forehead, then her cheek, then her lips, lingering there, not pressing for anything more.

Trace broke the kiss and smiled at Rachel, who kept her lips pursed, eyes closed, and face angled up, waiting expectantly for another kiss. When Trace obliged with only a peck, Rachel blinked at her. "That's it?"

"For now. Elizabeth and Matthew are due here any minute and I'm not about to start something I can't finish."

"Big talker," Rachel teased. "You better be able to back those words up tomorrow night..."

"Don't you worry your pretty little head about that, Miz Rachel," Trace said with a knowing smirk that made Rachel shiver. "I don't think you'll have any complaints."

"Pretty sure of yourself, aren't you?"

Trace shrugged and held Rachel tighter. "Guess you'll just have to wait and see." She felt Rachel stiffen a little in her arms and heard her breath catch.

"Trace…" Rachel's voice was hesitant. "What's that?"

Instantly knowing what Rachel was feeling against her belly, Trace released her, shoving her hands into her pockets, trying to extend the material of her pants outward to hide the shape of the socks. She rocked back and forth from her heels to the balls of her feet like a little kid who'd been caught in a tough-to-explain situation. "Uh…Insurance?"

Rachel stared at Trace's crotch, seeing a slight bulge where there shouldn't have been one. "Insurance? Insurance for what?"

The sound of a creaking wagon pulling up to the house interrupted their conversation. "Oh, my, look at that, the Reddicks are here," Trace said with relief, escaping into the kitchen for the container of eggnog.

Reluctantly taking her eyes off Trace, Rachel stepped out onto the porch to greet the Reddicks.

Matthew Reddick entered the house just as Trace lifted the can of the whiskey-laced potable. "Here, let me help you with that."

"No, I've got it. Just make sure my way is clear to the back of the wagon." And with that, they flew by the two women, who backed away from the door to let them through.

"Oh, my," Elizabeth murmured, watching Trace. "Got yourself a strong one, don't you? And good looking, too."

Rachel smiled at the compliment, the adoration on her face and in her body language apparent. "Yes, I think I got mighty lucky."

The women walked inside the house, while Trace and Matthew situated the can on the wagon. "Sure you want to do this, Trace?" Matthew asked.

"Do what? Go to town and have a good time?"

"No, get married." Matthew grinned. "Your life won't ever be the same."

Looking toward the doorway, Trace sighed. "I hope that's true, Matthew. I hope that's true."

They met up with Isaac as they were leaving. Trace filled the boy's pint flask like she had promised and then they parted ways.

"How come Isaac won't be at your stag session?" Matthew asked in surprise.

"He's doing me a little favor."

"Keeping an eye on the house for you?"

"Yep."

"I thought of suggesting that myself, but I was hoping it was just me being spooked."

"Ed Jackson is a coward, Matt. And right now he's desperate. I wouldn't put anything past him."

"You think it's wise to leave the ladies? I mean, we could bring them into town and take them to visit with Miz Ledbetter."

"We could, but then that opens a different can of worms. Jackson is a snake but I don't think he would burn the house, barn or stable down with Rachel and Elizabeth there. He doesn't want to kill Rachel, he just wants to save her for Ben Crane. But I don't think he'd have any qualms about torching the place if no one was here."

"What do you think he'll do if he finds Rachel and my wife there?"

"You've been dealing with him a lot longer than I have, what do you think he'll do?"

"He'll try to scare them, threaten Rachel, try to warn her off getting married."

"Yes, that's what I think. Rachel can handle that; Jackson doesn't scare her anymore."

"So, if the sheriff shows up, what do you think Isaac can do?"

"He's got a fast horse. He can ride to town and get us."

Reddick nodded. "You sure you aren't biting off more than you can chew here, Trace? I mean, Ed Jackson's one thing, the Cranes are another mess of vipers entirely."

Trace looked at the man seated next to her. "You want your town back, Matt? Your freedom? The chance to live your own life and raise your kids not to be afraid?"

"That's a nice dream, Trace...but it's just that — a dream. You don't know what it's like, but you will. And unfortunately, by marrying the one and only woman Ben Crane really wants, you're gonna see it a lot clearer than any of the rest of us."

Trace sighed. "I think I can turn things around, Matt, but I can't do it alone."

Matthew cocked his head. "Not that I think you have an ice block's chance in hell, but I'd be interested to hear how you think you can do that. And, no one's ever called me Matt before." He grinned. "I like it."

"You've got the whole town talking, Rachel," Elizabeth said as they sat out on the porch with cups of tea. "This mysterious drifter comes to town, shakes everything up, makes Ed Jackson face every day like he's got a hornet under his hat, and then claims you as his bride? What's going on?"

"I love him, Elizabeth. I think I fell in love with him the moment I laid eyes on him, I just didn't know it. He's strong and loving and protective and fearless, everything a..." She stopped and considered her words. "Everything a spouse should be."

"It's that fearless part that concerns me, and it should full well concern you, too," Elizabeth said, as though she were reprimanding Rachel. Then her tone softened. "But I can certainly see why you fell for him."

The sun had set two hours earlier and there was a chill in the air, unusual for that time of year. Isaac pulled his collar up around his neck and considered dismounting to sit by one of the bigger trees to shield himself from the strong breeze that had come up. Positioned between two rows of trees thick in the forest on the north side of the house, he could see the porch from his viewpoint and was pretty sure no one from the house had seen him, or could see him now. He was three-quarters through the contents of his flask, and feeling cocky and unconquerable, when he heard a voice behind him.

"Whatcha doin' here, Isaac? Gettin' an eyeful or planning on gettin' a piece of that pretty little blonde before she gets taken?"

Reining his horse around, the boy's eyes narrowed when he saw the sheriff. "Don't talk about Miss Rachel like that."

"Funny...not too long ago, you was thinking about her like that," Jackson reminded him.

"No, I was just goin' along with you because you threatened my father's store."

"Well, just remember, son, I can still put your father out of business. Now, why don't you run along back into town and let me do what I have to do. You're missing the festivities. After all, ain't you the best man? How you ever got yourself mixed up in that, I'll never know. There's still time to get smart, boy. Now get out of here."

"No." Isaac sat tall in his saddle. "Leave Miss Rachel and Miz Reddick be, Sheriff."

Jackson was clearly startled by the boy's defiance and then he laughed. "And just what do you think a scrawny little thing like you is gonna do to stop me?"

"Ride to town and get Trace and Mr. Reddick."

Jackson considered this. "You know, I could shoot you right here, boy, and no one'd be the wiser."

"You could, but you won't."

The sheriff unholstered his six-shooter and pointed it Isaac. "And what makes you think I won't?"

Holding his head high, Isaac feigned composure he did not really have. He pressed on, not wanting Jackson to see his fear. "Because you're afraid of Trace Sheridan and you know he'd kill you in your sleep if anythin' happens to Miss Rachel."

"Why, you snot-faced little..." he sputtered angrily. "I ain't afraid of nobody, 'specially not that half-breed lookin' cowboy. All I'd have to say is that I caught you out here gettin' ready to do somethin' to Rachel and I had to shoot you to stop you."

"Nobody would believe you, Sheriff," Isaac said, not sure if it was courage, whiskey, or idiocy propelling his words. "Miz Reddick is in there with Miss Rachel. Mr. Reddick was with Trace when they left, and Mr. Reddick knows I'm here and why, and it ain't to give either of them ladies trouble. But they was expectin' you would. I ain't tryin' to show you no disrespect, Sheriff, but I was asked to make sure you nor nobody else went anywhere near them ladies, and that's just what I aim to do."

Locking stares with Isaac, Jackson shook his head and holstered his gun. "You just bought yourself a whole heap a trouble, boy. You know that, don't ya?"

"I 'spect so, Sheriff." And trouble for his father, too, he was sure. But he didn't back down. He believed what Trace promised him about not letting the Cranes take his father's store. "It's up to you, course, but if I was you, I'd ride outta here and save yourself a heap a trouble."

"Well, you ain't me, now are ya, boy?" Jackson spat out.

Amen to that, Isaac thought. "No, sir. Just sayin' 's all."

Jackson glared Isaac, distaste showing in his eyes. "You'll regret this, boy," he said through clenched teeth.

Isaac knew there was probably truth to that, as he swallowed hard. "Yes, sir."

No one was more surprised than young Isaac Tipping when Ed Jackson turned his horse around and rode away. It was only after he could no longer hear the horse's hooves trotting over dried twigs that he let out his breath in a sigh of relief. It was then he realized that his saddle was wet.

The party at Wilbur's was winding down. All of Trace's new friends had been in attendance — Jed and Joseph Turner, Caleb Tipping, Luther Foster, the goldsmith, the banker, the usual men who played cards with Matthew every time Trace was there. Even two of the Indians she was doing business with stopped in for a couple shots of whiskey. Trace was surprised, but pleased, when the four old gentlemen who sat in front of the barbershop dropped by, and they didn't turn out to be bad company at all.

As the evening wore on, more and more men joined the festivities, deciding they liked Trace very much and appeared sincerely happy that Miss Rachel had found someone who seemed honest and would be good to her. When the subject finally got around to the contemptible things Ben Crane had said about the bride-to-be, everyone discreetly admitted they did not believe it and never had.

Everybody had only kind things to say about Rachel and the more the group imbibed, the more the conversation leaned toward grumbling about the Crane reign and how it affected each one of them, not just as business owners but as citizens of Sagebrush and husbands, fathers, and sons, as well. Normally, the fact that John Carver and his son, Seth, were drinking at the bar, listening to every word, would have put a damper on any grousing out loud, but for some reason, Trace's presence was empowering and seemed to make everyone just a bit bolder. The Carvers were not there to listen in as much as they were there to keep an eye on Trace while the sheriff was making a little visit to the Triple Y. The two men allowed the celebration to continue without incident as they were quite sure there would be no wedding the following night.

The highlight of the evening turned out to be Cassandra's seductive dance, ending with her plunking herself down abruptly in Trace's lap. This pleased the mayor, who cackled his delight by slapping his own knee and then Trace's. He patted Cassandra's behind and winked at Trace.

"Tell you what, son," Jed began, signaling Silas for another shot of bug juice for the groom-to-be. "It's your last night as a free man. Now, I know you're gettin' yourself a hell of a little gal tomorrow. She's a damned good woman from damned good stock and I know she'll make you a good and faithful little wife. But something tells me she's not going to be as, uh, let's say 'bold' as someone like Cassandra here might be. Least not 'til you teach her." He winked again at Trace, this time lecherously. "So, what say, as a weddin' gift, I buy you an hour with the best whore in the place?"

Trace cringed at the harsh title, but Cassandra, who just snuggled in tighter, didn't seem to mind it. Trace cleared her throat as Silas placed a shot of whiskey on the table before her. "Mr. Mayor, I think that's mighty generous of you, but I just couldn't let you spend your money on me like that."

"Why, Trace, I'd be honored to give you an hour or more for free as a wedding gift, if you're concerned about Jed's bank account," Cassandra said in Trace's ear. "In fact, I'd give you the whole night on the house if you were willing."

Trace looked over at Jed and the others gathered at the table. The mayor chomped on his cigar, eyebrows raised in expectation. The others seemed to be holding their breath in suspense. She picked up the shot glass and drained the contents quickly, closing her eyes until the burn passed. "I thank you both," she nodded to Jed and gently squeezed Cassandra's upper arm, "but I must respectfully decline. My future wife is saving herself for our wedding night and it is only fair that I do the same." When there was dead silence at the table, Trace realized that she'd made it sound as though her virtue was as intact as Rachel's. "I mean, you know, save myself for Rachel, not like I've never done it before," she added hastily. The group nodded and laughed and the conversation picked up where it had left off.

"Ya had me worried there, Trace. I didn't think a fella as good lookin' as you would still be a virgin. Hell, if Caleb's son can get his boyhood busted by one of them girls upstairs, I know a handsome stud like you couldn't've gone this long without havin' yourself a good time."

"Jed!" Caleb Tipping shouted. "That's not the kind of stuff you should be spreading around. It's personal. Why, if Isaac's mother found out, she'd kill us both."

"Oh, hell, Caleb, it ain't no secret. Your boy practically rang the church bells after and announced it to everyone hisself," Jed said dismissively. He returned his attention to Trace. "You're an honorable man, son. It don't matter none that I think you're plumb crazy." He looked pointedly at Cassandra. "I know what you're missin' out on, but I guess I can understand why you might wanna save your strength."

"I promise not to wear you out, Trace," Cassandra said, not moving off Trace's lap.

"I'm sure you would be most accommodating," Trace said diplomatically, "but Rachel deserves better from me. Thank you anyway."

"Hmmmm...too bad," Cassandra said, nuzzling Trace's neck.

Trace found herself very uncomfortable with the redhead's persistent attempts to get her to change her mind. She had to fend off predatory hands roaming toward her crotch. Had she actually been a man, the wool in those socks would have turned to steel very quickly. She must be in love if she wasn't even taking advantage of the invitation to openly cop a feel whenever she wanted.

All too soon for some, but not soon enough for Trace, the party was over and Silas amiably kicked everyone out. All of the attendees promised they would be present at the chapel to witness the marriage of Trace Sheridan and Rachel Young, which pleased Trace because she knew it would be a nice surprise for Rachel.

Singing *Buffalo Gals* raucously, and off-key, Trace and Matthew shushed each other as Isaac rode up to them. He must have heard them long before they reached the entrance to the property. In fact, Trace was sure they could probably be heard in Sagebrush. The pair weren't totally drunk, but neither were they sober.

"Hey, Isaac." Trace grinned. "Quiet night?"

"Well, the sheriff came by just as you 'spected he would."

"What! Why didn't you come and get us?"

Isaac took a deep breath. "I told him to leave."

"And he left?" Matthew blinked in shock.

"Well, not right off. But I told him that you wouldn't take kindly to anything happenin' to Miss Rachel, Miz Reddick, or me, and he saw my way and rode out."

Trace was impressed. "Well, obviously, I picked the right man for the job. You *are* the best man." She could actually see Isaac's chest expand as he grinned proudly at the compliment.

"Thank you, Trace."

"No, thank you, Isaac." Trace smiled then sniffed the air, sure she detected the distinct odor of urine and wet leather. "What's that smell?"

"Well, I gotta get goin'," Isaac said, quickly. "I'll see you tomorrow at the church, okay, Trace?"

"Sure. Thanks again, Isaac, I appreciate it."

"Me, too," Matthew shouted after the retreating Arabian.

They looked at each other, shrugged, and continued to the house, resuming their horrendous rendition of *Buffalo Gals*.

"Ooooh, my head," Trace wailed from the sofa. She never made it to the loft and Rachel was so annoyed that she didn't try to assist her. Trace awoke fully dressed, including her boots. "Oh, God, oh, shit," Trace moaned, her head hammering. Her stomach lurched and the room spun. Trace remembered that sometimes it helped with the whirlies if she put one foot on the floor. First, she had to find the floor.

"Trace, your language," Rachel said.

"I think I'm going to be really sick."

"Then you'd best get yourself outside to throw up."

"I can't move; my head hurts too bad."

"And whose fault is that?"

"Oh, God, God, please, if you get me through this, I'll never drink again, I swear."

"That's a hangover talking." Rachel shook her head. "Funny how you're calling for the Lord now."

"Rachel, don't you have anything to get me through this?" Trace still didn't dare to move.

"I'm making you some cabbage soup." When Rachel heard Trace make a noise that sounded like gagging, she said, "It'll work." Then she looked pointedly at Trace prone on her sofa. "It better work."

Two hours later, Trace's head had stopped pounding and ginger tea was starting to ease her nausea. Puking a few times into the bushes hadn't hurt either, and the cabbage soup had worked miracles...once Rachel convinced her to try it. Rachel's comment, "I've seen more life in a corpse," was made with a little more sting than it should have had, but her point was made. The last thing Trace wanted was Rachel to be mad at her, especially not with what was at stake following the wedding.

If Trace hadn't looked so pathetic, Rachel might have been able to stay mad at her, but now that Trace was beginning to become human again, all Rachel wanted was for her to feel better so their special day would go as smoothly as possible. Within a couple hours, the contrite "husband-to-be" was almost back to normal.

Taking her shower, Trace angled the straight razor carefully, running the freshly sharpened blade over her underarms and legs, acquiring only a few minor nicks. She had never before used an archaic implement such as the ivory-handled razor and respected it immensely, knowing the edge could probably cut off a limb if need be. Oh, how she longed for the gels of the modern world, which softened and moisturized the skin and made shaving a more tolerable event. However, the matching ivory shaving cup and brush with badger bristles that belonged to Rachel's father came in handy, as she was able to work up a decent lather with the borax soap. The water had been warmed by the sun, which made it a bit more enjoyable and not having to shave over goosebumps made it easier to remove all the body hair she had accumulated.

Rachel had already been picked up by Matthew and Elizabeth Reddick, who had taken her to Molly Ledbetter's, where she would bathe, address any last minute alteration issues, and then get dressed for the wedding. Trace had another half hour before she had to saddle up Chief and head to town. She wished she could ride in on Rio, but the mustang wasn't ready for his public debut.

After binding herself down, Trace put on the white, button-down, shirt that Rachel had boiled clean the day before, her wedding slacks, a gray satin vest, and a string tie. The swallowtail coat, with satin lapels that matched her trousers, was waiting at the church. Rachel had taken it in on the wagon with her so it wouldn't get wrinkled. She asked Trace to wear different clothes in and change at the chapel, but Trace didn't want to take the chance of anyone seeing her undressed.

Trace took one last look around the cabin, then closed the door behind her, knowing that when she returned, she would carry the love of her life over the threshold and they would start a new journey together, beginning with a much anticipated consummation. A rush of heat boiled through her body and then subsided as quickly as it had come. She shook the sensation out of her system, then walked down the steps to Chief, who she had saddled up prior to her shower.

"You have a good wedding. Do not worry about here."

Trace turned to smile at Little Hawk, one of the four Indians who were going to deliver cattle to the ranch. "Thank you. I'm grateful to you and Black Feather for watching over the house while we're in town. You will not go unrewarded."

"You standing against Crane is reward enough." Little Hawk was anything but little. He was burly and barrel-chested and almost as tall as Trace. He had weathered skin and a wrinkled face, but he had kind eyes. Trace had not asked the two warriors to come and guard the house. They decided on their own that it would be done. She knew she could not have left the homestead in more capable hands.

At five o'clock, Trace took her place at the altar with Isaac standing next to her, dressed in his Sunday best. The small church was packed with the men Trace had mingled with at her party, and women she had never seen before, who she assumed must be "the wives".

Trace was not accustomed to feeling anxious. She wasn't afraid of getting married to Rachel, or regretting her decision in any way, yet she was suddenly cold and her insides were shaking. She drew in several deep breaths to steady her nerves.

"Stop fidgeting." The firm, yet melodic, voice of Pastor Edwards snapped Trace out of it as the organ music pealed forth Mendelssohn's *Wedding March.*

Everyone turned and looked toward the entranceway as Molly Ledbetter, attired in a dusty rose-colored velvet dress, proceeded down the aisle, beaming as though it were her own wedding. When she reached the chancel rail directly in front of the altar, she winked at Trace, who smiled in reflex.

Then Rachel stood in the doorway and began her walk down the aisle. Trace's heart skipped a beat at the sight of the gorgeous woman floating toward her, radiantly beautiful in her mother's wedding gown, altered just enough to personalize it as Rachel's. Her hair was braided and held back by sapphire-studded silver combs, family heirlooms borrowed from Elizabeth, and she carried a shower bouquet of white asters.

At the altar, Rachel handed her flowers to Molly and Trace took a step forward, standing next to the stunning apparition who, within a matter of minutes, was to be her wife. Even though they faced Reverend Edwards, neither woman could take her eyes off the other. When Trace mouthed the words, "I love you," she thought Rachel just might pass out then and there.

The organ music was the cue for Ed Jackson and the Carvers to enter the church. Their plan was to stand in the back and wait for the preacher to ask if anyone had reason to object to the union and they would all object...for different made up reasons. And being that Pastor Edwards was never one to cross the sheriff, the marriage ceremony would not be completed.

So it was a great surprise when Jackson and his sidekicks ascended the steps of the church and found their entry blocked by two members of the neighboring Indian tribe, carrying Remington rifles. With bowie knives, bows slung across their backs, and full quivers of arrows, they looked like they meant business.

"Out of my way, Injun; we got matters to attend to in the church." It was John Carver who spoke. Then he made the mistake of trying to push the native out of his way. The next thing he knew, he was flat on his back, five feet away from the doorway.

"Big mistake, son," Jackson told the young warrior.

"I am not your son. You have no business here," the young man said.

"I'll throw you in jail, savage!" Jackson yelled.

"White man's laws do not mean me. You lock me up, you deal with my father."

Jackson and the Carvers blanched. Could this young warrior blocking their way be the son of Moving Elk, one of the best known, and bravest warriors, of the Plains nations? It had been rumored that he migrated his tribe to a stretch of land a few miles from Sagebrush. Things might be friendly now, but there were stories about how the tribal chief had single-handedly cut down platoons of cavalries who dared to attack his family. Did they want to take that chance?

John Carver decided for them by getting up, dusting himself off, and keeping his distance. Extremely irritated, he crooked his finger at Jackson.

"Now what, Ed?" Carver glared at the sheriff. "This cowboy ain't turning out to be quite the little pantywaist you thought he'd be. Jacob ain't gonna be happy with you."

Jackson stood in the middle of the street, stewing. "Maybe it's time we paid a little visit to the Triple Y. If everybody's here, no one will be out there."

With that, the three men ran in the direction of the sheriff's office to mount their horses. The two warriors smiled after them.

Immediately after the ceremony, where for the first time in the history of Sagebrush, people actually cheered when Pastor Edwards said, "I now pronounce you man and wife," the invited guests assembled at the home of the minister, where a sumptuous wedding supper was served. The house was attractively festooned in pink and lavender, tastefully arranged with ferns and asters.

While everyone ate and drank and had a merry time, all the bride and groom could think of was how soon would be an appropriate time to leave. After the dinner, Trace and Rachel were driven by Isaac in a double horse-drawn coach, courtesy of grocer Luther Foster, to the photo gallery, where they had their wedding picture taken.

Returning to the pastor's house, they thanked everyone, bade them goodnight, hitched Chief up to the Reddicks' wagon, and were taken back to the Triple Y.

Chapter Eighteen

At the front door of the house, Trace swept Rachel up in her arms in an impressive move that was typical of her. It shouldn't have surprised Rachel, but it did. It also made her giggle at the chivalrous manner in which Trace was behaving, taking her role as husband very seriously.

"What are you doing?"

"Indulging in a tradition." Trace pushed the door open with her foot and carried her bride over the threshold. Kissing Rachel with loving abandon, Trace set her down and bolted the door behind them. She turned and admired her wife, who seemed to be glowing, even in the dim light of twilight, enhanced only minimally by a kerosene lamp Rachel lighted. "Hi, Mrs. Sheridan." There was unbridled affection in Trace's voice.

"Hi, Mr. Sheridan," Rachel said, her voice thick with allure. "It was a nice ceremony, wasn't it?"

Trace removed her suit jacket, hastily undoing her tie and shedding her vest. She nodded. "The reception was nice, too. A lot of people in this town love you, Rachel."

"Thanks to you. You brought them all back to me."

Grinning, Trace put on her best Old West accent and said, "Why, 't warn't nothin', Miz Rachel. I jes' set 'em straight, 's all." Trembling with anticipation, she touched Rachel's perfectly proportioned nose. "Now what do you want to do?"

Rachel blushed, peering up at her through honey-hued eyelashes. "I was thinking maybe...another tradition?"

Trace studied her for any hint of hesitation. "Are you sure? I mean, really sure?"

Her eyes not straying from Trace's for a second, Rachel exhaled a shaky breath. "I'm absolutely sure. I've never been more sure of anything in my life."

Trace enclosed Rachel's hands in her own. "Then let's go up." She nodded toward the loft.

"Why up there?" Rachel asked, still not relinquishing eye contact.

"Total privacy. I overheard a few drunken whispers at the reception about peeking in our windows. Going up there will guarantee our privacy. And I don't want to have to think about any interruptions. I want to be free to be me making love to you, not the Trace Sheridan everyone in town knows."

"I want that, too," she said, her voice a low quiver. The fever of emotion passing between them was jarring and Rachel seemed enchanted by it, and by Trace.

"Are you ready?"

"I've been ready," she admitted as she doused the lantern.

Trace nudged Rachel as they headed to the stairs. "You were the one who insisted on waiting until the wedding night."

"That's the proper, and traditional, thing to do."

"Sweetheart," Trace said, as she followed her up the steps, "there's nothing traditional about this relationship."

"I haven't been in this bed since my Mama died," Rachel said softly, staring at the quilt her mother had stitched for her when she was a little girl.

"Is it okay that we're up here? If it brings up too many sad memories, we can go back downstairs."

"No. This was my bed. I just started sleeping downstairs because that room smelled like my folks and it made me feel close to them. But you've been sleeping up here and now the pillows will smell like you."

Trace wrapped her arms around Rachel's waist, lacing her fingers together, and kissed Rachel on the top of her head. Rachel leaned back into the embrace and covered Trace's hands with her own. "I love you Rachel Young," Trace whispered.

"Rachel Sheridan," the new bride corrected, slapping one of Trace's hands lightly.

Trace grinned, swaying slowly toward the bed, moving Rachel with her. "Right, right... Best I don't forget that, huh?"

"Not if you don't want me to neglect my wifely duties," Rachel teased. Trace turned her around and stared into her eyes, the look so mesmerizing, Rachel forgot to expel the breath from her lungs.

"What we're about to do... I guarantee you won't ever consider it a 'duty'."

Breathlessly, Rachel said, "Show me?"

"Exhale, sweetheart." Trace smiled. "I don't want you passing out...at least not from this." She dipped her head and placed a gentle kiss on Rachel's lips, intensifying the pressure as Rachel urged her on, following her lead. One thing Trace had learned was that Rachel was an extremely quick study, a thought that made her body fairly vibrate with expectation.

Rachel dissolved into the kiss, absorbing the sensation of Trace's tongue swirling around the inside of her mouth, sensually pillaging everything it touched. Rachel wasn't sure how their making love was supposed to go, all she knew was the room was sweltering and spinning and she wanted nothing more than to be lying on the bed with Trace holding her, kissing her, doing things to her that just thinking of made her cheeks burn deeply. Drawing away from Trace's lips, Rachel sat on the bed and gasped for air.

Proud of the spell she could cast on Rachel, Trace smiled. "Are you all right? I'll go slow, okay?"

"This can't hurt the baby, can it?"

"Nothing we do tonight, or any night, will harm the baby, I promise." Trace removed her shirt and began to take off her binding when Rachel stopped her.

"Let me...please?"

Trace nodded and handed Rachel the loose end of the wrap. She slowly spun while the material was unwound. Before Trace turned around to reveal her naked breasts, she drew a deep breath. It was not that she was suddenly shy, and the word "inhibited" would never be used to describe her, but she knew that anything that happened between her and her bride tonight would deeply impact Rachel and how the younger, impressionable woman would think of their making love from here on.

Trace had never been concerned about what she did in bed, or what her conquest might or might not feel emotionally, although her ego demanded that she perform well enough to evoke a highly vocal response from whoever was the object of her lust. Actually caring about whatever nameless, faceless woman happened to be in her embrace was never an issue. Trace was out for Trace, and would have said and done whatever it took to get her selected sex partner into bed. But this — being in love thing — was having a profound effect on her. She felt that their first time together would be an awakening for both of them.

Trace stood before Rachel feeling exposed. It wasn't that she was naked from the waist up, fully displaying her breasts to Rachel for the first time; it was the way Rachel's appreciative eyes took in every inch of her skin, the reverence with which Rachel regarded her, and how time seemed to stand still as Rachel touched her. Fingertips chilled from excitement and fear raised instant goosebumps on Trace's flesh, as Rachel lightly circled the areola. The dark ring on Trace's breast got smaller as the nipple became impossibly erect. It was torture, and they hadn't even begun yet. Raw hunger swallowed Trace. Her desperate need for Rachel, was becoming intolerable. Her body ached to feel Rachel against her. It was the height of restraint, and a testimony to how Trace had changed, that she didn't just overpower Rachel and have her way with her.

Rachel could not stop staring at the physique before her. She'd been so used to seeing Trace bound down that she'd almost forgotten she even had breasts, much less the glorious pair she was now touching. She had no idea that seeing another woman's breasts would provoke such a feeling of desire deep inside her.

Trace gasped out a short breath, as if she hadn't even realized she had been holding it. She exhaled and pressed Rachel's fingers against her. Trace watched her as she looked up expectantly into Trace's eyes, now dark with desire. She could not hide that she was overwhelmed and a little unnerved by what was happening between them and within her own body.

Rachel didn't have a clue as to what she needed to do to make love to a woman. It was up to Trace to create the atmosphere in which this night would be one neither of them would soon forget. "I...I...don't..." Rachel could not get the words to come out of her mouth, could barely raise her voice above a whisper.

Trace put a finger to Rachel's lips. "Shhhh...I know," she soothed. Trace's eyes sparkled as they held the emerald gaze, conveying a deep love and sensitivity. Almost imperceptibly shaking her head, awed that Rachel was about to give herself, Trace kissed Rachel's palm, then the inside of her wrist.

Releasing Rachel for just a moment she sat on the edge of the bed and removed her shoes and socks, then her trousers, Rachel's eyes following as the material slid off the smooth skin. Trace wasn't wearing any underwear. She stood up and turned to face Rachel again, silently letting Rachel absorb the look of her body. Rachel's eyes automatically fell to the dark triangle of curls at the apex of her thighs. She seemed transfixed. It made Trace chuckle.

"Like what you see?"

Rachel's eyes closed as she blushed and turned her head away. "I'm sorry. I feel so bold. I've never seen another woman bare before."

Trace gently guided Rachel's face forward. "Sweetheart, please open your eyes." When Rachel hesitantly obeyed, Trace said, "I want you to look at me. I want you to get comfortable looking at me like this. You have no need to feel embarrassed or bold, no need to apologize. I intend to make love with you every chance I get, and I refuse to do it with my clothes on. Okay?"

"Okay," Rachel said, but did not drop her gaze from Trace's face.

Trace sat back down on the bed. "And I want you to get comfortable with me looking at you with no clothes on. Because I intend to do that a lot."

"Even when my belly gets big?"

"Especially when your belly gets big."

"Oh my Lord, Trace, whatever you're going to do, would you hurry up and get started? My blood is starting to stir something awful."

If Rachel hadn't sounded so serious about it, Trace would have laughed at the tension breaker. She could not suppress her smile at Rachel's admission of being ready to burst. "Stand up, please. I'd like to undress you."

In no time at all, Rachel was standing nude before her. Ranching and farming were certainly a workout, and Rachel's body showed it. Except for a slight, almost imperceptible, bulge of her abdomen, there was not one ounce of excess anywhere. Rachel's creamy white complexion was all muscle, femininely defined. Her breasts were in perfect symmetry with the rest of her figure, tantalizingly round and firm and just begging to be caressed. Trace moistened her lips. Suddenly the lush, heady aroma of arousal was everywhere.

"Oh my God, Rachel, you're so beautiful."

"Like what you see?" Rachel asked, not feeling as shy as she'd expected.

Trace took Rachel in her arms and kissed her feverishly, pressing their bodies together, craving the full contact. At first, Rachel was stiff, but within seconds she relaxed, molding to Trace's warm contours.

Trace knew they both needed to lie down before passion caused them to collapse, and eased Rachel back onto the bed, breaking contact only once to position herself on top. She kissed Rachel's lips until they were swollen. Moving over forehead, nose, and cheek, Trace then nibbled on the nearby earlobe and Rachel's entire body trembled. From there she blazed a trail of kisses down her neck and shoulder and skimmed her hand along the inside of Rachel's thigh. She sailed a feathery touch up her side to her arm, where her fingers finally came to a rest on Rachel's cheek. As Trace stared at her bride for a moment, the only movement in the room was the rise and fall of Rachel's chest.

"Oh, my, Trace, I never knew the places you are kissing could feel like this."

"You ain't seen nothin' yet," Trace promised, her voice a mere murmur. She kissed the base of Rachel's throat and then rested her face there. "Rachel...I know what I want to do to satisfy your desires, but if I do anything that hurts or makes you uncomfortable, I want you to tell me, all right?"

"Must we discuss this now?" she asked impatiently, breaths coming in spurts.

"Yes. I'm just making sure you know that you don't have to do anything you don't want to do."

"Trace?"

"Yes?"

"Please hush up and make love to me."

That did prompt Trace to laugh. "As you wish, my Lady." She kissed Rachel passionately. If dizzying desire could have made Rachel melt, Trace was sure her bride would be a puddle in her arms.

She knew, because Rachel was pregnant, hormones would make her erogenous areas much more sensitive. She would have to be careful not to stimulate her partner to the point of irritation. It was all about giving Rachel pleasure, and hopefully replacing the brutal experience of her first time.

Trace placed her mouth over Rachel's nipple and began flicking it with her tongue. Hearing a sharp intake of breath and a hiss, Trace knew Rachel was experiencing a new, welcomed sensation. When Trace started to lightly suck on the rigid tip, Rachel grabbed a handful of Trace's hair and squeezed with the same intensity she was feeling. Lingering on the left breast until Rachel appeared to be nearly hyperventilating, Trace moved over to give equal time to the right breast, still rolling, pulling, and slightly pinching Rachel's nipple between her thumb and forefinger.

Rachel watched, as Trace kissed down her chest, fascinated as Trace hovered over her breast. "Oh, Lord in Heaven, Trace..." Rachel sighed, holding on to Trace's head.

"You like this?" Trace's voice was low, husky, thickly laced with desire. She only lifted her face long enough to formulate words, her warm breath on Rachel's wet nipple sending another shiver through them both.

"It...it feels wonderful. Please don't stop." If this was all Trace did to her, it would surely be enough. But she knew there was more to being made love to. She had figured out that since Trace didn't have the proper equipment to penetrate her, and her loins were begging for it, that Trace would no doubt use her fingers. The thought of that was exciting but when Trace began kissing down her ribcage, taking special care to lavish extra attention on her belly and then went further down... That certainly had never occurred to her. *Where is she going? What is she going to do? What — Oh, Jesus, Jesus, that feels...oh good God!*

Trace nuzzled the soft blonde curls that smelled like sex and lavender soap, then kissed the line that, when parted, would reveal the secrets of Rachel's being, and make her feel born again. Running her tongue the full length, Trace pushed through, feeling Rachel startle, then settle as she let out an involuntary moan. Slowly, gently, Trace located that little bundle of nerves — the only spot in the human body solely put there for pleasure and no other purpose — and ravished it with desperate tenderness, gauging Rachel's reactions, taking cues when to go faster, when to slow down, when to add pressure and when to back off. Tasting this woman, remembering that this was all new to Rachel, knowing what she was doing to her brought Trace to the edge herself, the tingling warmth between her own legs building to its own crescendo.

Rachel had never felt anything like this before. She had no idea anyone could make her feel this way, could make her feel like her entire body was about to explode in a sensation of such ecstasy she didn't think she was going to survive it. She didn't even realize she was rocking to a rhythm Trace set with every stroke and thrust of her tongue. Suddenly, an indescribable, wonderful feeling ignited and radiated outward to every nerve in her body and then intensified to a glorious white heat that continued to burst until she lost her breath.

She rode out every ripple as it surged around her, a whirlpool creating a vortex she never wanted to stop. Her body spontaneously convulsed, wracked with waves of pleasure, and as Trace sucked every last drop of orgasm from her, she thought she was going to lose her mind from sheer bliss.

And then, so taken by the emotion of what she had just experienced, Rachel began to weep.

Moving quickly up Rachel's spent form, Trace embraced her securely. "Shhh, shhh, it's okay," she soothed, kissing Rachel's forehead.

Holding Trace as though her life depended on it, Rachel cried against Trace's neck. "I...I've never felt anything like that before... it...you..."

Although it wasn't quite the reaction she'd expected, she found it touching and endearing. The fact that she could draw that kind of emotion from Rachel made her heart pound. She had never before brought anyone to tears. Giving her an extra squeeze, Trace cuddled Rachel. "It's okay, baby, I understand."

With many soft words of love and reassuring kisses, Trace ran her fingers in wide, lazy circles over Rachel's stomach, moving ever closer to the still quivering core.

"Oh, Lord, you're going to touch me there again."

"Mmm hmmm. Unless you would rather I didn't..."

Green eyes snapped open and glared at her. "Don't you dare stop now, Trace Sheridan. Why, that would just be cruel."

Trace erupted in a deep, throaty chuckle as she fondled damp curls that now appeared almost auburn. She began to gently stroke, Rachel clinging to her shoulders until a second orgasm rocked her.

Not waiting until Rachel was completely recovered, Trace gathered some moisture and inserted a finger very slowly, drawing it out and pushing it in a little further with each thrust. Trace locked eyes with Rachel, watching for any signs of emotional or physical discomfort. She saw nothing but wanting and incapacitating need. While Trace steadily drove her finger into Rachel, she gently kissed her, conveying her love and desire.

"Baby," Trace whispered in Rachel's ear, "does this feel good?"

"Oh, yes." Rachel was almost beyond speech as thrilling, titillating sensations seized her brain, holding her body hostage, releasing itself only when she no longer had the strength to grip Trace or even form a fist to grasp a handful of sheet.

"I'm going to add a second finger...I think I can make it more enjoyable for you. But if it's too much, you tell me, okay?"

"Okay." She trusted Trace implicitly and if Trace thought it could feel even better, then she would believe her. Still, when Trace removed the one finger, Rachel grabbed her wrist. "No..."

"Shhh, it's all right." Trace ran her fingertips around Rachel's opening and then easily slid inside, increasing the depth of her penetration with each push.

Rachel didn't think she could feel rapture beyond anything that she had already experienced. Any more would certainly drive her to madness. Yet what Trace was doing, and the way Trace wouldn't take her eyes off her, enticed Rachel to a near frenzy, and as close to Heaven as she was sure she would ever get without actually dying. The feel of Trace's fingers thrusting inside her in a bliss-creating cadence was exhilarating, but when the fingers curled and began rhythmically massaging a sensitive spot, Rachel's eyes rolled back in her head and she uttered moans of ecstasy with each expelled breath. She was quickly approaching orgasm but this one felt different, this one felt almost ethereal in its origin, and when her insides exploded, the climax shook her to her core, sizzling out to her extremities then back to her groin.

Rachel lay there, chest heaving, not at all sure she was even going to survive, not having the strength to fight it if the Lord wanted to take her at that very minute. When she was able to focus, she looked up into loving, caring eyes.

"How're you doing?" Trace wanted to make the experience memorable for Rachel; she was pretty sure she had succeeded. She'd almost had a sympathetic orgasm with Rachel on the last one.

When Rachel regained the capability to vocalize, she said, "I love you, Trace. I never knew my body could do that."

"So...you've never..."

"Never what?"

"Never...um...done that to yourself?"

"What? Oh, Heavens, no!" Since her whole body was already flushed, it was hard to tell if she was blushing. "Do you...do that?"

"All the time."

Rachel's eyes grew wide. "You do?" When Trace nodded, Rachel said, "Is that because you don't have anyone to do that for you?"

"Partly."

"Well, now you have me." Rachel's smile was so sincere and her words so decisive, that Trace fell in love with her all over again. "In fact," she took Trace's face in her hands and pulled her toward her, "let me do it for you now."

She kissed Trace with such wantonness that all she would have had to do was touch Trace and it would be over.

Trace rolled them over so that Rachel was now above her and, after a few deeply probing kisses, Rachel bowed her head, nuzzling it into the crook of Trace's neck. "I don't know what to do." She knew what she wanted to do, but wasn't quite sure how to put her thoughts into actions. She could try to mimic what Trace had done, but she'd been so invested in just feeling the new sensations, she had not paid as much attention to the execution of the acts as she probably should have. Not that she would have done things any differently if she'd had the chance.

"Well, first, you need to relax." Trace ran her hands lightly up and down Rachel's back. "And then you need to think about what you want to do and what you don't."

Rachel raised her head and looked into a blue sexual haze. "I want to do it all. I want to give you as much pleasure as you just gave to me."

"Rachel, your responsiveness gave me a great deal of pleasure. And there might be a few things that might be a little too, uh, over-whelming for you this first time."

Adamant, Rachel said, "I want to do everything."

Trace caressed her face, pulling her in for another fiery kiss. With one hand, she guided Rachel's fingers to her breast and moved them in a circle around her nipple. Breaking the kiss, Trace said, "I know you've never felt another woman's breast before tonight. I don't want you to be afraid of touching me here, of touching me anywhere. I want you to get very familiar with how it feels to have my nipple harden between your fingers." Whispering into Rachel's ear, she commanded, "Put your mouth there."

Without hesitation, Rachel brushed her thumb over Trace's nipple before sealing her lips around it. Her mouth on Trace's areola elicited a satisfying groan and Rachel decided that she enjoyed causing Trace to make that particular noise. Concentrating her attention on both breasts equally, Rachel determined from Trace's reaction that her nipples were very sensitive to certain stimulation and quickly learned what drew out the strongest response, committing it to memory. "What would you like me to do next?" Rachel asked in a hushed tone.

Trace's voice cracked when she said, "I need you to touch me...down there."

Rachel briefly studied the stunning face of her excited spouse then said, "With my mouth or my hand?"

"Oh, Jesus." Trace sighed at the thought of Rachel's face burying into her. "Right now, let's try it with your hand."

Had Trace not showed her first what it felt like to be indulged and pleased orally, she might have been more reluctant to engage in that particular sexual act, but after what Trace had done to her, had caused her to feel, she was eager to try it, almost greedy in her need to cater to her lover's desires. She was looking forward to experiencing that. Her hand trailed the length of Trace's torso, making her shiver. Rachel stopped when she felt the dewy thatch of hair covering Trace's mound and idled there, playing with the damp curls.

Not being able to stand it any longer, Trace covered Rachel's hand and moved it two inches lower, positioning it exactly where she needed it the most. She held Rachel's index and middle fingers together and began rubbing them over her clit, ensuring the pressure, motion, and rhythm were just right. "Just keep doing that," Trace said breathlessly, releasing Rachel's hand.

"Until when?"

"Oh...you'll know, trust me." Trace almost immediately began to tense. She only had to reposition Rachel's fingers once as Rachel had been distracted by Trace's rocking and unrestrained moaning. Trace's legs wrapped around Rachel's thighs, holding her in place and she brought Rachel's face to her own, her lower body convulsing. As Rachel stopped to watch her raptly, Trace's words came out in short gasps, "No...Jesus...don't stop!" Trace moved herself aggressively against Rachel's fingers until Rachel got the hint and resumed what she had been doing with as much, if not more, vigor than she had before. Panting, trembling, Trace exploded in a powerful climax. "Oh, fuck...fuck, that's beautiful. Oh, Jesus!" Trace continued to quiver until she reached down and stilled Rachel's hand.

"Trace...your language," Rachel commented sotto voce, breathing almost as heavily as Trace. Her admonition carried no sincerity this time. In this context, she was embarrassed to admit, she liked the vulgarity. It heightened her excitement.

"God, Rachel, I need you inside me right now." Bracing Rachel's wrist with her left hand, she directed Rachel's fingers to her opening with her right and propelled them inside, expelling a relieved breath at the sensation. At first, Trace thrust herself onto Rachel's hand until Rachel got the idea and then Trace let the small, strong fingers work her. "Please...I need another finger..."

Again, stopping, Rachel looked at her questioningly.

"It's all right, baby, you won't hurt me. Come on, it's fine."

Skeptical, Rachel obeyed, and seeing the ecstasy on Trace's face eased any apprehension that three fingers pumping inside her lover was anything even remotely close to unpleasant. Having to reposition herself for comfort and maximum effect, Rachel marveled at how this felt, the almost sacred closeness of a part of her connected to Trace in the manner it was. Never in a million years would she have believed that a bond so intimate could exist between her and another person, especially not another woman. Yet Rachel knew, although she could not explain it, that this was where, and with whom, she was meant to be, despite all that had happened and regardless of what the Bible indicated. More than anything in the world, Rachel was sure that Trace Sheridan had specifically been brought to Sagebrush to save her...in more ways than one.

When the warm, velvety flesh contracted around her fingers and pulsing wetness coated her hand, she heard Trace's sensual voice prompting her to increase her pace. Rachel watched with awe at what her touch did to her lover.

Holding her breath, Trace nearly sat up, clutching Rachel to her, anchoring Rachel's hand in place while she screamed her release into the air, rocking until every last ounce of orgasm had left her body. She fell back on the bed, with Rachel on top of her, and stared up into two startled green eyes.

"Did...did I hurt you?" Rachel asked with concern.

Her breathing coming in bursts, she said, "No. You did exactly what I wanted you to do. That's how I...uh...um...express myself."

It took a moment for what Trace meant to sink in and then Rachel blushed furiously. "Oh."

Laughing, Trace pulled Rachel close to her. "Get used to that, Rachel Sheridan. I expect you'll be hearing it a lot."

Late into the night, an hour after both women had finally fallen asleep, Trace's arm circled around Rachel's waist, Rachel snuggled tight against her solid frame. Trace awoke to kisses on her eyelids. The soft lips moved to Trace's cheek and then mouth, an insistent tongue finding its way inside, provoking Trace's body to respond, regardless of being oblivious in slumber. Without too much coaxing, Trace came fully awake to find Rachel half on top of her, lips fused to her own and Rachel's hand stroking her with such precision, it was as though she had been doing it all her life.

With very little guidance, Rachel found the exact spot that incited a rush of arousal, a sharp, electrifying passion that enveloped Trace and took her in a way that was new, freeing, and more exciting than she had ever known.

Growling, Trace flipped Rachel onto her back and wasted no time spreading her legs, putting them over her shoulders, and diving in. She was a little less gentle this time, a little less patient, as Rachel seemed almost ravenous for the sensory overload Trace knew would be deliciously inevitable. Rachel came quickly and Trace wasted no time working Rachel up again. "Baby?"

"Yes?" Rachel panted, clearly concentrating on her nicely building orgasm.

"May I make a small suggestion?" Trace stopped orally servicing her and was using the pad of her thumb in place of her tongue, while she spoke.

"Must you make it now?" Rachel asked, mild exasperation puffing in her voice.

Trace chuckled, resting her face on Rachel's thigh. She silently agreed she couldn't have chosen a less convenient time to suddenly have a conversation. She looked up at Rachel, who was breathing so heavy she was almost gasping. "When the climax hits you? I want you to let it out. You don't have to hide it. I want to hear you. I want to know that you enjoyed what I did to you. If you feel like you have to scream then I want you to scream. If you want to rock against me or buck, I don't want you to hold back. I know you were probably taught it's not ladylike, but that's not true." When Rachel nodded vigorously, Trace said, "Whatever you feel, I want you to show me."

"Trace...hush...up...please..."

Shaking her head, Trace went back to her mission of gratification. Excellent student that Rachel was, instead of anchoring herself down by holding on to the bed frame, the sheet, or Trace, she allowed her body to rear up with the momentum of the orgasm, crying loudly at the intensity of the release instead of holding her breath and holding it in.

"Yeah...kind of like that." Trace kissed her way back up Rachel's body, settling over her.

"Sweet Lord in Heaven, I didn't think it could get any better." She held to Trace tightly while their breathing calmed. "Just give me a minute and I'll—"

"No, baby, I'm just fine. How about we try to get some rest?"

Rachel hadn't noticed that Trace pleasured herself while bringing Rachel to climax, coming about thirty seconds after her. Rachel had seemed a little aghast at the idea of masturbation and Trace didn't want Rachel to think that she couldn't do the job, but being that Trace was just so ready, she didn't want to wait. Contentedly settling Rachel back in her arms, both women fell asleep, spent and sated.

Two hours later, Rachel's kissing the back of Trace's neck and fondling her breast stirred her awake again. Trace shook her head. "I think I've created a monster."

Chapter Nineteen

The newlyweds did not get out of bed until later that afternoon. Some of that time had been spent sleeping.

As much as Trace was used to the muscle aches that could occur as a result of vigorous marathon sex, even she was mildly surprised at the stiffness and the soreness she was feeling. She looked over at Rachel, who was baking an apple pie and humming. *Humming.* Trace had never heard Rachel hum. There was also a bounce in her step that had not been there before. Trace knew Rachel had to be experiencing some physical discomfort, but if she was she certainly wasn't showing it.

Chuckling, a sound that was deep, throaty and, most of all, contented, Trace drained her coffee cup and approached Rachel from behind. "I think married life suits you, my love." She ensnared Rachel with an arm around her waist, catching her off-guard. Rachel blushed and grinned.

"Being in your bed suits me," Rachel said boldly. She spun in Trace's embrace and lovingly looked up into radiant blue eyes.

"How are you feeling? Does anything hurt?"

"Everything hurts." Rachel smiled. "That's the pain and glory of consummation, isn't it?"

Trace blinked, mulling over Rachel's statement. "As long as it was more glory than pain."

"It was...wonderful, Trace. I just never...had any notion...that it could be like that."

"Well, then," Trace grinned proudly, "glad I could be of service." She leaned in and kissed waiting, luscious lips, a kiss so heated that Trace's stomach fluttered and Rachel actually growled. Reluctantly breaking the contact, Trace held Rachel closely against her. "And you, my lovely wife, were amazing."

"I pleased you, then?"

"Oh, yes. You couldn't tell?"

"I figured I did, but not having anything to liken it to—"

"Oh my God, Rachel, you did just fine." Trace held her at arm's length and gazed directly into her eyes. "I've never been more in love or in lust in my life. And 'disappointed' would be the last word I would use to describe last night...and this morning. Your instincts are, well, impressive."

Trace wasn't just being kind. She was awed by the fact that Rachel had never participated in anything like that before and still was able to bring Trace to the heights of sexual satisfaction. And Rachel would only get better as she became more relaxed with her role as Trace's wife.

In appreciation of Trace's praise, Rachel stood on her tiptoes and initiated another long, sensual kiss, which Trace finally ended with a gasp. "Sweetheart, I would like nothing better than to carry you right back up to that loft and make love to you again, but I need to check on the animals."

Rachel smiled at her complacently. "We'll have time tonight."

"Oh, that we will." The thought of Rachel writhing beneath her set her on fire.

Trace finished riding Rio bareback around the corral and was leading him back to the stable when she saw Matthew Reddick approaching. His buckskin advanced at a gallop then slowed to a trot. When Rio began to toss his head at the scent of the unfamiliar animal, Trace put up her hand and Matthew reined his mount to a halt.

Matthew's horse snorted, nodding his head repeatedly and prancing sideways.

"Let me just put him inside and I'll be right with you, Matt." Trace admired her neighbor's steed. She was learning that a man's horse was analogous to the type of car the modern man drove. It was a status symbol and representation of his personality.

Nodding, Matthew dismounted, tying his spirited horse to the hitching post in front of the house. He met Trace back at the stable, and he appeared troubled. "I apologize for interrupting your special time, Trace, but...have you seen Sheriff Jackson?"

"Why would I have seen that useless waste of oxygen?"

"Well...the last anyone knew, he was supposed to have been heading out this way with the Carvers who, by the way, are also missing." They strolled back toward the porch.

"When was this?"

"They had a confrontation with one of the Pawnee at the church yesterday. When they couldn't get in, they were overheard saying they were coming out here."

Trace couldn't help smiling. Little Hawk and Black Feather had not been at the house when she and Rachel returned from their wedding. She had assumed they were still around, just making themselves inconspicuous. Maybe they had found something better to do.

"All three horses showed up at the Crane spread late this morning, but with no riders. Hannah Burnett came to town looking for the sheriff to ask him where John and Seth were."

"Who is Hannah Burnett?"

"The only Crane daughter."

Trace wondered just exactly how many Cranes there were. *The family must breed like bunnies.* "I haven't seen them, Matt.

But...maybe we should take a look around the ranch, make sure they didn't get lost somewhere on the property."

"Yep, that's what I was thinking."

"Let me tell Rachel where I'm going and I'll be right with you."

Trace saddled Chief. Rio was only predictable in his own familiar environment.

As their mounts ambled along, Trace scanned the countryside while Matthew focused his attention straight ahead of them. "So... Trace...how was your wedding night?"

Trace looked over at her neighbor and new friend. She chuckled at the smirk he wore, which bordered on lewd. "It was just as it should have been. That's all you need to know."

"Think there might be a little Sheridan running around come winter?"

Grinning proudly, as if she had actually made a baby with Rachel the night before, Trace said, "I have no doubt."

"Good. I can't tell you enough how pleased Elizabeth and I are that Rachel has found happiness."

"Matt, when I got here, she was alone. It looked to me like everyone had abandoned her, like they didn't care. She told me that you wouldn't allow Elizabeth to even come visit her. That hurt her a lot."

He hung his head in shame. "I know. You don't understand what it's like. These Cranes...they want Rachel's land bad and have tried everything to get it, short of burning her place down or maybe even killing her. If it wasn't for Ben's being sweet on her, I can't imagine what could have happened before you came along. We were all warned off from going near her, cautioned that if we didn't stay away things might start happening to us and our land. I have to be honest with you, Trace, none of us could understand why Rachel didn't just sell. It would have been easier on her. Hell, would've been easier on everybody."

"I know why she didn't and I'm proud of her for not giving in. This ranch is all she has left of her family, her heritage. Yes, she's paid dearly for her defiance, but if they take this land, they take her soul. No amount of money is worth selling your soul for, I don't care how much it is." Trace was startled by her own words. Before she'd landed here, she would have sold her soul to the highest bidder. Who was this person inhabiting her body? Just when had this momentous change taken place, anyway?

"Well, I apologize, Trace. Things looked pretty hopeless. You've kind of showed us all that we have a choice. No one's ever stood up to Ed before so they never knew he'd back down so easily when he doesn't have one of the Crane brothers standing behind him."

"Matt, I guess I can understand that it's been easier for everyone else to go along with things the way they were, but it hasn't been easier on my wife." Trace liked the sound of that... *My wife.* She realized that in the era she was living in, it implied Rachel was her property, but she liked the message the word sent to others — especially the one it would send to Ben Crane: Rachel was off limits. "Whether you stand with us or we stand alone is your choice, but I'm telling you plain — that family terrorizing Rachel is over. I may go down protecting what's mine, but if I do, I'm taking as many of them with me as I can."

Matthew mulled that over. "I don't know if that's being courageous or downright crazy, Trace...but I've got to admire your determination."

"If everybody in town decided to do the same, the Cranes' threats would lose their fear factor. Once that's gone, it's an even fight. If they suddenly realize that people have had enough and not only are they willing to go down fighting but take out the family bullies along with them, you might see a big difference in how things happen around here."

"You'd be willing to kill a Crane?"

"The Cranes won't think twice about killing me," Trace said. "And now that Rachel is no longer available to Ben, they won't think twice about killing her, either."

"You might be right."

They were riding in silence when they heard faint calls for help. Heeling their horses to a canter, they headed in the direction of the voices. They stopped their mounts abruptly as they entered a small clearing. Trace slid off Chief and surveyed the scene before her, wishing she had a camera. Tied naked to three separate trees were Ed Jackson, John Carver, and his son, Seth. The expression on the sheriff's face at being found in such a state was a blend of fury and embarrassment. His attitude was purely indignant.

"You know how much trouble you're in, Sheridan?"

"Me? Looks to me like you're the one who has a little problem here." She let her eyes fall to the sheriff's lower anatomy. "And I do mean little."

Matthew couldn't help but laugh at Trace's insolence.

Looking down at his penis, then back up into the twinkling eyes of his nemesis, Jackson's face went beet red. "I don't get no complaints!"

"Yeah, but your hand doesn't count." Smirking, Trace continued, "Gee, Ed, other than yourself, who you gonna satisfy with that shriveled up little talliwacker?" Despite their unfortunate situation, the two Carvers snickered.

"Damn it, Sheridan, untie me this minute or I'll—"

"Or you'll what? Doesn't look to me like you're in a position to do much of anything, least of all give orders, Ed."

"You...you...you're behind this, Sheridan, I know it. Untie us right now."

"When did you boys get tied up, anyway?" Matthew asked, taking his cue from Trace.

"Yesterday evening," Seth said sullenly.

Trace shrugged. "Then you know it wasn't me. I was getting married; I have plenty of witnesses."

"Then you had them Injuns do it."

"You mean you didn't see who did this to you?"

"No. We was attacked from behind and knocked out. Next thing we knew, we was here...like this."

"Sheriff, those two Pawnee at the church never left town," Matthew said. "Everyone who was at the wedding, and then at the preacher's, saw them."

"Well, I see it like this, Ed," Trace said. "You and your friends here, entered our property — and it is our property now, mine and Rachel's, as marriage gives me that claim of co-ownership — without permission. That's trespassing, and you were previously warned about trespassing. I have the right to designate anyone I damn well please to act as my agent while I'm away, to protect my home and my land. The way I see it, Ed, you should be the one who's incarcerated in your own jail." She absorbed Jackson's speechlessness with a sense of triumph. She knew she was using legalese that likely was confounding the three captives, but she also knew that, in actuality, she and Rachel were the wronged parties. "And, hmmm, let me recall how you put it to me a while back: you didn't see who did this to you so they can't be identified...just who are you supposed to arrest?"

"Hey, Sheridan," John Carver said, his tone more defeated than angry, "we get your point, we really do. But do you think you could show us a little mercy and untie us? I can't feel my arms or legs no more."

"Show you mercy? Show you mercy?" Trace repeated incredulously. "Just for saying that I should leave you all tied there for the scavengers to pick over. When was the last time you boys showed any mercy to anyone in this town, most specifically my wife?" Angry, Trace turned and walked back toward Chief, as though she was actually going to leave them there.

"Wait! Wait." It was the younger Carver speaking up this time. "What do you want? What will make you let us loose?"

Trace spun and walked back to the three pathetic looking men. "Do you think I'm foolish enough to believe anything any one of you would promise me? You guys are at an extreme disadvantage right now and I know you'd do or say anything to get freed. I've been dealing with criminals like you—" she looked pointedly at Jackson, "especially like you — all my life. I know how you think. You'll be agreeable until you get your clothes and your horses back, and then you'll hate me twice as much and come after me with a vengeance."

No one said a word as Trace pulled her knife from its sheath and walked toward the younger Carver, whose eyes grew wide with fear. Matthew held his breath, apprehensive. Raising the blade menacingly, she swung it down in a blindingly fast arc that sliced the rope, freeing Seth's hands. "That's all I'm going to do. You want out of this situation, you do the rest yourself."

Trace returned to Chief and mounted, waiting for Matthew to follow.

"Reddick, you ain't gonna leave us here like this, are you?" Jackson asked, still hostile.

Stepping into the stirrup and swinging his leg over the saddle, Matthew settled in. "It's not my property, Sheriff, so it's not for me to say. But to tell you the truth, I wouldn't even have freed Seth's hands. You boys deserve anything you get. And my sentiment is that it's about damned time."

"Why, you ungrateful, no good—"

"Shut up, Ed!" John and Seth Carver chorused.

"This is your final warning, Ed," Trace told him, evenly. "If I see you on this property again without official business, I will kill you."

Wisely, the sheriff stayed quiet while Seth looked like he was trying to figure out how to untie his legs.

That night, lying in bed with Rachel in her arms, basking in the afterglow of more passionate and inventive lovemaking, Trace asked about the tribe of Native Americans who had saved their wedding day and possibly their house, barn, stable, animals, and whatever crops they had left.

"What do you want to know about them?" Rachel asked, snuggling deeper into Trace's embrace.

"Everything. I find their immediate loyalty to me fascinating," Trace said. She went on to advise Rachel about the events of her afternoon. As Rachel covered her mouth and laughed, Trace related her warning to Ed Jackson.

Gently patting Trace's belly, Rachel said, "It surprises me that I'm no longer afraid of that old turkey buzzard, even though laying a straw in his way usually means rankling the whole lot of those Cranes." Looking lovingly into Trace's eyes, she beamed. "I feel very safe in your presence, Trace, and most definitely in your arms. I mean, I know you're only one person and there are many more of them than you, but with you here, I don't feel that sense of doom that was always there before. You know, like my situation was hopeless." Then Rachel said soberly, "If the Cranes still win and everything ends tomorrow, I want you to know that you've still made me the happiest person alive and I'd never, ever want to take back the last couple of months."

Trace nuzzled and kissed Rachel's neck. "I couldn't agree more. But I promise you the Cranes will not win, even if it was just me and you against the whole lot of them, and I don't believe it is anymore." Trace described what she suspected was the work of Black Feather and Little Hawk that had resulted in the situation with the three naked men tied to the trees. "I guess another reason I would like to know more about their background is that... Listen, Rachel, I hope you don't get upset about this, but I kind of made a deal with them."

"Them who?" Rachel asked cautiously.

"The Indians."

Relaxing, Rachel asked, "What kind of deal? Will they protect us?"

"Well," Trace pursed her lips in contemplation, "I suppose that would be automatic under the circumstances."

"Tell me those circumstances and I'll tell you if I'm upset — although I can't imagine ever getting upset with you, Trace."

Trace leaned in and kissed her on the tip of her nose. "Sure, you say that now." She told Rachel about the deal she had made with the four tribal members regarding the cattle.

Deeply touched by Trace's generosity, Rachel began to cry. "I cannot believe you, Trace Sheridan," Rachel sobbed. "I have never met anyone like you in my life. I never knew one person could love another person so much." She softly caressed Trace's cheek and Trace lowered her lips to Rachel's, bestowing a tender kiss. Rachel's emotional release led to more steamy sex, depleting the energy reserve of both women.

"So..." Trace began, her voice losing its tremble after some cuddling, "now that you have me as a captive audience, I want to hear about our new business partners."

Rachel expelled a deeply satisfied sigh, her body feeling momentarily boneless. "I'll tell you what I know, but a lot of it is just folklore. I suppose we could get the real story from them if we really want to know, and if they want to share, but seeing them in town is as scarce as hen's teeth, so I don't think anybody really knows about them." Rachel shrugged. "Sometimes legends are better."

"I won't argue with you there, my love." Trace adjusted her position so Rachel could comfortably cover half of Trace's body with her own. "Matt told me they are Pawnee."

"From everything I know, that's a generalization. What I've been told is this band is a mixture of Chaui, Skidi, and the most rare, Quiveras, which are really three smaller groups of The Pawnee Nation.

"As the story goes, Moving Elk, depending on who you believe, is either a charmingly persuasive leader or a savage of infernal size. After most of his tribe was slaughtered by particularly violent groups of

Plains Apaches, British-armed Sioux, and Osage Indians, he supposedly took what was left of his family from a burned Platte River village in Nebraska and migrated southwest, picking up other stray Pawnee along the way.

"These other warriors had survived raids that killed many of their men, and caused their women and children to be sold into slavery to the Spanish and Pueblo Indians. Those who weren't murdered were lost to white men's diseases like small pox and cholera. The original aim of the direction of the migration was to hopefully find and rescue lost family members. It turned out to be a futile mission because none were located.

"So about fifteen years ago, this mixed band of Pawnee settled in an area not more than five miles from Sagebrush. Even though they have always seemed to be a peaceful tribe, Moving Elk's legend continues to grow, and I'm quite sure that tribal members boost that lore with each shot of whiskey at Wilbur's, knowing it will make the white men think twice about treating them badly."

"Matt said something about the male members of the tribe offering female captives as a sacrifice to ensure good crops." Trace ran her fingers lightly up and down Rachel's back. "Do you know anything about that?"

Rachel's body shook with laughter. "I've heard that, too, but I don't know of anything that backs that up. Taking women from Jefferson City wouldn't make sense; it's a lot farther away, and no one has gone missing from here. Besides, why do you think they were so quick to accept your offer of corn? They don't have hardly any fertile land to grow crops on. My daddy used to tell me that the Pawnee were known for their bountiful maize crops and skill at hunting buffalo. The buffalo aren't a problem, but it seems as though they don't do so well with the corn growing. At least not around here.

"Traditionally, in Pawnee settlements with better farm land, corn was plentiful and considered a sacred gift, one which they called 'mother'. The Pawnee linked various spiritual rites to its planting, hoeing, and harvesting, and their lifestyle revolved around that and hunting buffalo. This tribe doesn't seem to have a lot of fertile land to grow on."

Trace smiled. "No wonder they were so eager for the corn deal. Maybe with our new friendship and business arrangement, I'll be able to go visit their village. I can't recall ever seeing a real tepee."

"You won't see one in their village, either," Rachel told her. "They live in an earth lodge. They only use tepees when they're out on the buffalo hunt." Rachel then went on to explain about the circular, dirt-roofed, dome-shaped dwelling which housed all seventy some tribal members.

"You mean they all live together, like in a commune?"

"What's a commune?"

"It's a, uh, a group of people who live together and share possessions and responsibilities."

"Well...I guess I don't really know." As Trace's hands lightly caressed the cheeks of Rachel's firm rear end, she swatted at Trace playfully. "Maybe you can find out on your visit to the village." Trace suspected her lazy finger activity was stirring Rachel to arousal again. At least she was hoping.

"Maybe I will," Trace said, fascinated by what Rachel told her.

Rachel rose up and leaned on her elbow, looking into Trace's eyes. "How come you don't know anything about Indians? Weren't there any around Cottonwood?"

Trace wished that she didn't have to keep lying to Rachel about her hometown, but she knew that the truth was too unbelievable...even for her at this point...and her relationship with Rachel was too fragile to try to tell her the truth yet. Trace vowed that she would be the last person to ever betray Rachel again, but this was one myth she would have to keep up. "Where I come from, they're called Native Americans and they live on a reservation, which is now sovereign land. The closest tribe was well over sixty miles away and they ran a cas— a gambling house called the Mystic Sun."

Rachel looked bewildered by what Trace was telling her. "Indians run gambling houses?"

"Yes. And quite successfully, too. Cottonwood is very different from here..."

"So you keep saying. Too bad you don't want to ever go back there." Rachel sighed, settling back into the comfortable position of her head on Trace's shoulder and one leg slung over Trace's abdomen. "Because I would love to see it someday."

"Unfortunately, sweetheart, I can never return. I'd be killed if those men ever found me."

"Then we'll never go there," Rachel said simply. "My goodness. Gambling houses..."

"Tell me more about my silent business partners," Trace asked, enjoying what she was learning. While one hand had returned to massaging Rachel's backside, Trace's other hand began to circle Rachel's breast. Even though Rachel appeared to be ignoring the touching, Trace could feel the heat start liquefying Rachel's lower body.

"Well, again, this tribe of Pawnee has always been kind of mysterious. It isn't that they aren't friendly, they just mostly keep to themselves...until now. They come to town to—" Rachel closed her eyes when Trace's fingers brushed over her nipple. She took a breath and continued. "They come to town to barter and do business and to drink and Lord knows what else at Wilbur's."

"What about Moving Elk? Does he ever come to town?" Trace could not keep the smirk from forming as she assessed her own body's rising readiness and could feel the wetness of her lover even more when Rachel ground her center against Trace's hip.

"I don't know as anyone's ever seen him. Maybe he doesn't even exist." Rachel's words were sporadic, as though she were finding it difficult to concentrate. "Maybe on your visit to their village, you can... see...if..." Not being able to stand it any longer, Rachel turned Trace's face to hers and seized her lips hungrily. When she broke the sizzling kiss, Rachel said, "My word, Trace, I'm beginning to wonder if I'm turning into some kind of sex monster. The more you touch me, the more I crave you."

Trace loved Rachel's unabashed honesty, the way she could just come right out and say whatever she felt. Trace carefully positioned Rachel fully on top of her, cupping Rachel's behind and pulling her up the length of her body to a sitting position. Straddling Trace's rib cage, Rachel looked down at her lover questioningly. "Trust me?"

"Of course." Rachel's voice was hoarse with want. Trace slid underneath her and guided her down. "Wh—?" When Trace's tongue inside her hit her full force, she grabbed on to the headboard and threw her head back. "Ohhh, sweet Lord in Heaven..."

Chapter Twenty

Trace could barely put one foot in front of the other one. She just didn't seem to have any energy in reserve. Rachel's stamina, however, appeared undiminished, which surprised Trace, considering they had been up half the night indulging each other's desires, and then spent a good portion of the morning with Rachel's vomiting. Shaking her head at the irony of the smaller, inexperienced, pregnant woman having more vigor than she, Trace smiled to herself. "God, I must be getting old," she mumbled. "If we're going to keep up this pace, we're going to have to start going to bed a lot earlier."

Trace was not expecting Isaac to bring her the rest of the fence order until Saturday, as it was a one day trip to Jefferson City and a one day trip back, so her plan for the day had been to work on reinforcing the fence and begin marking off an acre of land to start plowing for Rachel to grow the herbs and vegetables she used in her natural remedies. Now that the town was embracing her again, Trace was sure they would start calling on Rachel for her concoctions. That and selling her vegetables to Luther Foster had been lucrative for her in the past and Trace was going to make sure it was profitable for her once more. She shook her head again. The chores would have to wait. She just couldn't muster the energy.

Rachel was heating water to wash clothes, and Trace tried to think of something to do that would be productive but not too taxing. She decided to try her hand at fishing. Locating the pole and a pail in the barn, she headed down to the river, equipment in hand, sleeves and pant legs rolled up, ready for business. *If I had a straw hat, I'd feel like Tom Sawyer.*

About five feet from the river, where the ground was softer, Trace dug for worms. It didn't take her long to find a handful of fat juicy ones, which she stuck in the pail with a clump of dirt. The big, tough detective made a terrible face at handling the slimy little creatures and when she speared one on a hook, she looked even more distressed.

Trace settled in on a comfortable patch of ground and leaned her back against a smooth boulder. She leisurely tossed her line in, noticing for the first time the beauty of the shimmer from the sun on the river. She looked up at cottony white, billowy clouds, and marveled at how vibrant the bright blue of the sky was. Her eyes focused on how those same clouds cast shadows on the green crown of the mountains in the distance. The sparkling water and the faint stirring of the leaves from a small, warm breeze prompted Trace to shake her head in amazement at the changes in herself. Never in her world would she have noticed these things, if they even still existed in such a pristine state, much less taken the time to appreciate them.

Two hours later, she had forgotten all about her admiration of nature. She had caught no fish but lost plenty of worms to their hungry, conniving little mouths. "Frustrated" did not even begin to describe how Trace felt at her inability to catch the cold-blooded creatures with brains far inferior to her own. She had never tried fishing before, and it was proving to be a lot harder than the cocky woman had originally anticipated. She had one worm left, which she skewered several times onto the ordinary hook that was still sharp enough to poke her and draw blood. Tossing the line back in the water, Trace told the worm, "Bon voyage," and tried one last time.

Rachel took a break from doing the washing to wonder what Trace was doing. She couldn't be too far, especially since Rachel checked the corral and found all of the horses grazing and accounted for. She grinned at Zelda, who was getting big and starting to feel her oats as she bounded around the pasture. It was then she heard yelling coming from the direction of the river. Approaching from behind, Rachel stopped a few feet away from Trace and just observed, crossing her arms in amusement.

"Augh! I can't believe this! Son-of-a-bitch!" She held the pole in one hand and the empty hook in the other; her frustration was clear as she looked directly into the water. "All I want is one little fish, just one...okay maybe not so little but that's not the freakin' point here! Can't one of you give me a break?" Exasperated, she threw the pole to the ground and spun around, finding herself face to face with Rachel.

"You tryin' to catch a fish or scare it to death?"

"I thought I could bring home dinner, but the fish have other ideas...and don't say I need to be smarter than the fish."

"Well..." Rachel drew the word out as though she was contemplating just that. "You gotta admit it when you're licked." She didn't miss the lascivious smirk that crossed Trace's face, and when she realized what Trace was thinking, she swatted her arm, a blush suffusing her whole body. "Trace Sheridan!"

"What?" Trace asked in mock innocence. Wisely, she directed the focus back to her annoyance. "I will not concede defeat to a fish."

"There's a fish trap in the barn. It would be easier to set it up and just let the current of the river guide them in."

Trace blinked at her. "You have fish traps? Why aren't they already set up?"

"Well, I just have one and it needs to be repaired. A section of wire rotted out a few months back. Wasn't very useful. The fish could swim right through."

"I can fix it. In fact, maybe I can get to that tonight after supper. In the meantime, I'm not coming back to the house until I catch a fish."

"You going to will it onto your hook?" Rachel asked, nodding toward the empty pail.

"No. I'm going to dig up more worms," Trace told her, unconsciously making a face at the thought.

Rachel stared at the ground, shaking her head at Trace's stubbornness. "Okay." Turning and walking back to the house, she called back, "I'll make something else to eat, just in case."

"Hey!" Trace hollered after her. "Where's your faith?" She smiled fondly as Rachel waved her off and disappeared through the trees on her way back to the house. Not wanting to disappoint Rachel, Trace fell to her knees and began digging through the soil for bait.

She was baiting the hook with a very long worm, when she felt a presence before she saw one. Tensing, she prepared herself for anything.

"You want to catch fish, Tsápaat?"

Trace relaxed as she recognized the voice of Little Hawk, who stepped up to stand beside her. "You move like a damned ghost," she said.

The solid-framed man took the comment in stride. "You found the sheriff." It wasn't a question. His English was broken but comprehensible.

"Kind of took a big chance with that one, didn't you?" She couldn't keep the smile out of her voice. Neither looked at the other when they spoke, both preferring to stare out over the gleaming water.

"We knew you would find them."

Trace was about to throw her line in when Little Hawk raised his hand to stop her. "Yeah, I'm not having much luck at this," she said with a chuckle. If nothing else had come of this journey back in time, she had learned to stop taking herself so seriously, as she had in the twenty-first century.

Little Hawk stuck his hand into a pouch on his cloth tunicle and pulled out a fistful of the contents. Taking a step closer to the edge of the river, he let the substance fall into the water. "Now we wait," he said.

"What's that you dropped in there?"

"Walnuts." At Trace's questioning expression, he said, "You will see."

Nodding, Trace set her pole down. "I really appreciate your help two days ago, Little Hawk. The day would have been a disaster had it not been for you and the others."

"Crane's time has come, Tsápaat. It only needed the right leader. We knew you would come; we just did not know when."

Trace should have been rattled by the fact that she had been a part of the Pawnee prophesy but curiously enough, she was not. When Little Hawk began walking along the bank, she followed. "I'm hopefully going to be planting the corn at the end of next week," she told him, making small talk.

"We will make sure you have some help and we will bring you seeds to plant squash. We have very little land that is not barren." About twenty feet downstream from where they'd previously been, Little Hawk stopped and waded into the river until he was submerged to his waist. He looked at Trace. "Come. You must learn."

Trace joined him in the water, which was not as cold as she expected. She watched in astonishment as one fish, then two, then four more floated to the surface. She grabbed three and Little Hawk plucked out the others. "Are they dead?" she asked as they made their way back to where her pole and bucket sat on the riverbank.

"No. Just sleeping," Little Hawk said as they dumped their catch into the pail.

"Walnuts put fish to sleep?" Trace asked, incredulous.

The Pawnee hunter nodded. "The meat from the walnut holds powerful medicine." He pointed to the fish. "Bring them home to your wife, Tsápaat. She needs to eat well. She has another growing inside her."

Trace attempted to speak, but nothing came out. "How could you possibly know that?" His face remained impassive.

"I am a father. I have three wives and eleven young ones and another coming. There are many ways to know when I will be a father again. The way a woman walks, even when she does not know that she is with child, when the seed is small, shows me. There are many signs. It does not matter how. I do not question knowledge when it comes to me. And you should not, because you will learn. I also know you are not the father, Tsápaat." The sage, brown eyes captured astonished blue ones.

Trace felt as though the wind had been knocked out of her. It was one thing to sense someone was pregnant; that had been explained away. She knew Indians were very spiritual people and had insight to so much more than, well, white people, but to know the baby was not hers was another matter entirely. Did she dare ask him how he knew? And what was this name he kept calling her? "Why do you keep calling me Tsápaat? What does that mean?"

For the first time, Little Hawk cracked a hint of a smile. "Woman."

Oh. That's how he knew. Trace stood speechless and wide-eyed. They strolled back to her original fishing spot, Trace walking beside him, a little dazed.

"Your wife is pure of heart, but I see dark spirits around her when she thinks about the child," Little Hawk said. "This child was not created from love. Even if I did not know you are woman, you love her too much to have brought her the pain she feels for the planting of this seed."

"No," Trace said bitterly. "If the baby was mine, if I'd had the ability to give her this child, there would have been nothing but joy surrounding us." She looked at Little Hawk, her expression clearly showing her sincerity. "I will raise this child as mine, as though he or she really is a part of me."

"You will belong to the child as much as the child will belong to you." He put a reassuring hand on Trace's arm. "What you are doing is noble and brave. I am proud to know such an honorable woman."

Trace was deeply touched, to the point where she had to choke back tears. No one had ever said — nor had she ever given anyone any reason to say — words like that to her before. Swallowing the lump in her throat, she said, "Does it bother you that I am a woman living as a man, that I love Rachel the way a man loves a woman?"

"My people weigh worth by deed and self-respect, not by bounty or if you are man or woman. You are more man than most white men I know, Tsápaat. You will make a great leader someday. Perhaps someday soon."

After Little Hawk's departure, Trace walked up the steps, pail full of fish in hand, laughing to herself. All mysticism aside, Little Hawk admitted that he had been on the other side of the river, tracking a deer a month earlier, when he saw her bathing in the stream. He also told her that he would have known anyway after their actual meeting. There was a different scent to a woman than there was to a man.

She did not have to ask him not to tell anyone. It went without saying that he would respect her secret. He had been aware of her deception for some time and had not spoken of it.

Inside the cabin, Trace set the pail on the table and approached Rachel, who was slicing vegetables.

"You're back early. Did you give up?" Rachel's teasing tone indicated that she fully expected Trace to say yes.

"Ha. Ye of little faith." Trace gently took her by the elbow and led her to the table.

Seeing the contents of the pail, Rachel looked at Trace in surprise. "You did it."

"Of course I did it." Trace was all but preening.

Setting two carrots down on the table, Rachel grabbed the pail and carried it out to the porch, Trace right behind her. Sitting on the top step, Rachel removed the first fish. "You never stop confounding me." Trace joined her on the step. "I'm so proud of you; you never give up."

Trace flashed her a dazzling smile and was about to lean over and kiss her when Rachel unceremoniously lopped off the head of the fish, which caused Trace's stomach to lurch. Her queasiness lasted only until the smell of dinner cooking titillated her nostrils.

After a delicious supper of trout grilled over an open flame, Trace repaired the fish trap, replacing one entire side with new wire, while Rachel boiled the trout heads, bones, and skins for stock. Taken by a bout of nausea, Rachel suddenly ran to the edge of the porch and expelled most of her supper. Trace went inside — at Rachel's request — to check that the pot on the stove was not bubbling over. Whatever was in there smelled damned good. Taking a towel to lift the lid, Trace stirred the soup stock with a spoon and stopped dead when at least three sets of eyes, attached to three very ugly heads, were suddenly staring at her from the steaming water. In a matter of a minute, Trace was joining Rachel, heaving up her trout consumption.

Trace wondered when her stomach had gotten so weak. Or maybe it was sympathetic morning sickness. *Or maybe it was those damned fish heads.* That thought reminded her of Rachel beheading and gutting the trout earlier and her insides turned again.

Later, when their stomachs had settled and the mood was more tranquil, the couple sat on the porch and watched the sunset. "The reds and purples sure are pretty on the leaves as the sun is turning in for the night behind the mountains," Rachel said quietly.

Trace picked up her guitar and sang a few songs while Rachel started sewing a new binding from a remnant of stretchy material she'd gotten from Molly.

Who'd have ever thought that being so domestic would make me so happy?

By the time they went to bed that night, Trace was feeling guilty about not being up front with Rachel earlier. "Sweetheart?" Trace climbed into bed beside Rachel.

"Hmm?" Rachel snuggled into Trace, resting her head on Trace's shoulder.

"I, uh, have a confession to make." Trace wore a hangdog expression.

"You didn't like the way I cooked the fish?"

"No, no." Trace smiled, kissing the top of her head. "The fish were delicious. It has to do with the way I caught them." She explained about Little Hawk and the walnuts.

Rachel searched Trace's eyes, not hiding the disappointment in her own. "Why did you lead me to believe you caught them the traditional way?"

"I know it was wrong, but I felt like you challenged me and I wanted to prove to you I could do it."

"I wasn't challenging you, Trace. I was challenging your experience."

"I just didn't want to come across as incompetent...again." She leaned in and kissed Rachel's forehead.

Snuggling down in Trace's arms, Rachel said, "I've never thought you were incompetent. You just seem, um..." She appeared to be searching for the proper word, "...unseasoned at some things. But you learn fast."

Holding Rachel tight against her, Trace said, "Well, I certainly learned a lot today." She wasn't just referring to fishing.

"I'm not surprised by the effect of the walnuts, though."

"Really?"

Rachel shook her head. "Little Hawk is right. But it isn't just the meat of the nut, the sweet fragrance of the shell shavings has a soothing and relaxing effect as well. They act as a natural sedative."

Trace rubbed Rachel's belly lightly. *Well, it certainly worked on the fish. I can see I'll have to lay in a supply of walnuts for after the baby is born.*

Isaac brought a wagon load of barbed wire the next morning and he and Trace got to work on the fence. Within an hour, Black Feather and two other Pawnee appeared and silently began to help affix the hazardous wire to the wooden rails. Ninety minutes later, a few men from town arrived with their own tools and began on another section. Soon after that, Matthew Reddick and his card playing buddies were there to complete the last fifty feet of reinforcement on the fence. A project that should have taken three or four days was suddenly done in one.

After the fortifications to the fence were finished, Trace made the rounds and thanked everyone for their help, starting with the Pawnee.

"We help each other, Tsápaat," Black Feather said. His two companions nodded. "This land will bring my people bounty again. It must be safe."

Trace sighed. "My concern is the two-legged predators."

Black Feather mounted his horse. "Game will come here to survive. White men will come here for greed. Game will learn boundaries. White men never will."

How prophetic. Trace watched the three Pawnee hunters ride away, then went over to where Matthew and the others were cleaning up and loading their tools back onto their wagons. "I want to thank everyone for coming out to help me today. Your generosity is touching and I promise I will pay you all back somehow."

"Trace," Matthew secured the gate on his wagon, "we've been talking and the boys and I all agree that you can repay us by helping us do the same things with our land."

She searched the faces of the men from town — her neighbors, and now her friends. "Are you telling me you want to do this to start standing up to the Cranes?"

"Yep. It's about time, don't you think?" Caleb Tipping said, as he ruffled his son's hair.

Grinning at his declaration, Trace clapped Matthew on the shoulder. "I'll be more than happy to help every one of you."

They all shook hands on it and then rode in a group toward the ranch house. When they reached the corral, Trace saw a buzzing of activity around the cabin. While the men had been out toiling, the women had converged on the homestead with food, plates, cups, and utensils, and created a feast to feed the tired, hungry workers.

Trace washed up before supper and caught Rachel on her way out of the house. They smiled, inspecting each other appreciatively and standing very close together, the urge to be inappropriately physical nearly overwhelming. Trace nodded her head in the direction of the crowd and said, "Did you arrange this?"

"No. This is as much a surprise to me, Trace." The genuinely bewildered but pleased look on Rachel's face backed up her words.

Reaching over and affectionately rubbing Rachel's shoulder, Trace watched as Rachel then mingled with their neighbors, obviously thrilled to have them back in her life. Struck with adoration for her wife, Trace took a deep breath, focusing on the horizon.

As the light bathed the summit of the purple mountains in the distance, the reality of what was happening washed over her as surely and as richly as the inevitability of the sunset. The surrounding conversation of loud and different timbered voices filtered through her head like a chorus behind the echoing of Little Hawk's words: *You will make a great leader someday. Perhaps someday soon.* It was indeed happening — an army, one person at a time.

A repeat of the same spirit of community occurred the next week when Trace began plowing and harrowing the ground. A few tribal members and several residents of Sagebrush showed up at different intervals to help till the deep, black soil, uproot weeds, break up crop residue, then plant and cover seeds.

A task that should have taken seven days at the least, took three, and instead of one acre for corn, Trace now had two, and Rachel's vegetable and herb garden was stretched out another half-acre. If they could keep the varmints away — animal and human — they might actually reap a good harvest.

Over the next six weeks, with the new property barrier in place and the contents of the garden and cornfield beginning to break through the earth, Trace and Rachel concentrated on helping their neighbors strengthen their defenses. Time was of the essence if they were going to take a stand against the Cranes to get their town, and their liberties, back.

The Reddicks came by every Sunday morning and picked Rachel up for worship services while Trace and some of the Pawnee would patrol the property, ensuring that everything remained as it should. Then they would go back to the river, fish with walnuts, and imbibe grain alcohol, a double distilled spirit derived from the fermentation of different grains.

Torn between exasperation and amusement, Rachel discussed Trace's new "routine" with Molly Ledbetter. The newlyweds were in town for supplies and Rachel stopped by Molly's to buy material so that she could sew a few maternity dresses for herself.

"Every time Matthew and Elizabeth bring me home from church, I find Trace and the Pawnee all the same way," Rachel said to Molly. She sipped at a cup of hot tea while Molly brought out fabric from the back room. "They're sitting by the river, splitting their britches, laughing over nothing, and there are empty bottles of that darned sour mash everywhere."

"Oh dear. That stuff is just dreadful. Harvey would partake every once in a while and I don't know why. The consequences never seemed to match his enthusiasm for drinkin' it in the first place. I never understood why anyone would take a second drink after the first one nearly killed 'em." Molly placed a sign on her door stating she was having lunch. She wanted to visit with Rachel uninterrupted. "You say this happens every week?" Molly shook her head, "Trace seems too smart to drink mash regularly."

"Trace is smart, but he also likes his liquor, I've learned."

"I remember Harvey and your daddy sneakin' off one day when he and your mama came to town. It was gettin' late and we had to go lookin' for 'em. When we found 'em, they were flat out cold in Daniel Baines' barn."

"Tommy's daddy?"

"One and the same. Your mama was seven months along, expectin' you, so we couldn't lift them. We could smell the alcohol so we figured the damned fools deserved a night in that cold barn. We left 'em there to sleep it off. When we went back the next day, they begged us to chop their heads off."

"Mama never told me that story." Rachel smiled, wondering whether her mother handled her father the same way she dealt with Trace.

"No, I 'spect not. Your daddy was pretty embarrassed and I don't think your mama let him forget it none too soon. Far as I know, he never touched the stuff again, but I don't know if that was due to how it made him feel or not wanting to have to face your mama afterwards."

"Wish I could get Trace to stop." Rachel sighed. "I have to spoil their fun and send the Pawnee on their way. Then I have to help my drunk-as-a-lord husband into the house and onto the couch, where he usually spends the night."

Molly raised an eyebrow, giving Rachel a knowing smirk. "Punishing him by withholding your wifely favors?"

"Oh no." Rachel blushed, bowing her head, demurely. "Trace promised me on our wedding night that he would never make me feel like...that...was a duty. And he never has."

Studying Rachel's suddenly shy demeanor, Molly's smile transformed from teasing to warm. She was thrilled to see that Trace was doing right by Rachel in every way. "Well then, if he is pleasin' enough to put that kind of look on your face, why would you make him sleep on the couch?"

"I'm not punishing him, Miz Ledbetter. I've just learned that it is fewer steps from the couch to the bushes when Trace gets sick the next morning."

Molly shook her head. "That's exactly what I mean. If that stuff makes everyone feel so blessed rotten, why would they want more?"

Rachel shrugged her shoulders. "Trace says it's a guy thing, whatever that means."

"A guy thing? Huh." Molly mulled that over. "It must be, because I don't know of any gals who even want to try drinking grain alcohol, much less drink it every week. Sometimes men don't have the sense God gave a goose."

Laughing, Rachel nodded, then finished her tea. "I love being married to Trace, Miz Ledbetter," Rachel said without prompting. "He's the most wonderful man in the world."

"You haven't met all the men in the world, so how would you know?"

"I don't need to. I have the one for me."

Her hand fluttered to rest over her heart as Molly said, "Rachel, you don't know how good that is to hear. Before I got to know Trace, I was afraid you married him just to get back at Ben because I knew how desperate you were. But that boy so clearly loves you and I can see that you love him without you even tellin' me. You're the envy of everyone in town. 'Cept Ed Jackson and the Carvers. Not that they count for much of anythin' other than trouble. Looks like you two are settlin' into married life just fine."

"Yes, ma'am, I swear it is as if we were always meant to be together. Matthew says that one of us without the other is like having half of a whirleygig."

That made Molly snicker. "He loves you, that's plain. Does he treat you well, respect you? It doesn't bother him that, well, Ben, you know..." Molly didn't want the conversation to take an uncomfortable turn but she wanted to make sure Trace wasn't holding the rape against Rachel.

"It bothers him a great deal." Rachel's voice was subdued. "I think he hates Ben as much as I do, if not more, but he never treats me like used goods. He tells me all the time what Ben did to me wasn't my fault. He treats me better than I think any other man would if they knew what you and Trace know. I'm so grateful for that. He makes me very, very happy and I know I do the same for him."

"I hope it stays that way, but you two are still honeymoonin', more or less." Molly winked at Rachel, making her blush again.

"I'm not saying we don't have our disagreements. Trace has a stubborn streak that I'm never going to break, I know that for sure."

Trace had told Rachel she was happier than she had ever been, then further confessed that she was not used to sharing every aspect of her life with someone. Sometimes her self-sufficient, headstrong, solitary ways got on Rachel's nerves. However, with Rachel's hormones fluctuating to opposite ends of the spectrum at lightning speed, it didn't take that much to perturb her and Trace was temporarily in the doghouse at least once a day. The best thing about that was making up afterward, which never ceased to be passionate and fulfilling.

The grandfather clock in the corner of her shop chimed twelve, and Molly patted Rachel's hand and stood. Walking to the door, she said, "So when are you gonna start workin' on givin' me some babies to spoil?" She removed the sign and put it to the side. When she turned back, she stopped in her tracks at the elated expression on Rachel's face. "Rachel? Are you—?"

"Yes, Miz Ledbetter," Rachel said proudly. "Trace and I are expecting."

Molly's eyes teared. "What? When? Are you sure?"

"Yes, I'm positive. I think it happened on our wedding night, so I figure nine months from then. Come winter, there will be a baby in the Sheridan household."

"Oh, Rachel, congratulations!" Molly pulled Rachel to her feet and into a hug. "Is that why you need material? To make some dresses to fit your growin' belly?"

"Yes, ma'am."

"Well, don't that beat all. I was wonderin', because you just bought fabric a couple months back and you don't normally go through clothes that quick. You keepin' it a secret or can I tell Harvey?"

"If I was trying to keep it a secret, I wouldn't be able to for long, so please, tell Mr. Ledbetter. I know he'll be happy for me."

She hugged Rachel again then stepped back, appraising her. "On your weddin' night, huh?" She shook her head. "I knew that boy was fertile from the minute I laid eyes on him."

None of the new community activity went unnoticed by Sheriff Jackson. With every passing day, the lawman grew angrier and more nervous. It wasn't just the strangely charismatic Trace Sheridan that made him jittery, it was the unmistakable change in the townspeople that also gave him pause. For the first time since the Cranes had established their rule over Sagebrush, and ensured Jackson's continued election into office, the sheriff was losing his control-by-proxy. In the past, just the use of the Crane name had been enough to cow the townspeople, but now the concern about doing something, anything that might provoke the Cranes' wrath no longer had the terrifying impact it once had.

To make matters worse, he had to stand by and watch it happen, because ever since that humiliating incident in the woods, John and Seth Carver wanted no part of anything that had to do with Trace Sheridan...at least not until all the Cranes were back and a family meeting decided just exactly what strategies would be put into place to deal with that upstart. As Sheridan apparently had the Indians on his side, that would require a whole different method from how Jackson — and the Cranes — normally handled dissident behavior.

"I'm just thinkin' that maybe Jacob and the boys have gotten a little complacent about them Pawnee," the sheriff said to Seth as they idly sat in chairs outside Jackson's office. The boardwalk was not congested with the usual daily traffic and the two men watched as tribal members helped Trace load supplies into her wagon. "Just 'cause they're peaceful now don't mean they're always gonna be that way. They're still savages. 'S in their nature."

Seth lazily pared an apple. "Ed, you're just ruffled 'cause they're dealin' with Sheridan and not you."

"Course I'm ruffled," Jackson spat, his tone harsh. "You and your daddy should be ruffled, too. You seen how persuasive Sheridan can be. Ain't it obvious these Injuns are partnerin' up with Sheridan 'cause it suits 'em right now? Didja forget about bein' tied nekkid to that tree? If it weren't Sheridan what did that, then it had to be the Pawnee."

Seth stopped peeling his apple and discarded the skin between the cracks in the boardwalk. "You're fixated on Sheridan, Ed, you know that? It could have been anyone who did that. It ain't like we got a lot of friends in this town. 'Specially not you. Now my pa said to forget about him until Uncle Jacob gets back. He'll deal with Sheridan. And the Pawnee. You should be careful, 'cause you ain't soundin' so loyal to my kin right now. You keep talkin' that way and you may be findin' yourself in more trouble than Sheridan."

Jackson's glare matched that of the young Carver. "I ain't being disloyal, you little puke. I know your uncle can handle a lot, but he ain't never dealt with these Pawnee before. These are Injuns, you damned fool! They ain't afraid of war. They ain't afraid of killin'. They also ain't afraid of takin' our women and offerin' them as sacrifices to their Great Spirit after they've done who knows what to 'em."

"Come on, Ed, that ain't never happened yet. My pa said that was somethin' told to us all just to scare us." Seth took a bite of the apple.

"Well, that's 'cause we ain't never riled 'em up before. You and your daddy wanna give Trace Sheridan the freedom to do whatever he damn well pleases until Jacob gets back, but I can tell ya, that ain't smart. These Pawnee are pledgin' their loyalty to that damn upstart and we're all gonna be sorry for it; mark my words."

"Those Pawnee ain't gonna cause us no fuss, Ed," Seth said dismissively. "They don't want to cross us. If they did, they woulda done it a long time ago when Uncle Jacob kinda hog-tied their tradin' and barterin' business with Sagebrush and Jefferson City."

Jackson shook his head in frustration. "You're a bonehead, ain't ya, boy? Don't you know nothin' about the Pawnee? They ain't afraid of fightin' but they don't want a fight if they can help it. They been goin' outta their way to keep the peace, but they ain't yellabellied. They already lost too much and they don't wanna lose any more, but that don't mean—"

"Then why would they fight now?" Seth finished his apple and tossed the core off to the side. "Don't make no sense."

Jackson nodded his head in Trace's direction. "That's why. I swear that boy is half-Injun hisself. I'm tellin' ya, he's partnerin' up with the Pawnee, probably rilin' 'em up just by defyin' us. If they see that he ain't afraid to stand against us, they're gonna start thinkin' 'bout standin' against us, too. It's about profit, Seth, and the Pawnee need that just as much as any of us. Yeah, they been goin' along with bein' cut out of everythin', but even they got their limits. We need to do somethin' about that damned Sheridan or there's gonna be an uprisin'."

Seth laughed. "An uprisin'? You got you a wild imagination, Ed."

"Yeah, you think it's funny? You think I'm crazy?"

"I think you're crazy when it comes to Sheridan, that's a fact."

"Well, let's see how hard you laugh when a rebellion happens, especially if it's led by Movin' Elk."

At the mention of the Pawnee legend's name, Seth's flippancy ended abruptly. Tilting his head in thought, he decided that wasn't possible. "He's gotta be an old man by now, too old to lead anythin'."

"He's a chief. Just 'cause maybe he can't ride don't mean he can't still command his tribe. If Sheridan stirs them into an uprisin', that means we're all lookin' at a serious shift in authority. Jacob ain't gonna be very happy about that."

"Y'know, Ed, ain't that your job — to make sure that don't happen? You're gettin' paid enough to keep things goin' our way. Uncle Jacob ain't gonna be very happy if he gets back to find he's lost this town, 'specially not to an uprisin' led by a half-breed who took Rachel from Ben."

The sheriff didn't need to be reminded of that fact by someone he was hoping to cement as an ally in doing something about Sheridan. Seth was a violent young man and usually didn't need too much provocation to ambush and beat someone up. But Seth was being steadfast to his father's order to let Ed handle everything that had to do with Sheridan until the Cranes returned home. Suddenly Jackson had heartburn.

Jackson was not happy that Sagebrush seemed to be coming alive again under the guidance and leadership of Sheridan, and he had no way of stopping it. He would threaten people with arrest or retribution, and that damned Cottonwood cowboy would advise them how they could lawfully avoid it. Every day that passed seemed to empower the townspeople more and more. Jackson knew it was reaching a critical point when he went around to collect the monthly tax from the store proprietors and homeowners — the payment that insured they be allowed to stay in business and keep their houses and properties from getting burned to the ground — and they refused.

When fifteen head of prime cattle suddenly showed up at the Triple Y, Jackson nearly bit his cigar in half. Performing his daily patrol of the exterior of the ranch, he heard the bovines grazing beyond the new barbed wire fence. Nobody, except the Cranes, was allowed to own cows and steers. How and when the animals had gotten there, as well as where they could have come from, was a mystery to Jackson. One day they weren't there, the next day they were. The sheriff's rising suspicion that there was more to this Sheridan character than met the eye grew with every incident.

The news that Rachel was with child was the last straw. He actually broke out in flop sweat when he sent the telegram to Webb City, where he knew it would reach the Cranes. The wire, intended for Ben, stated that Rachel was now married. He didn't dare mention a baby. He'd let Ben find that out for himself. Just the fact that Rachel was with another man would be enough to turn the youngest, most volatile, Crane into a tornado. Jackson hated to send the telegram, loathe to admit he needed help, but that was something he could no longer get from the yellow-bellied Carvers. Maybe if Ben's focus was on Rachel, his own ineptitude wouldn't be as noticeable. Sheriff Jackson was no longer complacent about his position in town or his worth to Jacob Crane, and he began having nightmares about being at the serious end of a hemp rope wrapped around the center beam of the Cranes' barn. Betting that they would not react to his inability to put a muzzle on this anarchy was not the sort of odds even a desperate gambler would have wanted to draw to.

In four short months, the sheriff had gone from feared tyrant to town laughingstock. The Cranes weren't going to care how it happened, just that it had happened and he had not been able to prevent it. Nor had he been able to keep order in the jurisdiction they had been so successfully terrorizing and controlling for the past ten years.

And the one thing he had never thought twice about — ever — was that anyone would have the balls to take Rachel Young away from Ben Crane. Who was this Trace Sheridan, anyway? How could a total stranger just waltz into Sagebrush, rile up the townspeople, steal the object of Ben's misguided affection without a second thought, befriend the Pawnee to the point of blind loyalty, and cut him down to size with so little obvious effort?

There was only one thing Ed Jackson could do to rectify this situation before Ben Crane got back. Trace Sheridan had to die.

Chapter Twenty-one

Plumes of dust billowed up as the dirt was kicked back underneath thundering hooves. The animal's ears were pinned, his nostrils flaring. He was snorting and almost to the point of wheezing, sweat shining as it gathered on his forequarters, his rider huddled low over the horse's withers, pushing the animal hard.

Ben Crane had received Sheriff Jackson's telegram. He left his father and brothers and the drovers behind in Webb City where they had detoured to purchase racehorses. A lone rider on a shorter path, it would take him a little over four weeks to reach Sagebrush as opposed to another six weeks. Crane didn't know who this son-of-a-bitch was who had taken his woman, but when he got back to Sagebrush, the man would be one dead son-of-a-bitch.

Rachel was in her sixth month of pregnancy and could not have been happier. Even though it was not so, she felt as if the child she was carrying belonged to her and Trace. When her morning sickness had subsided, she had other symptoms that were just as annoying and she was glad she had the understanding, compassionate companion she did and did not have to suffer any more abuse and humiliation at the hands of Ben Crane.

Sitting out on the porch one evening, sharing a quiet moment, listening to the chirping crickets, Rachel reached over and gently took Trace's hand, pressing it into her own. Trace smiled in contentment as she stared out over the empty horse paddock. Rachel absentmindedly rested her teacup on her distended tummy and took an occasional satisfied sip. "I love you, Trace," she murmured.

It wasn't odd for Trace to hear those words from Rachel, but tonight Rachel's inflection was more impassioned than usual. "I love you, too. So very much."

Rachel believed it, was confident that Trace had never been in love before, at least not anything like the intimacy they shared. "You know, Trace, you make my heart swell almost as big as my belly."

"Do I now?" Trace's voice was low, sexy.

The expressive blue eyes flashed in the moonlight and it made Rachel's skin burn. It was amazing how quickly Trace could whip her into a frenzy. "Yes." She tried not to sound as breathless as she felt. "You saved me."

"It's only fair, my love. You saved me," Trace said, bringing Rachel's hand to her lips, kissing her fingers and the inside of her wrist. "In more ways than you know."

Trace had said so more than once, providing only brief details of what she meant, but she had said enough to let Rachel know that sharing their lives was mutually gratifying. Rachel blushed as the fire in her veins bolted to her loins. Although their lovemaking was frequent and satisfying, she could never quite come to grips with how much she always wanted Trace. Rachel cleared her throat and tried to remember what she was originally going to say. "Had you not come along when you did, I really think I would have been doomed to be at the mercy of the Cranes."

"But you said you would never surrender to them," Trace said.

"I know what I said. But I'm carrying a Crane child inside me and it would not have been long before the whole town knew it and that would have grimly altered my options. You showing up and marrying me changed everything. And I'm endlessly grateful for that, for you being in my life. You have shown me unquestioning love, Trace. I feel like what we have together has no boundaries. I am eternally beholden to the Lord above that it is you and not Ben who is here for me when I get a little ornery, when the baby causes my temper to make me say and do things I really don't mean. Ben would have only made my life worse if he and I had been married, Heaven forbid." Rachel shook her head in despair. "I just cannot think of that." She sighed. "You gave me choices. You gave me my life back. I cannot even imagine being with anyone else. You're a wonderful...husband, Trace."

Yes, it was her tall, sable-haired lover who massaged her head, neck, and back when her daily chores caused everything to ache unmercifully. It was Trace who applied a bruised fresh peppermint leaf to her forehead, rubbing in the oil from it to avert an impending migraine. And it was her dearly beloved who tolerated her tantrums and tears, who told her she was stunning and glowing, and held her when she felt bloated and frustrated. Traced bestowed gentle kisses on her growing belly, constantly reassuring Rachel she was going to be a wonderful mother.

When leg cramps startled her out of a sound sleep, it was Trace who pushed the ball of her foot back to stretch the muscles and ligaments so the pain stopped. It was Trace who never complained at being awakened when Rachel's numerous nightly uses of the chamber pot became more urgent and her foraging in the pantry for a snack became more frequent. And it was Trace, not Ben Crane, who was working her firm, tantalizing ass off to get the Triple Y back to being a prosperous working ranch again so as to provide the family with a comfortable living.

It was also Trace who enthusiastically, regardless of how tired she was, satisfied every whim Rachel was now having due to heightened sexual arousal. Sometimes it would be in the middle of the day when Rachel would get amorous and Trace always obliged her, always ensured that Rachel was satiated, that every carnal need was lovingly indulged.

One early afternoon, Matthew Reddick stopped by to give Trace and Rachel the news that Elizabeth was expecting again. He knew they had to be about because Rio was tethered to the front hitching post.

"Trace! Rachel!" Matthew approached Rio slowly so that he would not spook the spirited animal. "Hey, Trace!"

Inside the cabin, the women were making love furiously, the delicious friction of their perspiring bodies driving them both near to climax. Trace was working her magic on her responsive wife, Rachel riding Trace's hand while clutching Trace impossibly close.

"Trace? You in there? I've got great news! Rachel?" Matthew shouted.

The women heard him as though he was yelling through a filter, but continued with their pleasurable activity. At the sound of their names, closer this time, Trace groaned in frustration. Matthew was perilously close to walking through their front door.

"Oh, Lord, don't stop, Trace, please!" Rachel begged, her breath coming in spurts as she took Trace's earlobe between her teeth.

"I don't want to, baby," Trace huffed, "but—if—we—don't—stop—him— Oh, fuck, you are so beautiful."

"Hey — everything okay? Where are you two?" Matthew yelled, his voice showing his bewilderment.

"No, no, no, no..." Rachel said, straining to reach her climax before their unexpected guest made it impossible. She could hear Reddick's horse snort as he stopped out front.

Knowing Rachel was close, Trace was torn between bringing her to completion or preserving their dignity. Avoiding an embarrassment for all three of them finally won out. "Sweetheart, listen...listen." Trace tried to still Rachel's frantic movement. "You need to go to the door and stop him before he gets in here."

Rachel collapsed on Trace in frustration. "Jesus, Mary, and Joseph, I could kill Matthew right now." She slid off Trace who swatted her on the behind when her feet hit the floor.

Matthew tied his horse to the post and hurried up the steps, about to go inside to make sure everything was okay when a tousled, flushed Rachel met him at the door in her housecoat.

As inconvenient as it was, especially since Trace had gotten her *right there*, Rachel knew that she had to prevent Reddick from entering the cabin so that Trace had time to get dressed. It was much easier for Rachel to throw on clothes in a hurry than it was for Trace. As Matthew took in her appearance, she knew she didn't need to explain that she and Trace had been occupied.

It was an awkward moment for Rachel and her neighbor, but Matthew told Trace later that he had left with a healthier respect for Trace that Trace could get Rachel into bed in the middle of the afternoon and that Rachel obviously had no complaints. He didn't believe it when Trace told him that Rachel was the initiator and in a few months, if Elizabeth carried this baby to term and experienced the same hormonal changes, Matthew would be in for a big surprise himself. At first, Rachel was a little bothered that Trace spoke of something so personal with Matthew, but Trace assured her that was what men did and then she told Rachel that she would never disrespect her by going into any detail of anything they did in the bedroom.

The first time the baby kicked, Rachel wasn't quite sure what had just happened. She was sitting on the porch sewing another maternity dress when she experienced a peculiar feeling. The only thing she could liken it to was what it must feel like to swallow a large swarm of butterflies which were now flitting around in her stomach.

Trace had just returned to the outdoor pump for a cup of water and was about to take Rio out for a perimeter check when she saw the strange look on Rachel's face. "What's wrong?" Trace asked, more curious than alarmed.

"I don't know...something's fluttering in my belly."

Rachel may not have had a clue as to what was happening to her, but Trace knew. With one leap, she cleared the steps and was on her knees at Rachel's side with her hand on Rachel's abdomen. "It's the baby kicking, I bet!" However, even when Rachel had the sensation again, the baby was still too small for Trace to feel the movement on the outside. That didn't stop Trace from nuzzling Rachel's belly and speaking softly to the child within.

"Did you know that the baby can hear me talking to it? It can hear noises outside your womb."

Rachel's heart swelled with overwhelming love at Trace's enthusiasm. "How on earth would you know that?"

"Lamaze classes," Trace answered without thinking.

"La— what?"

Avoiding Rachel's curious gaze, Trace kept her cheek to Rachel's tummy. She hated lying to her. "Uh...in Cottonwood, there was this doctor and he went to one of those fancy medical schools back East that taught him all this stuff. He was the town doc and he tended to all of the sheriffs' and deputies' wives when they had babies. He told us all about it."

Rachel was fascinated. "The baby can hear us talking? Right now?"

"Absolutely. And the baby has eyebrows and toenails and fingernails and has hair and can suck its thumb." She grinned at Rachel.

"How would a doctor know that without being able to crawl up inside and look?"

"Well, I can't tell you all the technical stuff because I haven't been to medical school. But it has to make sense, right? The baby just doesn't come together when it's born, it has to develop along the way. This doctor can also do a test to tell you if the baby will be a boy or a girl."

"Before it's born? Trace Sheridan, you're making that up."

Trace stuck her right hand in the air. "I swear to you, I'm not."

"I've never heard of such a thing. And I have never heard of this Doctor Lamaze. If he can do all these things, why isn't he famous?"

"He is. I'm surprised you haven't heard of him. But then, if the Cranes are controlling everything else, they might be controlling what kind of news comes into town, too."

"I never thought of that. It wouldn't surprise me if they did exactly that." Rachel was quiet for a moment. "He can really tell if it's a boy or girl?"

"Yes." Trace looked up at Rachel's contemplative expression. "Would you want to know, if you could?"

"I don't know. I guess...no. I think I'd like to be surprised."

"Really? I'd want to know."

"You would?"

"Sure. It would make it so much easier — choosing names, whether to knit pink or blue..."

"I never thought of that." Rachel pondered a little more. "I still think I'd like to be surprised." She reached down and smoothed Trace's hair. "Can it hear you when you sing?"

"Yes."

"Would you?"

Smiling, Trace kissed Rachel's belly and began to sing a lullabye.

The kicking in Rachel's abdomen intensified, as though the baby was reacting to Trace's voice. It was times like this that made it so easy to convince herself that Trace was this child's other parent. Even if Ben Crane figured it out, Rachel would make sure that the idiot would lay no claim to the little boy or girl growing inside her. Now she just needed to persuade the townspeople when the baby was born, it was arriving two months early.

Trace pestered Rachel about names for the baby to the point of obsession. Rachel smiled indulgently as she looked up from the booties she was knitting. "Trace, you ask me the same question ten times a day, and ten times a day I tell you that it's too soon to pick out names." She sighed deeply. "I'd like the middle name to be after my mother or father — either Frank or Minnie — if you have no objection to that."

"None at all. I just wish we could tell if it was a girl or a boy. That way, we'd be more ready with the right color clothes and things."

"You're just anxious. This baby will be here before you know it; don't wish it here too soon. We're not ready. At least I'm not." Rachel winked.

"I know, I know." Trace fidgeted. "I just think picking out a name now would help us get used to it and give us a chance to change our minds if we decide we really don't like it." Trace didn't want to tell Rachel, but she was hoping for a daughter who would look more like Rachel than Crane. She would not be disappointed with a boy, but with a female offspring it might be easier to deny ancestry than with a boy who might be the spitting image of his father. And then a thought hit her. *Hmmm. The Pawnee are intuitive. Maybe the medicine man can help with this.*

Daily visitors to the ranch, Little Hawk and other tribal members helped till the fields and tend the stock, and, as the cows were dairy cattle, they further made sure that the expectant parents had fresh meat. Trace appreciated that contribution especially, as hunting was not something she wanted to do, but Rachel put her foot down and was insistent that the Pawnee take Trace with them when next they went in search of game. As Rachel's wrath was nothing to be trifled with — especially lately — Trace accompanied Black Feather and two of their Sunday drinking buddies, brothers Rising Moon and Red Sky, the next time they went hunting.

Trace rode along quietly at first, hoping they would not see anything she would have to kill. Then she decided to start telling jokes, which, unfortunately, went right over her companions' heads, until she told the only Indian-related joke she knew. "...so then the boy goes to the Chief and says, 'how do we get our names?' and the Chief says, 'when you are born, you are named after the first thing I see, like a blowing leaf or a howling wind. Why do you ask, Two Dogs Fucking?'" One thing she had learned from her first visit to Wilbur's was that the word "fuck" was just as widely used in the Old West as it was in her era.

Her Pawnee friends were silent at first and then laughed uproariously, which pleased her on two levels. The first was that the noise would probably scare away any game in the area and the second, she loved to make her new friends laugh, and that wasn't easy unless they were all rip-roaring drunk.

"You do not like to hunt, Tsápaat?" The observation came from Red Sky.

"I've never done it before. I don't like to kill animals unless they are sick, gravely injured, or about to kill me."

"Out here we kill only what we need to live," Black Feather said.

Trace smiled. "I could live on fish and vegetables."

Black Feather shook his head. "That may be so, but Caskí Custíra'u needs the meat for the young one growing inside her."

The Pawnee now always referred to Trace as Tsápaat and Rachel by a name which, loosely translated from their native language, meant "little mother". Suddenly things got very still and Black Feather reined up, raising his hand for the others to do likewise. He sniffed the air. "We need to find game soon. Rain is coming. Not a good time for hunting. Rahúrahki holes up when it rains," he said, meaning the wild animals.

Not more than ten minutes later, in the uppermost quadrant of the north side of the Triple Y property, Red Sky, who obviously had ears like a cat, directed the party to the right of the path, where they spotted a few antelope grazing in an open area. They all stopped and looked at Trace, who returned their stares skeptically.

"You're going to make me kill one of them, aren't you?"

Rising Moon didn't understand Trace's reticence. "You must be the one. You must learn to do this. For Caskí Custíra'u. For the little one who will learn from you how to hunt."

Trace did not want to do it. Every fiber of her being silently protested having to execute an animal just to fill their bellies, when she knew they could survive on fish, rabbit, eggs, and vegetables, and it would be just as good for the baby. But she also knew that her refusal would not be met with understanding; it would be looked upon as a weakness and would damage her credibility as a warrior. It was critical that she continue to do all she could to prove her mettle so that she would not lose the respect of the Pawnee.

Trace knew it was hypocritical that she readily ate the meat the Pawnee brought them, but eating it was one thing, killing it was quite another. She didn't have to look the target in the eye and shoot it, watch it drop to the ground, and die. When a cut of meat was put on the table in front of her, she could overlook how it got to her plate, blocking out any consideration of the details of its demise. Today, right now, she could no longer do that. She had to prove her manliness. She knew if she didn't kill this antelope, it would go no further than the four of them in that group. She also knew if she did kill the animal, the word "hunter" would be added to her growing reputation, and news would spread quickly.

Come on, Trace, buck up, she told herself. *How hard can it be? Just aim and pull the trigger and it'll be over quickly, you'll have proven yourself. Hell, you can kill a man and not think twice about it; this shouldn't be such a dilemma.* But it was.

She stared into the expectant eyes of the three Pawnee. They dismounted to find concealment behind tall shrubbery as Trace reluctantly drew her Winchester from its sheath on the saddle then joined them in hiding. She watched the antelope grazing peacefully and drew a deep breath. Sensing slight movement to her left, Trace glanced over to see a waterskin offered to her from Black Feather.

"*Kiiráhkata?*" he asked.

Trace knew that could mean whiskey, corn liquor, or anything alcoholic. Accepting the deerhide container, she removed the small stopper and took a long swig of the light amber liquid that burned all the way down her throat. The spirit made her eyes water and there was a small part of her that wondered what she had just drunk, while a bigger part of her didn't want to know. She was about to raise her rifle when Black Feather nudged her again, indicating she take another swig.

"*Raahikuuc.* Courage."

Trace shook her head. She wanted to get it over with. It wasn't courage she lacked; it was desire. She raised the Winchester and took careful aim, catching the exquisite, unsuspecting animal squarely in her sights. After a brief wave of panic, her nerves steadied. She took a breath, relaxed her stance, and squeezed the trigger. Trace was a dead shot with any kind of weapon; she did not miss, but when the antelope fell, so did her tears.

Other than her scent, it was the first indication the Pawnee had that Tsápaat was indeed a woman, with emotions accordingly. Sad and angry, she stoically, robotically participated in the skinning and gutting, and rode back to the cabin. When they reached the house, the Pawnee gave her the best cuts of meat and took the rest and the hide and directed their horses toward their village as the rain began to fall.

The minute Trace stepped through the door, Rachel knew something was wrong. She could see it in Trace's demeanor, feel the chill in the air when Trace handed her the meat and then brushed past her. Her bewilderment apparent, she said, "Trace?"

Trace spun on her heel and stalked back. "Don't you ever ask me to do that again, Rachel. Not ever!" Trace was almost spitting every word. "I hate killing animals unless I absolutely have to and it's something I will not do again unless I am faced with those circumstances. I don't mind doing anything else around here but if you want fresh meat, from now on you can do it yourself or we can barter with the Pawnee. I will not do that again!"

At first, the vehemence in Trace's voice frightened Rachel, but when she realized Trace was not as angry as she was heavyhearted, it became easier to understand what had motivated her outburst. "I'm sorry...Trace...I had no notion hunting would affect you like this, I—"

"Well, it did! I will forever have the memory of that magnificent creature falling to the ground, dying because of something I did, the memory of those beautiful eyes staring at me while we took its meat."

"Honestly, Trace, I've seen you shoot. If you hit it directly between the eyes, it was most likely dead before it even dropped. It would have been a quick and painless death."

"You know, that doesn't make me feel any better."

"But, Trace, we need red meat, I need it for—"

"Then you kill it next time. I don't need it; I can live on whatever we've been surviving on without it." She walked to the bedroom and pulled out clean clothes. "I'm going to take a shower and wash this blood off me."

As Trace stomped toward the front door, Rachel followed. "Trace, at least let me—"

She stopped and looked at Rachel. "Don't...don't come near me for a while."

The flash of anger in the expressive blue eyes stopped Rachel in her tracks. Tears welled as she watched Trace disappear from view. She had never seen that side of Trace and wasn't sure she liked it. Her emotions fluctuated from hurt to indignation and back to hurt. Wiping away tears with her sleeve, Rachel began to prepare the meat for storage, leaving one cut out for supper.

Ignoring Trace's strong protestations, she had practically demanded that Trace go hunting with the Pawnee. She honestly believed it was something Trace needed to learn, to get used to, since food became scarce in the winter. Killing an animal for food never bothered her; she had been doing it since the first time her father took her hunting when she was seven. It was not a matter of liking it or not liking it, it was a necessity and it served a purpose. Well, if she had to be the hunter of the family, then so be it. Trace was a good provider in everything else, and this was the first time she ever balked at one of Rachel's requests. *If hunting is the only thing Trace won't do, I'm still pretty fortunate.*

After Rachel stored the haunch of meat for later meals, she cleaned up the mess and readied the thick portion of flank she had put aside for supper, spicing it with herbs, skewering it with a metal rod, and setting it to broil slowly over a small flame. As she began to peel potatoes, Trace re-entered the house.

Taking in the aroma of dinner starting to cook, she stated flatly, "I don't want any." She crossed to the bedroom, running her fingers through her hair to help it dry faster.

"You have to eat," Rachel said softly, as she continued to fix the potatoes.

"I don't have to eat that." Trace pointed at the fireplace.

Rachel put her knife down, wiped her hands on her apron and went into their bedroom, where she sat on the bed, watching Trace search for a pair of socks. "Trace...I won't ever ask you to do that again."

"It wouldn't matter if you did, because I won't."

"Please don't be mad at me, sweetheart," Rachel pleaded. "I can't bear it." The thought of Trace really being angry with her tore her apart and she began to cry, burying her face in her hands.

"Now, don't start that, Rachel," Trace said, exasperated. "You know your tears always get to me and I'm not done being pissed off yet. And I'm not backing down on this."

"I don't want you to," Rachel sobbed. "I shouldn't have made you go. I was wrong and I'm sorry."

Emitting a deep sigh, Trace said, "No, you shouldn't have, you shouldn't have made me feel like less of a person because I hadn't put meat on the table that I killed. Who cares how it gets there? If the Pawnee don't mind bartering for it, then what's the problem?"

"There isn't one."

"No, there isn't. So, we'll never have this discussion again, all right?"

"All right."

Trace looked over at Rachel, who was obviously distraught, much of the emotion undoubtedly fueled by raging hormones. When Rachel could not stop crying, Trace sat beside her on the bed and enveloped her in a secure embrace. "Shhhh, it's okay, baby. Shhhhh," Trace soothed. "I know you didn't understand my feelings about this. I should have made myself more clear."

She kissed the top of Rachel's head, reassuringly, as Rachel settled down in her arms. Lightly stroking Rachel's back and arms, Trace held her for a while, until it smelled like the meat was beginning to burn in the other room.

"I think dinner might be done," Trace said quietly.

"I'm suddenly very tired," Rachel said, guessing that it was the fight that had drained her.

Without further conversation, Trace gently laid Rachel back on the bed, helped her into a position as comfortable as possible, and went to tend to dinner.

A few days later, Little Hawk rode up to Trace and Isaac working on repairing a trough that had been kicked in by one of the steers. The Pawnee dismounted, carrying something in his hand as he approached.

"Ráwa," Little Hawk greeted.

"Hey, Little Hawk." Trace smiled. "Whatcha got there?"

Trace and Isaac went to meet the Pawnee, who held out his hand. On his palm was a tiny, sleeping puppy. "For you and Caskí Custíra'u, Tsápaat. And for your little one."

Deeply touched by the gesture and immediately in love with the precious little gift, Trace took the puppy and cradled him beside her neck. He was gray and off-white and had an area of black on his head that made him look like he was wearing a World War II flying ace's cap with goggles. "He's beautiful; thank you, Little Hawk. He's so tiny. How old is he?"

"Old enough to be away from his mother. He is special, Tsápaat. He is mostly wolf. He will be loyal to you and to your family. He will be calm but he will be fierce in his loyalty."

Isaac was also smitten and reached over to scratch the little dog behind his ears. The puppy yawned, making a small whining noise, and then went back to sleep.

"I have to show Rachel. Come with me?" The offer was directed to Little Hawk, as Trace knew Isaac would follow her, regardless.

"No. I am needed back in my village."

"Anything wrong?"

Little Hawk shrugged. "One of my wives is giving birth," he said nonchalantly.

"What?" Incredulous, Trace shooed him back to his horse. "Then, yes, you should be there."

"I have seen it before," he replied, not exactly disinterested but not enthusiastic, either. "This will make twelve."

"I know, but, Little Hawk, you should still be there."

Little Hawk mounted his horse and grinned. "She is not ready. It takes time. You will see, Tsápaat."

"Why do you call him that — Tsápaat?" Isaac asked, curious. "What does that mean?"

Exchanging glances with the Pawnee hunter, Trace said, "Uh...cowboy," at the exact same time Little Hawk said, "Warrior." Looking at each other again, Trace then said, "Warrior," as the tribal hunter said, "Cowboy."

Isaac appeared confounded and Trace spoke up and said, "It means Cowboy Warrior. Let's go show this little guy to Rachel." Isaac seemed okay with that and beat Trace to the steps. Turning to Little Hawk, she rolled her eyes in mild relief and patted the flank of the Pawnee's horse. "Thank you again."

Putting his hand up in response, Little Hawk heeled his stallion to a trot and rode away.

Rachel gushed her approval and appreciation when presented with the puppy, and Trace didn't get to see him or hold him again until sometime after midnight when he began whine and cry for his mother. Trace knew it was wrong but both she and Rachel were exhausted and the only thing that would quiet the puppy was to bring him into their bed, where he promptly curled up between them and went back to sleep.

As Rachel smiled fondly at the dog, rubbing his warm little tummy, Trace shook her head, laughing. "This will not happen with the baby."

Rachel leaned over the dog and kissed Trace on the forehead. "We'll see."

Rachel gingerly carried the puppy out to the porch and set him down by Trace's feet. "He piddled inside."

"On you again, or the floor this time?"

"On the floor," Rachel said. She didn't understand why Trace found it so funny that the dog had peed on her. Twice.

"He's a baby, honey, he needs to be trained." Trace watched the puppy waddle around her ankles. He sat down abruptly and began gnawing on a piece of rawhide dangling off the bottom of Trace's chaps.

"He needs to be trained outside," Rachel said, trying her best to sound irritated. "Dogs should be outside, Trace."

Trace scooped up the puppy and turned him belly up. She kissed his round, soft stomach, and cradled him. "I love puppy bellies," she said as the dog chewed on her fingers. "Little needle teeth and little puppy breath." He wriggled in her hand, making high-pitched growling noises, and she held him out to Rachel. "Come on, how can you stay mad at a face like that?"

As if on cue, the puppy looked at Rachel with an expression so precious, she gave up all pretense of annoyance. "You fight dirty, you know that?" Rachel took the puppy from Trace. He began licking her chin. "All right, okay, you're forgiven."

"You're going to have to toughen up there, mommy," Trace patted Rachel's stomach, "if all it takes is looking adorable to get out of trouble."

"It's never worked for you," Rachel teased, raising an eyebrow.

"Now that I know it's a weakness, I'll have to try harder." Trace scratched the puppy behind his ears. "We need to pick a name for this little guy."

"I thought we decided on Sparky."

"No, you decided on Sparky." Trace laughed. "He's going to grow up to be a ferocious looking wolf. What self-respecting wolf would want to be called Sparky? All the other wolves will beat him up on the wolf playground if we name him that."

Rachel snickered. "What are you talking about? What wolf playground?"

"It's a joke, sweetheart. Seriously, we can't name him Sparky."

"Fine, what's your suggestion?" Rachel held the puppy against her to get him to stop squirming, and petted him in an attempt to make him settle down.

Trace studied the dog, then her expression became melancholy. "Let's name him Ramiro."

"Ramiro? That's unusual. Why Ramiro?"

"When I was growing up, we had a neighbor, a Basque woman, Mrs. Segura. She was very kind to me. She fed me meals when my mother was too busy, which was most of the time. I spent a lot of evenings and weekends at her place. She had this beautiful dog, a German Shepherd—"

"A what?"

"A German Shepherd." At Rachel's look of confusion, she added, "It's a kind of dog that our little guy here might look like when he grows up."

"Oh. And he reminds you of that dog?"

"Not yet." Trace smiled. "But Ramiro was my best friend. The only time we were apart was when I was at school. And when he died of old age, I grieved like I never had for any human in my life. Mrs. Segura told me that Ramiro means 'great judge'."

The puppy yawned, looking little like a great judge, but Rachel knew that it was important to Trace. "Ramiro. It's settled. I can think of no greater honor for him than to name him after someone so very special." Rachel handed the dog to Trace.

"Thank you, sweetheart." Trace cuddled Ramiro to her, rubbing her cheek against the velvety-soft fur on his head. "Yes, you're my good boy. You're my little Ramiro, you're—" Feeling something wet on her shirt, she held him away from her and looked down. "Oh, man! Rachel, your dog just peed on me!"

Two weeks went by with Ed Jackson's appearances uncharacteristically rare, and that made Trace suspicious. Even when she went to town, with or without Rachel, the sheriff was not out performing his usual routine of making himself annoyingly present where he was not wanted, which was pretty much everywhere. Silas, who was always a fountain of information, advised Trace that, for some reason, Jackson had been sticking close to his office, not even going home at night, preferring instead to sleep in a little room behind the area of the cells. While everybody else seemed okay with the sudden scarcity of Ed Jackson, Trace didn't like it. A warning bell tolled in her gut and she had learned a long time ago never to ignore that alarm. He was up to something, she was sure of it, and she was even more sure that whatever it was, she was going to be the target.

Ben Crane was two weeks from home. His rage was so all-consuming that he felt he could walk the rest of the way to Sagebrush and still make it in the same amount of time as it would take his horse to get him there. He wouldn't have stopped at all if his horse hadn't been too exhausted to travel any further. After he and his mount got a drink from a stream, he hobbled his ebony Friesian to a grassy shelter by some large boulders and a few trees, where he decided to bed down for the night.

He stripped the saddle from the sturdy horse and the sweaty animal rolled on the ground. Crane rubbed him down with handfuls of dried grass, then hitched the stallion to a low branch where the horse foraged on the rich vegetation at his feet. Crane also needed to think about dinner, something substantial, as he had been living on whatever he had in his pack since he had left Webb City. Within the last half mile or so, he had seen the tracks and droppings of both deer and elk, so he was pretty sure he would eat well before he went to sleep that night.

Ben was the baby of the Crane family, the only one who hadn't yet married, and he was under a lot of pressure from his family to do so. Considered roguish by his father and brothers, he was known in the town as a violent womanizer. Ben was a mean drunk who preferred the company of the wayward women who resided above the saloon because he knew he could treat them any disrespectful way he pleased and pay them enough to take it.

The past year, with his family's unyielding insistence that he take a wife, he had cast his eye upon Rachel, the most comely of any female Ben had ever seen. After all, why shouldn't he have the best? He figured it would also solve the twin problems of gaining ownership of the land she owned, land that was blocking his family's direct route to drive cattle to Kansas, as well as their intent to own all of the property east of Sagebrush. It never occurred to him that she wouldn't be interested, that she would decline his offer, that she would have the audacity, much less the courage, to turn down a Crane.

So my reputation ain't the best, maybe that's what stuck in her craw. He tossed a couple more sticks on his campfire. The sun was setting and he could feel the cool dampness in the air. *Still, that shouldn't have mattered. As my wife, she coulda had everything she ever wanted. I'm rich, I'm good-lookin', and I can be downright charmin' when I've a mind to. It ain't every woman I bathe for, dress up in my Sunday best for, and bring flowers to. That shoulda told her she was special. Why did she have to be so damned difficult?* Although, he had to admit, right up until the day he took her, she had been polite but firm in her refusal. She was right when she told him a Crane never took no for an answer. He thought that he could just wear her down, if not one way then definitely another. *It wasn't right that she was livin' on that big spread by herself. She had to be lonesome, and she needed a man to take care of her and the ranch. Well, I guess she does want a husband, it just ain't me. That'll change when I get back to Sagebrush. If she ain't my wife, she ain't gonna be nobody's wife!*

His back hairs bristled at the thought of Rachel being with anybody else, at the visual of some other man having her every night and getting it lovingly, willingly and, he had no doubt, eagerly. Crane could not bear the thought of that pretty little face and body that just begged to be touched again and again, warming anyone else's bed. Well, if there was one thing he could tuck up under his belt, it was the knowledge that he'd had her first. He grinned at the memory and wondered if Rachel's husband knew that he hadn't married a virgin. *Of course he knew. All men know. And the son-of-a-bitch obviously stayed married to her anyway.* That put him right back into another sour mood.

Few men had ever gone up against him or his family, and the ones who tried, lived to regret it, if they lived at all. What could possibly be so different about this drifter that Jackson, his uncle John, and cousin Seth couldn't keep him in line? The man had to be downright crazy in the head and, for that matter, so did Rachel, to think that someone, anyone, would keep him away from her, keep him from taking her whenever he damn well pleased. However, if the man *was* a touch insane, it would make the confrontation a little more interesting; crazy people weren't afraid of anything. Crazy didn't scare him...but he'd learned to never underestimate it. Regardless, he could not stop thinking of Rachel and what it felt like to have her and, after he killed her husband, what it would be like to have her again.

Without realizing it until it became almost painful, he'd sprouted an erection that was straining the fabric of his trousers. He wasted no time unbuttoning his pants and immediately went to work on taking care of that little problem, fantasizing about a certain feisty blonde resisting him while he did.

The fence was in place and strong, the cattle were healthy and productive. The crops were starting to thrive, Ramiro was growing like a little weed, and Rachel was really showing. The reality that there would soon be an infant in their lives was becoming more and more the focus of their days, and Trace began preparing the house for the arrival of the baby. She found some items packed away in the barn that had been Rachel's when she was a newborn and Trace pulled out all the clothes and set to work reinforcing a lovely cradle with intricate carvings on all sides.

Trace reflected on the last few months with mixed emotions as she sat on the porch working on the cradle. She was so settled into her new life that what memories she had of her past were beginning to feel like figments of her imagination, as though she'd really never been anywhere but on the Triple Y. She knew that wasn't so.

She could recall mostly everything up to the circumstances that resulted in her being in 1879, and try as she might, she could not get past that dead end. She was thinking maybe she should be grateful that she couldn't remember, that maybe it was the horror of whatever had happened that caused her to forget. She accepted that she hadn't been a good person in her former life; she worked both sides of the law and selfishly lived for more money and the next cheap thrill. She realized that she would have most likely worked for the Cranes had she been born in this time period. She shuddered to think she might even have been so despicable as to be the one who went after Rachel to get her land for her bosses. She could now admit that she was repulsed by the person she once was, and thankful she could bring her modern experience to an old fashioned world and use it to her benefit. She knew the Cranes would never concede in any situation, just as she never would have. However, her advantage was in knowing how they thought, and knowing she could use it against them. Trace hoped she could eventually accomplish a peaceful arrangement with no one getting killed, but she doubted it. Too much was at stake. For everyone.

She could not think of anywhere she would rather be, anyone she would rather be with, in spite of the impending inevitable showdown with the Cranes. She had been given a second chance and she was not going to screw it up. Redemption was a funny thing. She had never felt she needed redeeming, but now that she had been, she didn't know how she could have existed the other way. She knew beyond any doubt that she would die for Rachel and this unborn child, and that came as a revelation to someone who never would have believed she had that kind of selflessness inside her. The sudden need to confess her shortcomings to Rachel became so overwhelming, it made her physically ill.

That evening, Trace enjoyed a hearty supper of steak and sliced potatoes, all fried in deliciously unhealthy bacon grease. "By the way, Rachel," she said casually, "the Pawnee are having a celebration tonight, so they won't be around the property. It doesn't really make a difference. I'll be home all night."

"That will be a little strange. There are always at least one or two of them around." Rachel finished up her last bite of beef.

"That's because they like to keep an eye on the ranch buildings, as well as on their own interests in the growing corn and squash. They trust the Cranes and anyone affiliated with them less than we do." Trace drank from her water glass.

"I didn't think that was possible," Rachel said. "I'm glad the Pawnee are always around, but I trust you to keep us safe."

"We'll be fine. I just wanted you to know."

"What are they celebrating?"

"I didn't ask them. I figure if they wanted me to know, they'd tell me."

"Trace, you seem to understand the Pawnee real well and they almost treat you as one of their own. Are you sure you don't have any Indian blood in you?"

Trace wiped her mouth with a linen napkin. "I honestly don't know. I guess it's possible."

Rachel hesitated, gathered her courage, and asked a question that had been bothering her. "Trace, I've been wondering, why don't you ever really talk about your past. I mean, you've told me bits and pieces, but you don't talk about your family, or things that you did kind of just every day."

Taken aback for a moment, Trace decided to open up to Rachel — at least about the things she hoped Rachel would understand. "Are you sure you want to hear all this?" she asked, as Rachel started to clear the table.

"Of course. I want to know everything about you. I just never thought you were comfortable talking about it. You always changed the subject." Rachel grinned. "I guess I talk enough for both of us."

Trace grabbed Rachel's wrist as she passed and pulled her onto her lap. Kissing her lingeringly on the cheek, Trace said, "I love to hear you talk. You are such a gift to me, Rachel. You have no idea."

Rachel stared deeply into Trace's eyes. "Gosh. No one has ever said anything like that to me before. A gift? That's so romantic. I love you so much, Trace. You are a gift to me, too." She hugged Trace fiercely and while her head was nestled against Trace's neck, she said, "Is this your way of changing the subject again?"

Trace eased back and kissed Rachel's forehead. "No. I'm ready to talk about it."

"Should I make tea?" Rachel stood.

"No. Not just yet. Unless you want a cup."

Alert to the pensive tone, Rachel shook her head. "How bad is it?" she asked cautiously.

"I'll let you decide." Taking a deep breath and clearing her throat, Trace began. "You already know that I don't know who my father was and my mother was a prostitute. She was what was known as a crack whore and spent more time in jail than out of it before I came along."

Rachel winced at the harsh name Trace called her mother. "What does crack mean?"

"Crack is a drug, a medicine, sort of, that gives you a short burst of euphoria and energy. My mother became addicted to it, you know — having to have it all the time, so she had to do something to be able to buy this medicine. She always used to say she was sitting on a gold mine so she sold her, uh, services to men so she could afford the crack."

"Is that why she was in jail so often? I know prostitution is supposed to be against the law but I don't understand. I mean, here, the sheriff just looks the other way as long as he gets the girls to lay with him for free."

"Well, in Cottonwood, the law makes prostitution and the drug she bought and used illegal."

It seemed beyond Rachel's comprehension. "A medicine is against the law?"

"This was not a useful, helpful medicine. It was a bad medicine that people misused, and it killed them."

"Is that what killed your mama?"

Trace felt a twinge of guilt. *Is Zelda still alive? If she is, she's probably just a shell of a woman. What she hasn't paid for with her life, she paid for with her soul long ago.* "I honestly cannot tell you what finally killed my mother." She wasn't lying. If her mother was still alive, Trace would never know what would be the cause of her death.

"I can't imagine being a little girl, growing up like that."

"I don't think I ever felt like a little girl. I don't think I was ever allowed to be a little girl, to have the kind of childhood most little girls — or even little boys — have, for that matter." Trace shrugged. "I never knew anything different. It wasn't until I went to school and met other kids my age that I realized every kid didn't live like I did."

"Did your mama still, you know, um...see men after you were born?

"She actually cleaned herself up, uh, behaved herself for the first couple years of my life. But it was too much responsibility and she went back to her old ways. Men and crack always came first. So I grew up being cast aside and always having to fight for whatever little crumb of affection she tossed my way. I still loved her very much, but I was a bitter and angry child, Rachel, and although I didn't turn to drugs or prostitution, I wasn't a very nice person. Nothing was ever given to me and even the things I worked for when I was younger never seemed within reach. So I began taking, because I thought it was the key to my survival."

Rachel held her breath. "Taking how? Stealing, robbing people?"

Trace hung her head and then looked out toward the porch, purposely avoiding Rachel's gaze. "In a way, yes." She glanced back at Rachel.

"B-but weren't you a sheriff?" Rachel's eyes were wide with disbelief, as though she were not willing to believe what Trace was telling her.

"I was a police detective," Trace said, "which is very much like a sheriff. But—" She hung her head, the burning in her cheeks an indication of the shame she felt. "I was a lot like Ed Jackson. In fact, I was much worse than Ed Jackson could ever think of being."

Rachel's hand fluttered to rest over her heart. "I don't believe it," Rachel said in a whisper. She shook her head. "It's not true. You're honorable and caring and—"

"It is true. I'm so sorry, baby. I know this probably changes your mind about me, but I had to tell you." She reached for Rachel's hand, which was chilled, and enclosed it in both of hers. "I used to think honor and integrity and truth and benevolence were for suckers, because that's the way I grew up. Honorable and benevolent people never wanted to help me, never wanted anything to do with me. I never got a break. So I took the breaks for myself. In my old life, I would have run roughshod over people like you and the Reddicks and the Tippings and, well, everybody else who didn't seem to be able to do something for me."

"The Bible says the meek shall inherit the earth," Rachel said, her voice laced with disappointment.

Trace was surprised that Rachel did not withdraw her hand. "Rachel, in the place I come from, the meek won't inherit anything but unending bruises from always turning the other cheek. And that's what the Cranes are counting on: that everyone in this town, like you, obeys the teachings of the Bible and stays passive. I know how they think because I used to be like them."

"You were never like them!"

"I was."

"You have never been like that since I've known you. What changed you?"

Tears welled in her eyes. Before Rachel, she never would have thought it possible, that one person could show her so much love and goodness that she would do anything to atone for the sins of her former self and commit herself completely to a decent way of life. She never would have believed it achievable. "You did."

Rachel's eyes also teared up and she squeezed Trace's palm. "Are you saying I made you want to be the respectable person you are now?"

"And much more." Trace tugged on Rachel's hand and pulled her over onto her lap again. "I never want to do anything to shatter your faith in me."

"You haven't. I don't know that person you just told me about. I only know the upstanding, loyal, righteous person you are now. The one Sagebrush knows. And the woman I know has rescued my family's good name, and I love her and she loves me beyond all reason."

"I do, Rachel. Truly. The Cranes are done hurting you. And they're done abusing the good people of Sagebrush."

Snuggling, Rachel was momentarily quiet, then she said, "So, who are those men who are looking for you — good men or bad men?"

"Bad men I betrayed." The answer came out before she even thought about it, as it had the other time Rachel had inquired, the very first day they met. Trace didn't need to wonder if it were true; she knew it had to involve the DeSiennas. She just wished she knew the why and how. She smoothed Rachel's silken hair. "I promise you they will never find me. They'll never come here looking for me."

"How do you know?"

"You just have to trust me on this, sweetheart. I just know. We won't have to worry about them. Ever."

After clearing the dishes from the table, Trace stepped out onto the porch, about to pick up her guitar when she had a sense something was amiss. Focusing on the herd that was grazing, she saw that one was missing.

"Sweetheart, I don't see all of the cows," she said as Rachel joined her on the porch.

They searched the immediate area and the errant heifer was not found. It was unusual for one of the cows to have separated on its own, especially when it was closing in on night time for them. Trace wished she wasn't so suspicious and dismissed her own skepticism. "I'm sure she just wandered off. It will be dark in an hour or two, so I'm going to take Rio out and look around the property."

"Is that necessary? She'll come back on her own."

"Let's hope. I'll just feel better if I find her and bring her back as soon as I can. Will you be okay here by yourself?"

"I'll be fine."

Trace knew Rachel could stand up for herself. She felt confident that if Rachel had to use the Winchester or the carbine, she would. Or would she? Rachel had never shot a human being. She had used the rifle on plenty of animals but never on a person. When it came down to it, could she, would she pull the trigger? Trace guessed it depended on the circumstances and she hoped Rachel would never have to find out.

"Go round up our cow. I'll just sit here on the porch and get some fresh air." Rachel looked down at the puppy dancing around her feet. "Ramiro will protect me." She smiled as she reached down to pick up the dog.

Trace kissed Rachel, patted her belly, ruffled the fur on Ramiro's head, and went to the stable to saddle the mustang.

She sat atop Rio, gazing out over the landscape, sweeping an appreciative eye over what Mother Nature was offering her. Sunlight suddenly poked through the clouds and dropped through the trees, the oaks and pines posed in almost regal beauty. She could hear the river babbling as a soft breeze whispered by her, and the moss on the nearby rocks was of the deepest shade of kelly green. No artist could recreate Nature's majesty on canvas; no photographer would be able to capture the dazzling display on film.

Trace heeled her mustang to an ambling walk and came out over a small rock landing. Before her was a lovely meadow and beyond that loomed the northern wall of the mountains, cut by deep ridges and furrowed by shallow folds. Scanning the area thoroughly, she could not see or hear any signs of the runaway cow. Nor could she shake the feeling that Ed Jackson was somehow behind its disappearance.

As the sky darkened into night, Trace decided to head back to the house. As it was, she had left Rachel alone in the cabin longer than she cared to. Trace reassured herself with the thought that, sacred celebration or not, one or two Pawnee were never very far away, but she would never forgive herself if something happened and she wasn't there to help deal with it. Hopefully the cow would be fine until morning; she would start looking for her at first light. *And if I find that heifer in any condition other than whole and healthy, there'll be hell to pay.*

Chapter Twenty-two

It had been dark for nearly thirty minutes and the bushwhacker lying in wait was getting restless. He shifted his weight, shook out the numbness in his hands. He had just resettled into a motionless position when a noise alerted him that the time had come to take care of business before his bosses got back to town.

Sheriff Ed Jackson brought his rifle to bear, trying to estimate the distance to the bane of his existence, sitting tall on the mustang. He drew a careful bead on the silhouette with his Winchester and then squeezed the trigger, the sound of the shot splitting the night. The noise echoed to the mountains and back. A satisfied smile crossed the sheriff's face. He knew Rachel had to have heard it and imagined the terror that would fill the traitorous woman's heart.

Trace heard the rifle bark, then saw the stab of its flame an instant before the bullet stung her like a whip. The jarring impact of the slug as it entered her shoulder tumbled her from the saddle. It took her a moment to realize what had happened and then instinct told her to get the hell out of there. Rio had already retreated at a thundering pace and now it was his rider's turn to do the same.

The wound was on her left side, which was fortunate as she was right-handed. Drawing one of her Colts, she knew she had to move behind something that would provide her with some cover. Trace started to rise but another shot slammed her back to the ground and she felt a stab of agony in her side. The coppery smell of blood told her she was in trouble.

Trace used her legs to scoot herself behind a clump of bushes and stayed as still as she could. Drawing in shallow, careful breaths, she listened for the slightest movement, the remotest of sounds. She heard nothing.

Suddenly a wild barrage of pistol fire flew inches over her head, into the trees behind her, the flash from the barrel coming from the south band of forest to her right. Then there was silence. Trace knew it was searching fire, that her attacker was shooting blindly, either hoping to hit her again or provoke her into firing back so that he could see the location of the barrel flame. *Six shots, he must be reloading.* Her shoulder was throbbing and she knew that every beat of her heart pumped blood from her body. Quickly checking the wound on her side, she was relieved to see it was only a graze, even though it stung like an entire swarm of hornets, and oozed like honey seeping out of a comb. She knew it had to be Ed Jackson. The Carvers had made it clear that they were staying out of the vendetta the sheriff had for Trace. When the Cranes got back, that would be a different matter, but until then, Ed was on his own. It didn't surprise her in the least that he would ambush her, and she quietly cursed herself for letting her guard down. Her right hand removed the revolver from her left holster and laid it on her lap. Her left side was starting to feel as though it was weighted down with cement. Propped up against a stump, waiting, Trace heard dry twigs snapping and knew the sheriff was closing in on her.

"Hey, Ed," Trace said as the sheriff came into view. Her Colt was trained on him, her hand steady. "I figured you'd pull a sneak attack. Glad to see you didn't disappoint me." Her voice was strained, her pain evident. "You're a dirty fighter, Ed, no way around it. No Code of the West for you." Trace's wavering voice reflected her weakening condition.

"Say what ya gotta, Sheridan, but it ends here." He put his pistol away and aimed his rifle at her.

"You do realize if you shoot me, reflex will make me shoot you back, right?"

"That's if you can even hit me. You look to be in pretty bad shape. I know I can kill you with one shot...I don't think you can do the same." He snickered. "I'm gonna love taking your head off, son. Then you know what I'm gonna do? I'm gonna bring your corpse back to your wife and drop it on her doorstep. And then, I'm gonna ease her grief and get me a little piece of that. And since we don't need no more little Sheridans running around, I'm gonna—"

His eyes opened wide in disbelief as the bullet struck his belly. Dropping his Winchester, he simply sat down, staring at the hole in his shirt, the ring of blood surrounding it spreading. "Y...you shot me. I ain't never been shot before," he wheezed. As shock washed through his body, he looked up at Trace, whose gaze was focused beyond him.

Rachel held the carbine steady, smoke spiraling from the barrel. Trace had never seen the look that was in Rachel's eyes. She hoped she'd never see it again, at least not directed toward her.

Rachel took a step closer, looking down at Trace. "How bad are you hurt?" Rachel's voice was scarcely louder than a whisper.

"I'll live." She hoped that was true. Her breath was coming in gasps and each one hurt more than the last.

Rachel looked back at Jackson, her eyes narrow slits, her voice even and deliberate. "You know, Sheriff, you got away with tormenting and threatening my parents, you got away with killing my fiancé's folks and bullying me ever since they've been gone. You stood by, knowing that Ben Crane raped me, and now you try to take away the most precious thing I have in my life. You're right, Sheriff...it ends here. We'll tell them to bury you face down, so you can see where you're going." Squeezing off another shot, Rachel didn't react when Jackson's head snapped back. She watched, rifle steady, until the sheriff slumped to the ground. Then she passed out.

When Rachel woke, she was lying on her sofa, her forehead covered by a cool, damp cloth. Standing over her were Little Hawk and another Pawnee she didn't recognize. Her first thought was not for herself. "Trace?"

The other Indian placed his hand gently on Rachel's shoulder to stop her from trying to rise. "She is strong, like a horse. The bullet did not stop in her body. Her wounds will heal quickly."

Rachel looked up at Little Hawk, who nodded. "She is resting. She lost much blood. Not enough to stop her. She said you saved her life."

"I...I guess I did. What about the sheriff?"

"He no longer walks this earth. He will not be missed."

She supposed she should feel something — remorse, guilt, shame...but all she felt was relief. The fact that she had killed a man, taken a life, did not affect her like she would have expected. At least not yet. Perhaps her indifference was due to shock. Perhaps because she was defending her own. Her hand flew to her belly. "My baby?"

"The child is strong...like you...like Tsápaat," Little Hawk assured her. When Rachel looked over at the other Pawnee, Little Hawk said, "This is Fire Arrow. He is medicine man."

Sitting up slowly, she glanced toward the bedroom. In the semi-darkness she could see a figure on the bed, covered by the thick quilt. Standing, gaining her equilibrium, Rachel extended her hand to Fire Arrow, who took it warmly in his own. "Thank you, Fire Arrow."

"We are never far away, Caskí Custíra'u."

Rachel found a smile for the medicine man. Even though they had never met before, he referred to her by the pet name bestowed on her by her Pawnee friends. It made her feel like she had known him a long time.

Still a little unsteady on her feet, she slowly walked into the bedroom and sat on the bed, taking one of Trace's hands in her own. She watched her sleeping, worrying about the clamminess of Trace's palm and her ghostly pallor, wondering how much blood Trace had lost. Fire Arrow had cooked pine resin and fashioned a poultice for inflammation and pain, but the wound areas were still seeping. Before daybreak, she would replace the Indian's dressing with nettle tea and honey. The thought of the honey elicited a memory that made Rachel smile and sad at the same time, as it reminded her of the first time she ever patched Trace up, the day they met. Trace had never before looked so helpless and debilitated, not even on that first day, and regardless of what Flaming Arrow told her, she was afraid of losing the one and only thing in her life that made her feel whole. A tear trickled down her cheek.

"I was hoping the lead had not yet been molded that had your name on it," Rachel said quietly.

Ramiro curled up by Trace's side, and Rachel and the puppy remained with Trace over the next several hours while Pawnee stood guard over the house and property.

While sitting vigil over Trace, a sudden shiver went through Rachel as she thought about the chilling events of that night. She had been sitting on the porch, waiting for Trace and wondering whether the missing heifer was some sort of trick. If Ed Jackson had decided to make a move, he could easily have sneaked up to the corral gate while they ate supper and lured one of the herd away, knowing Trace would go looking.

Then she heard the shot that shattered the night, echoing through her soul as her heart stopped. *Oh, no, not again.* She had already lost one love to a sheriff's bullet... Could the Lord really be so cruel? Instinct made her reach for the carbine. The sound had come from the woods behind the house and that was where she headed.

At that point, Rachel was not thinking; pure adrenaline pushed her forward. While she had just been mildly cursing the starless night only minutes earlier, she was now grateful for it. It was the pitch blackness that allowed her to see the glow of the muzzle flashes when six shots rang out in rapid succession and led her to where she was sure she would find Trace. The closer she got, the more she was seized with dread. What would she see there? What if Trace was dead and she was walking into a trap, too? Well, if Trace was dead, she didn't want to live.

When she heard Ed Jackson's voice, she stopped running and slowed to a standstill to get her bearings, positive he could hear her heartbeat from where she was standing. It was pounding so forcefully in her ears, she could barely make out the sheriff's words. But then she heard Trace's weak, but impossibly welcome voice. She was still alive!

Stepping quietly up to the scene, she saw Jackson facing her, but focused on the ground just in front of a clump of bushes. His Winchester was aimed at what she assumed was Trace. When she heard the horrible things the sheriff was saying, the carbine fired as if of its own volition. She didn't remember raising the rifle or aiming. However, the second shot would stay with her forever; she would never forget Jackson's head jerking back before she passed out.

The first time Trace moved, she groaned softly. The sound went through Rachel like a shiver; it was the most beautiful noise she had ever heard. The bleeding had stopped, and Rachel attended to Trace's wounds with a poultice of chamomile flowers for the swelling, and honey to draw out the infection.

Over the next few days, Trace was asleep more than she was awake. Rachel fed her broth made from venison, with healing ingredients of cabbage and garlic, and only left her side to make trips to the outhouse.

"You're tougher than post oak, Trace." Rachel smiled, looking into precious blue eyes. It was a week after the shooting and things had begun to settle down. They were together, in bed, alone in the house; the first night that a Pawnee, or someone from town, wasn't with them. With Ed Jackson gone, and the Carvers idle, the need for a guard seemed less urgent.

"I love you, Rachel. Slap me if I don't say that to you every day, at least once a day." The graze on her side had already scabbed over and looked a lot worse than it felt. The wounded shoulder was mending, and with Rachel's natural remedies and devoted nursing abilities, it felt much better than Trace thought it should. Her mobility was limited but she was getting more of it back every day. As soon as she could, she would begin working her left arm with the punching bag in the barn.

Rachel leaned over and lightly kissed Trace's bandaged shoulder. "Jed Turner stopped by today while you were napping."

"What brought him all the way out here?" It was odd, Trace thought, that the mayor made a trip to the Triple Y. According to everyone else, he seemed mighty disturbed about being left with making the funeral arrangements for the sheriff. "He wasn't nasty to you or anything, was he?"

"Jed? Oh, no, he was fine. He told me he was upset that there was no one to do all that stuff for Ed, seeing as he had no family anywhere, and Mrs. Crane refused to, denying that Ed Jackson was ever on the Crane payroll."

"That's bullshit."

"Trace...your language," Rachel said automatically. "Anyway, everybody knows it's a lie, but Jed's griping was not why he was here." She gingerly ran her fingers in wide circles around Trace's wound, then down her arm, to her side, to her bare abdomen.

Trace wondered if Rachel was aware what her light rubbing might lead to, if Rachel was purposely or unconsciously trying to arouse her. That morning, Rachel had shamelessly admitted that if it was one thing she missed the most while Trace was infirm, it was their lovemaking.

"So why was he here?" As much as everything ached and pulled and was generally uncomfortable, Trace's brain was engaging in strategic maneuvering as to how she could position herself so that they could both be satisfied with a minimal amount of pain. *And if she doesn't stop stroking me like that, to hell with the pain.*

"He said that the town needs a new lawman. Elections were held this morning." Rachel's fingers were now lightly massaging Trace's taut lower abdomen, making her stomach muscles quiver. Smirking, making eye contact with Trace, Rachel was obviously enjoying the effect she was having.

"So...now who's the sorry sucker in that thankless job?" Trace's breath caught as Rachel's hand began to float lower. There was no mistaking her intention. "Don't start something you can't finish here, blondie."

Rachel dipped her head, nuzzling Trace's neck, nipping at her earlobe. "Who says I can't finish it...Sheriff?"

Trace's eyes closed as Rachel began leaving a trail of kisses and nibbles along her throat and jawline. She was surrendering to the stimulation when Rachel's words sank in and her eyes snapped open. "What!" Bolting up, she forgot her injuries and nearly tore the stitches in her shoulder. "Ow! Fuck!"

"Trace!"

Ramiro hopped around the bed, yapping.

"Don't you 'Trace' me, Rachel Sheridan. You just called me sheriff." The look in the blue eyes was not pleased and it was not because she had nearly wrenched all her body parts, again.

Rachel shrugged. "You won the election."

"I wasn't running!"

"Seems the people of Sagebrush didn't care about that. Your name was brought up at the emergency town hall meeting and the vote was unanimous. No one associated with the Cranes showed up to dispute it."

"No! No way in hell, Rachel. I am not going to be sheriff."

Rachel began her feather light touches again. "The community has decided, Trace. They look up to you. You give them hope." She leaned in and kissed Trace's jaw. "You give everyone the promise of fairness." Rachel pushed Trace's hair aside and kissed a sensitive spot behind the ear. Fingers found their way to damp curls covering a bundle of nerves that seemed to have a mind of its own as Trace pressed in for firmer contact. "And you give them an expectation of getting their freedom back. They need you, Trace." Burying her fingers between hot, wet folds and stroking, Rachel's mouth hovered over Trace's. "I need you, too. Right now," she whispered.

Trace put her hand on the back of Rachel's neck and drew her down roughly so their lips met, grinding together in passion. Trace pulled Rachel on top of her to give her better access and to make it possible for her to touch Rachel's most intimate areas, which she was taking full advantage of.

The pressure of Rachel's body was painful, but she was not about to call a halt when she was ready to explode, and Rachel was not too far behind her. She had missed this, missed how readily Rachel responded to her, missed how much Rachel so thoroughly enjoyed all the things they shared in bed.

Their sexual compatibility still amazed Trace and she didn't care how much agony her body was in, or that she'd just been sacrificed to the Crane family by being named the town cop. She would deal with all that in the morning. Right now, she wanted to watch her beautiful, pregnant wife come all over her hand, cry out her name in ecstasy, and then she wanted to take her again, sinking her tongue where her fingers had been.

Rachel had her own ideas. Following a jarringly satisfying climax, she continued to carefully straddle Trace, drawing her fingers out and removing herself from Trace's fingers as well. When Trace moved as though she were going to try and reverse their positions, Rachel placed a firm hand in the middle of Trace's chest. "No."

"But..."

"No, Trace," she said firmly. "You lay right there and let me tend to you. I wish I could put into words how grateful I am to still be able to make love to the woman who has become my reason for waking up in the morning. Knowing that you could have been taken from me is almost too much to bear." Rachel placed kisses all around Trace's wounds, then marked a path with her lips down over Trace's chest and abdomen to the heat between her legs. Intoxicated by the scent of arousal, Rachel drank in a deep breath before putting her mouth on the source of Trace's excitement and then flattened her tongue against it, causing Trace to inhale sharply.

Trace relaxed into the pleasurably intense sensation. *Fuck the pain. It's going to be a long, glorious night.*

Chapter Twenty-three

Sheriff Trace Sheridan.

After saying it to herself for two days, it had started to sound not so bad after all. It was an overwhelming commitment, but it entailed a lot less responsibility than she'd had before she ended up in 1879. Trace had basically been slowly taking on the duties without the badge, anyway; at least now she would have the legal authority to back up what some might have passed off as bravado.

The Cranes were going to be a problem, there was no way around that, but if anyone in Sagebrush was a match for the nefarious family, it was the twenty-first century detective. As she got used to the idea of her new job, she realized it was meant for her to do this.

The hardest part was going to be leaving Rachel alone on the property while she did business in town. Jed Turner had visited the ranch again and told Trace she would be paid the sum of sixty dollars a month, that was as high as he could go, and with that extra money, she could hire someone — not so much to work the land and do what she normally did on a daily basis, but to act as a lookout. Just in case.

"But Ed Jackson's gone," Rachel argued mildly at Trace's suggestion. "The Pawnee are out here every day...and usually most nights...helping out. Do you really think one more person is going to make a difference?"

"The Cranes are coming back, sweetheart." Trace carefully eased herself down into the porch chair, enjoying the cool breeze that came with the sunset. She was feeling more like herself and was much more mobile, her shoulder now free from its sling.

"You don't need to remind me, Trace. As much as I don't like to think of it, I know they're going to be back soon. I just don't see where hiring another person is going to—"

"It will make me feel better, okay? Knowing even one more person is out here to spot trouble before it gets here will make me feel better." Trace picked up her guitar, barely wincing as she did so.

Rachel smiled, pleased with the healing results of her natural remedies. "Looks like you're just about able to use that shoulder normally," she said.

Trace rotated her shoulder forward and back. It moved easily and with little pain. "Thanks to you, my love," she said. "I confess I'm glad we had all that meat to help build my blood back up. Though I'm just as glad I'm not the one who had to kill it." She laid the guitar over her lap and slid her fingers deftly along the neck. She strummed a few chords to see if the instrument needed tuning, tightened the stubborn

E string, then plucked out a chord progression that sounded like she was going to play *Stairway to Heaven*.

"I love that song," Rachel said. "That one and *How Do I Live?* I think that's one of the most beautiful songs I've ever heard." She settled in to enjoy Trace's singing. "The message in it is so clear, and the way you sing it gives me goosebumps. Even makes me cry a little." She adored Trace's voice and would drop just about anything to listen to her sing. Listening to Trace's light strumming, she thought about the admonition concerning the Cranes' return. "You know, the Cranes aren't due back for a while. They're supposed to take a detour and look at more horses to buy or something."

"There are still the Carvers and whatever assorted ranch hands were left behind to keep the place running. I don't trust any of them and you shouldn't either."

"I don't, Trace. I would never dismiss anything the Cranes or their hands might try," Rachel said, feeling unnecessarily lectured. Although Rachel knew she could be too trusting and naïve, at least compared to Trace, she would never underestimate the Cranes again. Especially after Ben's last visit. She appreciated Trace's protectiveness but no longer felt weak or defenseless. After all, hadn't she just killed a man because Trace's life had been threatened? Didn't that prove her timidity was a thing of the past? She sat, mildly stewing, wondering if she was being overly sensitive.

Trace picked out notes on individual strings. Suddenly she stopped playing and an impish grin crossed her face. "Oooh, Rachel, I have just the song for you." She strummed the chord of G and crooned the lyrics to *I Shot The Sheriff*.

Rachel's eyes widened then narrowed while she listened to the rest of the song. "Trace. I can't believe you would treat my killing someone so frivolously."

"I'm just trying to get you to lighten up about it, baby."

"Lighten up? I don't understand."

"To get you to take it easy on yourself and stop taking on unwarranted guilt. We both know you saved my life. And you saved your own and the baby's, as well."

"I'm okay with that part, Trace, I am." Rachel's voice was quiet. "I'm no longer feeling sinful; that has passed and has been replaced by the great relief that my family is safe and the threat of Ed Jackson is gone forever. But whether Ed got what was coming to him or not, I still took a life and I need to make peace with that."

Trace reminded herself that Rachel had not dealt with the reprehensible elements of life like she had done on a daily basis, that Rachel was not desensitized to what Trace considered righteous killings. Not that the evil Rachel had experienced wasn't horrible, but Rachel had retained most of her purity, whereas Trace had to dig deep to find hers, if there was any left. Reaching over and taking her hand, squeezing it, Trace said, "I'm sorry. You're right. Take all the time you need."

Linking her fingers with Trace's, Rachel smiled. "Sing something that will take my mind away from remembering the night I almost lost you."

As much as Rachel wanted to think of other things, the memory of that night was still like a bad dream. She recalled sitting on the porch for quite a while as sunset became dusk, then evolved fully into night, and she was getting a little concerned that Trace was not back. And then... Rachel snapped out of it and absorbed the moment as Trace ended the song, again feeling grateful that Trace was still there and able to finish *anything*. The baby kicked a few times, as if agreeing.

Trace smiled fondly at Rachel who, totally lost in thought, was unconsciously massaging her bulging belly. "Where'd you go?"

"Huh? Oh." She grinned, looking down at her stomach. "Just thinking about how you make every day worth rising and every night worth retiring." She glanced up at Trace with an unmistakable twinkle in her green eyes. "And about how much I love you and how much in love with you I am. And about how our baby is so lucky to have you for a father... Well...you know what I mean."

Trace let Rachel's words sink in and set the guitar aside. Her voice was low and seductive. "What do you say we retire right now? I'll make it worth your while."

That tone always sent a jolt of heat right through Rachel, which settled like a brewing volcano between her thighs. It amazed her how Trace could so completely mesmerize her, making her feel weak in the knees just by a certain vocal inflection or a look in those baby blues that reflected pure want, meant for her and only her. "But...you have your monthly..."

Trace recognized the hesitation and reached over, intertwining her fingers with Rachel's. Bringing Rachel's hand to her mouth, Trace kissed the fingers that brought her so much pleasure. "Yes, but you don't."

From the flush on Rachel's face, it was obvious she was already too aroused to say no.

Anticipating the rest of the evening, a rush of unmitigated lust surged through them. Trace stood and eased Rachel up with her. They kissed passionately and walked arm-in-arm inside the house, closing the door behind them.

Seven days after her election, the new sheriff rode into town and started her first day as The Law in Sagebrush. It felt odd to be wearing a badge again, especially so openly on her rawhide vest. She had been used to wearing a flat shield clipped to her belt or on a chain around her neck, which only needed to be visible when she chose to show it.

Now she sported a shiny brass star with five points, with the words "Sheriff" engraved in a half-circle above the middle and "Jefferson County" in a semi-circle below. Whereas in her former career, she kept a low profile while working, in her new life a bold presence would be an advantage.

She looked around the filthy, musty sheriff's office — the only building in the small community made mostly of brick — and her first official decision was to clean the place up and personalize it, exorcising the spirit of Ed Jackson, and removing any physical reminders of him. Not knowing who Jackson may have given keys to the cells, she also arranged to have the locks changed. If she did get a Crane behind bars, she wouldn't keep him there for long if he could just reach in his pocket, produce a key, and unlock the door.

Isaac Tipping knocked on the door then stepped inside, bringing with him a young woman who looked to be about his own age. "Trace, this here is Lydia Canfield." He blushed but manfully continued, "My sweetheart."

The young woman was a little slip of a thing with reddish-blonde hair, big hazel eyes, and freckles. The last time Isaac had worked on the ranch, he'd not spoken of anyone in particular, much less a girlfriend. With a smirk and a raised eyebrow that made both teenagers blush, Trace said, "When did this happen?" Trace suddenly wondered what Rachel looked like at Lydia's age, which triggered a tender smile.

"Well...we were always kinda sweet on each other, but two weeks ago at the dance at the schoolhouse, we promised ourselves to each other."

"Promised? Is that like being engaged to marry?"

"It's kind of like promising to get betrothed," Lydia said shyly.

"Well, then, that's a big commitment." Trace extended a hand to Isaac, who shook it enthusiastically. "Congratulations." Trace took Lydia's hand and kissed it. "And congratulations to you, too."

Flushed for a different reason now, Isaac's girlfriend was charmed.

Seeing the expression on Lydia's face, Isaac reached over and politely, but firmly, removed his girlfriend's hand from Trace's grasp and held on to it tightly. "We thought we'd stop by and see if you needed any help. Sheriff Jackson never put much effort into keeping the place clean."

Amused by the boy's possessive action, Trace shook her head and looked around in disgust. "He was a pig. But then, I guess we all knew that. If you really want to get your hands dirty, be my guest. I'll go clean up the cells as best I can. Lydia, if you want to start in the office, and Isaac, you take the room in the back. That would be great."

"Anything you don't want us to throw away?" Lydia asked, untying her bonnet.

"Whatever looks official, I guess. I'll need to look over the paper-work and see if there is any unfinished business that might come back to haunt me. So if you could just put it all into a neat pile, it would be much appreciated."

As the two teenagers rolled up their sleeves, Trace stepped over to the detention area and took a deep breath. The holding cells smelled like urine and vomit. Some things never changed.

Before the day was over, almost everyone in town stopped by to con-gratulate Trace, wish her well, and bring her a gift, mostly home cooked food or dessert. Since she had ridden in on Rio and had no way to transport any of it back home, what she, Isaac, Lydia, and the visi-tors to her office did not eat, she decided she would take over to Wil-bur's at the end of the day.

After helping tidy the place up, the teenagers left and Trace sat down behind the desk to look over the paperwork Lydia had put into neat piles. Nothing out of the ordinary jumped out at her, for which she was grateful, but with Jackson as her predecessor, she wasn't com-pletely comfortable that things associated with his office were on the up and up. Until she had things in order, she would err on the side of caution.

Around mid-day, Trace walked over to the lumber mill and bought three wooden crates to use as file boxes. She organized her paperwork to separate the forms, reports, dockets, and ledgers.

Scanning Jackson's entries in his daily incident log book dis-gusted and disturbed Trace deeply. It was documentation of the exact types of behavior for which he should have been arresting criminals — fraud, deception, forgery, perjury, and extorting the very people he had sworn to protect and defend. She shuddered, knowing that was exactly what she used to do. Trace put that book aside to take home with her. She wanted to keep it somewhere safe as evidence against the Cranes, should they ever be brought to trial.

Mayor Turner made a visit to the office on his way back from his nooner with Cassandra. "You sent word for me to come by, Trace?"

"Hope my message didn't get delivered at an inopportune moment, Jed," she said with a smile. "I want to know exactly what the town expects from me, and I figured the mayor would be the man to ask."

Settling in the uncomfortable chair opposite Trace, Jed enjoyed a slice of Mrs. Edwards' peach pie as he rattled off some of the sheriff's duties.

"Lessee here, well...enforcin' the law and arrestin' people, surely, that's the big ones," he began, shoveling a forkful of pastry into his mouth. "When the circuit judge comes to town — transportin' and escortin' prisoners, if ya got any, to and from the courtroom — which here is usually the schoolhouse on a Saturday. Then there's... uh...servin' and executin' writs and warrants, enforcin' injunctions..." He paused to take another few bites, washing them down with coffee. "Then there's conductin' property sales and collectin' fees and funds. That's where ol' Ed seemed to go astray."

"Your Honor, 'ol' Ed' went astray long before that became an issue, trust me." Trace could have expounded on that from what she had read earlier, but she had no doubt it would have been telling Jed Turner something he already knew.

"Guess you'd be right about that, son." He held out his coffee cup for a refill. As Trace reached for the graniteware pot, Jed shook his head. "Ain't ya got something a little bit...stronger...than that layin' around? My mouth's dry as a cactus."

It was beyond her how anyone could be dry after drinking almost a whole gallon of coffee, but she knew what he meant and returned the pot to the small iron woodstove. Trace stood and went over to a pile of discards that were to be thrown out before she closed the office for the night. From it she plucked a half-empty bottle of pale, orange-colored liquid. Having sniffed it earlier, she knew it was alcohol, some kind of rotgut, but what kind escaped her. She had opted to toss it out; anything that had touched Ed Jackson's lips would never touch hers. Turner's eyes lit up when she brought it back to the desk. "Is this what you mean?"

"That'll do. Can always use a little whiskey to keep the fire in my belly stoked." The mayor took the bottle from Trace and filled his cup half way. "A snootful in the afternoon never hurt nobody," he said, throwing the cup back, swallowing the contents with minimal reaction. "Now...where was I? Oh, yeah...if there's a trial— There ain't been one in near ten years. Jacob Crane seen to that with his havin' everythin' his way, but now that you're sheriff, I reckon things'll change a mite."

"Count on it."

"Yep, I figgered as much. Anyways," he poured another shot into his coffee cup, "if there's a trial, you and me, we get to select a jury. Not that we've had any for a long while, but if there is any kind of unlawful assembly or disturbances, you'd be the one to break that up and arrest anyone who don't mind ya respectful and proper. If you need deputies, you can call on the powers of the county to deputize anyone or pick yourself a posse."

"Ever been the need for a posse around here?" Trace asked, pouring herself another cup of coffee, feeling the need for the caffeine. Her weariness was probably due to not yet having regained all her strength.

"Oh, hell, no. The only posse that's ever been needed here was one that shoulda gone over to the Crane spread. But any sheriff that tried that, he'd be a dead sheriff." Turner's eyes met Trace's. "No offense, son. If anybody can do it without gettin' hisself killed, I'd bet a month's pay, it'd be you."

"Why, thank you, Mayor. I appreciate your confidence."

"Whether or not you can actually round up enough men to ride with you will be another thing. As it is, if you don't get Sagebrush back to an orderly town and, Lord help us, Jacob and his boys get the best of you— Well, let's just say that might lead to some unpleasantness, like scaffolding and ropes, and none of us want to see that."

Especially not me. "How can Crane legally hang anyone without a trial?"

"Without a sheriff to testify against him, no judge will ever lock up him or his boys. And there are some circuit judges who pass through here who, it won't matter if you do testify against them; they still won't lock him up. Jacob has money and them judges are greedy." Turner reached for a piece of apple pie, sent over by Molly Ledbetter.

"Tell me, Mayor, why did the town elect me? Especially since I had no interest in running."

"'Cause you got sand, boy. Ain't no one else in this town ever stood up to Ed Jackson. Not only did you stand up to him, you killed him, gettin' him out of our hair."

Only the Pawnee knew that Rachel had been the one who shot Jackson. They'd all agreed it would be better if the town thought Trace had killed the sheriff. Regardless of the circumstances, no one looked too kindly upon ladies who killed anyone. And, although Trace very much wanted to give credit where credit was due, she had gone along with it because Rachel asked her to.

"I gotta tell ya, Trace, even them snooty ol' gals who only leave home to go to Sunday meetin' ran into town to vote for you. They never come to town. Too damn scared they'll get dirt in their dimples." Finishing up the pie, Turner held out his cup. "Any of that coffee left?"

Trace picked up the pot and swirled the contents, feeling the weight. "Just about one more cup. If you're going to want more, I'll have to make another pot." She poured him the last cup.

"Gotta tell ya, boy...even before Ed Jackson got hisself planted, you had him shakin' like a congressman at a revival meetin'. Damned worthless, pickle puss of a man, he was. It was always my fondest wish to knock Ed Jackson colder'n a wagon tire; he caused so much trouble in this town..."

"Why couldn't you stop him?" Trace asked pointedly.

"The Cranes, plain and simple. When they get back, you'll understand. Although I do think you'll make a difference, I don't believe you can perform miracles."

Trace smiled inwardly. No, miracles were not within her capabilities, but insight into a modern world of strategy and self-defense were. Maybe Jed Turner was afraid of the Cranes. Trace Sheridan was not.

Chapter Twenty-four

Soon after Trace's election, she and Rachel were asked to attend a celebration at the Pawnee settlement two miles northwest of Sagebrush.
It was a singular honor, which both women recognized.

"Trace, do you realize that in the fifteen years since the tribe laid
claim to that land, no one — and I mean no one — from Sagebrush has
ever been invited into their village?" Rachel's voice carried a hint of
excitement.

Hitching Moses to the wagon, Trace said, "Not even the mayor?"

That made Rachel giggle. "Jed? Jed Turner would only go if they
promised him a squaw."

"At least the man knows where his priorities are." Trace placed
Moses' reins over the wagon footboard. She was actually quite
impressed with the mayor's unassisted sexual prowess. In Trace's
time, a man his age would be running to the drugstore to enhance his
stamina in the bedroom. Her admiration was short-lived.

"One of those Pawnee women would kill him in the bedroom. Why
do you think he goes to a prostitute instead of finding himself a wife?
Elizabeth said Matthew told her that unless Jed orders lunch while
he's in Cassandra's room, he's only up there for ten minutes."

Trace reached over and pulled Rachel into a tight embrace.
"Aren't you glad I'm not Jed Turner?" She kissed the top of her head.

"Yes. In more ways than just that one." She squeezed Trace back.
"We should get going."

Trace helped Rachel up to the wagon seat. "So we're the first?"
She climbed up beside Rachel and snapped the reins.

"Yes, and I'm not about to refuse that privilege."

Trace was proud of Rachel's enthusiasm. Other than her hatred
for the Cranes, there didn't seem to be a prejudiced bone in Rachel's
body. She studied her beautiful, glowing lover. "You know, Rachel, I
just want to say that...I have never once regretted my decision to stay
here, will never ever regret making a commitment to you." Rachel
looked over at Trace with reverence and devotion. "You keep looking at
me like that and we'll have to stop so I can take you in the back of this
wagon right here and now," Trace warned playfully.

"You surprise me sometimes with the things you say." Rachel's
hand rested over her heart. She looked down at her swollen belly, now
at the end of her seventh month. "I sure don't feel very appealing right
now."

Trace reached over and took Rachel's hand. "Well you should, because I find you adorably appealing right now. Despite your unpredictable mood swings," Trace said with a smile.

"My what? What does that mean?" Rachel tried not to be defensive. She knew Trace meant it in a teasing way.

"It means I love you no matter what."

When the couple arrived at the village, they were welcomed as though they belonged there. Black Feather and a gaggle of women, mostly around Rachel's age, assisted the pregnant woman down from the wagon. They surrounded her, laying hands on her belly as though consecrating the baby. Rachel was cloaked in a colorful poncho by one of the older females in the group and then escorted away from Trace to join the Pawnee wives. Rachel was fascinated by the flatbreads and cornmeal creations that were being put together. The food smelled delicious and her stomach rumbled with hunger. As a guest, the mother-to-be was not expected to help prepare the meal, but Rachel, true to her nature, pitched right in.

Trace was greeted by Little Hawk, who, in respect for her custom, shook her hand, and then offered her a ceramic pipe with a long stem, which connected the wide mouthpiece to a tall, deep bowl. She didn't dare venture a guess as to what the bowl might hold.

"Thanks, Little Hawk, but I don't smoke," she said politely.

"I do not smoke, either. Only when we have raahisii." He extended the pipe again. "It is custom, Tsápaat, to take haaktuu'at when it is offered."

Used to Little Hawk's droll sense of humor, Trace accepted the pipe hesitantly. "What's in it?" She fully expected him to admit to peyote. She had heard all kinds of stories about the effects of the cactus plant, the least of which was that hallucinations from ingesting it lasted twenty-four hours. Maybe if she only took a brief hit, she could escape the typical side effects. She wasn't opposed to getting high, but she couldn't risk losing control for an entire day.

"Cannabis."

Trace's eyes popped open, looking at the pipe and then back at Little Hawk. *Why didn't I smell it? Are the cooking smells so strong that I completely overlooked the odor of burning leaves?* Bringing the bowl of the pipe closer to her nose, she inhaled. *Ah, yes. There it is.* "Cannabis, huh?" It was a welcome surprise. Taking a quick draw off the pipe, she let the smoke slowly burn down her throat and sear into her lungs with a pleasant familiarity and the forbidden sensation she suddenly had very much missed. *And it's some damned good shit.*

"You have smoked cannabis before?" There was surprise in Little Hawk's voice.

"Oh, yeah." Trace took another hit, holding her breath, savoring the tranquility that settled over her before handing the pipe back.

She was pretty sure marijuana was not yet illegal, something she had not even considered until that moment. She smiled. It was a habit she had picked up in high school and one she continued after she graduated from the police academy. Hypocritically, she had arrested people for selling, buying, and possessing pot and then, after her shift, she had gone home and gotten high. It wasn't a habit, but she did not hesitate to smoke pot following a very stressful day.

"Where did you get this — the cannabis?"

Little Hawk made a sweeping gesture with his hand. "Hemp. It grows everywhere."

Hemp. Of course. It's probably flourishing all over the Triple Y. She'd never even thought to look for it. It raised a dilemma. Even though hemp wasn't against any laws yet, she did not want to get back into the routine of relying on weed to get her through her tough situations. Before, it hadn't mattered. Her life had become quite meaningless so it made no difference whether or not she got high. Now she had a responsibility — to her wife, to the child she would raise as her own, and, most importantly, to herself — to not return to being the kind of ruthless, self-centered person she had been before she arrived in Sagebrush. Pot neutralized all her emotions, dulling her senses and making her unobservant and sometimes downright negligent. She could not afford to be that way here and now. Still, there was no reason she could not occasionally get together with her new friends and enjoy herself recreationally, when her accountability was not as front and center, when Rachel was in a secure environment. Like tonight.

Trace smiled, feeling much more relaxed already. "I thought you guys all sat around smoking peyote."

Little Hawk shrugged. "Peyote is not as strong through the pipe. We take peyote by mouth, whole. We suck on it slowly and then chew it and swallow. We will share some later, if you wish."

"No, no, thanks. I'm fine with this right here. But I am curious — what's the difference?"

Little Hawk thought a moment before responding. "When we both smoke cannabis, we both feel the same. If I eat peyote and you eat peyote, we will not feel the same. It is personal...how you would say...individual. My visions would not be like your visions. If one of my wives is ill, I can ask the Great Spirit why and what I have to do to make her better. I can ask the Great Spirit if she will heal or if she will meet Him. If you or Caskí Custíra'u is ill, you would have to ask why and what you have to do to make it better and the answers would not be the same as mine. It is the Great Spirit's message to me. For you, it would be His message to you."

"So peyote allows you to have a religious experience?"

Little Hawk tapped his own chest. "Spiritual. Between you and The Creator." He held up the pipe. "This — between you and everyone. We all feel the same."

"But what about hallucinations — seeing things that aren't there? Nausea? The amount of time it takes for it to wear off?"

The Pawnee shrugged. "It is a choice, Tsápaat. Sometimes the reward of the wisdom you acquire is worth the bad things that happen to gain that knowledge."

Trace stared at him intently. *Isn't that the truth.*

Before the festivities began, Little Hawk and Howling Wolf took Trace on a tour of their earth lodge, a large dome-shaped, structure, fifteen feet high in the center with a hole open at the top that served as a combination chimney and skylight. The floor was semi-subterranean, three feet below ground level, the framework of the building covered with layers of willow branches, grass, dried mud, and dirt.

"The earth lodge have two part." Howling Wolf extended his arm, indicating north, "Iriiïrakaahuraahkatiitu." He pointed south. "And iriiïrasakuhaku." He and Little Hawk escorted Trace into the north sector. His arm made a sweeping gesture of the area and then he held up three fingers. "This part have kusaar, eh…" He struggled to find the right word.

"Stations," Little Hawk supplied.

"Yes. Three station where our women sleep and have riiksuhur — re-responsibility. Our older women, they do most labor. They live here." He pointed to an area where elderly and middle-aged female tribal members were stooped, gathering blankets. He then walked to another large section, followed by Trace and Little Hawk. "This kusaar…station…is where our wives sleep who take care of our children and earth lodge. There," he pointed to another big room beyond where they were standing, "is for our young women. They live together to learn what they must know to be tribal women. Duty to Pawnee."

Howling Wolf watched Trace to see that she understood. When she nodded, he continued. "When hunters bring back the buffalo meat, we sometimes return to a woman in a different station than the one we left."

That certainly explains how Little Hawk has twelve children by different wives. The males moving from household to household supported Trace's supposition that the Pawnee lived in a communal environment.

After touring the lodge, Trace joined Rachel and they were seated to start the meal. Even though they were both females, they were also guests of honor, and were not required to help serve the food. Under normal circumstances, Rachel would have protested and insisted on doing what the other women did, but she did not want to insult their customs, and now, heavy with child, she was grateful to get off her feet.

She was a little taken aback by Trace's ravenous appetite, and by her sudden propensity to think everything was absolutely hilarious. Trace also seemed unusually relaxed. Rachel was not unhappy to witness that, she just didn't understand it. She had not seen Trace imbibing any spirits and in any event, Trace was not acting like she typically did when she had been drinking. And her irises were not visible. The gorgeous eyes were nothing but black pupils with blue rims.

Trace was also acting on sexual impulses, her usual public restraint absent. When she wasn't grabbing at anything edible that passed by her, her hands were pawing at Rachel. The mother-to-be blushed and playfully swatted her advances away, though no one else seemed to notice or care. *What has gotten into Trace? And how soon before we can leave and do something about this amorous behavior at home, if we make it that far.*

After the remnants of the meal had been cleared away, just as Trace was threatening to whisk Rachel behind a tree somewhere, the atmosphere stilled and there was the sound of a softly beating drum. Accompanied by a vocable, a procession emerged from the earth lodge.

Leading the regal group was the tribal chief, an elderly man wearing an eagle feather headdress, which reached the ground and trailed two feet behind him as he moved to the distinct rhythm. There was a fiercely proud nobility about him and his weathered skin advertised his age, which the couple guessed later was maybe in his eighth decade. They were told this was Moving Elk. Although he was frail, he had an undeniable presence and bearing that made Trace and Rachel feel like they should bow in respect when he passed.

Behind Moving Elk walked his children, grandchildren, and great grandchildren, elders, the warriors and the hunters, then the women. Once they were all gathered into a circle, the drumming and the song ended. The Pawnee chief recited a prayer in Skiri, blessing the celebration. This was followed by a full tribal dance.

As Moving Elk stood tall in the middle of the circle, the dance stopped and Little Hawk stepped next to his leader. Moving Elk nodded and the Pawnee hunter looked directly at Trace. "Tsápaat. Come." He gestured her forward.

Confused, she nevertheless released her hold around Rachel's waist and entered the sacred circle. She stood before Moving Elk, who sang something in his native tongue. When he was finished, he said another prayer, waving his hand over Trace's head and then moving his arm in a circle three times. He spoke two words: "Cki'ri" and "Awataarihur".

The Pawnee broke into a raucous cheer and then a spirited song and dance. Moving Elk placed his palm against Trace's breastbone and bowed his head, then he took two steps backward and quietly returned to the earth lodge. Rachel joined her, just as confounded as Trace.

"What was that about?" Trace asked Little Hawk.

"You are now a member of our tribe."

A speechless Trace was rescued by Rachel. "Wait — do you mean this whole ceremony was for Trace, to induct her into the tribe?"

Little Hawk nodded and looked at Trace. "We knew if we told you, you would find reasons not to come."

"That's true." Rachel patted Trace's arm. "She doesn't like being the center of attention." She looked up at Trace, who had been clearly thrown off-balance by the distinction. "She does what she has to, not for the glory or the reward but because it's unavoidable." She hugged Trace. "I love you so much."

Thinking back to her days as bad cop, playing both ends against the middle, Trace reflected on why she didn't want any attention brought to her, and it wasn't for any praiseworthy reason. *I so don't deserve this. If they only knew.* "I'm...I'm...I'm honored. Thank you."

"Does she have a tribal name?" Rachel asked, bursting with pride.

"Yes. Awataarihur. Raging Fire."

It was Rachel's turn to laugh. "My goodness, he certainly got that one right." Immediately after she said it, the import of her comment made her turn crimson.

Moses had them halfway home and Rachel had control of the reins, the rifle across her lap and Raging Fire snoring in the back of the wagon. *So much for the romantic plans I had for bed time. Raging Fire, my behind,* Rachel thought, shaking her head. *More like Fading Ember.*

The next morning started out badly. Trace had awakened with a pounding headache that put her in a horrendous mood. As Rachel had not seen Trace drink any kind of potable the night before, the headache seemed to have been provoked by nothing obvious and even in their short, impromptu lovemaking — a session initiated by Trace rousing Rachel out of a sound sleep — she was a little rougher, more aggressive than she had ever been. It was not that it wasn't enjoyable, just...different.

Trace's surly disposition got worse when she got out of bed, tripped over a stick Ramiro had dragged in the night before and, to keep her balance, grabbed on to the bedroom door. It was not a well thought out movement as the momentum of her solid body propelled the door shut, causing Trace to slam into it, stubbing both big toes and pinching her fingers in the process.

Rachel had never heard such a string of obscenities in her life. Every day something proved to her that Trace had made the right decision to pretend she was a man. Although her mannerisms were neither male nor female, her strength, skills, and confidence were like nothing Rachel had ever seen in a woman, and ladies definitely did not have the earthy, blasphemous vocabulary Trace did.

Trace cursed Ramiro for leaving the damned stick where he had, even though she knew the dog had not done it on purpose, cursed not being able to get the damned lamp lit on the first, second, or third try, cursed the damned stubborn cattle for not getting out into the corral exactly when she wanted them to, and even clipped her words to her new Pawnee brothers, who showed up to help with the crops.

Trace explained this behavior to Rachel once, calling it "pee em ess" or some such thing, but those incidents of temperament never reached the level of Trace's current unexplainable irritation. The normally affable woman even complained about breakfast, which she never did. Rachel cured Trace's throbbing head with a spoonful of honey and was almost relieved when Trace went out and saddled up Rio to go to town. When she came in to kiss Rachel goodbye, Trace still appeared to be out of sorts.

Despite Trace annoying her greatly that morning, Rachel would not have traded her for anything in the world. But she was puzzled by the behavior. "Sweetheart, what's wrong?" Rachel asked, loosely hanging on to Trace's waist.

"Nothing. Well, nothing I can put my finger on, exactly." Trace sighed, hugging Rachel very close to her. "I'm pretty sure it's the aftereffects of the cannabis, I almost always end up with a mild headache."

"Why do you smoke the stuff?"

"Because it makes me feel better."

"Right." Rachel nodded, giving Trace a patient stare.

"I don't know, though. The agitation that's come along with this headache is not something that usually happens, and that bothers me. Something else is." She shook her head. "Anyway, I should head out. I have that meeting this morning with Caleb Tipping. He's filing a complaint to get back the money that the Cranes have extorted from him." She kissed Rachel. "I think Caleb is a brave man to start the ball rolling like that. Once he follows through, I think everyone else will follow suit."

Reluctantly releasing Trace, Rachel said, "Please try to have a better day than you have had so far."

Trace waggled her mildly bruised fingers, glared at the dog, and pouted. "Don't remind me."

It wasn't two minutes before Rachel heard Trace yelling outside. Wiping her hands on her apron, she stepped out on the porch to see Trace atop Rio, shouting at Ramiro, who was bouncing around and barking. "No! Go back to the house right now!" Ramiro sat. "I mean it!" As she reined the mustang around to leave, the wolf puppy trotted after her, which made her stop again. "Goddamn it, Ramiro!"

Rachel knew better than to remark about Trace's language when she was in such a mood. "Oh, for Heaven's sake, Trace, take him with you. What harm can it do?"

"I want him here to protect you."

"Good Lord, Trace, he's just a puppy. The only thing he could do right now would be gnaw at someone's ankle bones."

"That's not the point! He needs to learn to—"

Exasperated, Rachel pointed toward the field. "Little Hawk, Red Sky, and Thundercloud are here. I'll be fine. Let him go to town with you. He pines until you come home, anyway." Rachel heard a growl and wasn't sure if it came from the dog or Trace. Without another word, Trace rode away with Ramiro following happily.

Returning inside, Rachel shook her head, blowing out a deep breath. Hopefully the proverbial bee that had flown into Trace's bonnet, would fly out before she came home for lunch.

The morning went by quickly for the new sheriff. The paperwork for Caleb Tipping's complaint was easy to fill out and so most of their meeting became a bitch session about how the Cranes had taken advantage of the town for so long. When Trace ran out of coffee, Tipping decided it was time to go back to work.

After that, Trace visited Emmet Hallack, Esquire, a defense attorney who had stayed out of the Cranes' hair as much as possible. In return, the Cranes allowed him an acceptable amount of success in all minor legal matters that did not involve the cattle baron or his family. Trace had heard that Hallack was a decent man and was constantly looking for a bigger case that would allow him to do better than break even, maybe even make a name for himself. With Ed Jackson gone, and the not-so-easily intimidated Trace now in the job, maybe Hallack could actually start practicing law and be backed up by the authorities.

Trace decided to make an appointment to meet the man and judge for herself. She showed the rotund lawyer the complaint and assured him there would no doubt be more.

"Well, Sheriff, I think if you want to have any success at all, you should write an official letter to the governor requesting an impartial circuit magistrate to come to Sagebrush, or Jefferson City, to try all five Crane men on whatever charges we can file against them."

Trace found Hallack's enthusiasm for helping nail the bastards reassuring.

She was ready to go back to the ranch for a quick lunch when John and Seth Carver walked in. Surprisingly cordial, John said, "We'd like to put in a claim for a couple more acres of land southwest of the Crane spread. If you have the map, I could show you just where."

Great...that land touches the Triple Y. Just what we need...closer proximity to the devil's minions. And just when the day had actually started to go well.

Chapter Twenty-five

Rachel finished chopping the vegetables Thundercloud had brought in from the field and she dropped them into the beef stock boiling on the stove. She turned to the pantry to get the spices to flavor the soup, freezing when she heard a noise behind her.

"Howdy, Rachel."

She didn't have to turn around to know who the voice belonged to. Panic seized her. The carbine was across the room, and Trace was in town. She closed her eyes and took a deep breath, trying to rein in her fear. She knew she couldn't let him know she was terrified, but that horrible, violent night replayed in her mind and she started to shake.

Her hand went protectively to her growing belly, the other hand clutching a chair for support. She thought her knees were going to buckle and she knew she mustn't faint. Calling up all the strength she possessed, she forced her voice to be firm. "You have no business here, Ben. You need to leave before my husband gets back."

He was leaning against the doorway. "Nope. Don't think so. Seth and Uncle John are keeping the new sheriff busy in town. And those Injuns you got watching the place? They're putting out a small fire in that nice corn crop right now. So, looks like I got you all to myself." He took a few steps inside. "You goin' and marryin' someone else just wasn't right, Rachel. He know I had you first?"

"He knows all about you, Ben. He knows what kind of vile vermin you are."

"Aw, now that just ain't nice. Maybe you and me need to get reacquainted. No man with any respect for hisself would stay married to a woman who cheated on him, especially with her very first."

She knew she could no longer keep her back to him; she had to know where he was, watch what he was doing. She nonchalantly reached over and took hold of her broom. If nothing else, she might be able to wield the handle defensively if Crane tried to attack her, hit him in a sensitive area like Trace had taught her, so that she could get to the loaded rifle by the bedroom door. "You were only my first because you took me against my will."

"Don't matter none how it happened, now does it? I'm still—" Crane stopped dead when Rachel faced him and his steel gray eyes fell to her bulging stomach. "Well, well, well...lookie what we got here. Don't that just beat all."

"That's right, Ben. I'm with child. Trace's child. Sure you don't want to think about touching a man's expectant wife? I think even you might not stoop to that."

The veins in Crane's neck were pulsating and he was clearly trying to control his temper while not hiding his disappointment. *No one told him that I was in the family way. Were they afraid he would go berserk?* She took a deep breath. *He probably would have.* Rachel knew his obsession with her. He was looking at her in a way that made her uncomfortable.

"Damn, Rachel, you're still the prettiest creature that ever drawed a breath. You make my insides ache. I bet you still got a smile that could melt snow caps."

"You'll never see it again." She gripped the broom handle so tightly, her fingers grew numb. "You really need to go, Ben. Trace won't be happy when he finds out you've been here."

Crane fingered the hammer of the Smith & Wesson six-gun hanging low on his side. "Well, you know, I'd kinda like to stick around and meet this Trace fella. Been hearin' a lot about him; kinda expectin' him to walk on water. Wonder if he can stop bullets. Oh, that's right. He can't. Didn't Ed plug him a few times? Yep. Sorry to hear about ol' Ed becomin' worm fodder. Hope your Trace don't follow in his footsteps."

"I swear, Ben Crane, you touch one hair on Trace Sheridan's head and I'll kill you myself." The cast in her green eyes was pure venom, enough to make Crane take a small step back, leaving him looking a little unsettled.

"Now don't go gettin' yourself all riled up, I never said I was gonna kill 'im, just that bein' sheriff is a dangerous job."

"Especially when the sheriff isn't working for you."

Crane smiled. "I have no idea what you might mean by that, Miss Young," he said sweetly.

"Mrs. Sheridan," Rachel corrected stiffly.

"Right. My apologies, Mrs. Sheridan," he said with a sarcastic half-bow. He had been studying her intently since he'd discovered she was pregnant. His eyes suddenly narrowed in suspicion. "How long you been married?"

"Six months."

"Huh. Belly's mighty big for six months, ain't it? He musta nailed you on the first night. Unless you and he got friendly before that."

"I'm sure I conceived on my wedding night," she said defensively.

"All's I'm sayin' is my sister, Hannah, and my brothers' wives were all about your size just shortly before they birthed them babies. Now, if that follows, then that would mean you're lyin' and that baby was made maybe a little over eight months ago. When your husband was nowhere around...but I was. You carryin' a Crane baby, Rachel?"

"I would cut any child out of me before I spawned another Crane! Fire Arrow says this is just a very big baby."

"Fire Arrow? Who the hell is that? What does Doc Smith say?"

"Doc Smith will never get his hands on this baby or me. He's as far into your back pocket as Ed Jackson was." She was trying not to sound panicky, hoping it was coming out more like indignation.

"Who's this Fire Arrow? One of them crazy Pawnee?"

"I'm done talking to you. I want you to leave my house this instant."

He laughed. "You ordering me off your property, Rachel?"

"Yes. You're trespassing, Ben. I'll have my husband arrest you."

"Oh, I don't think that would be a good idea at all." The intent in his eyes was purely sinister. "I'd bet real big money that I planted the seed that's growin' inside you. And if that's so, then I got more rights to you than that sonuvabitch you're married to."

Rachel's heart was in her throat. "No, Ben, you're wrong, wrong in every way."

When he leapt for her, she was prepared but her body didn't move fast enough. She raised the broom handle but Crane knocked it out of her grip and sent it flying across the room. The force of his body suddenly against her, he pushed her backward. Getting one hand free, she slapped him hard across the face. Retaliating, he swung at her with the back of his hand. Deflecting his blow threw her slightly off balance, and that was enough for him to regain the advantage. He grabbed her shoulders and forced her against the wall.

She screamed, though she had no hope that anyone was around to hear. "No, Ben, Stop it! Stop!" *Oh, dear Lord, this can't be happening again.* He tried to kiss her and she moved her head to evade him. "Please, Ben, don't — you'll hurt the baby."

He ignored her pleas as he spun her around, pushing her face against the rough logs, attempting to corral her flailing arms with one hand and pull up her dress with the other. She was hysterical, her sobs loud and coming out in gasps, and when his feet moved apart in an attempt to spread her legs open, she saw her opportunity and brought her heel up as hard as she could.

Everything suddenly stopped and she heard him suck in air as a strangled noise choked from his throat. Freed, she spun around, prepared for a fresh attack. He was no longer focused on her as he crumpled to the floor in a fetal position, his hands clutching his crotch. Enraged, Rachel kicked him several more times — in the face, in the back, and in the side — then reached down and pulled his revolver from the holster. She emptied all six bullets from the cylinder, dropped them into the pocket of her apron, and threw the pistol out the front door. Then she ran and picked up her rifle. Raising the carbine, she cocked the hammer back and took aim. She was breathing hard and fast, and shaking like a leaf, but she pointed the rifle in the general direction of the groaning man writhing on the floor.

Trying to slow her breathing, Rachel wrestled with her conscience. *What is happening to me? Am I capable of taking another life?* Ed Jackson was barely cold in his grave and there she was, ready to kill someone else. But this wasn't just anyone, this was Ben Crane, and if anyone deserved to die, he did.

The injured man rose slowly to his knees. "Son-of-a-fucking-bitch, Rachel..."

His voice was hoarse and he was still holding his damaged manhood. His face was bruised and bloody from her kicking him, and it startled her to see the results of her violence. But her moment of weakness did not last as her eyes constricted with fury, knowing he would have raped her again.

Rachel brought the carbine to bear. At that moment, despite her emotional turmoil, she felt a presence beside her and a hand wrapped around the barrel of the gun, pushing it downward. She looked into the gaze of Little Hawk. He shook his head gently. Willing her fingers to release the carbine, she allowed him to take possession of it.

The Pawnee held the rifle loosely, muzzle pointed toward the floor. He looked over at Red Sky, who was standing in the doorway, and spoke to him in Skiri, then quietly guided Rachel behind him. When Red Sky left quickly, Little Hawk spoke, his voice strong and commanding. "You will go, Crane, before Red Sky fetches this woman's husband. And you will thank whatever spirit you pray to for letting you live."

Crane struggled to his feet. Bent at the waist, he rested his palms on his thighs, grimacing. He raised angry eyes to glare at Rachel, the expression he wore no longer filled with lust or wanting. "You just made the biggest mistake of your life, Rachel. You should have killed me while you had the chance." He let his gaze fall to Rachel's stomach again and then met her eyes. "Tell you what...that baby comes out of you in another month instead of two and looks anythin' like me? I'm comin' to get it."

"Over my dead body!"

He pointed at her. "Careful what you wish for, Mrs. Sheridan."

"You come back here, you die." The words from Little Hawk were not a threat, rather a promise. There was no mistaking the tone or intent, and his eyes burned holes through Crane as he left.

When she heard Ben's horse ride away, Rachel sank to the floor and wept uncontrollably, her face in her hands.

Rio splashed through the river, his hooves clicking on stone as he crossed the wide base of rocks that covered part of the stream bed. Trace, belly down and riding hell bent for leather, was pushing him hard, the staccato hoof beats thundering over the ground from the river to the house. Instead of the usual half hour by wagon, it took her only ten minutes to cover the ground from Sagebrush to the ranch.

"Rachel!" Trace jumped off Rio and ran up the steps. Flying through the door, she searched for her wife, spotting Little Hawk first. "Rachel?" When the Pawnee cast his eyes downward, Trace saw the top of Rachel's head and nearly overturned the table to get to her.

Trace dropped to her knees, not missing the bruise on the side of Rachel's face where she had been pushed into the wall. She held Rachel's chin and inspected her for additional damage. The wounded look in the wet and swollen green eyes clawed at Trace's heart. She took Rachel into her arms, not even daring to breathe until Rachel spoke. Trace gently rocked her as Rachel began to cry again. Through clenched teeth, Trace asked, "Did he touch you?"

Rachel could not seem to find the breath to answer, but her head nodded against Trace's shoulder. The very idea of Ben Crane laying one finger on Rachel again made Trace's heart pound like a trip hammer as rage seethed through every pore of her body. She positioned herself on the floor so that she could look in Rachel's eyes, see her face.

"What...did...he...do?" Trace could barely get the question out; her body shook with white-hot anger.

"He...he...tried...to...have...his...way...with...me...again..." Every word was punctuated by a ragged drawing of breath, as Rachel tried to get her tears under control.

Trace stood slowly, helping Rachel up with her, pulling her into a full body hug. Rachel clung to her as though for dear life. "What did he do to you? How did he touch you? Did he hit you across the face?"

"No. He pushed my face into the wall and tried to keep me there while he was pushing up my dress and...and I kept begging him not to hurt the baby and—"

"He was trying to rape you from behind?"

Again, the movement of Rachel's head against Trace's shoulder indicated she had understood correctly. Trace felt as if she would explode from the hatred and fury building inside her. "But he didn't succeed..." She could not even phrase it in the form of a question, instead making it a statement, as if that would make it so. She did not think she would be able to control her urge to kill if Rachel said he had even partially succeeded. It was taking every ounce of self-discipline for her not to leave Rachel in the custody of Little Hawk to track the bastard down and tear him limb from limb with her bare hands.

"No."

If Rachel did not have to look at her, she seemed to have more strength to talk about the attack without breaking down. Trace adjusted her embrace, supporting Rachel's full weight against her. "How did you get away from him?"

"I kicked my heel back and caught him between the legs. He let me go and fell to the floor. Then I kicked him and took his gun and emptied it. I got to the carbine and I swear I would have shot him if Little Hawk hadn't stopped me."

Trace shot a sharp glare at the Pawnee, who met her eyes and then casually looked away. She returned her attention to the shattered woman in her arms. "You did great, baby; you did everything you should have. You beat him, Rachel. You stopped it from happening again. You took your power back, sweetheart."

She kissed the top of Rachel's head several times and then led her into the bedroom. "I really think you should rest, honey. It's been an exhausting trial for you." Rachel laid her head back on the pillow and Trace covered her up with the shawl from the foot of the bed. "It's going to be all right now. Okay? I'm not going to let anything happen to you or the baby." Trace rubbed the back of her hand over the nasty looking contusion on Rachel's cheekbone. "You're going to be okay."

When Trace withdrew her hand, Rachel grabbed it. "Trace...it's not going to be okay. He knows."

Seeing her precious wife becoming distraught again, Trace tried to calm her. "Shhhh, shhhh...everything is going to be fine. I won't let anything happen to you, I promise. What does he know?" Her gentle tone of voice didn't reveal the explosiveness she was feeling inside.

"He knows the baby is his."

Seeing the hysteria rising. Trace began lovingly stroking Rachel's face. "Sweetheart, you have to calm down. This is not good for the baby. Now — tell me exactly what he said that makes you think he knows the baby is his."

Rachel described Ben Crane's realizations and Trace cradled her comfortingly. "It'll be all right, Rach. I promise." She leaned away. "I just need to go and talk to Little Hawk for a few minutes and then I'll come back. Is that okay?" Rachel hugged her, then reluctantly released Trace.

Stalking by her Pawnee brother in the kitchen, Trace plucked a cup from the cupboard and pumped water into it. She approached Little Hawk, trying to keep her voice quiet enough to keep Rachel from hearing. "What the hell is wrong with you?" she whispered harshly. "Why did you stop her from killing that bastard?"

Gazing intently at her, he said, "It is not meant for Caskí Custíra'u to kill Crane. It is your destiny to do this."

"Why? Why is it my destiny? What does it matter who takes this prick out, as long as he's gone?"

"You will understand when the time comes." Little Hawk patted her on the shoulder and went to the door, setting the carbine by the arch.

"Wait! If it's supposedly my destiny to kill the son-of-a-bitch, you stay here with Rachel and I'll go after him now!"

Little Hawk turned and walked back toward her. "No. You ride after Crane and you will die. He will be waiting for you. Your wife needs you here tonight. Tomorrow, we will find him. Tomorrow, you will send him back to his Creator."

There was wisdom in his words. For Rachel, she would wait until tomorrow. "All right," she said, "but if he comes back here before tomorrow, he's a dead man."

"Yes. He has been warned. I am going back to my village now. I will send warriors to stand guard."

"What if he returns?"

"Then you do what you must."

"What if your warriors get to him first?"

"Then he will be captured and brought to you."

"And after that?"

"The warriors will follow your lead." Before he rode back to his settlement, Little Hawk instructed Red Sky to keep vigil on the homestead.

Trace thought Rachel would nap for a while, having cried herself to sleep, but she slept only as long as it took for Trace to heat a kettle of water for tea. So infuriated she thought her head would implode, Trace did not notice Rachel at the bedroom door until she heard her sniff back tears.

"Baby, what are you doing up? You should be resting."

"I feel so dirty..."

It was a desperate whisper. Rachel sounded tormented, lost. Even when Trace pulled her into a hug, Rachel's arms remained folded across her chest. Resting her chin on the top of Rachel's head, Trace knew what she needed to do. She led Rachel to the pantry area where the tub was. "I'm going to heat some water," she told Rachel gently. "Then I'll help you get your clothes off."

Trace made sure that the bath was not too hot; she remembered reading somewhere about the dangers of raising the body temperature while pregnant. Rachel was semi-submerged in the warm water, arms encircling her knees, hugging them as close to her body as she could get them, given the size of her belly. Even though Rachel was not saying a word, trying not to make a sound, tears were streaming down her face, her body shuddering with every drawn breath.

Trace's eyes misted over as she lightly scrubbed Rachel's back with a cloth. "Rachel...I am so sorry..." Trace's voice slid from soft to repentant to barely controlled wrath. "I should have been here. I should have known better than to start working in town before that bastard got back and things were taken care of." She soaked the wash-cloth and sluiced the water over Rachel's shoulder, then did the same to the other. She gently pressed Rachel back and began to wash her neck and chest.

"I should have known something wasn't right when those Carvers showed up wanting to claim land — land that's been there all along. They were being so damned nice. I should have known."

"Trace? It's all right. Really. You couldn't have known." Moist green eyes connected with deeply rueful blue ones. A single tear fell from Trace's eye. Rachel wiped it away with her thumb, then caressed Trace's cheek and chin. The love conveyed by that one gesture caused Trace to break down. Rachel drew Trace closer, into a tight embrace. "You can't be everywhere at once."

"You needed me here, Rachel, and I wasn't. God, baby, I love you so much and I failed you." Trace went back to tenderly bathing Rachel. "I'll never do that again, I promise you. Anyone ever comes near you again, meaning you harm, and I'll kill them with my bare hands. You are the best thing in my life and if anything happened to you, I...just couldn't go on. I know it.

"In just a few months you've changed me completely, made me want to be a better person, made me want to spend the rest of my life just pleasing you. And the thought of all that being taken away from me..." She couldn't go on, devastated in a way that defied words.

Crying again, Rachel pulled Trace to her and kissed her. "I never want to find out what that's like, either, Trace."

In a silence that was now more comfortable, Trace went back to lovingly cleansing her wife. *Funny...but bathing Rachel is making my soul feel cleaner.*

Chapter Twenty-six

It was a sleepless night for Trace, and knowing she would be killing Ben Crane the next day had very little to do with it. It was Rachel's recurring nightmares that were keeping her awake. Each time Rachel woke, it was with a frightened yelp or agonized sob, along with sweating and shaking. Knowing that she couldn't stop Rachel's horrific dreams, left the normally fearless Trace feeling helpless, an emotion so alien to her, she wasn't even sure that's what she was experiencing. Trace hated Ben Crane for what he did to Rachel, what he tried to do again, and what that had done to her — made her feel weak and ineffectual.

Every time Rachel roused, Trace calmed her and kissed her, hoping to reassure Rachel that she was safe. Trace liked being Rachel's protector, her knight in shining armor. It was the one pure thing, other than her love, that she could offer her, and now...now this monster had destroyed that surety between them.

She couldn't recall ever in her life wanting so badly to see a man dead. She was sure revenge would taste powerfully sweet.

Trace would have preferred to leave Rachel with a familiar female, like Elizabeth Reddick or Molly Ledbetter, until her task was completed. But the fewer people who knew what Trace was about to do, the better.

Little Hawk, Fire Arrow, and Dancing Leaf — one of the women of the tribe who served as midwife — stayed with Rachel inside the cabin. Fire Arrow thought it best to be there, in case the harrowing events should cause Rachel to go into premature labor. Trace agreed.

Howling Wolf and Black Feather rode with Trace to find Ben Crane. They settled in the woods just beyond the border of the Crane property line and waited there for an opportunity to present itself. From their perch on the side of a hill overlooking the main ranch house and several outbuildings, they waited and watched. Trace knew she didn't need her Pawnee brothers there; she could handle an overgrown punk like Ben Crane. However, on the off chance she could not fulfill her destiny, as Little Hawk had predicted, their presence would ensure that Crane would never lay his hands on Rachel again.

While they waited, Black Feather spoke to Trace concerning the retribution against the cattle baron's youngest son. After listening to the reasoning of the warrior, Trace concurred that a severe ass-kicking and then a prolonged, painful death were well deserved.

After an hour's wait, Howling Wolf saw movement in the bunkhouse as a few ranch hands emerged and ambled over to the cookhouse. Not long after that, the cowboys moved out to start their day. It took another two hours before the target of their vengeance showed himself on the porch, stretching what seemed to be stiff and sore muscles.

Rachel was trying to find something to keep her from worrying about Trace. Housework, baking a pie, or tending to the garden were not going to provide enough diversion. She had already knitted enough booties to warm the feet of every infant in Jefferson County, and taking Chief out for a leisurely ride was out of the question. Ramiro's barking caught her attention and she went out on the porch to see what the commotion was. She was greeted by a very dirty puppy, who began happily jumping around at her feet.

"My goodness, boy, where have you been?" Rachel's nose wrinkled. At least he didn't smell like he'd been in the pasture, rolling in something one of the cows left behind. He'd done that last week. But it solved the problem of what she could do to busy herself. *Someone else is going to have to catch him*, she thought, and she went inside to ask Dancing Leaf if she would help get the ten gallon bucket ready.

Rio was tied to a low branch, feeding on tall grass while Trace waited for Crane to pass. She had removed her gunbelt. She did not want to do battle with him from a distance; she wanted to feel her hands on him when she hurt him. Her Pawnee brethren had remounted and stayed concealed.

Trace watched as the cocky bastard and his horse ambled along the path, moving in a direction that would take him to the Triple Y. *Is he really so clueless that he would try again? Does he honestly think I would leave Rachel alone again to give him an opportunity? His arrogance is evidently only matched by his stupidity.*

He pulled the brim of his hat down, shading his face from the sun and looking around in a lazy manner, either unaware that anything might be amiss, or just disinterested. In the next moment, she went flying at him, hard and quick, and knocked him off his horse without giving him a chance to react. Lying on the ground, he picked his face up from the dirt and eyed a pair of boots.

"Hello, Crane." Trace's voice was shaking, not from anything having to do with fear. She found it difficult to restrain herself while the man got to his feet. She was in a defensive stance, ready for anything from this bully.

Ben rolled onto his knees. "Sheriff Sheridan, I reckon."

Trace's heart went up in her throat. *That voice...where have I heard that voice before?* And then he stood up and lifted his face, steel gray eyes meeting her ice blue ones. Trace reeled back from the shock, nearly losing her balance. Suddenly the curtain rose on her amnesia and everything became clear: why she had run from the twenty-first century; why she had given up everything and risked her life to be in Sagebrush. Her blood ran ice cold through her veins. Ben Crane was the spitting image of Vincent DeSienna, the man who had ordered her death for double-crossing him.

Crane silently appraised her. "You look like you've seen a ghost, Sheriff."

She felt as though she had. Everything about him was identical to the only man who had ever really intimidated her: vocal inflection, height and build, and most of all, conceit. DeSienna was the culmination of generations of interethnic unions. Ben was the lighter, uneducated, less savvy version of Vincent. Those eyes...that voice... Could this possibly mean that Rachel was carrying an ancestor of a horrendous family to come? Was she going to help raise a distant relative of the man she hated most in the world?

On the verge of hyperventilating, she forced her focus back to the situation at hand. How much better would it feel now, as though she were killing Ben Crane and Vincent DeSienna at the same time? Oh, how she wished that were true. Trace abruptly relaxed and steadied herself, suddenly feeling very much in control. Now she knew what Little Hawk meant, that it was her destiny to kill Ben Crane...but how did he know? A question for another time.

She stared at Crane's bruises and regarded him with a smirk. "My wife do that to you? She did a nice job. Too bad she didn't kick your nuts off in the process."

His eyes narrowed in contempt. "You gotta lot of nerve, Sheridan, comin' to this town and takin' over, takin' my woman."

"She was never your woman, Crane. I think she proved that yesterday. And now you're going to answer to me. Let's see how big a man you are when you're facing someone your own size, someone who's not afraid of you."

He snorted. "My size? You tall, skinny shit, a strong wind could blow you over. Why, you ain't nothing like I suspected. Who the hell would be afraid of you?"

"A scumsucking pig rapist like you." She watched his expression change and his hand move to his hip and hover above his holster.

"Fill your hand, Sheridan!"

Trace gestured to her waist where there was no gun. "No. We're going to settle this without weapons. Shooting you would be way too easy, way too quick."

"There's just one thing wrong with that...you ain't running this show." He was able to pull his pistol from his holster but that was all. Her lightning fast front roundhouse kick disarmed him with an accuracy that startled him speechless.

"You fucking ball-less, piece-of-shit coward." She punctuated that with a wicked backhand blow that sent him sprawling. "Get up, you son-of-a-bitch; we're going to do this right." She planted her feet and beckoned him forward. "What's the matter, Crane? You can only beat up on girls?" Clearly furious, Crane hopped to his feet and charged, a move she anticipated, stepping aside and sweeping his feet out from under him, sending him bouncing on his ass. She let out a little snicker. "Where do they teach you boys how to fight?" He looked up at her, a little dazed. "What's pissing you off more, Crane? The fact that you haven't even got a punch in yet, or that I'm laughing at you?"

"Nobody laughs at a Crane...and lives to tell about it!" Scrambling to his feet, he adopted a boxer's stance, hopping around a bit, one fist extended in front of his face the other curled in front of his chest. "Take your best shot, Sheridan, 'cause it'll be your last."

Trace shook her head. "Silly boy." She wound up and jumped. While in the air, her right leg shot out as if she were going to perform a side kick and, instead, her other leg launched to the left in a ball kick, executing a scissor kick after her rotation, striking him with the back of her heel. That caused his own fist to smack him hard in the face. He took a few off-balanced steps backwards, befuddled. The eye that Rachel hadn't blackened immediately started to swell.

"You don't fight like no man I ever seen," Crane spat, getting madder and more frustrated.

"Neither do you," Trace said. Gifted with a natural hand and eye coordination that enhanced her precise fighting skills, she was good at what she did and she was not used to losing in hand-to-hand combat. Ben Crane was no match for her and she knew it.

There was a part of her that just wanted to grab him in a head lock and break his neck, but he deserved to be punished. If Trace had been a different type of individual, she would have done it in the exact same manner in which he had brutalized Rachel, so he could know exactly what it felt like — not just the physical pain, but the loss of control, security, self. Most of all, she wanted him to feel humiliation as he had never felt it before.

Still, Trace was many things but a rapist was not one of them, and even as tempting as it was in this situation, she was not ready to add that to her résumé. It would be enough that Crane would know that she was capable of killing him, and would, if she chose to do so. She could degrade, demean, and emasculate him by not letting him land one blow, and then when he was well weakened, she would hand him over to Black Feather and Howling Wolf. Until then, she had some serious ass kicking to do. Crane had resumed his previous fighting stance, doing his best imitation of a banty rooster, advancing toward Trace in a menacing posture.

"Obviously, you don't learn from your mistakes, asswipe."

Her center of gravity low, Trace moved out of Crane's path, executing a stepping side kick. Thrusting her leg out, she connected solidly with Crane's hip. It stopped him dead in his tracks and she moved her foot in a crescent, kicking him in the posterior and planting him once again in the dirt, face first.

Not waiting for him to recover, Trace walked over to Crane and dragged him up by the back of his shirt. Using her anger and adrenaline for momentum, she swung him around, releasing him so that he was propelled headlong into a tree. Bouncing back from the unyielding fixed object, the cattle baron's son staggered backward before he fell on his butt.

"Get up, you sorry fucking excuse for a man!" When Trace approached him, he promptly scooted away from her. "What's the matter, Benjy? You afraid of me? Huh? How does it feel to be afraid? How does it feel to have no control? How does it feel to know someone else holds your fate in their hands?" She grabbed the collar of his shirt and hauled him to his feet. Releasing him, she stomped her foot as though she were going to let loose with another side kick and he backed away, nearly whimpering.

Relaxing her body, Trace baited Crane into thinking she was letting her guard down. He didn't disappoint her when he raised his fist, shooting it forward with all the strength he had. She raised her hand in an upward motion, blocking his attempt. Crane tried again with his other hand but Trace deflected his movement again, never taking her eyes off his. He repeated the futile attack several times, more overcome with exasperation with every swing.

Backed up against a large oak tree, seeing the look in Sheridan's eye, all color drained from Crane's face. He flinched when Trace slowly, deliberately, raised her arm. She let her hand hover in front of him threateningly.

His eyes twitched back and forth from Trace's face to her hand. "What are you going to do to me?"

"Exactly what you did to my wife," she growled. His eyes grew wide with fear and she knew exactly what he was thinking.

"Is your asshole puckering, Crane? It should be. No, I'm not going to do that, although nothing would give me greater pleasure than to see you suffer that way. No, I'm not going to rape you because that would make me just like you. I realize I may have been as bad as Ed Jackson at one point in my life, but I was never anything like you, and I will never be. Make no mistake, though, Benjy, I am going to hurt you. Bad. And then you are going to die."

Trace thought she could actually hear his heartbeat. Crane hesitated and then drove his head forward in an attempt to smash it against hers. She caught him by the forehead and slammed the back of his skull against the tree.

Having him pinned, she performed a penetrating power punch she had learned from a Shaolin sensei, a remarkable woman who personified the word self-control. The move had required a lot of concentration and discipline to perfect. With just a touch, energy was used to penetrate her opponent's body. Following the strike, the surface of the body looked untouched but the internal organs in that specific area were destroyed.

She had only used it once before, on a henchman of DeSienna's. She had disarmed him, but he was huge and starting to get the upper hand. Having exhausted all of her other fighting skills, and having practiced the move on a heavy punching bag for years, she felt she had nothing to lose by trying it. After the punch, the man had gotten in a few more hits before he slowed down and passed out. He died from internal injuries.

Now, she could not think of a better subject on whom to repeat that scenario. Staring into the strangely familiar wide eyes of Ben Crane, Trace felt a sudden vindication. He wasn't Vincent, but he was the next best thing. "That was for me," she said without remorse. "What happens next will be for my wife." When she let go of him, he fell to his knees.

"What...did you...just do?"

"Something that would eventually kill you if you weren't going to die before then. You probably have a small ache in your gut right now. In about five minutes, it's going to be a throbbing, searing pain. But, trust me, that won't be anything compared to what you're going to feel."

She knew that whatever justice was going to be meted out to this man would have to be administered by her. There was no law other than herself to turn him over to; no jail would hold a Crane for very long. A territorial prison might serve, perhaps, where an unbiased warden could keep him behind bars, but who knew when Crane would be able to be transported. By that time all hell could break loose. Jail might be fine for the rest of the Crane clan, but Ben didn't deserve the courtesy of a trial. He didn't deserve any of the considerations that someone would who might actually be innocent of the crimes she knew for a fact Ben Crane had committed.

Once Trace was satisfied that Crane was terrified and suffering, she dragged him over to Black Feather and Howling Wolf, who picked him up and tied him between two small trees. One arm and one leg were tied to each tree so that he was spread eagled between them. Normally, that kind of death would be a little gruesome, even for her, but not when it came to this subterranean piece of shit.

The two trees would be easy to chop through, but heavy enough so that when they fell in opposite directions, they would take Crane's limbs with them. It would be an agonizingly slow and painful death and when his body was found, it would look like he had been torn apart by a wild animal. It wasn't that Trace wasn't willing to take responsibility for Ben Crane's demise, but she wanted to play by the Cranes' rules. Ben would be found right outside his own property, in pieces, the circumstances surrounding the incident, an unsolvable mystery. It would serve as a warning to the rest of the Cranes: they weren't invincible.

Trace glared at the evil staring back at her, his eyes now as fixed and dull as a dead man's. "Any last words?"

"Yeah, I found fulfillment in the arms of your pretty little wife, Sheridan, and she was eager and willin'."

Defiant and arrogant to the end. "You raped my wife, Crane. You came up behind her, and like the coward you are, ambushed her and beat her into submission, and then you took her against her will. You violated her. You humiliated her. You degraded her. You stole her virginity. You took away her security. But as much as you wanted to, you never took her dignity. You couldn't take no for an answer. No, she didn't want to sell her land. No, she didn't want to be courted by you. No, she didn't want to marry you, and the biggest no of all, she did not want to have sex with you. But being the despicable creature you are, you took her anyway. And then, you disgusting bastard, you came back and tried to do it again."

"You don't know what happened in that cabin, Sheridan. All you got is that little bitch's lies and the word of these Injuns, which ain't much better."

"My wife doesn't lie, Crane. And neither do my brothers."

"She doesn't lie, you say? You think that baby inside her is yours? She lie to you about that? 'Cause it don't matter what she told you, she knows and I know — that kid is mine!"

Trace stepped up to Crane, almost nose to nose. "You may have injected the seed, you fucking scrote, but that child will never be yours. My wife — yes, my wife, not yours — would have never let you be a part of that baby's life. Whine, piss, and moan all you want, but Rachel would have convinced the town that the baby is mine. And, you know what? Since everybody hates your family's guts, they would be quite willing to believe her. As much as it would kill you, my wife would have gotten the best of you in the end."

"Ain't no woman ever gonna get the best of me, Sheridan."

"Oh, really?" A smirk crossed her face and she stepped back, raising an eyebrow. Looking up at Black Feather, who smiled back at her and nodded, she returned her attention to Ben Crane.

As the Pawnee began to chop, Trace unbuttoned her shirt and removed it, revealing a chest wrapped in a stretchy, binding cloth. Slowly, she unwound the material until it fell to the ground. Crane's eyes popped at the sight before him.

"What in the hell!"

The last thing he saw before the trees fell and ended his life were the breasts of the woman who got the best of him.

The scream that ripped from deep within his being echoed in Trace's ears for barely a second and, as he went into shock, the guttural, pleading moan that rose up from his throat, died quicker than he did. Trace didn't even flinch, watching Ben Crane's limbs separate from his body as he bled out. Once the trees had done their job, as disturbingly bloody and repulsive as the process was, Trace felt a satisfaction that almost alarmed her. She experienced no guilt or remorse over Crane's death.

They removed the ropes, covered their tracks, dug up the tree stumps and filled the holes with dirt, leaves, and other vegetation, making the area look as undisturbed as they could. As they left the scene of Ben Crane's death, hauling the trees back with them to chop for firewood, Trace was sure she would immediately fall under suspicion, that she would be held responsible, even if not accountable, for what she considered this justified act of reprisal. She shrugged it off. The important thing to her was that the most immediate threat to Rachel was gone forever. With that knowledge, she felt no qualms about the potential outcome of taking on the rest of the family.

The ride back to the ranch was quiet. Trace knew Black Feather and Howling Wolf thought her contemplative silence was due to the murder they had just committed. They couldn't know it was fueled by her getting her memory back.

She had been on a special detail for the department. She thought it was funny that she'd been pulled from her regular assignment to work with a sting team that was haphazardly thrown together. It was funny until they were set up and ambushed, and a hail of bullets meant for her slammed into her colleague instead, critically wounding him. Instinct told her that her luck and time had run out and she knew she was a dead woman walking, as Vincent would not stop until he finished her off. So she had run. Far and fast. And then something directed her to the secluded home of Mark Teranovich, her first patrol partner and dear friend. She didn't know whether it was a fluke or destiny that she knew someone who dabbled in unproven and untested scientific inventions, that Mark happened to be experimenting with what he called a retromolecular transference device. An amateur time machine.

Mark had cut her hair, dressed her in appropriate clothing, and given her many items of his great grandmother's jewelry to carry with her to pawn. He reluctantly used Trace as his guinea pig, both of them knowing if the process didn't kill her, that Vincent or his hired men would. She wished she knew of a way to tell him that she had made it, that it had all been successful in so many ways.

She wished she could have thanked him for finding the only way to give her a second chance.

Chapter Twenty-seven

Ben Crane's body was discovered by Seth Carver, who vomited several times before he could remount and return to the Crane spread to report what he had found. He told his father first, who called for three ranch hands to saddle up and accompany them back to Ben's corpse.

"What do you think happened, Pa? Looked to me like he got tore up by animals of some sort," Seth called to his father from afar.

"Seth, get over here," John demanded.

"No, Pa. I can't bear to look at that again. It's just too damned grisly. Just recallin' it makes me sick. Scavengers was feeding on him when I rode up the first time. So what do you think? A wolf?"

John shook his head. The death was going to be hard on Jacob, but it was absolutely going to kill Priscilla, Ben's mother. "A pack of wolves, maybe. Aw, Ben..." John sighed. "You really did it this time." The older Carver was pretty sure the only animal who had gotten to Ben Crane was a man named Trace Sheridan. He didn't have any proof, but the timing was just too coincidental.

Ben had come home the day before and bragged about paying a little visit to Rachel, swore up and down that the baby she was carrying was his, not the sheriff's, and further boasted that he'd taken Rachel again, right there in her own parlor. If that was true, the sheriff had every right to go after Ben. Regardless of how willing Ben said Rachel was, he shouldn't have gone messing with another man's woman, especially when that woman was in the family way.

And John knew better than to believe Ben's claims of consent. Rachel Young never wanted his nephew. If she had, they would have been married by now and starting their own family. Ben was the only one who considered himself suitable for the likes of Frank Young's daughter. John had been there when complaints filtered back to Jacob about Ben's abusive behavior toward the "painted doves" over Wilbur's Saloon, and even more telling, when his brother-in-law paid off a few of the hands to keep them quiet about Ben's unwanted advances towards their wives and sweethearts. Although John was loyal to Priscilla and Jacob, he considered Ben a mean, spoiled, unruly swine, and if he'd had Rachel, John guessed that it was by force. If his nephew hadn't been planning something wretched two days ago, why had he instructed them to keep the sheriff occupied for a while so he could let Rachel know he was back?

Looking at the mangled corpse before him, John thought it was too brutal an ending, even for Ben. No, Jacob wasn't going to be happy about this at all.

"You boys go back to the ranch and get a box out here and pick him up," John said. "I'll go tell his mama."

When a shaken Trace and her companions got back to the Triple Y, Little Hawk greeted them solemnly. "It is done?"

Trace nodded. "Yep. He won't be bothering Rachel — or anyone else — ever again. How is she?"

"She is resting."

"Good." She removed her fingerless rawhide gloves and looked directly at him. "How did you know?"

She didn't have to clarify; he knew what she was asking him. "I cannot explain this, Tsápaat. There are things I just know. Do you know why?"

"Why it had to be me and not Rachel who caused his death? Yeah. It was clear to me once I saw him."

The face and voice of her personal antagonist not only haunted, but taunted her as well in the person of Ben Crane. The irony was not lost on her; she'd felt almost mentally sucker punched by the shock. Had she not reacted purely on instinct, Rachel's rapist could have gotten the best of her, instead.

She could only hope through karmic synchronicity, that while she was killing Ben Crane, her own adversary was experiencing a death of similarly torturous conditions. And, because she was sure she would never know for certain, it gave her great sadistic pleasure to assume that he had. The recollection of Crane's agonized scream resonated in her ears, sending a shiver of satisfaction through her. When Ben Crane laid his filthy hands on Rachel again, he had reawakened the sanguine nature that Trace had kept dormant. She took several deep breaths, consciously swallowing her rage. *If only I could have gotten to him before he found Rachel alone, if only...*

"You killed him? Ben is dead?"

They turned to see Rachel entering the room, her expression a mixture of curiosity, incredulity, and relief.

"Yes, sweetheart. Ben Crane will never bother you again."

Rachel threw herself into Trace's arms, not unexpectedly, but with a fervor Trace had not anticipated. Trace held her comfortingly, securely.

Little Hawk moved toward the door. "I will leave you two alone."

Kissing the top of Rachel's head, Trace said, "Thank you, Little Hawk."

"I will be in the field. There is maize to harvest." It was his subtle way of letting them know he would not be too far away...just in case.

The full impact of the removal of the relentless threat hit Rachel like a dam breaking. Safe in Trace's loving and protective arms, Rachel broke down and wept.

John Carver's sister broke down and wept. "How did it happen, John?" she asked, not needing to ask why. Though she would never have said it out loud, Priscilla Crane knew that Ben had a mean streak in him that her other children did not have, and a pattern of behavior that eventually was going to take him to an early grave. It was one of those things a mother just knew. She was surprised it had not happened sooner.

Ephraim, her first born, despite having Jacob's temper, was more like her, possessing a quiet strength and an almost regal bearing. Gideon was more like his father in that he was sometimes too stubborn and too proud, never admitting to mistakes and having little patience with people who did not see things his way. Then there was Micah, who was a combination of the best parts of Jacob and the worst parts of her. Although he was virile and decisive, her middle child had a tendency to be gullible and easily manipulated. Like her. She hated to admit it, but those traits had allowed her to be unwillingly matched up with the most eligible bachelor in her parents' elite circle.

It wasn't that Jacob Crane hadn't been devastatingly handsome, and hadn't provided her with a secure future and a fine family, it was just that she had not been impressed with the sneaky, petty, and tyrannical way Jacob's father and grandfather had done business and, most importantly, she had been in love with another young man. James Powell, the preacher's son, who had nothing to offer her but his devotion and a meager subsistence as a minister's wife, at best, was the man she had secretly promised herself to, the man she really wanted to marry and have children with. Her parents wouldn't hear of it. Certainly the ministry was a noble calling, but it was in no way suitable for the only daughter of Omaha's most aristocratic banker. She would learn to love Jacob, her mother told her, just the way her mother had learned to love Priscilla's father.

And, learn to love Jacob, she did. But that did not stop her from occasionally thinking wistfully about what might have been with James and how, maybe, he would have helped her raise *their* children with different values.

Hannah, her only daughter, was beautiful and took full advantage of her privilege as a member of the most influential family in the county. She had grown up to be a disagreeable and bitter woman. Priscilla could only think that was due to constantly being overshadowed by her brothers. Regardless of how subtly Hannah competed, she never got equal amounts of attention from the father she adored. As much as Priscilla loved her husband, he made no secret that he favored his sons over his daughter and that damage was irreparable, and unforgivable.

And then there was Benjamin, whom she named after her father. He had been spoiled from the day he was born. She had nearly died giving birth to him and that pretty much guaranteed that he would be the last baby. He was eight years younger than Ephraim and treated like a little prince by all his siblings, including Hannah. By the time young Ben was in school, he already had the idea in his head that he could do no wrong, and that anyone who wasn't a Crane, owed him. She tried to rectify that, tried to discipline him for his bad conduct and manners, but her husband always overruled her. Jacob had wanted at least ten children, preferably all boys, and it seemed, perhaps because Ben was the last of Jacob's sons, punishment of any sort involving Ben was not tolerated.

So Priscilla stood by and watched her youngest child slowly become the monster he grew up to be, powerless to stop him. And now he was dead, something she had known was just a matter of time. She grieved for the loss of her son and she prayed for his soul, ashamed to entertain the thought that a child of hers might be too evil to get past the Pearly Gates.

"I really don't think I should tell you what happened to Ben, Priscilla. His death was pretty gruesome. I think that the sheriff was somehow involved." Giving her a few moments to absorb that, he continued, "Jacob and the boys will have to know and, I reckon he will declare all out war on the town and that there renegade lawman."

Priscilla just nodded. She held no ill will toward Trace Sheridan...in fact, in spite of the fact that it may have very well resulted in the death of her youngest child, she almost respected the sheriff for having the courage to stand up for what he believed was right.

It had to stop sometime, somewhere. She just wasn't sure if she was ready for it to be right now.

John and Seth Carver paid Trace a visit that afternoon at the sheriff's office to report Ben's death. The younger Carver still looked a little peaked and both men seemed as though the wind had been taken out of their sails. Although the older Carver scrutinized Trace suspiciously, he never once leveled an accusation at the sheriff during the entire time spent in the office.

Trace knew they were watching for her to do something, anything that might betray her guilt. But she was good at playing the passive game, experienced at donning a façade that hid her real emotion. No one had ever been able to see through that mask...except for Rachel. Looking with the eyes of love.

Filling out paperwork, recording all the details, Trace assured the Carver's, "I'll certainly look into the possibility of wolves roaming out near the Crane property."

"Yeah, maybe a Pawnee named Howling Wolf and a few of his friends," Seth said.

"Those are pretty serious allegations. You got any proof?"

The younger Carver shook his head. "I reckon you'll be coverin' tracks, just like when we was found stripped naked and tied to a tree."

John laid a silencing hand on his son's arm before he could say too many accusing words. "I think our business is concluded, Sheriff. I'm sure that when he returns, Jacob Crane will be around to hear what you find out."

John Carver was surprised that the sheriff had displayed no incriminating behavior, nothing indicative of a guilty conscience. He wondered whether Trace did have anything to do with Ben's death. The sinewy young lawman sounded almost compassionate while asking questions about what Seth had found in the woods not too far from the Crane property. In fact, Trace remained so professionally neutral that the older Carver stopped just short of apologizing for Ben's violent actions toward the sheriff's wife. Despite the fact that the new sheriff had kicked the crap out of him that night outside the barn, Carver was beginning to conclude that Trace wasn't such a bad guy after all.

Thinking back, brother-in-law of Jacob Crane or not, he'd had no business going along with any of Ed Jackson's hairbrained schemes for avenging the former sheriff's cowardice. It had been a mistake to make any kind of a move like that without Jacob's okay. The Crane patriarch really had no claim on Rachel or the Young ranch, either, but the situation definitely would have been handled face-to-face as opposed to the sneaky, underhanded manner in which Jackson decided to retaliate for a wounded ego. Carver had a feeling that Trace Sheridan wouldn't lay down like a kicked dog every time Jacob spoke like Ed Jackson had. Sheridan had already proved he wasn't afraid of anything.

Hmmm. Maybe a new sheriff running this town isn't such a bad idea, after all. It sure is going to make life interesting.

Trace watched the Carvers ride out of Sagebrush, then headed over to Wilbur's. Appearances be damned; she needed a drink. It wasn't so much because she had suddenly recovered her memory, or that Ben Crane bore a shocking resemblance to her modern day, would-be executioner. Or even that the Pawnee had carried out the actual execution on her behalf while she witnessed the death of the vaunted Ben Crane. It was the realization that she had more than likely just started an unstoppable war, one that might get innocent people killed.

Trace knew the Cranes had no clue what they were really up against now that she had the entire Pawnee tribe behind her, but they were a family used to getting their own way, regardless of the means they had to use, or the consequences of their actions. The citizens of Sagebrush were stronger now and more aware of their cooperative power but, in the long run, very few of them could stand up to the dangerous dynasty that had terrorized them for ten years. At the very least, someone undeserving was going to get hurt, would end up a casualty of her actions and decisions. For the first time in her life, that really bothered her.

When she pushed through the double doors of the saloon, even Silas stopped what he was doing and observed with tacit fascination the almost reverent silence that fell over the room as all eyes watched the sheriff stride to the bar. Most of them were sitting in the exact same places they had been the day before when one of the Pawnee came in and told Trace that Ben Crane was at the Triple Y.

Matthew Reddick laid down his cards and was the first to speak. "Hey, Trace...did you hear about Ben Crane?"

Trace nodded as she stepped up to the bar. "Yep. John and Seth Carver were just by my office." She looked at Matthew pointedly and decided she might as well face the town gossip sooner rather than later. "How did you find out about it?"

"It wasn't more than an hour ago that Pete Mason, one of the Crane ranch hands, stood over by the stairway trying to wash away what he'd seen with shots of that rotgut Silas keeps under the counter. He looked really spooked, and he couldn't stop shaking. When I asked him what was wrong, he said they'd found Ben and he was trying to forget that he had just shoveled what was left of him into a box."

"What do you think happened?" the usual jovial bartender inquired as he brought Trace a shot and an ale.

Trace shrugged nonchalantly, downed the shot, cleared the burn out of her throat and said, "I have no clue. Sounds like wild animals got him."

"You don't sound too upset," Joseph Turner said.

"Should I be?" Trace pinned the pawnbroker with a glare. "The man went to my house and attacked my wife yesterday. I don't need to remind you that Rachel is having our child, Joseph. He could have hurt her something bad, or hurt my son or daughter. If you're looking for me to be sad or upset that the son-of-a-bitch met his Maker, then you're going to be disappointed."

"Did you have anything to do with it, Trace?" The question came from Cassandra, who was descending the stairs.

Trace gauged the prostitute's intent and decided that she was being straightforward. She took a long swallow of cool beer, then shook her head in amusement. "Now if I had, do you think I'd actually stand here and admit it to a roomful of people?" A smirk curled Trace's lips and everyone exhaled a collective relieved breath.

"Well, I certainly can't speak for anyone else in this room, but nothing would give me greater pleasure than to know you'd been the one to call out Ben Crane," Cassandra said. "It's been a long time comin'."

Amid the murmurs of agreement, Matthew spoke up. "We're with you, Trace. Whatever happened, we know Jacob will probably come after you. We've been talking, and we want you to know that we'll all stand with you."

Trace slowly turned and faced the men in the saloon. Each and every one of them was nodding in support of Matthew's statement.

Joseph Turner grinned sheepishly at her. "Tell ya the truth, Trace, I'm not real upset by the news, either. That man gave me nothing but headaches."

Trace broke into a relaxed smile and signaled Silas for another shot. As the bartender refilled the sheriff's glass, she inclined her head toward the prostitute, who had joined her at the bar. "And give Cassandra one, too. On me."

The bartender set the shot glass next to Trace's and looked at Cassandra expectantly. The prostitute pointed to a medium-priced bottle of scotch, which Silas retrieved. "How much of this you want, Cass?"

Just as Trace brought her glass to her lips and threw the shot back, the prostitute stood inseparably close to Trace and purred, "I'll take three fingers."

Trace discovered that whiskey being expelled from the nostrils hurt like hell.

Cassandra returned upstairs with a seductive wink and smile, and Trace sat at the table with Matthew and a few others. "What's John Carver's story?" she asked of the table, as she wasn't sure who might have the best information. She should have known it would be a toss up between Joseph Turner and Silas.

"You mean other'n him not knowin' one end of the horse from t'other?" That came from Clay Canfield, the father of Isaac Tipping's sweetheart, Lydia.

"That's not true," Joseph corrected, sniffing. He pulled up a stool next to Matthew and sat. "John Carver causes the least amount of trouble of anyone related to the Cranes. My wife and I had him and his late wife to dinner many times. He changed after Margaret died, got a little cantankerous, but I think he's still the most honorable of that bunch."

"Something tells me that's not saying much," Trace said wryly. She distinctly recalled Carver saying he'd like a little piece of Rachel for himself. That was the night he and Isaac had set out to attack them on the Triple Y. He'd said that if Rachel didn't cooperate, she just might have to be taught a lesson. That didn't make him very honorable in her estimation. "How did his wife die?"

"Nobody really knows. He told around that he accidentally shot her," Joseph said.

"What?" Trace asked, incredulous. "And that's honorable, how?"

"Story goes like this...supposedly Seth came back early from Jefferson City and caught his mama warmin' the bed of one of the ranch hands and the boy shot her on the spot, cold as Satan's breath about it. Probably would have shot the hand, too, 'cept he took off and was never seen again. John got back, found out about it and needed to save face. So, he told everyone that he was shootin' at targets and Margaret walked into his path, not knowin' he was there."

"And there were actually people who bought that story?" Trace asked.

"Oh hell, nobody bought it," Clay said, "That's cuz if you gave John Carver a gun and told him to shoot hisself, he'd miss. There was all kinds of crazy stories goin' around about that day. There was even one that said Priscilla was the one that shot her for betrayin' her brother." He stared blatantly at the pawnbroker. "What's with that hair on your face, Joseph? Those whiskers tryin' to make up fer what ye're losin' on top?" He dipped a big, dirty hand in a bowl of peanuts on the table.

"Winter's coming. You know Joseph always grows a beard to keep his face warm," Silas said.

"You know, Clay, you've always been one rude sonuvabitch. I'm telling you that I knew Margaret Carver better than anyone in this town and—"

"Yeah? Just how well did you know her, Joseph?" Canfield teased crudely.

"He didn't know her like that." Silas laughed. "Why, if Ruth ever thought Joseph was bein' unfaithful, she'd shoot that little dauber square off him."

"Well, I always thought your wife was right handsome, Joseph, so if worse comes to worst, I promise I'll do all your fuckin' for ya."

"Gentlemen, please," Trace interrupted, "we're getting off track here." She ordered another round for everyone at the table, hoping it would give Turner a chance to get his blood pressure down. The last time she'd seen something that red, it was a fireplug. Silas delivered everyone's drinks and collected the tab out of the change Trace had left lying on the bar.

"Joseph is right." Silas leaned his elbows on the counter. "John really isn't as bad as the rest of them. He always stays behind during the drives to handle everything for Jacob, makes sure everything stays running smooth, makes sure the women are all safe and protected. When none of the Crane boys are around, John is the number one man there."

"Personally, I think he shoots long range with a short gun, if you know what I mean." They turned around to see Emmet Hallack, who had strolled in unnoticed. He removed his derby and joined the others at the table.

"You think he's not quite all there?" Her question was meant to clarify the expression, which caused the others at the table to look up at the attorney, puzzled by his words. She'd have to remember that expression since "one french fry short of a Happy Meal" wouldn't cut it in this era. "Why?"

Hallack shrugged. "Something has to be wrong with him. He's the son of Benjamin Carver, who was one of the most influential businessmen in Omaha. Why isn't John a man who has his own fortune? Francis, the older brother, had money. He lived right well until he died from whooping cough five years ago. Old Benjamin arranged for Priscilla to marry well... So, what happened with John? Instead of being a man of his own means, his life has been spent following his sister around like a lost puppy — marrying her best friend, making his livelihood working for her husband instead of making his own way. It's not right, doesn't add up."

Hallack made a good point. "Anybody know why John Carver isn't a rich man in his own right?" Trace asked.

No one answered...but it certainly gave them all something to speculate about...which they did far into the evening, and were still discussing when Trace left.

When she arrived back at the Triple Y, she was greeted by a not-so-happy wife, apparently upset at Trace's intoxicated condition. Watery, bloodshot blue eyes tried to fix their gaze on green eyes and Trace could only equate Rachel's glare with one that might belong to a pissed off grizzly bear.

"Sorry, Rach. I stopped off and had a couple of drinks at Wilbur's."

Rachel raised an eyebrow. "Really? It doesn't look as though you stopped at a couple, Trace. I know you've had a day beyond my imagining, but did you have to get this drunk?"

"Yes," Trace said simply. Barely acknowledging Dancing Leaf with a nod, Trace collapsed on the bed, sideways, and Rachel pulled her boots off and left her there.

Loud snores immediately came from the bedroom and Dancing Leaf quietly rose to go. She embraced Rachel. "There will be a headache tomorrow. I can mix something for you before I go."

"Thank you, Dancing Leaf. My own remedies will work extremely well, but what I'd really like is to cure Trace's penchant to get this drunk whenever she drinks. I think I'll just let her suffer through this one." She shrugged. "Although that means we'll both be suffering."

The next morning, Trace awoke, unable to focus or to move. She was pretty sure if she did, her head was going to explode. She felt the presence of someone by the bed and knew from the scent of what smelled like fresh milk with honey in it, that it was Rachel. Even though it was a fragrance she normally cherished, at that moment it was making her stomach turn.

"Morning, sweetheart!" Rachel yelled, right next to Trace's ear.

"Oh, Jesus Christ..." Trace bit off her words, squeezing her eyes shut tighter, riding out the wave of agony in her pulsating skull that resulted from the loud voice.

"Language, dear. You promised not to take the Lord's name is vain in this house."

She was sounding way too sweet, enjoying the hangover entirely too much. "I'm not taking His name in vain," Trace whispered. "I'm praying that He will be merciful and take me right now."

"What's the matter? Head big as a washtub, is it? Or does it feel more like a shriveled up prune?"

"Yes. Please, baby, please stop talking and do your thing with the cabbage soup. I'm dying here."

"Well maybe next time you'll remember this and not drink so much."

"These were mitiga...miti...mitigat...exten..." Concentration was eluding her. Thinking hurt. "It was different this time."

"It was different last time. Now get up and haul yourself out of here so I can fix you some tea."

"Can't you bring it to me in here?"

"Trace, you have not moved since you got home last night, not one muscle. I couldn't even move you so I could fit on the bed. I had to sleep on the sofa."

"I'll make it up to you, I promise." Her eyes felt crusted shut, her teeth felt like they were wearing slouch socks, and her hair throbbed.

"Oh, you bet you will," Rachel promised. "Now get up and I'll fix you a nice big breakfast of greasy bacon and runny eggs and—"

"Oh, Rachel, you can be a hateful woman sometimes." Trace defied gravity and stood abruptly, ignoring the anvil that was clanging inside her head and raced outside to throw up. When she was done, she returned inside and sat at the table, awaiting further punishment.

Hands on her hips, Rachel sighed. "You know, Trace, when this child gets here, you're not going to be able to get this way, all liquored up. I can't have you as helpless as the baby, and it shouldn't fall to the Pawnee to do your chores around the house. You understand that, right?" Her tone was reasoning, not nagging.

Trace was slumped over the table, so low that she almost bumped her nose on it when she nodded.

Her voice softening, Rachel bent over and kissed the top of Trace's head. "Your forehead's hotter than a pistol and I've seen corpses with more color."

"No matter how bad I look...I feel worse."

"I was going to really make you regret coming home drunk again but I just don't have the energy, and it's too hard to watch you like this. I think you've suffered enough. I'll make you your soup now."

Resting her cheek on the cool wood surface of the table, Trace sighed a heartfelt, "Thank you."

Chapter Twenty-eight

The day the Cranes rode into Sagebrush, autumn was in an early, full foliage. The welcome, crisp fall air, the brilliant colors of the trees that dotted the mountains, and the burnished leaves painted brightly by Mother Nature, that were quickly gathering on the ground, did not reflect the cutting chill the town felt as word got around that the feared family had returned. What made this annual occurrence different from all the other times was that this time the Cranes had a score to settle. At least that's how the townspeople believed they would feel. Things were bad enough when Jacob Crane and his brood were behaving like their typical selves, but when there was an obligation to retaliate for the death of a son, regardless of whether or not he'd earned the right to die, the collective mood in Sagebrush was grim.

Jacob and his remaining sons had learned about Ben's death less than a week earlier from a terse telegram. They were looking to get the details when they got back to their ranch and spoke with John and the ranch hands, who had scooped up Ben's remains and buried him. As they tried to cut across the Triple Y to get to their property, they ran into a surprise. Not only were they blocked by nearly a mile of barbed wire fencing, there were flourishing cattle grazing on the Young land and evidence of recently harvested corn and crops on what looked like acres to the east, inside the fence line.

Had there not been nearly an entire tribe of Pawnee on horseback roaming close to the boundaries of the Triple Y, Jacob would have ordered the fence torn down and taken his entourage through, ignoring the hand painted signs that announced it as being private property and warning against trespassing.

Jacob and his sons exchanged stunned looks. Ed Jackson had wired them about all the changes going on in Sagebrush, but since Ed had a tendency to embellish to the point of exaggeration, none of them were expecting the sophisticated set up they found. "This Sheridan fellow is going to be a bigger problem than we anticipated."

The eldest Crane did like a worthy adversary, but only if he could pretty much guarantee he could defeat the opposition. Jacob was returning home to one less son, a sheriff who was not under his control, and still coveting land that was no longer owned by a frightened young woman but by what appeared to be a strong, respected married couple and guarded by a band of possibly hostile Indians.

Hmmmm...maybe I can appeal to this Sheridan's financial shrewdness. Money is almost always the great equalizer. He might prove to be a greedy son-of-a-bitch. Though that tack hasn't worked with Rachel, she's a woman and stubbornly sentimental about the property. Men are much more reasonable about these things, especially if the offered monetary amount is...appropriate. Although, if the fortress this Sheridan has set up around the Triple Y is any indication, he might not be as easily swayed as those other landowners. Ah well, if that's the case, sheriff or not, we'll just burn them out. Had that Young bitch just accepted Ben, all of this could have been avoided.

Jacob was running out of patience and options, especially now that it may have cost him the reign over the town's legal quarrels and, most importantly, a son. So, if neither the sheriff nor his wife cooperated, then they had no one to blame but themselves for whatever death and destruction was brought onto their land.

On the other hand, there would be the Pawnee to deal with. Not knowing much about them, Crane deduced that if they had been a savage bunch, they would have shown that side of themselves by attacking the townspeople long ago. With that in mind, Jacob reasoned that the Pawnee could probably be bought, too. Everybody had a price.

Jacob had no real idea as to what he was up against until he returned to his home and spoke with his family and ranch hands. After hearing how Trace Sheridan mysteriously appeared just weeks after they had left for their drive, how the drifter took up residence on the Young property, and how he'd defied Ed Jackson, Jacob Crane was puzzled. For some reason, the whole town was disregarding the threat of Crane retaliation and supporting and following the new sheriff like the Pied Piper. Jacob had more questions than answers about why the Pawnee were getting involved, and whether Ben was right in claiming that the baby the Sheridans were expecting was really his. Finally, he still had no solid information about Ben's suspicious death.

Whatever was going on with the clearly charismatic lawman, his luck would have to start running out at some point. Maybe it would serve him and his sons well to bide their time.

"Ephraim, you and me are going into town in the morning and we'll have a little chat with the new sheriff. I want to meet this Sheridan fellow face to face, get a feel for him, see if he can be reasoned with."

"And if he can't, Father?"

"Then we'll start planning our attack." He knew that Rachel would be a weakness, as would the unborn child, especially if the infant was the sheriff's. "If that baby is Ben's — which makes sense, given what he told Priscilla and John — that would put a whole new twist on things, specifically if the sheriff don't know that he's not the daddy."

They were exhausted from their nearly eight month trip, a trek that had taken two months longer than it usually did because of the race horses they had detoured to buy for the track they wanted to build outside Jefferson City. Jacob wanted a good home-cooked meal, a glass of his expensive scotch, and his own bed with his wife in it, fulfilling her conjugal obligations. It wasn't that he had not entertained a lady of the evening or two while they had been away, but it was Priscilla's duty to serve him, her responsibility as his wife to satisfy his needs when he told her to. Even after twenty-eight years of marriage, she had never once resisted him when he demanded she indulge him in the bedroom. Unless she was having her monthly, and then she would still be expected to service him even though he would not touch her.

And if it was that time for his wife, perhaps Ephraim's wife would be willing to...fulfill his needs. Though Priscilla never refused him the missionary position or manual stimulation, any other kind of copulation was out of the question for his proper spouse. However, he knew that Julia, Ephraim's wife, secretly liked being ordered to engage in the sometimes degrading sexual acts he could only get from a prostitute, and that excited and fascinated him.

Jacob knew his oldest son was a washout in the bedroom. One evening not too long after the couple was married, the patriarch had found Julia crying out by the stables. The young minx confessed to Jacob that Ephraim could not perform and would get drunk and pass out because of it. Jacob had gotten her so excited by telling her what he was capable of that he took her right then and there in the hayloft. He knew that what Priscilla wouldn't give him, Julia would. Smiling lasciviously, he put aside all thoughts of the new sheriff until morning.

Isaac Tipping slid off his horse in front of the sheriff's office, dropped the reins, and ran into the building. "Trace! Jacob Crane and the rest of his clan are back! They tried to get through your property but were stopped by the barbed wire and the Pawnee. Jacob didn't look happy."

"Well, Isaac, I guess that one or more of them will be paying me a little visit, then. Maybe even this afternoon. Thanks for letting me know. You'd probably better ride out and spread the word. I don't want anyone getting caught unawares."

Isaac nodded his understanding and dashed out as quickly as he'd entered. Trace checked her pistols and sat behind her desk to wait. Primed though she was for the confrontation, she was relieved when it didn't happen. It would give her a chance to steel herself for what she knew was going to be the beginning of the end. Trace had no intention of losing to the Cranes, but if things went awry, she would arrange for Little Hawk to get Rachel away from Sagebrush, somewhere safe from harm, maybe even staying with the Pawnee. They would protect her, and she and the baby would at least be alive, regardless of whether or not Rachel was happy with the plan. It had become a frequent debate between them.

"No, Trace!" Rachel had told her adamantly. "I cannot, will not entertain the thought of losing you. It's just not negotiable. Don't you understand?"

"Rachel, you need to be reasonable."

"Reasonable? About the possibility of losing you? To what? A noble cause? It's not noble to me if you're gone. I think not."

"Look, I'm pretty sure nothing will happen to me, but in case it does—"

"We are not discussing this, Trace. It is a price I'm not willing to pay. The ranch, the stock, the property — none of it is worth losing you or the baby over."

"But, Rachel, you've fought so long for your pride—"

"'But Rachel' nothing! Pride is all well and good but it's already cost me too much!"

"That's what I'm saying, sweetheart. You cannot give up now," Trace said.

"Yes, I can. I can and will give all this up if it means you, me, and the baby can walk away with our lives."

Trace was floored by what Rachel was willing to give up for her. However, they had come too far and at this point, it wasn't a matter of pride, it was more a matter of dignity. It was about giving the citizens of Sagebrush back what was rightfully theirs. Though she would have done so for Rachel's sake, there was too much at stake for her to surrender. Regardless of the reason, if Rachel ceded her property, the town would be lost to the Cranes forever and none of them would have any peace, least of all the Sheridan family.

Trace knew that on principle alone, just like the crime family she dealt with in her own time, the Cranes would not rest until they hunted her down and hanged her, killed Rachel or worse, and took the baby. None of those prospects were acceptable, especially knowing if those events took place, the child would be brought up as a Crane and that would cement the beginning of the mob legacy that would destroy many lives, including her own. Trace would do anything humanly possible to stop that.

She was not sure how the baby Rachel was carrying would lead to the founding of the DeSienna crime family, but after being bitch-slapped into realization by the sight of Ben Crane's face, she knew the link was undeniable. Was it possible to change what would happen in future decades by raising her enemy's great-grandparent in a healthy, law abiding, environment? Would instilling good, decent values in a child be enough to alter at least four generations of reprehensible criminal behavior? There was only one way to find out. And in order to have that chance, Trace could not allow the cattle baron to even touch the life of the child she was about to raise as her own.

She found it ironic that she, with her own questionable beliefs and morals, would be responsible for instilling ethics and character into the psyche of any child, much less one who could grow to wield enormous power, whose future offspring would have so much influence on her life and the world in which she grew up. Trace was also curious as to what would have happened had she not come along. Would Rachel have been forced to marry Ben? She shuddered at the thought. Would the Cranes have blackmailed Rachel in order to possess the baby, or worse yet, murdered her to get custody of the child? All of it was unthinkable and now, unnecessary, because she was very much present in this lifetime, knowing what lay ahead if she didn't do something to change the course of the future.

Also, as to the question brought up at Wilbur's the afternoon of Ben's death, Trace discovered why John Carver was not the man of means everyone thought he should have been. Rachel had found out through her former best friend and Seth's fiancée, Suzanne Beauregard. Seth had wallowed in a little too much drinking and had confessed it to her in the throes of his intoxication. The younger Carver was not a happy drunk and he became angry and resentful when inebriated, complaining about how his "grandparents" had mistreated his father, who was a good, hard-working man.

Suzanne had told Rachel in the strictest of confidence, as it was not something anyone wanted to get spread through the town. John was an orphan that Priscilla's mother and father had taken in when he was barely two years old. Although they eventually adopted him, he was never quite one of the family. He and Priscilla were very close and when she married, Priscilla refused to allow John to be left behind. Her younger brother went to live in the bunkhouse at the Crane ranch outside of Omaha. When John and Priscilla's best friend, Margaret, met and fell in love, they married and built a house on the corner end of the Crane property, and John had been at Priscilla's side ever since.

Trace reasoned that this must have been why John always seemed to be trying to prove himself. It made her almost empathize with him. Maybe Joseph and Silas were right, maybe the older Carver really wasn't the same level of thug as the rest of the family. He had backed off after the second time Trace got the better of him while he was following Ed Jackson's directions. That meant he wasn't a stupid man and obviously not ruled by his ego. Still, as Trace now knew, there were always choices, and John continued to make his in the wrong direction. Maybe, like her, he was salvageable, but it was not an immediate priority of hers to find out. If he had a noble side, his true colors would show themselves soon enough. In the meantime, there were the big boys to contend with.

The next morning early, Trace was tinkering with a jammed lock on one of the archaic handcuff bracelets, when she heard two sets of footsteps enter her office and the air was suddenly filled with an expensive smelling cologne, a perfect blend of sandalwood and vanilla. Without even looking up, she figured her visitors were Cranes. She had been expecting them, and this scent screamed money, money that no one else in that community had. If the men in Sagebrush wore any aftershave, the fragrance usually smelled citrus-based. Only Joseph and Jed wore something more flowery.

She glanced at them briefly. They had an air about them that bespoke pretentious tyranny. *Yep, Cranes. How did Silas refer to them? Oh, yeah. Highfalutin'. That's as good a word as any.* She had guessed that Jacob was going to look like Vittorio DeSienna and was relieved when he didn't. He was a roguishly handsome older man with distinguished wisps of gray hair at the temples and a widow's peak, and he was obviously used to people being intimidated by his presence, as he looked a little perturbed when Trace wasn't. For her part, she had expected the air to seem suddenly stifling and the atmosphere to be unnerving, which was what she had always felt in the presence of his descendants, but Jacob didn't have that kind of effect.

The demeanor of the man with him, obviously one of his three remaining sons, exhibited poise and an almost restrained dignity, unusual under the circumstances. He was a carbon copy of his father, with identical mustache and tempestuous, yellow-tinted brown eyes. Trace decided that Ben must have looked like his mother. Returning her attention to the handcuffs, her voice purposely casual, she said, "Something I can help you with?"

"I'm Jacob Crane and this is my oldest boy, Ephraim."

Trace gave them her undivided attention. She pushed the handcuffs aside and stood, extending her hand first to the older Crane. How they responded to her gesture would be very telling. "Trace Sheridan. My condolences regarding your son."

Jacob gracefully accepted Trace's hand and shook it firmly. "I appreciate that, Sheriff."

Ephraim's poise, however, stopped at his physical appearance. When he would not take Trace's hand, his father touched him on the shoulder. "Ephraim, you were brought up better than that."

Gripping Trace's hand, the oldest Crane son squeezed it with the intent of breaking it if he could. He had no idea that Trace had been prepared for the immature reaction and not only gave as good as she got but never flinched at the discomfort, something he could not manage, which clearly infuriated him even more when he had to let go first.

Watching the two stare each other down, Jacob chuckled. "Well, well, well...nothing like a good cockfight."

"What can I do for you, Mr. Crane?" Trace motioned for them to sit as she returned to her seat behind the desk.

"First, congratulations on your marriage and the upcoming birth of...your...child."

Trace smirked at the doubt Crane placed on the word "your". "Thank you. I'm very lucky to have found Rachel and we're very excited about...our...baby." Two could play that game and she was frankly a little surprised that — at least so far — Crane wasn't playing it better.

"Also, I wanted to tell you that you have done a nice job on the Young property and—"

"Mr. Crane, let's cut the crap, shall we?" She almost laughed out loud at the startled expression both men wore, but she swallowed it and kept her voice to a professional monotone that was not without its unmistakably dangerous edge. "You didn't come in here to congratulate me on my personal good fortune, nor did you come here to compliment me on my ranching skills. It's doing us all a disservice to dance around the fact that I know you've been told that I might possibly have been responsible for your son's death. So, let's just get it all out in the open right here and now. But be warned, Mr. Crane — the playground is mine now and I don't play well with others." Her enigmatic blue eyes pinned them to their chairs, rendering them momentarily mute. Trace suspected he wasn't used to anyone challenging him blatantly like that without so much as a quiver in their voice.

Finally Jacob cleared his throat and nodded. "Your, uh, candor, is much appreciated, Sheriff. I respect a man who likes to get right down to business." Crane stared at her. "Did you kill my son?"

"No." It wasn't a lie. "Next question."

"I don't believe you," Ephraim spat, his eyes mere slits, accusing.

"I don't care what you believe, Mr. Crane," Trace responded. "What reason would I have had to kill your brother?"

"Because of Rachel."

"What about Rachel?"

The oldest Crane son was about to respond, but Jacob put up a hand to silence him. "Sheriff, I don't think it was any secret that my son was in love with your wife," Jacob interjected, in an obvious attempt to stop the mental chest bumping between Trace and his son.

"No, it was not a secret, but as far as I know, him loving my wife wasn't a crime. Unlike my predecessor, I take my job very seriously, Mr. Crane, and I am not about to abuse the power and authority of this office to indulge any petty jealousy I might have. Besides, it's also no secret that my wife couldn't stand your son, so that was not a worry to me."

The Cranes' exchange of looks did not go unnoticed. Trace knew what they were thinking. If they didn't bring up the question of the baby's paternity, she was not about to. "I did an investigation and filled out a report that I sent to the state attorney's office to be kept on file just in case anyone wanted to make a big deal over this. It looked to me and, I might add, to your brother-in-law, nephew, and four ranch hands, that Ben had been killed by a wild animal or a pack of wild animals." She glared at Ephraim. "If you want to contest that, be my guest. But, under oath, in a court of law, your own people will back up my findings. Now, is there anything else I can do for you gentlemen today?"

"Well, Sheriff, there is the matter of the rents that are past due. Maybe the shop keepers just got a little behind while we were gone on the cattle drive. Ed Jackson was supposed to be collecting the fees in our absence, but I guess he didn't, due to his unfortunate demise, and all. Maybe you could look into that for us."

Trace raised an eyebrow. "Ah, you mean the 'insurance' most of them were paying. We all had a little talk about that and decided that I would be all the insurance they would need. I don't think anyone plans on paying you any more fees, Mr. Crane."

Ephraim bristled. "We own most of the property on Main Street, Sheriff. Ed Jackson had the deeds filed right here in this office. He was so inept, he must've lost them." He was used to no one disputing the word of a Crane, under threat of death.

"Well, if you gents can get copies of the filings from the land office, then you just bring 'em on in and you can go back to collecting your fees. Because," Trace added solicitously, "I'm sure that no businessman in his right mind would ever have papers that important and not have copies drawn up in case the originals were to get lost."

The Cranes left the office frustrated and furious. Diplomacy had not worked, nor had implied intimidation. Whatever they threw at Trace Sheridan, the sheriff had a legitimate response. Even though the suggestion was never made, it was clear that the principled sheriff could not, would not be bought. Well...they would revisit that prospect after the baby was born. If the sheriff had no idea that Ben may have fathered the baby his wife was carrying, that could be their ace in the hole. Until then, or if the child turned out to actually belong to the sheriff, they would have to come up with another plan, one that made it clear to the lawman that he wasn't in charge after all. After that, it would be easy to get the town back under their control.

The problem would be executing any plan without bringing the whole damned Indian nation down on them in the process.

Chapter Twenty-nine

Cold weather settled in, as though it had followed the Cranes into the county and stayed there, mirroring the clan's frigidity and nastiness since their return. They had uncharacteristically kept to themselves, doing business in Sagebrush only when necessary and avoiding Trace and the Triple Y. Although grateful, Trace was neither arrogant nor naïve regarding their self-imposed segregation. The Cranes were up to something and in order to figure out what that was, she would have to continue to think like one of them.

The first thought she had was probably the correct one because it was what she would have done had she been in charge: wait until the approaching annual Pawnee buffalo hunt when half the tribe was gone, and then come in force and take her out. She knew that the Cranes referred to her as "the viper" because of the way they felt she had snaked her way into the hearts and minds of the townspeople. Of course, it was true, but not in the manner the Cranes had envisioned.

Trace knew the Cranes had never encountered anyone like her before. With her in control, backed by the Pawnee and the more stouthearted men in town, they would never get their power back. But Trace figured they would think that if they cut the head off this serpent, the body would shrivel up and die, and the best way to do that would be when she was most vulnerable to attack. With that in mind, Trace knew she only had to formulate a defense.

In the meantime, she was pretty sure that Rachel was safe puttering around the house, getting everything ready for the birth of their child. That visual of the glowing young mother-to-be brought a fond smile to Trace's face as she tried to bundle deeper into her wool coat, walking across the street from her office to the livery. Snow from an early storm clung to her eyelashes as she made a futile attempt to tug her collar higher. She had a spare sock wrapped around her ears under her hat and sheepskin-lined gloves pulled over her hands. She didn't remember weather being quite so cold in her time, but maybe the tall buildings cut the wind and kept the chill at bay.

Mounting Rio, who was left in the stable during the colder days, she rode home, grumbling, muttering, and cursing as she took turns rubbing both thighs vigorously and moving her feet, trying to keep some feeling in them so she could reach the warm embrace of her wife before anything important froze and fell off.

Before she reached home, the flurries became a blinding blizzard, the intensity of which concerned her, though Rio forged ahead undaunted. She moved her hat lower and hunkered even deeper into her coat, which was becoming heavier by the second from the wet snow that fastened to the material. The sight of smoke from a chimney had never been so welcome, as she drew a breath into lungs scorched by the skin-searing wind that sliced into exposed flesh like little needles her last quarter mile to the house. By the time she walked in the door, she was bone-deep miserable. Even Ramiro's happy bark and wiggling, like he was trying to turn himself inside out, didn't bring a smile to Trace's face like it usually did.

Rachel was cooking dinner and turned to greet her with a kiss intended to melt anything frozen on her. It worked. Trace held Rachel and kissed her again, hoping the heat would get her mouth to the point where it could actually form words again.

"Brrrrrrr." Rachel playfully knocked Trace's hat off and helped her remove her coat. "Take your boots off; you're dripping on the floor." Looking at Trace's head, she laughed. "Did you know you have a sock wrapped around your head?"

"Yes and it saved my ears," Trace admitted, untying it. She took the weighty coat from Rachel and hung it up on a sturdy peg by the door. While Rachel finished getting dinner ready, Trace squatted on her heels by the hearth and fed some logs into the fire, rubbing her hands close to the heat, hoping to get some sensation back in them. "Is it always this cold here?"

"No, this is unusual for this time of year. I guess we were lucky we had a late summer and the weather stayed as pleasant as it did for so long." She tasted the stew to see how close it was to being ready. "Didn't it get cold in Cottonwood?"

"Oh, yeah, but not like this." Standing, Trace approached Rachel from behind, encircling her with her arms and kissing the side of her neck.

"Quiet day, I presume."

"Not a peep from the Cranes, if that's what you're asking, and no new rumors around town. How about here at home?"

"Nope. Nothing."

"As long as the Pawnee are a visible threat, I think it will stay that way."

"But the Pawnee aren't a threat. Why, they are the least threatening people I have ever known."

"Yes, but the Cranes don't know that and I'd like to keep it that way for as long as possible." Trace looked over Rachel's shoulder at the huge pot of stew simmering on the stove. "Wow...you expecting an army?"

"No." Rachel smiled. "Just a small tribe. A few Pawnee have been hunting elk all afternoon. They killed a big buck earlier and prepared the meat. They left the best cuts for us and kept the rest for themselves."

Trace made a face but didn't protest. *Better them than me.*

As if on cue, the door opened and Little Hawk entered, accompanied by Rising Moon and Red Sky, all stomping the snow off their high moccasins.

"Hey! Do that outside!" Rachel reprimanded, pointing.

They all stopped and looked at Trace's feet. "You heard her," Trace said. Looking down at her own wet boots, she added, "And I'll take mine off while I'm on my way out behind you."

With Rachel's fluctuating moods, Trace wasn't about to push her into a hormonal tantrum, as the littlest things seemed to set her off. Trace ushered the three Pawnee outside, then removed her boots and grabbed the mop to clean up the water on the floor that had melted from their shoes. Rachel giggled, which received a raised eyebrow in response. She thought Rachel must be getting a kick out of all these strong people afraid of the temper of a tiny, very pregnant woman. But at one time or another, they had all fallen victim to Rachel's hormonally tempestuous disposition and no one wanted to do anything to provoke the usually unreasonable outbursts, especially not Trace.

"Thank you!" she called out to them, hoping her appreciation helped with the ignominy of being sent outside.

Re-entering the house minus their footwear, everything but the hearty meal was forgotten when they sat down to eat.

"Phoebe."

"No." Trace rejected Rachel's suggestion of a first name for the baby. This name game was becoming a nightly discussion since they had begun the process of elimination, and so far they were not in accord on much of anything.

"Leah?"

"Leah Minnie Sheridan...ummmmm...no."

"Why?"

"Just doesn't do anything for me, sweetheart."

They still readily agreed on Minnie as a middle name for a daughter and on Frank as a middle name for a son. Trace had hoped she could sneak in the name Mark, in honor of her friend, the inventor, the man who had placed her in the situation that ultimately brought her and Rachel together, but regardless of what they came up with, the combination of names just didn't flow.

Rachel was adamant about having a biblical name but so far, everything she suggested just wasn't striking Trace's fancy. And it was driving Rachel crazy. "Bethany."

"Now, that's nice...but, like Naomi, which I also liked, it goes great with Sheridan but it doesn't go with Minnie as a middle name. Bethany Minnie. Naomi Minnie. See?" Trace was cleaning her guns.

Beside her, Rachel was rocking quietly, her arms resting on her stomach, facing the moderate flame in the fireplace.

"Good Lord, Trace, I'm running out of names. What are some of your ideas? I almost dread asking. The last time you suggested names like Dylan and Hunter and Tyler and Dalton. Although those names are nice, they're just plain odd. A baby needs a good, solid Christian name."

"They're not odd, they're just...modern," Trace protested.

"Fine. They're *modern*. What are some more of your *modern* suggestions?"

Trace ignored Rachel's sarcasm. "I really like Kylie but it suffers the same fate as Bethany and Naomi, so that's out."

"Kylie?" A blonde eyebrow rose skeptically.

"Yeah. And Lindsay. But again...not with Minnie."

"Lindsay??" A second eyebrow joined the first.

"What? I like that name. I like Chelsea, too." At Rachel's silent stare, Trace shrugged. "Okay, what about Nicole? That sounds good — Nicole Minnie Sheridan."

"It's not a name from the Bible, though."

"Does it have to be from the Bible?" Trace asked, frustrated. She held up one of the Colts and looked down the barrel, checking for grit.

"Yes, I think it should be." Rachel's tone reflected annoyance.

Trace sighed, trying not to sound peeved at a lack of agreement that was starting to become habitual. "Then let's keep trying until we can agree on something."

Trace's mild exasperation only served to increase Rachel's irritation. "Hopefully this child won't be married with babies of its own before that happens."

Trace smiled patiently, trying not to react to the moodiness that was increasing with every passing day. "I'm sure we can reach a compromise before little Travis or Brianna is born," she joked. She closed the cylinder of her pistol and set it aside with the other guns.

"Augh! Trace, you're impossible." Rachel was not amused. "We need to decide on this and we're running out of time and you sit there and poke fun and—"

Trace stood and stretched, then took a step toward her wife, addressing her in a soothing voice. "Rachel, we've got time. We'll settle on something we both like and everything will be fine. In fact, let's go to bed and," she winked at Rachel, "sleep on it."

"I don't want to settle on a name! I want to decide on something we both love and will be proud to call our child, and something that Pastor Edwards will approve of when he baptizes the baby!" She stood up with difficulty and when Trace reached out to assist her, she swatted Trace's hands away. "Don't touch me. You...you...piss me off," Rachel said, using an expression she had picked up from Trace. "We'll sleep on it all right, but you can sleep on it either upstairs or here on the sofa. Maybe then you'll start realizing how serious this is."

Rachel stomped off to bed, leaving Trace mildly stunned. *Hoo, boy. It's going to be a long night.*

"Have you decided on a name yet?" Molly Ledbetter asked Trace, who was in the shop to pick up more material for Rachel to make another maternity dress.

"God, I hope so. We've finally narrowed it down. Zachary Frank Jeremiah Mark Sheridan or Jared Frank Timothy Mark Sheridan, if it's a boy; Rebecca Minnie Abigail Sheridan or Chloe Anna Minnie Sheridan, if it's a girl."

Molly chuckled. "Honoring all the branches of the Young family tree in one fell swoop, are ya?"

"I guess. Except for Mark, that was my suggestion, after a good friend of mine — the only name I came up with she liked."

Molly smirked at the hint of sarcasm. "Well, you still have time to change your minds. Should be another month or two before the baby gets here."

"Yes, at least." Trace smiled and paid the dressmaker. She couldn't tell Molly that Rachel was due any day now. Of course Molly would know soon enough because since Minnie Young couldn't be there, Rachel wanted Molly present for the birth of the long awaited Young grandchild.

Trace recalled the day Rachel had asked, practically begged her, if Molly Ledbetter could come out when she went into labor. Big, green eyes blinked in desperation, as Rachel knew Trace wanted the birth as private as possible, hoping to keep the questions about timing to a minimum. Once she got a look at how big Rachel was, Molly probably wouldn't believe for a second that the baby was early. But Molly adored Rachel. It wouldn't matter if she figured out that Rachel was pregnant before she got married. Molly already knew that Ben had raped Rachel. Maybe she had already figured everything out.

Well, Rachel wanted her there and Rachel knew the consequences of anyone finding out. It was difficult for Trace to deny Rachel anything and if she wanted Molly Ledbetter there, then Trace would make sure the dressmaker was there, even if she had to carry her from town on her back.

"Listen, Miz Ledbetter...Rachel wanted me to be sure to ask you again if you'd be there when—"

"I wouldn't miss it for the world, Trace. I've already arranged for Ruth Turner to come over and stay with Harvey when the blessed event happens."

"Thanks. It will mean a lot to her." *Great. Ruth Turner. She's a bigger town crier than her husband and Henry, the circuit clerk.*

"But," Molly patted Trace's hand in a motherly manner, reassuringly, "as I said, we have plenty of time, dear."

"Trace...Trace...Trace!"

Trace raced inside. Rachel was gripping her belly, bent at the waist, standing in a puddle. The mother-very-soon-to-be looked frightened and confused.

"It's okay, sweetheart; it's fine," Trace helped her to a seat. "Your water broke. Have you been in labor?"

Sitting, Rachel looked up at Trace. "I didn't think so... My back really started hurting about two hours ago. I felt a lot of...um...pressure...but no labor pains that I know of."

"Baby, you're probably having back labor. Let me send Isaac for Fire Arrow and Dancing Leaf."

"And Miz Ledbetter? Please, Trace. I promised her I would let her know."

"Okay. I'll make sure Isaac stops and tells her." Her heart pounding, Trace sped outside to get Isaac, who had been helping her pile wood in a lean-to outside the barn. She couldn't believe how excited she was: she was about to become a father!

Trace had no idea that sitting in for a co-worker when his wife needed a coach for their fourth child would be a skill she would ever use again. She had cursed not being able to say no to the puppy dog eyes of her pleading patrol partner to take his place in the Lamaze classes while he was temporarily assigned to another shift.

His wife was a nice woman, not too hard on the eyes, and Trace hadn't really minded. She and her partner's wife bonded, and now Trace was grateful for the experience. Although she could not offer Rachel soft, soothing music or privacy, she could furnish the dim lighting, warmth, and semi-peaceful surroundings.

After Molly Ledbetter recovered from the mild shock of the size of Rachel's pregnant belly and swallowed her suspicions regarding the prematurity of the child, she watched in awe as Trace lovingly touched and ministered to Rachel during the long waiting process. He seemed almost womanly in his devotion to helping his wife through the trial as best he could. Molly had never before witnessed a husband so attentive by choice during his wife's labor. She had known men who were anxious and nervous in anticipation of becoming fathers, but as much as they loved their wives, she also saw them grow impatient after too much time had passed — as if the mother-to-be had any control over the birthing. *For Heaven's sake*, Molly thought, *if women had any druthers — especially in this matter — they certainly wouldn't choose to have a spirited, unborn infant flailing about in their loins, stirring so violently inside them, wanting to get out as much as their mothers want them out. But not this man...he seems more patient and understanding than Rachel.*

Molly felt her heart flutter a little watching the almost pretty man attend to Rachel. Where did he come from that he was so chivalrous and caring? She couldn't have dreamed up a more perfect husband if she'd tried. Tears stung her eyes knowing how proud and happy Minnie would have been at this moment, to see the birth of her first grandchild, to see her daughter so blessedly content, loved and in love.

Although Molly completely understood why Rachel did not want Doc Smith present for the birthing, she was a little nervous about having the Pawnee in charge of the birth of the closest thing she would ever have to a grandbaby. Grimacing, she chastised herself for having such thoughts. After all, the Pawnee had only ever helped Rachel and Trace.

While Molly knitted on a second blanket for the cradle, she watched as Trace cuddled Rachel, massaging and stroking her back, and placing either a cloth warmed by heated water, or cooled by water fresh from the indoor pump, on Rachel's lower spine when unbearably strong labor pains seemed to clutch at her.

Trace had Rachel up walking and, at one point, when Rachel seemed to be getting frustrated that the baby was taking so long, held her and slowly moved her around the floor as though they were dancing. He made his wife focus on breathing in a funny way and when Rachel would try her best not to cry out at the pain, Trace would speak to her in a quiet, soothing voice and ask her to pretend they were somewhere else, vividly describing the ocean and white sandy beaches, warm sun and something called "palm trees", or he tried to get Rachel to pretend they were in a mountain meadow with fresh flowers and warm breezes, and even Molly almost felt as though she were running barefoot through soft, green grass, smelling lilacs, her face hot under the summer sun.

Dancing Leaf and Fire Arrow were exchanging glances at Tsápaat's behavior. It wasn't something they would ever introduce into their birth ritual, but it certainly appeared to calm the white woman in a manner they had never seen. Although Rachel wasn't like any white woman they had ever dealt with in the past...nor was Trace. This young couple had restored their faith in the Taka'piíta, or at least the white man in Sagebrush. Not that the Pawnee had ever really been bothered by anyone in Jefferson County, but neither had anyone ever made them feel a part of the community, either. Not until Trace Sheridan.

"Shouldn't she be lying down?" Molly asked Trace as she wiped sweaty tendrils of hair away from Rachel's forehead with a cool cloth.

"Honestly, I have heard that it's better if she doesn't have to," Trace said, seated snugly behind Rachel, supporting her wife, who was in a squatting position and leaning back against Trace. "Gravity will help the baby descend the birth canal easier and—" She looked up and saw the startled faces of the others in the room, including Rachel in last stages of labor who, through very heavy breathing, glanced back at her with astonishment. "What?"

"How do you know all this without no doctor trainin'?" Molly asked. "I mean, it might make sense and all, but..."

"Uh...well...when I was back in Cottonwood, uh, I..."

"Oh, Lord, Trace, I think the baby's coming out!" Rachel parted her legs wider, squatting lower. Dancing Leaf and Fire Arrow got into position.

"Yes, *piiraki'ripahki* is here," Dancing Leaf announced as the baby crowned.

Sixteen and a half hours after Rachel's water broke, the baby drew its first breath. "Is *pii'raski* — you have a son," Fire Arrow told the waiting parents. Rachel and Trace broke into tears. Easing the new mother back into the chair as Trace slid out from behind her, Molly handed her a sharp pair of scissors that had been boiled clean. Trace cut the cord and helped Fire Arrow clean up the baby while Molly and Dancing Leaf waited for the delivery of the placenta.

"He's perfect, Rachel," Trace announced. "He has a shadow of strawberry blonde hair, ten fingers and toes, and I bet he weighs about six pounds and change." Trace didn't have to tell her he possessed a healthy set of lungs; she could hear that for herself.

Feeling as though she was going into labor again, Rachel delivered the afterbirth, watching as Trace lovingly bathed their son, put a diaper on him, and brought him to her for the first time. "Oh, sweet Lord, Trace, he's beautiful," Rachel gasped. Tears of joy fell on the infant she held close to her heart.

"Yes, he is. And he's hungry." Trace helped the waiting little mouth find its way to Rachel's exposed nipple and watched the baby suck greedily at her breast. "Yep." She smiled. "Just like a man." She leaned in and kissed the baby's forehead and then reverently kissed Rachel. "You did great, sweetheart."

"I couldn't have done it without you."

"Of course you could have," Trace reassured her. "You're the strongest woman I've ever known, Rachel."

Looking at Trace adoringly, Rachel's tears flowed freely. "Trace, you name him. Whatever you want," Rachel said, overwhelmed with emotion. Overcome with an unconditional love, his paternity now not even an issue, she fell totally and hopelessly in love with her baby.

Molly approached the new parents and spoke in a hushed tone. "Everybody has gathered. They have been staying out of the cold in the barn, but they're waiting on an announcement from you, Trace."

"Really? How many people are out there?"

"If I were to guess, I'd say the only ones left in town would be Ruth Turner and my husband."

Shocked but pleased that so many people cared, Trace nodded. "Give me a minute with my family and tell them I'll be right there." Smiling, Molly threw on a shawl and stepped outside.

When the baby seemed to have his temporary fill of milk and Rachel dozed off from exhaustion, Trace bundled the baby up and took him outside. Taking his fragility into consideration and making sure she supported his neck, she held him up to the waiting crowd like Mufasa had with Simba in *The Lion King*. Of course, the parallel was lost on them, but Trace loved doing it.

"May I present Mr. Wyatt Frank Sheridan!"

Chapter Thirty

Though neither one had any experience with children, much less an infant, the new parents quickly settled into a routine. The baby ate every two hours, and because Rachel was breastfeeding him, she didn't have time for much else. While Rachel caught up on her sleep, Trace eagerly helped out with the many other baby duties. She changed diapers and washed them out every day, sponge bathed Wyatt, and got up with him when he was fussy.

Rachel would sometimes wake up to find Trace cradling Wyatt securely against her as she spoke softly or sang to him. He made little squeaking noises as Trace rocked him and serenaded him. When he seemed especially restless, she would get his attention with a small rattle Black Feather had made for him. The sound fascinated him and he would quiet. Observing Trace's interactions with Wyatt, Rachel fell in love with her all over again.

Pawnee came every day to assist with the chores so Trace was able to spend most of her time inside with Rachel and their son. She had deputized Matthew Reddick to keep an eye on things in town while she and Rachel adjusted to their new life. Matthew rather enjoyed his new appointment, although he freely admitted that if the Cranes began misbehaving, he would happily hand the responsibilities back to Trace.

For a couple of hours every day, while Rachel and Wyatt napped, Trace busied herself in the barn. With Isaac's help, she made a crib with enclosed, slatted sides and then, with leftover pieces of wood, some fishing line, and the small cloth baby toys Molly Ledbetter had sewn, she fashioned a mobile. They placed the crib in the bedroom and hung the mobile above it. At three weeks old, the tiny boy was moved from the cradle to the crib, the mattress at eye level of the bed for Trace and Rachel so they could just look over and check on him. When he wasn't crying or sleeping, Wyatt was mesmerized by the sculpture dangling above his head.

Life was blissfully perfect. They knew it was just a matter of time before the Cranes changed that.

Molly Ledbetter stopped by unexpectedly to visit with Rachel and Trace, see her surrogate grandchild, and bring the baptismal gown she'd made for Wyatt. As she cuddled the baby, she watched with delight as Rachel admired the garment, marveling at the tiny light blue suit with its attachable robe and square collar and a lace appliqué cross over the front with a matching cap. "Oh, Miz Ledbetter, this is just exquisite. Trace, honey, feel this."

Trace obligingly reached over and rubbed the soft, delicate cloth. "Yeah. Nice."

"Nice? Well, ain't it just like a man to under appreciate such beautiful material," Molly said. "This is shantung silk, Trace, directly from China."

"Okay." Trace was pleased with the gift; she just didn't understand getting all gushy over cloth. She still didn't get the big deal. Nor was she all that enthusiastic about the upcoming baptism. She knew that to Rachel the ceremony symbolized the cleansing of sins and meant that the baby would be "saved", but she considered it all hogwash. She knew many ruthless killers who had been baptized. Ben Crane had probably been baptized and it certainly hadn't saved him, or any of his victims. However, the religious ritual was important to Rachel so Trace went along with it. Rachel had had precious little go right in her life until the last seven months, and Trace was going to ensure that — within her power — whatever Rachel asked for, Rachel would get.

"Trace, don't disillusion me now," Molly kidded. "Here I thought you weren't like most men."

"Trace isn't like most men." Blushing, Rachel smiled over at Trace, who winked back, and Rachel's heart fluttered.

"I've been meaning to ask you, Trace, about Wyatt's name," Molly said, cradling the squirming baby.

"What about it?" Trace wiggled her fingers at her son to get his attention. The movement caught Wyatt's eye and he focused on Trace's hand.

"I remember Rachel saying you could name him anything you wanted, but Wyatt isn't any of the names you told me you'd decided on, and it sure ain't from the Bible."

"You don't like it?" Rachel was still lightly stroking the gown material.

"No, no, it's not that. I do like it; it's a very strong name. Matter-of-fact, I heard stories 'bout a marshal in Dodge City a few years back with that name. I'm just wondering how this little fella got it when the choices were Zachary and Jared."

"Because when I looked at him for the first time, he didn't look like a Zach or a Jared. He looked like a Wyatt," Trace said.

"But what about wanting a Christian name?" Molly asked.

"Well, that's kind of a sore spot between us." Rachel shot Trace a mock look of reproach. Trace returned a smile. "However, I do agree with Trace that giving a child a Christian name doesn't always guarantee the good Lord's favor."

"It doesn't hurt," Molly countered.

"Wyatt will grow to be who he is whether or not his name comes from the Bible. We'll raise him the best we can with the same values my mama and daddy raised me and hopefully he'll become a good man," Rachel said.

Molly lifted the baby and kissed his cheek several times. "I s'pose you gotta point. Trace ain't a name from the Bible and Lord, Rachel, you do have yourself a good man."

"Why, thank you, Molly," Trace said, grinning.

"My how this child fidgets," Molly said, trying to calm the tiny writhing body in her grasp.

Rachel laughed. "Just like his daddy."

There was a sudden knock on the door and Trace instantly went on alert, reaching for one of the Colts from her holster, which was draped over the back of a chair. "Who is it?" she called through the door.

"It's Doc Smith! Open up!"

Trace's eyes flashed in anger. The town doctor was not welcomed in their home. Trace still had a bad taste in her mouth from the first time they'd met in Cassandra's room, but when Rachel told her he was also on the Crane payroll, it just cemented her own suspicion about him. She yanked the door open with such force, it made both Molly and Rachel jump and startled the baby into crying. Stepping outside into the face of Amos Smith, slamming the door closed behind her, she had to take a second before she could speak. "Are you insane? You ride onto my property, uninvited, and order me to open my door? You damned well better have business here, Doc, or I could shoot you for trespassing — and don't think I'm not considering it, depending on your answer. What the hell are you doing here?"

"I want to talk to Rachel." He still sounded ornery but his demeanor wasn't as challenging as it had first been.

"She's busy with our son and there isn't anything you have to say to Rachel that you can't say to me." With the barrel of the Colt pointed downward, she cocked the hammer. "Now," she intoned evenly, "you've got one more chance to tell me why you're here."

"I need to see that baby, Sheriff. It's my duty. You didn't have nobody medically trained seeing to the birth, and him being premature and all, he needs a doctor to check him out."

Trace raised the pistol and pressed the barrel against Smith's left nostril. "Now I know it doesn't say 'stupid' across my forehead. You go back and you tell Jacob Crane that my son is just fine. He's healthy and he's perfect, and he looks just like me, not Ben Crane — which is the real reason you're here, not my baby's welfare. As you can hear, he has a hearty cry on him. He was delivered with no complications and Rachel is doing fine, too, thanks for asking. You have ten seconds to get your sorry ass off my land and eight of those seconds are already gone. You ever try this again, I'll shoot you, Doc. Understand?"

Amos Smith nodded as best he could with the tip of six inches of iron prodding his nose. When Trace lowered the gun, Doc barely touched a step leaving the porch. Mounting up, he rode away as fast as his horse would take him.

Trace looked down at Black Feather and Wounded Dog, who were blandly staring back at her, arms folded. "Why didn't you stop him?"

Black Feather shrugged. "We wanted to see you cause him to make water in his trousers."

Wounded Dog nodded. "You are good at that. Little Hawk say we learn much from you."

The next day, Matthew brought Trace a letter that had arrived at the office. It bore an official state seal and was marked "Office of the Governor". He watched Trace open the envelope and read the contents. At the stunned look on her face, Matthew walked over to her. "Everything okay, Trace?"

She stared over at the flickering fire. "Yeah. Yeah, Matt, everything's fine." She folded the piece of paper and held it up. "Thanks for bringing this out."

"Is it bad news?"

"No. It's good news. In fact, when you go back to town, let the mayor know that the governor is planning to visit Sagebrush in about three weeks."

Matthew couldn't hide his surprise. "Governor Armitage is coming here?"

"According to this letter, yes. And stop by Emmet Hallack's office and tell him I heard from the governor. He'll know what that means."

Rachel was puzzled by Trace's demeanor, and after Matthew left for town, she approached Trace and gave her a hug. "What's really in that letter, Trace?"

Trace sighed. "It's from the governor, about my request for an impartial circuit judge to try the Cranes once I arrest them."

"Did he say he would send one?"

"Yes," Trace responded, still a little shocked by what she had read. "He said to let him know the time and the place; he had just the judge in mind."

"Wow, I take it Governor Armitage knows of the Cranes."

"He definitely is well aware of one of them." Releasing Rachel, Trace sat down at the table. "Seems that the governor has been looking for Jacob for a little over ten years."

"Jacob? Why?" Trace handed the letter to Rachel, who unfolded it and read silently. "According to this, Jacob fathered a child by his daughter. Seduced her, got her pregnant, and just left her. Looks like our rotten apple didn't fall far from the poisonous tree."

"You seem less shocked than I am."

Rachel refolded the letter and put it back in the envelope. "Nothing that man or his spawn do would shock me. Must be that's why he uprooted and moved his whole family to Sagebrush. So what are you going to do?"

"Definitely use it against him." Trace weighed the possibilities. "Now that I have assurance from the governor that a trial will not be a pre-decided farce, I can actually put together a posse and go arrest the lot of them."

"When will you do that?"

"As soon as I can arrange for a wagon to transport them all to the territorial prison. Emmet Hallack said he would put it together once the governor gave his okay."

Rachel sat in Trace's lap and snuggled against her neck. "Lord, Trace, I can't believe this town is finally going to be free of the Cranes."

Rachel woke to the smell of smoke, Wyatt crying, and the flickering of flames as the colors reflected through the bedroom window and onto the wall. "Trace! The barn's on fire!"

While Rachel snatched up the screaming baby, Trace raced out of bed, throwing on a wool shirt and jacket over her long johns and pulling boots onto her feet. Ramiro right on her heels, she flew outside. She herded all of the cows out of the barn as Howling Wolf and Black Feather threw buckets of water on the fire.

"No, knock it down!" Trace yelled. "We don't have enough water to stop it in time." She ran inside the dark, smoky interior and moved the rabbit cages outside, then picked up an iron shovel and smashed it against the wall furthest from the flames. She swung it like a baseball bat, weakening a main post while the Pawnee took up axes and began to chop. Before that side of the structure collapsed, Trace could see sparks jumping to the stable. "Black Feather, get the horses out of there!"

While the Pawnee moved swiftly to the stable, Trace and Howling Wolf worked feverishly to knock down the rest of the barn. Fortunately, the few embers that drifted to the stable burned out before they ignited anything. With the horses and cows safely in the fields and Ramiro sticking right to Trace, the two Pawnee continued to hammer at the burning wood, collapsing the barn one section at a time while Trace dug dirt and tossed it onto anything flaming.

Just when it appeared they had the fire out, cowboys were suddenly riding at them from all sides. Trace squared up to meet the threat, thankful that she had been keeping herself in shape. It was going to take all her fighting skills to fend off such a large number.

Unseen by the trio menaced by the riders, Gideon Crane and Hannah Burnett stealthily entered the house. Quietly crossing through the living room, they crept up behind Rachel, who was just putting the baby into the crib.

When Rachel stirred, her head hurt and everything seemed woozy. She sat up slowly, steadying herself, and then looked over into the crib. The baby was gone.

"No...nooo! Trace!"

Rachel had reached her breaking point. Propelled by rage, she pulled on a pair of Trace's dungarees, rolling them up at the bottom, and donned a denim shirt over her nightshirt. Determined, she marched over to the carbine, checked to see that it was loaded, and rushed out the door. She paused for a moment at the melee going on near the barn. Trace and the Pawnee were battling numerous attackers.

Where did they come from? She shook her head. *Crane.* She had to go after Wyatt and trust that Trace and their friends could deal with this new threat.

Finding Chief in the corral, she used the bottom rail on the fence to boost herself up onto him, swinging her leg over, gaining immediate balance. With a sharp kick to his sides and a vocal command in his ear, Chief broke into a dead run with Rachel on his bare back, holding his mane with one hand and the rifle with the other. She had not completely healed from giving birth and the pain of riding quickly became excruciating, but it was nothing compared to the anguish in her heart.

Catching Rachel's departure out of the corner of her eye, Trace became frantic. Why would she leave the baby alone in the house? "Rachel!"

As Chief disappeared into the night, Trace wasted no more time with the men fighting her. She effortlessly disarmed them, breaking a few ribs here, shattering a kneecap there, cracking a skull. Until she could go after Rachel, everyone else's welfare was irrelevant. As she was grabbed by three men and took a kick to the gut, an entire tribe of Pawnee warriors rode out of the woods. She might have been able to defeat the men who were holding her, but she needed to get away and go after Rachel. Trace had never in her life been so glad to see back up.

In a living room full of Crane men and their wives, Hannah Burnett gently handed the infant into the waiting arms of Priscilla Crane. As much as she had protested her disapproval of Jacob's plan, if the baby was the child of her youngest son, she wanted to at least get a good look at him. When she did, her heart melted.

"He looks just like Ben did when he was a baby," Mrs. Crane remarked admiringly as she cuddled him close.

The door splintered open, crashing against the wall. Rachel entered, her rifle trained directly at Jacob Crane's head. "Give me my son!"

There was a deafening silence. It was Ephraim who finally spoke. "Put the gun down, Rachel. You know you aren't going to shoot anybody."

Moving the carbine mere inches away from the Crane patriarch's head, Rachel fired off a shot, blowing a hole in the wall and making everyone in the room either jump or duck. The noise startled the baby awake and he began to cry. She pointed the carbine back at Jacob. "I want my son, Crane, and I want him now."

"This is Ben's child, Rachel," Hannah said in a challenging voice. "That boy is a Crane and he belongs with us."

Through clenched teeth, she said, "This baby is mine and Trace's. He belongs to us and he is going home with me."

"An eye for an eye." Jacob spoke up, standing beside his wife who was rocking the baby to quiet him. "Your husband took my son away from me and now we're taking your son away from you. Don't try to stop us, Rachel. You'll get hurt."

"No, I think you'll get hurt."

Recognizing the voice behind her, Rachel relaxed; however, she did not lower the rifle or change her aim as Trace stood next to her.

"We'll take our son now."

"You're a foolish man, Sheriff," Jacob Crane said, not taking his eyes off Rachel. "Your wife laid with Ben, got herself in the family way, and you married her anyway? Then she lets Ben take her again while you're in town? What kind of man are you to stand by a Jezebel like that? I don't want such a woman raising my grandson."

"Crane, you're the last one on this planet who should be talking to anyone about morals. Right now, let's focus on Ben. Your son was a rapist and you know it. He abused the women at Wilbur's and abused the women who belonged to your hands. No decent woman wanted him, no matter how much money your family has."

"How dare you speak of Ben that way!" Hannah spat. "He can't defend himself."

"Lady, your brother couldn't defend himself even when he was alive." She returned her attention to Jacob. "If my wife was the kind of woman you say she is, she would have been after the Crane fortune and would have married Ben in a heartbeat. Your son raped my wife and then tried to rape her again, which is how he got that black eye you never saw but your wife and daughter did. Now you can believe what you want about that baby's heritage, but I'm going to tell you one time and one time only: that child is Rachel's and mine." Trace put her hand on Rachel's shoulder. "And you will hand him over to me now or I swear my wife will splatter your brains all over that wall behind you."

"You can't come here and threaten us," Gideon said.

Trace cocked her head, not at all intimidated. "I can and I just did. You came to my house, on my land, and stole my child. Your hands set my barn on fire and attacked me, my wife, and my guests. That's all illegal. As sheriff, I have every right to be here."

When Priscilla walked forward and handed the infant to Trace, no one was more stunned than her own family. Rachel lowered the rifle, leaned it against Trace's leg, and gently took the baby, whose wailing softened to a whimper as Trace picked up the carbine.

Amid the cries of "Mother!" and "Priscilla!" the Crane matriarch stood beside Trace. "No," she said firmly. "Enough."

Jacob's surprise overpowered his typical condescension and irritation. "For heaven's sake, Priscilla, what are you doing?"

"I'm doing something right for a change. This child does not belong to us or with us, Jacob."

"But if Ben is the father—" Hannah was cut off by her mother.

"If Ben is the father, it was not because he intended to be. What the sheriff says is true — if this poor girl got in the family way because of your brother, I don't even want to think about how that happened. I'm not proud that we all had a hand in raising a boy who became nearly as evil as Satan himself. He always got his way and what wasn't given to him, he took." Priscilla looked deep into Rachel's eyes. "I'm suspecting that's how he was with you."

Stunned by Mrs. Crane's actions, Rachel held her gaze for a second before she returned her attention to her baby boy. "Yes."

Mrs. Crane looked over her family standing stock still in the living room of her home. "I loved my son, but thanks to all of you, he was a brute. And those inclinations seemed to make themselves most apparent when he got an ache in his loins."

"Mother!" Hannah exclaimed.

"He had nothing but contempt for anyone who would not kowtow to him and he would not brook any opposition. And he was worse when he took to the drink. He did horrible things to women, Jacob. I loved him with all my heart, but I'm ashamed to say he was my son."

"Priscilla, stop this foolishness this instant," Jacob commanded. "Take that baby back and get over here!"

"Jake, you lay one finger on my son and you'll live to regret it," Trace said. She had the Cranes right where she wanted them. "If you have half a brain, you'll shut up and listen to your wife."

"How dare you—"

"Shut up, Jacob," Priscilla said, empowered by Trace's authoritative presence. She glared at her husband, who stared back at her, speechless and beet red.

Comforting the baby, hugging him to her and enveloping him inside her shirt, Rachel took Wyatt outside.

Rachel was not at all surprised when she got to the porch and saw half the town and what looked like the entire contingent of Pawnee warriors there. She smiled when a resounding cheer rose from the waiting crowd. Several of the men dismounted and approached the porch, Matthew Reddick in the lead. He looked at Rachel expectantly.

"I think he's got it under control, but you should probably stand by out here until he calls for you or comes and gets you," she told the deputy. She looked at the group of men tied up in the back of a wagon. "Anybody get killed?"

"No, but quite a few of them need a doctor. Those boys weren't hired to be gunfighters and it showed. None of us are much good at that, either. Thank the Lord for the Pawnee. Soon as they showed up, everybody just kind of surrendered."

She dreaded asking but needed to know. "How's my home?"

"Fine. We'll need to rebuild the barn." He pointed to a wagon that just pulled up. "Elizabeth's come to take you and the baby back to our place until this is over."

"What was that noise?" Gideon Crane asked, reacting to the sound coming from outside.

"That? That's just the people of Sagebrush letting you know that as of tonight they have completely taken their town back. I think it's a long overdue sound, how about you?" Trace asked smugly.

"You know, Sheridan, you're a pompous, self-centered, high-handed son-of-a-bitch," Jacob sputtered.

"Kind of like looking in a mirror, isn't it, Jacob?" Priscilla said, once again stunning her family into silence.

"Yeah, what she said." Trace smiled, nodding toward Mrs. Crane. "Now, this is what we're going to do. I can place you all under arrest—"

"For what?" Hannah interrupted.

"Trespassing, kidnapping, assault, arson, extortion, cruelty to animals, fraud, deception, forgery. And let's not forget complicity, duplicity—"

"What are those?" Micah inquired.

Trace recited the definitions she recalled from her police exams. "Complicity is the association or participation in or, as if in, a wrongful act, and duplicity is contradictory doubleness of thought, speech, or action, especially the belying of one's true intentions by deceptive words or action."

"What does that mean?" Gideon spoke for the rest who, with the exception of Jacob, were still confused.

Trace rolled her eyes. "Being underhanded and then trying to cover it up through lying and trickery. You're all guilty of that, and I have enough deputies waiting outside to make sure it ends here."

"My God, you *are* a lawman, aren't you?" Jacob sounded almost impressed.

"We're not going anywhere, Sheridan," Micah told her stubbornly. "This is our home, our land; you can't make us leave."

"Oh, I think I can. Because if you don't, there are very angry people outside who are willing to burn you out." Trace looked around pointedly. "You have a lot of nice, expensive things here. It would be a shame to lose them."

"You wouldn't do that," Hannah gasped.

"Yeah, I would. That's how you would do it, isn't it, Jacob? That's what your boys were going to do to me, to my family. Why should you be treated any differently? You're nothing but a common criminal. The only difference between you and those boys up in the penitentiary is that they got caught and didn't have the money to get their asses out of trouble."

Hannah recoiled, offended. "Sheriff, your language."

"Mrs. Burnett, where you and your family are going, language like that is the least of what you will find offensive."

"No judge who travels this circuit will ever uphold charges against me or my family," Jacob said confidently.

"Don't worry. I have no intention of sending you before a judge on your payroll. You'll be going before the governor." Trace waited for his reaction and she was not disappointed.

"Governor Armitage?"

"Yeah." Trace watched Crane blanch. "Thought you might feel that way."

Priscilla looked at her husband curiously. "Jacob?" He shook his head, dismissing her.

"What's the matter, Jake? Don't want your missus there to know your dirty little secret?"

"Jacob, what's he talking about?"

"Tell her, Jake...or I will." It felt good to have this man by the short hairs. Now his whole family turned to look at him.

"Listen, Sheriff, there's no need to get into this in front of my family. Why don't we go into my study and talk. I'm sure we can come to some sort of...agreement."

"Agreement? Now I need to add attempted bribery to your charges. No. Let's share this news with everybody, shall we?" Trace turned to her rapt audience. "Ever wonder why you all moved so abruptly from your last home? Seems your daddy fathered a child with the governor's oldest daughter, Willa — who was only fifteen at the time. He didn't want to face the scandal, so he abandoned her and his paternal responsibilities and moved you all here to the nice, unknown little hamlet of Sagebrush. It's taken the governor, who if you all recall, was a prominent attorney at the time, this long to catch up with him."

Priscilla was white with shock and rage and Jacob took a step toward her. "You're certainly not going to listen to this nonsense, are you?" If he had not been sweating profusely, his outrage would have been more convincing. "Look, she was a little tramp...she threw herself at me."

"You son-of-a-bitch!" Ephraim punched his father, knocking him back against the wall.

Jacob looked at his oldest son, startled and wounded, wiping the blood from his lower lip. "What was that for?"

"You're a whoremaster! We're all supposed to look the other way on the drives while you disrespect Ma and take comfort with the saloon girls. You take what you want, it don't matter who it hurts. Everybody 'throws herself at you'. That's what you told Seth, too, when he caught you in the bunkhouse with Aunt Margaret. How much did you pay him not to shoot you, too, to say it was a ranch hand? I knew Willa Armitage and she was a sweet, innocent girl. So, tell me, Pa...did my wife throw herself at you, too? Huh? Did she? Tell me that my daughter is not really yours! Tell me, Father! I always suspected it but now I know. Of course you protected and praised Ben — he was just like you!"

Ephraim's wife tried to slink back into the background. Trace watched as the family fell apart before her eyes.

"You can't blame me, Ephraim, if you can't satisfy your own wife. She came to me for help and advice."

"And you helped her all right, didn't you?" He turned and looked at Julia, his voice dripping with venom. "You must be real proud of yourself. Well, if you want him, you're welcome to him."

Gideon and Micah turned to their wives, questioningly. "Don't you look at me like that, Gideon Crane, I wouldn't let that old coot touch me if he was the last man on earth," Esther Crane told her husband indignantly.

Micah's wife, Emily, looked insulted. "He never came near me."

Trace had heard enough. "So, this is what we're going to do. You're going to pay back all the money you extorted, and the revenue the businessmen lost because of your shakedowns. If you don't remember how much it was, no problem; Ed Jackson wrote it all down in a ledger, which I have in my possession. You will also compensate the farmers and ranchers whose land was burned and destroyed, and for the stock you crippled and killed, and then you'll live here under house arrest like good citizens until the governor and his personally appointed magistrate get here. In the meantime, you will be guarded and monitored so that you don't attempt to destroy your land or any of your possessions; they belong to the people you've swindled. When you've been taken away to jail, we'll have Joe Turner preside over a public auction, put the word out to Jefferson City and some of the other surrounding cities where the more well-off can afford to bid on your things. Any proceeds will be divided up equally among the towns-people who were harassed by you."

"You're making a big mistake, Sheridan," Jacob spat out.

"Shut up, Jacob," Priscilla said in disgust. "What can I do to help you, Sheriff?"

Chapter Thirty-one

It was effectively the end of the Crane empire. Within a month, their stranglehold over Sagebrush had been legally vanquished. It wasn't easy on anyone, especially Priscilla. With her assistance, Priscilla's family went from prosperous to paupers in a matter of weeks. The horses and stock were sold, most of the hands quit before they were ordered off the premises, and Joseph Turner held an auction — right on former Crane land — of all the Cranes' material possessions, with the exception of the bare minimum they needed to survive. They were kept prisoners on their property by emergency deputized citizens of Sagebrush and Jefferson City, and Pawnee warriors who patrolled the boundaries of the ranch, ensuring no one wandered too far away from the main house.

The trials were scheduled as soon as the governor could arrange for a circuit and a congressional district judge to co-preside over the proceedings. The indictments moved forward swiftly and Trace marveled at how both judges respectfully deferred to the governor when they could not agree on an evidentiary matter. Not surprisingly, no decision was made in Jacob Crane's favor, which caused the Cranes' attorneys to cry foul through most of the trial. It did them no good, as the governor was very popular and powerful, and Crane was neither.

"It didn't help matters any that you showed up every day and just egged those Crane men on," Rachel said as Trace finished her coffee. They had been discussing the events of the last few weeks, both glad when Sundays rolled around as it was the only day court was not in session.

Trace looked at Rachel nursing Wyatt, the baby suckling her contentedly. His eyes were open and he watched his mother, seemingly fascinated by her, his tiny hands reaching up, trying to pat Rachel's face. It was endearing. "I wasn't egging them on. It was my job to be there." Trace circled the rocking chair so that she could observe their son while he ate. Trace loved feeding time. The connection between Rachel and Wyatt was so intimate, it almost made her jealous. Almost.

"It wasn't your job to give Emmet Hallack advice on how to get Jacob and the rest to lose their tempers and essentially confess their many sins. Matthew told Elizabeth he'd never seen anything like it. Did you learn how to do that in Cottonwood, too?" She brushed her fingers lightly over the soft strawberry blonde fuzz on Wyatt's head. He blinked several times and continued to stare at Rachel. She kissed his palm, making smooching noises, and then cooed at him, which caused his eyes to widen as he briefly stopped nursing. Rachel blew softly in his face and he blinked again and smiled.

"There's nothing illegal about using the defendants' own words against them." Trace rested a hand on Rachel's shoulder, the movement also catching Wyatt's eye. "Who's my handsome boy?" she said, her tone not without pride. Wyatt began sucking again but now he couldn't tear his eyes away from Trace. "It's called entrapping them into self-incrimination. In Cottonwood, it's not quite allowed but the law prohibiting that hasn't made it to Sagebrush yet. All I did was tip off Emmet how to rile them up to get them to admit the things they were guilty of. It's not like I did anything wrong. Everyone, including them, knew they were guilty."

"Their lawyers raised enough of a ruckus about it," Rachel teased.

"That's only because their clients were moving themselves closer to a prison cell with every word out of their mouths."

Rachel wiped some moisture off Wyatt's chin with the edge of her apron. "Is four months old too early for him to get teeth?"

"Why? Is he biting you?"

"No, but he's been drooling an awful lot lately."

"Well...we haven't seen anything breaking through his gums yet, but he could have teeth ready to pop out there." Trace studied Wyatt, a broad smile creeping onto her face. She started talking in a high-pitched, childish tone of voice that had debuted the day Wyatt was born. "Is my big boy getting toofers? Is my Wyanator getting little tuskies?" She shot a glance at Rachel, who was staring at her in amusement. Trace stood up straight, regaining her poise and speaking in her normal voice. "What?" *Amazing how a gurgling, fourteen pound armful of baby can turn me into a babbling mushball. Thankfully my former co-workers can't see this. They'd be looking around for the pod.*

"Nothing." Rachel shook her head, laughing, and then returned her attention to her son. "Your papa is silly, huh?" In response, Wyatt smiled again then went back to nursing. "What do you really think is going to happen, Trace? I mean, after the Cranes are found guilty?"

Folding her arms across her chest, Trace stepped back and leaned against the table. "I have no doubt that Jacob, Ephraim, Gideon, Micah, and Hannah's husband, George, will be on their way to a territorial prison by the end of next week. That's what Emmet and Governor Armitage think. There's no way they won't be found guilty on all charges. And if they did get off — any of them, or all of them — they'd never stay anywhere near Sagebrush. Even if they weren't run out of town on a rail, they have no power here any more. As long as Armitage is governor, they'll never have any power in this state."

"It's hard to believe that John and Seth Carver are already in jail."

"Yes, but they were convicted of lesser infractions and are only in the Jefferson County jail for a year. They'd also be very foolish to try and come back here."

"Miz Ledbetter told me that Suzanne Beauregard still wants to marry Seth. Funny — when Rosalie was demanding she marry him, she didn't want to. Now that Rosalie wants to distance herself as far away from an association with the Cranes as possible, Suzanne is insisting she's madly in love with Seth."

"Maybe she sees something in Seth the rest of us don't."

"If she does wait for him and marry him, I think she's taking her pigs to a very poor market." She brushed her hand over Wyatt's head. "What do you think will happen to Mrs. Crane and Hannah?"

"Well, they are both expected to get hefty fines for their participation. If they can't pay, they'll be sent up to the women's facility in Butler."

"I don't understand," Rachel said to Trace in a typical show of compassion. Despite all that had happened, it was difficult for Rachel to condemn Priscilla. "Mrs. Crane has helped the authorities every step of the way. Why does she have to go through a trial?"

"It's not going to be a full trial," Trace explained patiently. "It is a hearing. It's a chance for her or her lawyer to state her case. Regardless of her last ditch effort to do right and try to correct things, she was still complicit in the family wrongdoing."

"Explain 'complicit' to me again."

"It means that she was involved in what was done. Just by going along with it, never saying anything and allowing it to happen, in the judges' eyes, it is the same as doing it herself."

"But Trace, this isn't Cottonwood," Rachel protested, switching Wyatt to her other breast. "Women here are not looked upon the same as men are. We vow to obey our husbands when we marry them. I think she has been very clear that she never approved of any of it." She looked down at her hungry son. His eyes were closed and his tiny hand was grasping at the pale flesh surrounding Rachel's nipple.

Watching Rachel slightly wince at Wyatt's vigorous feeding frenzy, Trace commented, "He's a hungry boy. You sure he's not biting you?"

"No, just sucking really hard," Rachel said. "Reminds me of someone else I know."

That made Trace laugh. "Is that a complaint?"

"Nope. Just that if I didn't know any better, I'd say he is truly your son by blood."

Trace smiled and leaned over Rachel. "He is my son." She kissed Rachel on the forehead. "I will never think of him any other way." She rubbed her thumb against Wyatt's chubby cheek, which caused him to squint and smile. Seconds later, he was sucking contentedly again.

Kissing Wyatt on the top of his head, continuing to rock him softly, Rachel said, "I'm sorry, Trace. I know the baby is as much yours as he is mine. Sometimes I speak without thinking first."

"I know what you meant, Rach. I promise you our child will be more like me than Ben Crane."

"I know you will do what you can." Rachel hoped Trace was right, that she could teach Wyatt to overcome any bad traits he might have inherited from his father. "Sweetheart? I just wish that Mrs. Crane would not have to be punished any further. Being married to that man and having Ben for a son was punishment enough. She's been so willing to help...and, I'm sorry, Trace, but she is Wyatt's grandmother."

"Baby, I don't wish to deny her that. And I understand she was in a very bad situation. If it were up to me, I would make sure Priscilla was freed and got whatever she needed to start a new life. But it isn't up to me. And the judges are going to look at the situation and what she didn't do, not what she did do. What Jacob and his family did is not a small thing. They murdered people, ruined an entire town, not just one or two ranchers or merchants. She had the power all along to put an end to it, and she didn't do it. That's something the town and the judges won't forgive her for."

"How was she supposed to do that, Trace? How would she have survived if she turned on her husband and her family? And that's assuming that Jacob would have let her live if he'd even an inkling she would betray him. I doubt Jacob would have valued her above his holdings and his ambition. She would have had to get a lot further than Sagebrush to reach an order of law beyond Jacob's clutches. No one in this town — until you — stood against any of the Cranes. What makes you think she had the power to stop anything?" Rachel's voice had a defensive edge to it.

"She was able to stand up to them that night. And they listened to her, didn't they?"

"Only because you were there, I reckon."

"There was nothing stopping her from coming to see me sooner. She could have come to me the day she realized I wasn't going to buckle under to her husband, especially since I became sheriff before Ben or the others returned."

"But this went on ten years before you showed up. Why should she be expected to do what no man in Sagebrush had the backbone to do? She's just one woman."

"A woman with the distinction of being the Crane matriarch. I think the townspeople thought that she had a lot more power, knowing her family connection to influential people in Omaha. Until recently I think the townspeople thought she agreed with her husband's methods and that if she wanted to stop it, had the power to do so. I think because of her affluence, regardless of her being a female, the citizens of Sagebrush thought she still wielded more power than any man in town, including the mayor."

"If she had any power, I don't think she was aware of it." Rachel tucked her breast back into her dress and lifted Wyatt to her shoulder to burp him. "I wish I'd gotten to know her before..."

"Please don't tell me that would have changed your mind about Ben."

"No. Never. But it would have changed my mind about her. In a way, I think she was trapped, like I was. I think she did what she thought was right. And...I sympathize with her for that."

"You're a good woman, Rachel. Not many people who have been victimized would think of it that way." Trace picked up a diaper and draped it over her shoulder. "Here. Let me take him." She gently removed Wyatt from Rachel and placed him against her shoulder, lightly patting his back until he let go with a thunderous burp.

Rachel grinned. "That only half reminds me of you."

Continuing to massage her son's back, Trace said, "That's why I rub him up instead of down. What comes easy, let go free, ya know?"

On a break from the primary Crane trial, while the governor attended to business elsewhere, the judges decided to move ahead with the proceedings against Priscilla and Hannah. Rachel and Trace testified at Priscilla's hearing and asked for leniency because of her circumstances and the fact that she helped make the case against Jacob. Her willingness to testify against her own husband left no doubt in the judges' mind of just how accountable the man was for everything with which he had been charged.

The judges were forgiving in Priscilla's case but a little less tolerant in Hannah's, even though Hannah got off more easily than a male defendant would have. The women were to pay fines and then be released. "After all," as one of the judges stated, "even though Mrs. Crane and Mrs. Burnett are just women, and women really don't count, their silence in this matter was not golden, as speaking up sooner rather than later would have freed Sagebrush and maybe even saved Ben Crane from wild animals gettin' to him."

Although Hannah was no longer speaking to her, Priscilla was generous enough to pay her and Hannah's fines with money she had set aside in secret for years. Priscilla held no ill will toward her daughter, despite Hannah's professed hatred toward her now. Hannah was a consequence of her father's actions, another of Jacob's victims just like so many others before her, even though Hannah would never see it as such.

Priscilla's sons were also victims, to a point, and then they had chosen, as she had, to go along with Jacob's tyranny. For her sons, it seemed to be a rite of passage. She wondered how far things would have gone if she had not chosen to side with the sheriff. Yet, even though that betrayal had cost her everything — her children, her grandchildren, her home, her livelihood, her security — it had been worth it.

After sentencing, and before taking Jacob Crane away, Trace led him out to the back of the courthouse and unshackled him. "Ten minutes is all I can give you, Governor," Trace told Armitage, "then I have to get him back to the jailhouse because the territorial marshal is waiting with his crew to get them all on the wagon to Amesville." She ignored Crane, who was standing between them. "Looks like it's going to be a family procession with the sheep — I mean wives and kids — following these undeserving pricks all the way, so if I don't have him back soon, someone is going to come looking for him."

"Ten minutes is more than enough time to show him how I feel about him," Armitage snarled, barely able to contain the rage that had been bottled up inside him for so long.

"Wait! Sheriff, you're not seriously going to allow this?" Jacob's tone showed both outrage and fear. He was a tall man but Armitage was taller, and outweighed him by at least fifty pounds. And the governor had been a fighter before he went into politics. His prize money from boxing matches helped put him through law school. Crane knew that ten minutes with Armitage would be like spending an hour being stomped on by a bull. An angry, vindictive bull.

"I can't think of one good reason why I shouldn't, Jake," Trace told him. "In fact, if I had more time, I'd take my turn after the governor. With everything you've done, you just had to do one more unforgivable thing. Why? What purpose did it serve to scream out after your sentencing that Ben was really Wyatt's father?"

"Because it's true!"

"What do you know about the truth?"

"The same thing he knows about honor. Nothing," Armitage said.

"I wanted this town to know that there is still one Crane left here. That boy is Ben's legacy."

"He will never be a Crane. Wyatt will never know about your son and he will never know about you. By putting that idea in people's heads, you just made it twice as hard for him."

"You Cranes are good at planting your seeds in gardens where they don't belong," spat Armitage. "And you've always had a misplaced sense of importance. Do you think I'm actually honored that my granddaughter is a Crane? If I did to Hannah what you did to Willa, would you not want revenge? You ruined my little girl, Crane! And now that you're ruined, I'm after a more personal revenge. Now," Armitage rolled up his sleeves, "get your yellow ass ready to take your punishment like a man."

"Sheriff..." Crane's tone was almost begging.

"I hear nothing, I see nothing," Trace responded as she removed Crane's handcuffs.

She wrote up Jacob Crane's injuries as due to a nasty spill en route to the transport wagon.

The rumor spread like wildfire: the Sheridan baby was really a Crane. Trace and Rachel maintained their claim to Wyatt's parentage and, as the citizens of Sagebrush really wanted to believe them, the gossip died soon after it started. Only those who mattered knew the truth.

Nobody expected Priscilla to be invited to Wyatt's baptism, much less to show up, but after all the things she had done to make amends, Rachel and Trace felt it was only fair to invite her. At the ceremony, most of the townspeople avoided Priscilla, and very few spoke to her. Afterwards, when Rachel saw Priscilla leave quietly through the back of the church, she waited a few minutes and then excused herself to change the baby's diaper. Finding Priscilla alone in Reverend Edwards' office wiping tears from her eyes, Rachel nudged the door closed and brought Wyatt to Priscilla, letting her hold him. She cradled him lovingly.

"Thank you," she said, able to get the words out at a whisper.

"What happens now, Mrs. Crane?"

"I don't really know. I'm moving back to Omaha. I'll divorce Jacob from there. I guess that means I'll be divorcing Gideon, Micah, Hannah, George, and all the wives and grandchildren, too. How they can stand by their father and husbands after all this, I'll never know. I still have hope for Ephraim, but I guess time will tell. Maybe I'll look up my one true love. I hear he's a widower." She gently kissed the baby on the forehead. "You and Trace have a beautiful son, Rachel. I'm grateful for the time you've let me spend with him, but it's time for me to move on. I'm not wanted here and I don't blame these people. What my family has done to this town is unforgivable. It was hard losing everything, but it was worth the price to regain my freedom, as well."

Trace knocked and entered the office, shutting the door behind her. She looked uncomfortable in the Sunday best that Rachel had insisted she wear.

"Mrs. Crane will be moving back to Omaha," Rachel said.

Trace nodded. "You'll let us know when you get settled? We could send you pictures of Wyatt when we have them taken," Trace offered.

The Crane matriarch smiled ruefully. "No. I appreciate it but it will be too difficult. My son did a horrible thing and I don't deserve the privilege of being this child's grandmother. If I have pictures of him I'll want to display them, and if I do that, I'll have to explain who he is and then there will be more questions and...well, I need to let go of my past when I get back to Omaha, start my life over. I can't do that with any ties to Sagebrush."

Rachel's heart broke for Priscilla Crane. "I understand."

As the older woman handed the sleeping Wyatt back to his mother, she leaned over and kissed him one last time. "I think I should get my things to the stage." And with that, she nodded gratefully at both women, her eyes tearing up again at her final look at her grandson.

Trace draped her arm over Rachel's shoulder. "There goes a very brave woman."

"And the last of the Cranes." Rachel looked up at Trace. "What do you say we finally get our life started?"

Squeezing Rachel closer to her, Trace kissed her passionately on the lips. Looking down at Wyatt, she said, "Oh, I think we've already got a pretty good beginning."

Trace sat on the front porch, strumming softly on her guitar. She adjusted the E-string and played a more pleasant sounding G-chord. *Next time I go to town, I need to buy some new catgut strings from Joseph.* She would have preferred nylon or steel because gut strings were brittle in the cold and would warp in the heat, making it more difficult to keep the guitar in tune. She knew steel strings were expensive and wasn't sure nylon strings had even been developed yet, so gut strings were better than nothing. She chuckled to herself as she picked out notes to no particular song, amused that the most pressing thing on her mind right then was guitar strings. *How life has changed.*

The creaking of the door alerted her that Rachel had finished putting the baby to bed for the night. *Gotta put some oil on those hinges. Pressing issue number two.* She smiled. Without turning around, she said, "Wyatt's down, then?"

"And a blessing that he's finally sleeping all night, unless he wakes up hungry." She sat beside Trace on the porch swing that Trace had rigged up a week earlier.

"I know these past few months have been really hard on you, but now that things have settled into a routine in town and I've got Matt and Isaac deputized, I don't have to be in Sagebrush so much of the time." She set the guitar aside and turned to Rachel. Motherhood agreed with Rachel; it had changed her physically and emotionally. Trace thought Rachel was gorgeous under any circumstances but by the light of the full moon, her beauty took Trace's breath away. "I'm hoping that means we can spend a lot more time together."

"Me, too. I guess that will depend on how able your deputies are. Not sure how Elizabeth feels about Matthew being a lawman. With one daughter and another baby on the way, she's not going to want him doing things that might get him shot."

"Oh, but it's okay for me," Trace teased with a smile.

"No, it's not okay for you," Rachel said softly. "But I know you..." she reached over and tapped the tip of Trace's nose, "can take care of yourself. I've seen you do it. I'm not so sure about Matthew."

"Matt is a good man for the job, Rachel," Trace assured her. "He has excellent instincts and the common sense to know when to stand firm and when to back down. People respond to Matt's ability to reason situations out before they have a chance to turn violent. If circumstances dictate a threatening outcome, Matt does not shy away from that and the message that sends is a strong one."

"Yes, but can he fight like you?"

Trace never tired of Rachel's admiration for her. "He has a different style. I know it might be hard to believe, but Matt is a very effective fighter and a crack shot."

"I just can't picture Matthew shooting anybody. He's usually so genteel."

"He hasn't had to make that decision yet and hopefully he never will, though that's not likely. Though shooting someone is not Matt's first course of action, I'm confident if he is faced with that challenge, he will not hesitate to do what he needs to do to resolve the situation. I wouldn't have appointed him if I thought he wasn't up to the job."

"And Isaac? Have you given him any more responsibility?"

"Nah, he still just follows me around all day, kinda like my third deputy." Trace looked down at Ramiro who wore a star on his collar and looked a lot more menacing than he could ever be, unless it came to defending his family. Most of his watch consisted of shadowing Trace and sleeping on the porch at the Sheridan household. "Isaac keeps the office clean, runs errands and the like. It gets him out of his father's store, and makes him look good for his sweetheart."

Rachel chuckled. "I can understand that. What you've done for this town certainly makes you look good for your sweetheart." She sighed. "Things sure are a sight different in Sagebrush since you came here, Trace, what with you being sheriff, and trading for the town with the Pawnee. And of course, me and Wyatt. The town couldn't do without you now, any more than me and the baby could."

A swell of pride and love choked the words in Trace's throat. She didn't know what she would have said if she could have spoken.

Misinterpreting Trace's silence, Rachel's insecurities rushed to the fore, and she forced herself to ask a question she'd been avoiding. "Trace, uh, is Sagebrush too tame for you now that the town is on its feet again and things are running smoothly? Or maybe all of us are expecting too much of you? I mean, I know that before you said you wouldn't want to go back to Cottonwood, but..."

"Back to Cottonwood?" Trace looked down into the upturned face of the woman she was willing to die for. Stunned at the sudden turn of conversation, she tried to look back over their last few words and see how Rachel had ended up so far from the truth of her desires.

"Well, you're always talking about it," Rachel said in a rush, "and it sounds like a place that gets more progress than we get out here. And, well, I was just wondering...if you did go back to Cottonwood, would you...take Wyatt and me with you?"

There is no Cottonwood. The words that would reassure Rachel once and for always could never be spoken. *How could I ever explain that I came from a future that was destroying me, that I came back in time and was given a second chance to live my life right? That if I had the opportunity to bring you and Wyatt back to the life I had lived before, if Mark had the capability to open that portal again, I would not do it.* It was not that she wanted to continue to deceive Rachel but she knew it would be unimaginable for Rachel to comprehend the concept of time travel no matter how it was explained it to her. *After all, I went through it and it is still hard for me to come to terms with it.* There was no way to tell Rachel that truth, and yet there was another truth, one that Rachel did need to hear.

She caressed Rachel's cheek then dropped her hand to her lap. "My dearest wife, in the time before I came to you, and to Sagebrush, there is nothing but a past that is regrettable and forgettable. Cottonwood is no longer even a part of my world. You and the baby, and even the people I have sworn to protect, are my whole life. And there is nothing that would ever make me leave you."

Tears shone in Rachel's eyes. "I was just afraid that maybe you... I mean, we haven't made love much since Wyatt was born and..." She heaved a deep sigh.

"Oh, sweetheart. As much as I've missed making love with you, I know our son has urgent needs right now, and I understand that those have to come first." When Rachel didn't speak, Trace said, "You know, Jacob Crane was right." Before Rachel could protest, Trace clarified. "He said that Wyatt is a legacy. That's true, but he is your legacy...and mine, not Ben's." *And who knows, through him, I might just have some small chance to change the future.* "And as for not making love so often, well, I've been pretty busy too, with the trials and getting things in order in town. That's not laid to your account."

Rachel took one of the strong, callused hands in hers. "I know you're just doing your job like it should be done, but between the baby and the townsfolk, there hasn't been much time for just the two of us." She snuggled against Trace's side and turned her face up, inviting a kiss.

Quick to oblige, Trace made it sweet and lingering, letting Rachel know that their rare moments of shared intimacy had been too few and far between for her, as well. "There's always the loft in the new barn," she said suggestively.

Rachel swatted the arm that encircled her. "Trace Sheridan! There's also a baby who's now sleeping through the night and who could sleep through a locomotive chuggin' through the bedroom."

"Well he would have to, considering your passionate vocalizations," Trace teased.

"Me?" Rachel tried to wriggle away but Trace's grasp held her firmly in place. "If memory serves me, Mr. Sheridan, I believe you are the louder one. Of course, it's been so long, it's difficult to remember." Her tone was mischievous.

"If that's a proposition, Mrs. Sheridan, I'm perfectly willing to test your theory as to how soundly Wyatt will be sleeping." Trace pressed another kiss on Rachel's lips, then strayed down to her throat as her fingers worked at the laces of the gingham bodice.

Glancing around to see if anyone other than the livestock was within viewing range, Rachel moaned as the warm hand slid inside the cloth and cupped a tender breast. "Good Lord, Trace..." she whispered, pressing closer.

"I love you, Rachel. I always will. And I want this," her unoccupied hand gestured around the house and property, "and this," her fingers tweaked a nipple gently, "and that little boy sleeping inside. Honestly, I can't think of one thing that could make my life any better."

Rachel leaned up for another kiss and pressed Trace's hand tighter to her breast. At last, she smiled. "Well then, you're just not the creative person I thought you were," she said with an expression that could only be described as naughty. Settling a restive hand on Trace's strong thigh, she squeezed hard. "Come on, Sheriff. There's no time like the present to see how much our son can sleep through." She disengaged herself from Trace's hand, laughing with delight as Trace stumbled over her own feet in her hurry to rise.

"Um, you go on ahead, will you? I just need to grab my guitar and I'll be right in."

"All right. But if you take too long, I'm going to start without you."

Trace flushed at the image as she plucked her guitar from the railing, hearing the door shut behind Rachel. She looked out at the darkening sky and the land that was theirs for as far as her eye could see. It had been a long and hazardous journey for her, one that defied the laws of time and space and wiped her slate clean. And the road ahead was not going to be a smooth one either. But with Rachel, and Wyatt, she was home.

Cheyne was born on Labor Day many moons ago in Vermont. She was raised in New York. Among the places Cheyne has lived (so far) are Vermont, New York, Alabama, Massachusetts, Minnesota, California, Pennsylvania, Delaware, Ohio, and Italy.

At 17, she toured with a production of "Jesus Christ Superstar" and in her 20's, she enlisted in the Army and became a military police officer. After the Army, she took a break and went back to doing theater until an opportunity came up to work in law enforcement again. She has been in and out of police work and related fields ever since. She is thankful to have had such an amazing life experience so far.

In 2005, she returned to Vermont to concentrate on her writing. In 2008, she relocated to Ohio, where she now lives with her partner Brenda, and their "kids" Nikki, a black lab/retriever mix, and Liam, a pound puppy mutt.

She still pines for the west.

LaVergne, TN USA
15 September 2009
157920LV00003B/5/P